Selecting the top tales from the reams of science
fiction short stories, novelettes and novellas
published last year is a time-consuming yet
fascinating task. But as always when your editors
are finished, there is a sense of surprise—because
somehow each of the finalists is a gem that fits
into place in the final collection quite rightly.

Here we have an unusual mixture of the old
giants such as Silverberg, Asimov, Pohl, and the
young giants such as Tanith Lee, Greg Bear, and
the new bloods including Mary Gentle, Rand Lee,
Don Sakers, and more.

So join us in this year of 1984 and see what
Orwell overlooked!

Anthologies from DAW

ASIMOV PRESENTS THE GREAT SF STORIES
The best stories of the last two decades.
Edited by Isaac Asimov and Martin H. Greenberg.

THE ANNUAL WORLD'S BEST SF
The best of the current year.
Edited by Donald A. Wollheim with Arthur W. Saha.

THE YEAR'S BEST HORROR STORIES
An annual of gooseflesh tales.
Edited by Karl Edward Wagner.

THE YEAR'S BEST FANTASY STORIES
An annual of high imagination.
Edited by Arthur W. Saha

TERRA SF
The Best SF from Western Europe.
Edited by Richard D. Nolane.

WOLLHEIM'S WORLD'S BEST SF
Edited by Donald A. Wollheim

THE 1984 ANNUAL
WORLD'S BEST SF

Edited by

DONALD A. WOLLHEIM

with Arthur W. Saha

DAW BOOKS, INC.

DONALD A. WOLLHEIM, PUBLISHER

1633 Broadway, New York, NY 10019

First Printing, June 1984

1 2 3 4 5 6 7 8 9

DAW TRADEMARK REGISTERED
U.S. PAT. OFF. MARCA
REGISTRADA. HECHO EN U.S.A.

PRINTED IN U.S.A.

CONTENTS

INTRODUCTION

It would seem reasonable when writing an introduction to a science fiction volume intended for the year 1984 to devote space to meditating on the significance of Orwell's book, *1984*. But I imagine that this has been done by many others by the time you will be reading this and I suspect that all that is relevant will have been said. However I do have a theme possibly connected to the social premise of 1984 that is worth thinking about in this strategic year.

While in London some time ago, I picked up a postcard in a small progressive book shop which carried this statement: "The money required to provide adequate food, water, education, health and housing for everyone in the world has been estimated at $17 billion a year. It is a huge sum of money . . . about as much as the world spends on arms every two weeks."

This struck me at first as a startling statement but the more I thought about it the more truthful it turned out to be. Perhaps the figures are a bit exaggerated and suppose therefore we doubled the amount required for remedying the world's ills—even so it would be a very small fraction of the annual bill for armaments the world's nations pile up every year. Consider it: food, health, housing. . . . With four billion people on Earth today, the great majority are very much in need. All could be resolved for all for such a small diversion of the moneys used to accumulate useless masses of people-killing apparatus drawn wastefully from this planet's finite resources.

What this means to me is that the world is really quite close to Utopia—in a practical sense. Or just perhaps one year away from Utopia once this financial diversion is set into action. Such a clearing away of the ills of the human race would serve as a vast deterrent to war, would it not? So—with modern technology and skill in all fields, medicine, agriculture, engineering, the world is a mere year away from the Ideal State. But then has it not been in this condition for at least the last half century? Yet it does not get any closer to that desired denouement although time passes and demagogues promise.

This, to me, is the underlying meaning of 1984. That all is deception—that behind all the noise and saber-rattling and A-bomb stockpiling there hides this single fact—that Utopia is realizable just one year away. And that every effort, outside of some occasional science fiction, is being made to keep this startling truth obscured.

Science fiction, too, does not generally recognize this, except in the unconscious creation of future worlds where the problems are of such interstellar scope that one has to assume that back on Old Earth there are no longer starving peasants or imprisoned reformers.

In fact, science fiction writers are forced to think about the physical reality of futures, near and far, and are presumed to be familiar with the development and implication of modern scientific studies. The outlook derived from such studies, reflected by the politics of the world, presents sharp contrasts, so that much of what ought to be Utopian is instead gloomy. It is not hard to decide that humanity, as a species of animal designed to think its way out of nature's problems, is an apparent failure and doomed therefore to disappear like the dinosaurs in some planetary catastrophe of its own making. Perhaps. Perhaps not.

Something of this can be detected in the stories which shaped up for this year's collection of the most memorable shorter science fiction of the past year. There are stories here of many colors, one or two of the deepest gloom. But there are also stories of hope and the belief that men will somehow bungle through safely. The theme—if there is one in the year's output—appears to be social and social speculation. And, of course, there are as always stories that are sheer escape—a necessary relief from the mental contortions of the mundane world.

Science fiction during the past year has held up well in the literary market, although the times generally were not the best. Books of a science fictional or fantastic turn of mind continued to appear in the bestseller lists, both for hard-bound and paperbound works. The various imprints of paperback books continued to show vigor, although hampered by a sharp rise in other categories and the continuation of inflation and recession. The magazines held their own quite well and continued their task of bringing forth the newcomers as well as the work of the old established names. Arthur Clarke, Isaac Asimov, Robert Heinlein, Frank Herbert, Marion Zimmer Bradley, C.J. Cherryh came through impressively with works of popular appeal.

So the world may be in a crisis and the crisis may be deepening, but science fiction continues to hold aloft a light that reflects in its own way the hopes and fears of all humanity. The science fiction field is the widest-angled lens of the imagination—in this book alone you will find stories that range from the day after tomorrow to the far-far future. Read, enjoy, and above all, think.

Donald A. Wollheim

BLOOD MUSIC
By Greg Bear

We have had much speculation on the next step in evolution—is there something coming beyond the mammal with the inquisitive brain? Considering the relentless development of life over the last couple billion years, there is no reason to doubt that there will be such a step. Speculations have turned on robots and on spiritual clusters of direct-energy consumers. Greg Bear considers a different aspect of biology. . . .

There is a principle in nature I don't think anyone has pointed out before. Each hour, a myriad of trillions of little live things— bacteria, microbes, "animalcules"—are born and die, not counting for much except in the bulk of their existence and the accumulation of their tiny effects. They do not perceive deeply. They don't suffer much. A hundred billion, dying, would not begin to have the same importance as a single human death.

Within the ranks of magnitude of all creatures, small as microbes or great as humans, there is an equality of "elan," just as the branches of a tall tree, gathered together, equal the bulk of the limbs below, and all the limbs equal the bulk of the trunk.

That, at least, is the principle. I believe Vergil Ulam was the first to violate it.

It had been two years since I'd last seen Vergil. My memory of him hardly matched the tan, smiling, well-dressed gentleman standing before me. We had made a lunch appointment over the phone the day before, and now faced each other in the wide double doors of the employee's cafeteria at the Mount Freedom Medical Center.

"Vergil?" I asked. "My God, Vergil!"

"Good to see you, Edward." He shook my hand firmly. He had lost ten or twelve kilos and what remained seemed tighter,

10

better proportioned. At university, Vergil had been the pudgy, shock-haired, snaggle-toothed whiz kid who hot-wired doorknobs, gave us punch that turned our piss blue, and never got a date except with Eileen Termagent, who shared many of his physical characteristics.

"You look fantastic," I said. "Spend a summer in Cabo San Lucas?"

We stood in line at the counter and chose our food. "The tan," he said, picking out a carton of chocolate milk, "is from spending three months under a sun lamp. My teeth were straightened just after I last saw you. I'll explain the rest, but we need a place to talk where no one will listen close."

I steered him to the smoker's corner, where three die-hard puffers were scattered among six tables.

"Listen, I mean it," I said as we unloaded our trays. "You've changed. You're looking good."

"I've changed more than you know." His tone was motion-picture ominous, and he delivered the line with a theatrical lift of his brows. "How's Gail?"

Gail was doing well, I told him, teaching nursery school. We'd married the year before. His gaze shifted down to his food—pineapple slice and cottage cheese, piece of banana cream pie—and he said, his voice almost cracking, "Notice something else?"

I squinted in concentration. "Uh."

"Look closer."

"I'm not sure. Well, yes, you're not wearing glasses. Contacts?"

"No. I don't need them anymore."

"And you're a snappy dresser. Who's dressing you now? I hope she's as sexy as she is tasteful."

"Candice isn't—wasn't—responsible for the improvements in my clothes," he said. "I just got a better job, more money to throw around. My taste in clothes is better than my taste in food, as it happens." He grinned the old Vergil self-deprecating grin, but ended it with a peculiar leer. "At any rate, she's left me, I've been fired from my job, I'm living on savings."

"Hold it," I said. "That's a bit crowded. Why not do a linear breakdown? You got a job. Where?"

"Genetron Corp.," he said. "Sixteen months ago."

"I haven't heard of them."

"You will. They're putting out common stock in the next month. It'll shoot off the board. They've broken through with MABs. Medical—"

"I know what MABs are," I interrupted. "At least in theory. Medically Applicable Biochips."

"They have some that work."

"What?" It was my turn to lift my brows.

"Microscopic logic circuits. You inject them into the human body, they set up shop where they're told and troubleshoot. With Dr. Michael Bernard's approval."

That was quite impressive. Bernard's reputation was spotless. Not only was he associated with the genetic engineering biggies, but he had made news at least once a year in his practice as a neurosurgeon before retiring. Covers on *Time, Mega, Rolling Stone*.

"That's supposed to be secret—stock, breakthrough, Bernard, everything." He looked around and lowered his voice. "But you do whatever the hell you want. I'm through with the bastards."

I whistled. "Make me rich, huh?"

"If that's what you want. Or you can spend some time with me before rushing off to your broker."

"Of course." He hadn't touched the cottage cheese or pie. He had, however, eaten the pineapple slice and drunk the chocolate milk. "So tell me more."

"Well, in med school I was training for lab work. Biochemical research. I've always had a bent for computers, too. So I put myself through my last two years—"

"By selling software packages to Westinghouse," I said.

"It's good my friends remember. That's how I got involved with Genetron, just when they were starting out. They had big money backers, all the lab facilities I thought anyone would ever need. They hired me, and I advanced rapidly.

"Four months and I was doing my own work. I made some breakthroughs," he tossed his hand nonchalantly, "then I went off on tangents they thought were premature. I persisted and they took away my lab, handed it over to a certifiable flatworm. I managed to save part of the experiment before they fired me. But I haven't exactly been cautious . . . or judicious. So now it's going on outside the lab."

I'd always regarded Vergil as ambitious, a trifle cracked, and not terribly sensitive. His relations with authority figures had never been smooth. Science, for him, was like the woman you couldn't possibly have, who suddenly opens her arms to you, long before you're ready for mature love—leaving you afraid you'll forever blow the chance, lose the prize, screw up royally. Apparently, he had. "Outside the lab? I don't get you."

"Edward, I want you to examine me. Give me a thorough physical. Maybe a cancer diagnostic. Then I'll explain more."

"You want a five-thousand-dollar exam?"

"Whatever you can do. Ultrasound, NMR, thermogram, everything."

"I don't know if I can get access to all that equipment. NMR full-scan has only been here a month or two. Hell, you couldn't pick a more expensive way—"

"Then ultrasound. That's all you'll need."

"Vergil, I'm an obstetrician, not a glamour-boy lab-tech. OB-GYN, butt of all jokes. If you're turning into a woman, maybe I can help you."

He leaned forward, almost putting his elbow into the pie, but swinging wide at the last instant by scant millimeters. The old Vergil would have hit it square. "Examine me closely and you'll . . ." He narrowed his eyes and shook his head. "Just examine me."

"So I make an appointment for ultrasound. Who's going to pay?"

"I'm on Blue Shield." He smiled and held up a medical credit card. "I messed with the personnel files at Genetron. Anything up to a hundred thousand dollars' medical, they'll never check, never suspect."

He wanted secrecy, so I made arrangements. I filled out his forms myself. As long as everything was billed properly, most of the examination could take place without official notice. I didn't charge for my services. After all, Vergil had turned my piss blue. We were friends.

He came in late at night. I wasn't normally on duty then, but I stayed late, waiting for him on the third floor of what the nurses called the Frankenstein wing. I sat on an orange plastic chair. He arrived, looking olive-colored under the fluorescent lights.

He stripped, and I arranged him on the table. I noticed, first off, that his ankles looked swollen. But they weren't puffy. I felt them several times. They seemed healthy, but looked odd. "Hm," I said.

I ran the paddles over him, picking up areas difficult for the big unit to hit, and programmed the data into the imaging system. Then I swung the table around and inserted it into the enameled orifice of the ultrasound diagnostic unit, the hum-hole, so-called by the nurses.

I integrated the data from the hum-hole with that from the paddle sweeps and rolled Vergil out, then set up a video frame.

The image took a second to integrate, then flowed into a pattern showing Vergil's skeleton.

Three seconds of that—my jaw gaping—and it switched to his thoracic organs, then his musculature, and finally, vascular system and skin.

"How long since the accident?" I asked, trying to take the quiver out of my voice.

"I haven't been in an accident," he said. "It was deliberate."

"Jesus, they beat you, to keep secrets?"

"You don't understand me, Edward. Look at the images again. I'm not damaged."

"Look, there's thickening here," I indicated the ankles, "and your ribs—that crazy zig-zag pattern of interlocks. Broken sometime, obviously. And—"

"Look at my spine," he said. I rotated the image in the video frame.

Buckminster Fuller, I thought. It was fantastic. A cage of triangular projections, all interlocking in ways I couldn't begin to follow, much less understand. I reached around and tried to feel his spine with my fingers. He lifted his arms and looked off at the ceiling.

"I can't find it," I said. "It's all smooth back there." I let go of him and looked at his chest, then prodded his ribs. They were sheathed in something rough and flexible. The harder I pressed, the tougher it became. Then I noticed another change.

"Hey," I said. "You don't have any nipples." There were tiny pigment patches, but no nipple formations at all.

"See?" Vergil asked, shrugging on the white robe. "I'm being rebuilt from the inside out."

In my reconstruction of those hours, I fancy myself saying, "So tell me about it." Perhaps mercifully, I don't remember what I actually said.

He explained with his characteristic circumlocutions. Listening was like trying to get to the meat of a newspaper article through a forest of sidebars and graphic embellishments.

I simplify and condense.

Genetron had assigned him to manufacturing prototype biochips, tiny circuits made out of protein molecules. Some were hooked up to silicon chips little more than a micrometer in size, then sent through rat arteries to chemically keyed locations, to make connections with the rat tissue and attempt to monitor and even control lab-induced pathologies.

"*That* was something," he said. "We recovered the most

complex microchip by sacrificing the rat, then debriefed it—hooked the silicon portion up to an imaging system. The computer gave us bar graphs, then a diagram of the chemical characteristics of about eleven centimeters of blood vessel . . . then put it all together to make a picture. We zoomed down eleven centimeters of rat artery. You never saw so many scientists jumping up and down, hugging each other, drinking buckets of bug juice.'' Bug juice was lab ethanol mixed with Dr. Pepper.'

Eventually, the silicon elements were eliminated completely in favor of nucleoproteins. He seemed reluctant to explain in detail, but I gathered they found ways to make huge molecules—as large as DNA, and even more complex—into electrochemical computers, using ribosome-like structures as "encoders" and "readers," and RNA as "tape." Vergil was able to mimic reproductive separation and reassembly in his nucleoproteins, incorporating program changes at key points by switching nucleotide pairs. "Genetron wanted me to switch over to supergene engineering, since that was the coming thing everywhere else. Make all kinds of critters, some out of our imagination. But I had different ideas." He twiddled his finger around his ear and made theremin sounds. "Mad scientist time, right?" He laughed, then sobered. "I injected my best nucleoproteins into bacteria to make duplication and compounding easier. Then I started to leave them inside, so the circuits could interact with the cells. They were heuristically programmed; they taught themselves more than I programmed them. The cells fed chemically coded information to the computers, the computers processed it and made decisions, the cells became smart. I mean, smart as planaria, for starters. Imagine an *E. coli* as smart as a planarian worm!''

I nodded. "I'm imagining.''

"Then I really went off on my own. We had the equipment, the techniques; and I knew the molecular language. I could make really dense, really complicated biochips by compounding the nucleoproteins, making them into little brains. I did some research into how far I could go, theoretically. Sticking with bacteria, I could make them a biochip with the computing capacity of a sparrow's brain. Imagine how jazzed I was! Then I saw a way to increase the complexity a thousandfold, by using something we regarded as a nuisance—quantum chit-chat between the fixed elements of the circuits. Down that small, even the slightest change could bomb a biochip. But I developed a program that actually predicted and took advantage of electron tunneling. Emphasized the heuristic aspects of the computer, used the chit-chat as a method of increasing complexity.''

"You're losing me," I said.

"I took advantage of randomness. The circuits could repair themselves, compare memories and correct faulty elements. The whole schmeer. I gave them basic instructions: Go forth and multiply. Improve. By God, you should have seen some of the cultures a week later! It was amazing. They were evolving all on their own, like little cities. I destroyed them all. I think one of the petri dishes would have grown legs and walked out of the incubator if I'd kept feeding it."

"You're kidding." I looked at him. "You're not kidding."

"Man, they *knew* what it was like to improve! They knew where they had to go, but they were just so limited, being in bacteria bodies, with so few resources."

"How smart were they?"

"I couldn't be sure. They were associating in clusters of a hundred to two hundred cells, each cluster behaving like an autonomous unit. Each cluster might have been as smart as a rhesus monkey. They exchanged information through their pili, passed on bits of memory and compared notes. Their organization was obviously different from a group of monkeys. Their world was so much simpler, for one thing. With their abilities, they were masters of the petri dishes. I put phages in with them; the phages didn't have a chance. They used every option available to change and grow."

"How is that possible?"

"What?" He seemed surprised I wasn't accepting everything at face value.

"Cramming so much into so little. A rhesus monkey is not your simple little calculator, Vergil."

"I haven't made myself clear," he said, obviously irritated. "I was using nucleoprotein computers. They're like DNA, but all the information can interact. Do you know how many nucleotide pairs there are in the DNA of a single bacteria?"

It had been a long time since my last biochemistry lesson. I shook my head.

"About two million. Add in the modified ribosome structures— fifteen thousand of them, each with a molecular weight of about three million—and consider the combinations and permutations. The RNA is arranged like a continuous loop paper tape, surrounded by ribosomes ticking off instructions and manufacturing protein chains . . ." His eyes were bright and slightly moist. "Besides, I'm not saying every cell was a distinct entity. They cooperated."

"How many bacteria in the dishes you destroyed?"

"Billions. I don't know." He smirked. "You got it, Edward. Whole planetsful of *E. coli*."

"But they didn't fire you then?"

"No. They didn't know what was going on, for one thing. I kept compounding the molecules, increasing their size and complexity. When bacteria were too limited, I took blood from myself, separated out white cells, and injected them with the new biochips. I watched them, put them through mazes and little chemical problems. They were whizzes. Time is a lot faster at that level—so little distance for the messages to cross, and the environment is much simpler. Then I forgot to store a file under my secret code in the lab computers. Some managers found it and guessed what I was up to. Everybody panicked. They thought we'd have every social watchdog in the country on our backs because of what I'd done. They started to destroy my work and wipe my programs. Ordered me to sterilize my white cells. Christ." He pulled the white robe off and started to get dressed. "I only had a day or two. I separated out the most complex cells—"

"How complex?"

"They were clustering in hundred-cell groups, like the bacteria. Each group as smart as a ten-year-old kid, maybe." He studied my face for a moment. "Still doubting? Want me to run through how many nucleotide pairs there are in a mammalian cell? I tailored my computers to take advantage of the white cells' capacity. Ten billion nucleotide pairs, Edward. Ten E-fucking ten. And they don't have a huge body to worry about, taking up most of their thinking time."

"Okay," I said. "I'm convinced. What did you do?"

"I mixed the cells back into a cylinder of whole blood and injected myself with it." He buttoned the top of his shirt and smiled thinly at me. "I'd programmed them with every drive I could, talked as high a level as I could using just enzymes and such. After that, they were on their own."

"You programmed them to go forth and multiply, improve?" I repeated.

"I think they developed some characteristics picked up by the biochips in their *E. coli* phases. The white cells could talk to each other with extruded memories. They almost certainly found ways to ingest other types of cells and alter them without killing them."

"You're crazy."

"You can see the screen! Edward, I haven't been sick since. I used to get colds all the time. I've never felt better."

"They're inside you, finding things, changing them."

"And by now, each cluster is as smart as you or I."

"You're absolutely nuts."

He shrugged. "They fired me. They thought I was going to get revenge for what they did to my work. They ordered me out of the labs, and I haven't had a real chance to see what's been going on inside me until now. Three months."

"So . . ." My mind was racing. "You lost weight because they improved your fat metabolism. Your bones are stronger, your spine has been completely rebuilt—"

"No more backaches even if I sleep on my old mattress."

"Your heart looks different."

"I didn't know about the heart," he said, examining the frame image from a few inches. "About the fat—I was thinking about that. They could increase my brown cells, fix up the metabolism. I haven't been as hungry lately. I haven't changed my eating habits that much—I still want the same old junk—but somehow I get around to eating only what I need. I don't think they know what my brain is yet. Sure, they've got all the glandular stuff—but they don't have the *big* picture, if you see what I mean. They don't know *I'm* in there. But boy, they sure did figure out what my reproductive organs are."

I glanced at the image and shifted my eyes away.

"Oh, they look pretty normal," he said, hefting his scrotum obscenely. He snickered. "But how else do you think I'd land a real looker like Candice? She was just after a one-night stand with a techie. I looked okay then, no tan but trim, with good clothes. She'd never screwed a techie before. Joke time, right? But my little geniuses kept us up half the night. I think they made improvements each time. I felt like I had a god-damned fever."

His smile vanished. "But then one night my skin started to crawl. It really scared me. I thought things were getting out of hand. I wondered what they'd do when they crossed the blood-brain barrier and found out about *me*—about the brain's real function. So I began a campaign to keep them under control. I figured, the reason they wanted to get into the skin was the simplicity of running circuits across a surface. Much easier than trying to maintain chains of communication in and around muscles, organs, vessels. The skin was much more direct. So I bought a quartz lamp." He caught my puzzled expression. "In the lab, we'd break down the protein in biochip cells by exposing them to ultra-violet light. I alternated sunlamp with quartz treatments.

Keeps them out of my skin, so far as I can tell, and gives me a nice tan.''

"Give you skin cancer, too," I commented.

"They'll probably take care of that. Like police."

"Okay, I've examined you, you've told me a story I still find hard to believe . . . what do you want me to do?''

"I'm not as nonchalant as I act, Edward. I'm worried. I'd like to find some way to control them before they find out about my brain. I mean, think of it, they're in the trillions by now, each one smart. They're cooperating to some extent. I'm probably the smartest thing on the planet, and they haven't even begun to get their act together yet. I don't really want them to take over." He laughed very unpleasantly. "Steal my soul, you know? So think of some treatment to block them. Maybe we can starve the little buggers. Just think on it." He buttoned his shirt. "Give me a call." He handed me a slip of paper with his address and phone number. Then he went to the keyboard and erased the image on the frame, dumping the memory of the examination. "Just you," he said. "Nobody else for now. And please . . . hurry."

It was three o'clock in the morning when Vergil walked out of the examination room. He'd allowed me to take blood samples, then shaken my hand—his palm damp, nervous—and cautioned me against ingesting anything from the specimens.

Before I went home, I put the blood through a series of tests. The results were ready the next day.

I picked them up during my lunch break in the afternoon, then destroyed all the samples. I did it like a robot. It took me five days and nearly sleepless nights to accept what I'd seen. His blood was normal enough, though the machines diagnosed the patient as having an infection. High levels of leucocytes—white blood cells—and histamines. On the fifth day, I believed.

Gail was home before I, but it was my turn to fix dinner. She slipped one of the school's disks into the home system and showed me video art her nursery kids had been creating. I watched quietly, ate with her in silence.

I had two dreams, part of my final acceptance. The first that evening—which had me up thrashing in my sheets—I witnessed the destruction of the planet Krypton, Superman's home world. Billions of superhuman geniuses went screaming off in walls of fire. I related the destruction to my sterilizing the samples of Vergil's blood.

The second dream was worse. I dreamed that New York City was raping a woman. By the end of the dream, she was giving birth to little embryo cities, all wrapped up in translucent sacs, soaked with blood from the difficult labor.

I called him on the morning of the sixth day. He answered on the fourth ring. "I have some results," I said. "Nothing conclusive. But I want to talk with you. In person."

"Sure," he said. "I'm staying inside for the time being." His voice was strained; he sounded tired.

Vergil's apartment was in a fancy high-rise near the lake shore. I took the elevator up, listening to little advertising jingles and watching dancing holograms display products, empty apartments for rent, the building's hostess discussing social activities for the week.

Vergil opened the door and motioned me in. He wore a checked robe with long sleeves and carpet slippers. He clutched an unlit pipe in one hand, his fingers twisting it back and forth as he walked away from me and sat down, saying nothing.

"You have an infection," I said.

"Oh?"

"That's all the blood analyses tell me. I don't have access to the electron microscopes."

"I don't think it's really an infection," he said. "After all, they're my own cells. Probably something else . . . sign of their presence, of the change. We can't expect to understand everything that's happening."

I removed my coat. "Listen," I said, "you have me worried now." The expression on his face stopped me: a kind of frantic beatitude. He squinted at the ceiling and pursed his lips.

"Are you stoned?" I asked.

He shook his head, then nodded once, very slowly. "Listening," he said.

"To what?"

"I don't know. Not sounds . . . exactly. Like music. The heart, all the blood vessels, friction of blood along the arteries, veins. Activity. Music in the blood." He looked at me plaintively. "Why aren't you at work?"

"My day off. Gail's working."

"Can you stay?"

I shrugged. "I suppose." I sounded suspicious. I was glancing around the apartment, looking for ashtrays, packs of papers.

"I'm not stoned, Edward," he said. "I may be wrong, but I think something big is happening. I think they're finding out who I am."

I sat down across from Vergil, staring at him intently. He didn't seem to notice. Some inner process was involving him.

When I asked for a cup of coffee, he motioned to the kitchen. I boiled a pot of water and took a jar of instant from the cabinet. With cup in hand, I returned to my seat. He was twisting his head back and forth, eyes open. "You always knew what you wanted to be, didn't you?" he asked me.

"More or less."

"A gynecologist. Smart moves. Never false moves. I was different. I had goals, but no direction. Like a map without roads, just places to be. I didn't give a shit for anything, anyone but myself. Even science. Just a means. I'm surprised I got so far. I even hated my folks."

He gripped his chair arms.

"Something wrong?" I asked.

"They're talking to me," he said. He shut his eyes.

For an hour he seemed to be asleep. I checked his pulse, which was strong and steady, felt his forehead—slightly cool—and made myself more coffee. I was looking through a magazine, at a loss what to do, when he opened his eyes again. "Hard to figure exactly what time is like for them," he said. "It's taken them maybe three, four days to figure out language, key human concepts. Now they're on to it. On to me. Right now."

"How's that?"

He claimed there were thousands of researchers hooked up to his neurons. He couldn't give details. "They're damned efficient, you know," he said. "They haven't screwed me up yet."

"We should get you into the hospital now."

"What in hell could they do? Did you figure out any way to control them? I mean, they're my own cells."

"I've been thinking. We could starve them. Find out what metabolic differences—"

"I'm not sure I want to be rid of them," Vergil said. "They're not doing any harm."

"How do you know?"

He shook his head and held up one finger. "Wait. They're trying to figure out what space is. That's tough for them. They break distances down into concentrations of chemicals. For them, space is like intensity of taste."

"Vergil—"

"Listen! Think, Edward!" His tone was excited but even. "Observe! Something big is happening inside me. They talk to each other across the fluid, through membranes. They tailor something—viruses?—to carry data stored in nucleic acid chains. I think they're saying 'RNA.' That makes sense. That's one way I programmed them. But plasmid-like structures, too. Maybe that's what your machines think is a sign of infection—all their chattering in my blood, packets of data. Tastes of other individuals. Peers. Superiors. Subordinates."

"Vergil, I'm listening, but I still think you should be in a hospital."

"This is my show, Edward," he said. "I'm their universe. They're amazed by the new scale." He was quiet again for a time. I squatted by his chair and pulled up the sleeve to his robe. His arm was criss-crossed with white lines. I was about to go to the phone and call for an ambulance when he stood and stretched. "Do you realize," he said, "how many body cells we kill each time we move?"

"I'm going to call for an ambulance," I said.

"No, you aren't." His tone stopped me. "I told you, I'm not sick; this is my show. Do you know what they'd do to me in a hospital? They'd be like cavemen trying to fix a computer the same way they fix a stone axe. It would be a farce."

"Then what the hell am I doing here?" I asked, getting angry. "I can't do anything. I'm one of those cavemen."

"You're a friend," Vergil said, fixing his eyes on me. I had the impression I was being watched by more than just Vergil. "I want you here to keep me company." He laughed. "But I'm not exactly alone."

He walked around the apartment for two hours, fingering things, looking out windows, making himself lunch slowly and methodically. "You know, they can actually feel their own thoughts," he said about noon. "I mean, the cytoplasm seems to have a will of its own, a kind of subconscious life counter to the rationality they've only recently acquired. They hear the chemical 'noise' or whatever of the molecules fitting and unfitting inside."

At two o'clock, I called Gail to tell her I would be late. I was almost sick with tension but I tried to keep my voice level. "Remember Vergil Ulam? I'm talking with him right now."

"Everything okay?" she asked.

Was it? Decidedly not. "Fine," I said.

"Culture!" Vergil said, peering around the kitchen wall at me. I said good-bye and hung up the phone. "They're always swimming in that bath of information. Contributing to it. It's a kind of gestalt thing, whatever. The hierarchy is absolute. They send tailored phages after cells that don't interact properly. Viruses specified to individuals or groups. No escape. One gets pierced by the virus, the cell blebs outward, it explodes and dissolves. But it's not just a dictatorship, I think they effectively have more freedom than in a democracy. I mean, they vary so differently from individual to individual. Does that make sense? They vary in different ways than we do.''

"Hold it," I said, gripping his shoulders. "Vergil, you're pushing me close to the edge. I can't take this much longer. I don't understand, I'm not sure I believe—"

"Not even now?"

"Okay, let's say you're giving me the, the right interpretation. Giving it to me straight. The whole thing's true. Have you bothered to figure out all the consequences yet? What all this means, where it might lead?"

He walked into the kitchen and drew a glass of water from the tap, then returned and stood next to me. His expression had changed from childish absorption to sober concern. "I've never been very good at that."

"Aren't you afraid?"

"I was. Now I'm not sure." He fingered the tie of his robe. "Look, I don't want you to think I went around you, over your head or something. But I met with Michael Bernard yesterday. He put me through his private clinic, took specimens. Told me to quit the lamp treatments. He called this morning, just before you did. He says it all checks out. And he asked me not to tell anybody." He paused and his expression became dreamy again. "Cities of cells," he continued. "Edward, they push pili-like tubes through the tissues, spread information—"

"Stop it!" I shouted. "Checks out? What checks out?"

"As Bernard puts it, I have 'severely enlarged macrophages' throughout my system. And he concurs on the anatomical changes. So it's not just our common delusion."

"What does he plan to do?"

"I don't know. I think he'll probably convince Genetron to reopen the lab."

"Is that what you want?"

"It's not just having the lab again. I want to show you. Since I stopped the lamp treatments. I'm still changing." He undid his robe and let it slide to the floor. All over his body, his skin was crisscrossed with white lines. Along his back, the lines were starting to form ridges.

"My God," I said.

"I'm not going to be much good anywhere else but the lab soon. I won't be able to go out in public. Hospitals wouldn't know what to do, as I said."

"You're . . . you can talk to them, tell them to slow down," I said, aware how ridiculous that sounded.

"Yes, indeed I can, but they don't necessarily listen."

"I thought you were their god or something."

"The ones hooked up to my neurons aren't the big wheels. They're researchers, or at least serve the same function. They know I'm here, what I am, but that doesn't mean they've convinced the upper levels of the hierarchy."

"They're disputing?"

"Something like that. It's not all that bad, anyway. If the lab is reopened, I have a home, a place to work." He glanced out the window, as if looking for someone. "I don't have anything left but them. They aren't afraid, Edward. I've never felt so close to anything before." The beatific smile again. "I'm responsible for them. Mother to them all."

"You have no way of knowing what they're going to do."

He shook his head.

"No, I mean it. You say they're like a civilization—"

"Like a thousand civilizations."

"Yes, and civilizations have been known to screw up. Warfare, the environment—"

I was grasping at straws, trying to restrain a growing panic. I wasn't competent to handle the enormity of what was happening. Neither was Vergil. He was the last person I would have called insightful and wise about large issues.

"But I'm the only one at risk."

"You don't know that. Jesus, Vergil, look what they're *doing* to you!"

"To me, all to me!" he said. "Nobody else."

I shook my head and held up my hands in a gesture of defeat. "Okay, so Bernard gets them to reopen the lab, you move in, become a guinea pig. What then?"

"They treat me right. I'm more than just good old Vergil Ulam now. I'm a god-damned galaxy, a super-mother."

"Super-host, you mean." He conceded the point with a shrug.

I couldn't take any more. I made my exit with a few flimsy excuses, then sat in the lobby of the apartment building, trying to calm down. Somebody had to talk some sense into him. Who would he listen to? He had gone to Bernard . . .

And it sounded as if Bernard were not only convinced, but very interested. People of Bernard's stature didn't coax the Vergil Ulams of the world along, not unless they felt it was to their advantage.

I had a hunch, and I decided to play it. I went to a pay phone, slipped in my credit card, and called Genetron.

"I'd like you to page Dr. Michael Bernard," I told the receptionist.

"This is his answering service. We have an emergency call and his beeper doesn't seem to be working."

A few anxious minutes later, Bernard came on the line. "Who the hell is this?" he asked quietly. "I don't have an answering service."

"My name is Edward Milligan. I'm a friend of Vergil Ulam's. I think we have some problems to discuss."

We made an appointment to talk the next morning.

I went home and tried to think of excuses to keep me off the next day's hospital shift. I couldn't concentrate on medicine, couldn't give my patients anywhere near the attention they deserved.

Guilty, anxious, angry, afraid.

That was how Gail found me. I slipped on a mask of calm and we fixed dinner together. After eating, we watched the city lights come on in late twilight through the bayside window, holding on to each other. Odd winter starlings pecked at the yellow lawn in the last few minutes of light, then flew away with a rising wind which made the windows rattle.

"Something's wrong," Gail said softly. "Are you going to tell me, or just act like everything's normal?"

"It's just me," I said. "Nervous. Work at the hospital."

"Oh, lord," she said, sitting up. "You're going to divorce me for that Baker woman." Mrs. Baker weighed three hundred and sixty pounds and hadn't known she was pregnant until her fifth month.

"No," I said, listless.

"Rapturous relief," Gail said, touching my forehead lightly. "You know this kind of introspection drives me crazy."

"Well, it's nothing I can talk about yet, so . . ." I patted her hand.

"That's disgustingly patronizing," she said, getting up. "I'm going to make some tea. Want some?" Now she was miffed, and I was tense with not telling.

Why not just reveal all? I asked myself. An old friend of mine was turning himself into a galaxy.

I cleared away the table instead. That night, unable to sleep, I looked down on Gail in bed from my sitting position, pillow against the wall, and tried to determine what I knew was real, and what wasn't.

I'm a doctor, I told myself. A technical, scientific profession. I'm supposed to be immune to things like future shock.

Vergil Ulam was turning into a galaxy.

How would it feel to be topped off with a trillion Chinese? I grinned in the dark, and almost cried at the same time. What Vergil had inside him was unimaginably stranger than Chinese. Stranger than anything I—or Vergil—could easily understand. Perhaps ever understand.

But I knew what was real. The bedroom, the city lights faint through gauze curtains. Gail sleeping. Very important. Gail, in bed, sleeping.

The dream came again, This time the city came in through the window and attacked Gail. It was a great, spiky lighted-up prowler and it growled in a language I couldn't understand, made up of auto horns, crowded noises, construction bedlam. I tried to fight it off, but it got to her—and turned into a drift of stars, sprinkling all over the bed, all over everything. I jerked awake and stayed up until dawn, dressed with Gail, kissed her, savored the reality of her human, unviolated lips.

And went to meet with Bernard. He had been loaned a suite in a big downtown hospital; I rode the elevator to the sixth floor, and saw what fame and fortune could mean.

The suite was tastefully furnished, fine serigraphs on wood-paneled walls, chrome and glass furniture, cream-colored carpet, Chinese brass, and wormwood-grain cabinets and tables.

He offered me a cup of coffee, and I accepted. He took a seat in the breakfast nook, and I sat across from him, cradling my cup in moist palms. He was dapper, wearing a gray suit; had graying hair and a sharp profile. He was in his mid sixties and he looked quite a bit like Leonard Bernstein.

"About our mutual acquaintance," he said. "Mr. Ulam. Brilliant. And, I won't hesitate to say, courageous."

"He's my friend. I'm worried about him."

Bernard held up one finger. "Courageous—and a bloody damned fool. What's happening to him should never have been allowed. He may have done it under duress, but that's no excuse. Still, what's done is done. He's talked to you, I take it."

I nodded. "He wants to return to Genetron."

"Of course. That's where all his equipment is. Where his home probably will be while we sort this out."

"Sort it out—how? What use is it?" I wasn't thinking too clearly. I had a slight headache.

"I can think of a large number of uses for small, super-dense computer elements with a biological base. Can't you? Genetron has already made breakthroughs, but this is something else again."

"What do you envision?"

Bernard smiled. "I'm not really at liberty to say. It'll be revolutionary. We'll have to get him in lab conditions. Animal experiments have to be conducted. We'll have to start from scratch, of course. Vergil's . . . um . . . colonies can't be transferred. They're based on his white blood cells. So we have to develop colonies that won't trigger immune reactions to other animals."

"Like an infection?" I asked.

"I suppose there are comparisons. But Vergil is not infected."

"My tests indicate he is."

"That's probably the bits of data floating around in his blood, don't you think?"

"I don't know."

"Listen, I'd like you to come down to the lab after Vergil is settled in. Your expertise might be useful to us."

Us. He was working with Genetron hand in glove. Could he be objective? "How will you benefit from all this?"

"Edward, I have always been at the forefront of my profession. I see no reason why I shouldn't be helping here. With my knowledge of brain and nerve functions, and the research I've been conducting in neurophysiology—"

"You could help Genetron hold off an investigation by the government," I said.

"That's being very blunt. Too blunt, and unfair."

"Perhaps. Anyway, yes. I'd like to visit the lab when Vergil's settled in. If I'm still welcome, bluntness and all." He looked at me sharply. I wouldn't be playing on *his* team; for a moment, his thoughts were almost nakedly apparent.

"Of course," Bernard said, rising with me. He reached out to shake my hand. His palm was damp. He was as nervous as I was, even if he didn't look it.

I returned to my apartment and stayed there until noon, reading, trying to sort things out. Reach a decision. What was real, what I needed to protect.

There is only so much change anyone can stand. Innovation, yes, but slow application. Don't force. Everyone has the right to stay the same until they decide otherwise.

The greatest thing in science since . . .

And Bernard would force it. Genetron would force it. I couldn't handle the thought. "Neo-Luddite," I said to myself. A filthy accusation.

When I pressed Vergil's number on the building security panel, Vergil answered almost immediately. "Yeah," he said. He sounded exhilarated now. "Come on up. I'll be in the bathroom. Door's unlocked."

I entered his apartment and walked through the hallway to the bathroom. Vergil was in the tub, up to his neck in pinkish water. He smiled vaguely at me and splashed his hands. "Looks like I slit my wrists, doesn't it?" he said softly. "Don't worry. Everything's fine now. Genetron's going to take me back. Bernard just called." He pointed to the bathroom phone and intercom.

I sat down on the toilet and noticed the sunlamp fixture standing unplugged next to the linen cabinets. The bulbs sat in a row on the edge of the sink counter. "You're sure that's what you want," I said, my shoulders slumping.

"Yeah, I think so," he said. "They can take better care of me. I'm getting cleaned up, go over there this evening. Bernard's picking me up in his limo. Style. From here on in, everything's style."

The pinkish color in the water didn't look like soap. "Is that bubble bath?" I asked. Some of it came to me in a rush then and I felt a little weaker: what had occurred to me was just one more obvious and necessary insanity.

"No," Vergil said. I knew that already.

"No," he repeated, "it's coming from my skin. They're not telling me everything, but I think they're sending out scouts. Astronauts." He looked at me with an expression that didn't quite equal concern; more like curiosity as to how I'd take it.

The confirmation made my stomach muscles tighten as if waiting for a punch. I had never even considered the possibility until now, perhaps because I had been concentrating on other aspects. "Is this the first time?" I asked.

"Yeah," he said. He laughed. "I've half a mind to let the little buggers down the drain. Let them find out what the world's really about."

"They'd go everywhere," I said.

"Sure enough."

"How . . . how are you feeling?"

"I'm feeling pretty good now. Must be billions of them." More splashing with his hands. "What do you think? Should I let the buggers out?"

Quickly, hardly thinking, I knelt down beside the tub. My fingers went for the cord on the sunlamp and I plugged it in. He had hot-wired doorknobs, turned my piss blue, played a thousand dumb practical jokes and never grown up, never grown mature enough to understand that he was just brilliant enough to really affect the world; he would never learn caution.

He reached for the drain knob. "You know, Edward, I—"

He never finished. I picked up the fixture and dropped it into the tub, jumping back at the flash of steam and sparks. Vergil screamed and thrashed and jerked and then everything was still, except for the low, steady sizzle and the smoke wafting from his hair.

I lifted the toilet and vomited. Then I clenched my nose and went into the living room. My legs went out from under me and I sat abruptly on the couch.

After an hour, I searched through Vergil's kitchen and found bleach, ammonia, and a bottle of Jack Daniel's. I returned to the bathroom, keeping the center of my gaze away from Vergil. I poured first the booze, then the bleach, then the ammonia into the water. Chlorine started bubbling up and I left, closing the door behind me.

The phone was ringing when I got home. I didn't answer. It could have been the hospital. It could have been Bernard. Or the police. I could envision having to explain everything to the police. Genetron would stonewall; Bernard would be unavailable.

I was exhausted, all my muscles knotted with tension and whatever name one can give to the feelings one has after—

Committing genocide?

That certainly didn't seem real. I could not believe I had just murdered a hundred trillion intelligent beings. Snuffed a galaxy. It was laughable. But I didn't laugh.

It was not at all hard to believe I had just killed one human being, a friend. The smoke, the melted lamp rods, the drooping electrical outlet and smoking cord.

Vergil.

I had dunked the lamp into the tub with Vergil.

I felt sick. Dreams, cities raping Gail (and what about his girlfriend, Candice?). Letting the water filled with them out. Galaxies sprinkling over us us all. What horror. Then again, what potential beauty—a new kind of life, symbiosis and transformation.

Had I been thorough enough to kill them all? I had a moment of panic. Tomorrow, I thought, I will sterilize his apartment. Somehow. I didn't even think of Bernard.

When Gail came in the door, I was asleep on the couch. I came to, groggy, and she looked down at me.

"You feeling okay?" she asked, perching on the edge of the couch. I nodded.

"What are you planning for dinner?" My mouth wasn't working properly. The words were mushy. She felt my forehead.

"Edward, you have a fever," she said. "A very high fever."

I stumbled into the bathroom and looked in the mirror. Gail was close behind me. "What is it?" she asked.

There were lines under my collar, around my neck. White lines, like freeways. They had already been in me a long time, days.

"Damp palms," I said. So obvious.

I think we nearly died. I struggled at first, but within minutes I was too weak to move. Gail was just as sick within an hour.

I lay on the carpet in the living room, drenched in sweat. Gail lay on the couch, her face the color of talcum, eyes closed, like a corpse in an embalming parlor. For a time I thought she was dead. Sick as I was, I raged—hated, felt tremendous guilt at my weakness, my slowness to understand all the possibilities. Then I no longer cared. I was too weak to blink, so I closed my eyes and waited.

There was a rhythm in my arms, my legs. With each pulse of blood, a kind of sound welled up within me. A sound like an orchestra thousands strong, but not playing in unison; playing whole seasons of symphonies at once. Music in the blood. The sound or whatever became harsher, but more coordinated, wave-trains finally cancelling into silence, then separating into harmonic beats.

The beats seemed to melt into me, into the sound of my own heart.

First, they subdued our immune responses. The war—and it was a war, on a scale never before known on Earth, with trillions of combatants—lasted perhaps two days.

By the time I regained enough strength to get to the kitchen faucet, I could feel them working on my brain, trying to crack the code and find the god within the protoplasm. I drank until I was sick, then drank more moderately and took a glass to Gail. She sipped at it. Her lips were cracked, her eyes bloodshot and ringed with yellowish crumbs. There was some color in her skin. Minutes later, we were eating feebly in the kitchen.

"What in hell was *that?*" was the first thing she asked. I didn't have the strength to explain, so I shook my head. I peeled an orange and shared it with her. "We should call a doctor," she said. But I knew we wouldn't. I was already receiving messages;

it was becoming apparent that any sensation of freedom we had was illusory.

The messages were simple at first. Memories of commands, rather than the commands themselves, manifested themselves in my thoughts. We were not to leave the apartment—a concept which seemed quite abstract to those in control, even if undesirable—and we were not to have contact with others. We would be allowed to eat certain foods, and drink tap water, for the time being.

With the subsidence of the fevers, the transformations were quick and drastic. Almost simultaneously, Gail and I were immobilized. She was sitting at the table, I was kneeling on the floor. I was able barely to see her in the corner of my eye.

Her arm was developing pronounced ridges.

They had learned inside Vergil; their tactics within the two of us were very different. I itched all over for about two hours—two hours in hell—before they made the breakthrough and found me. The effort of ages on their timescale paid off and they communicated smoothly and directly with this great, clumsy intelligence which had once controlled their universe.

They were not cruel. When the concept of discomfort and its undesirability was made clear, they worked to alleviate it. They worked too effectively. For another hour, I was in a sea of bliss, out of all contact with them.

With dawn the next day, we were allowed freedom to move again; specifically, to go to the bathroom. There were certain waste products they could not deal with. I voided those—my urine was purple—and Gail followed suit. We looked at each other vacantly in the bathroom. Then she managed a slight smile. "Are they talking to you?" she asked. I nodded. "Then I'm not crazy."

For the next twelve hours, control seemed to loosen on some levels. During that time, I managed to pencil the majority of this manuscript. I suspect there was another kind of war going on in me. Gail was capable of our previous limited motion, but no more.

When full control resumed, we were instructed to hold each other. We did not hesitate.

"Eddie. . . ." she whispered. My name was the last sound I ever heard from outside.

Standing, we grew together. In hours, our legs expanded and spread out. Then extensions grew to the windows to take in sunlight, and to the kitchen to take water from the sink. Filaments soon reached to all corners of the room, stripping paint and plaster from the walls, fabric and stuffing from the furniture.

By the next dawn, the transformation was complete.

I no longer have any clear view of what we look like. I suspect we resemble cells—large, flat and filamented cells, draped purposefully across most of the apartment. The great shall mimic the small.

I have been asked to carry on recording, but soon that will not be possible. Our intelligence fluctuates daily as we are absorbed into the minds within. Each day, our individuality declines. We are, indeed, great clumsy dinosaurs. Our memories have been taken over by billions of them, and our personalities have been spread through the transformed blood.

Soon there will be no need for centralization.

I am informed that already the plumbing has been invaded. People throughout the building are undergoing transformation.

Within the old time-frame of weeks, we will reach the lakes, rivers, and seas in force.

I can barely begin to guess the results. Every square inch of the planet will teem with thought. Years from now, perhaps much sooner, they will subdue their own individuality—what there is of it.

New creatures will come, then. The immensity of their capacity for thought will be inconceivable.

All my hatred and fear is gone now.

I leave them—us—with only one question.

How many times has this happened, elsewhere? Travellers never came through space to visit the Earth. They had no need.

They had found universes in grains of sand.

POTENTIAL
by Isaac Asimov

Dr. Asimov has established himself as a scoffer at astrology and similar pseudo-sciences. Nevertheless he is not close-minded about things just beyond the boundaries of established science. So here he is with a consideration of the potential of human genetics for something new.

Nadine Triomph checked the long list of symbols for—what was it?—the tenth time. She did not think she could get anything out of it that Multivac had not, but it was only human to try.

She passed it over to Basil Seversky. "It's completely different, Basil," she said.

"You can see that at a glance," said Basil, gloomily.

"Well, don't drag. That's good. So far the only gene combinations that Multivac has dredged up seem to have been minor variations on a theme. Now this one is different."

Basil put his hands into the pockets of his lab jacket and leaned his chair back against the wall. He felt the line of his hips absently and noted it was gaining a certain softness. He was getting pudgy all over, he thought, and didn't like it.

He said, "Multivac doesn't tell us anything we don't tell it first. We don't really know that the basic requirements for telepathy are valid, do we?"

Nadine felt defensive. It was Basil who had worked out the neurological requirements, but it was she who had prepared the program by which Multivac scanned the potential gene structures to see which might produce those requirements.

She said, "If we have two rather different sets of genetic patterns, as we now have, we can work out—or try to work out—the common factors, and this could give us a lead as to the validity."

"In theory—but we'll be working in theory forever. If Multivac works at its present speed for the remaining lifetime of the sun as a main-sequence star, it will not have gone through a duodecillionth of all the possible structural variations of the genes that might exist, let alone the possible modifications introduced by their order on the chromosomes."

"We might get lucky." They had held the same conversation—upbeat versus downbeat—a dozen times, with minor variations in detail.

"Lucky? The word hasn't been invented to describe the kind of impossible luck we would need. And if we do pick out a million different genetic patterns with potential for telepathy, we then have to ask what the odds are that someone now alive will have such a gene pattern, or anything near it."

"We can modify," said Nadine.

"Oh? Have you come across an existing human genetic pattern which can be modified by known procedures into something Multivac says will produce telepathy?"

"The procedures will improve in the future and if we keep Multivac working and keep on registering all human genetic patterns at birth—"

"—*And*," Basil continued sing-song, "if the Planetary Genetic Council continues to support the program adequately, *and* if we continue to get the time-sharing we need on Multivac, *and* if—"

It was at that point that Multivac interrupted with one more item and all a dazed Basil could say afterward was, "I don't believe it."

It seemed that Multivac's routine scanning of registered genetic patterns of living human beings had turned up one that matched the new pattern it had worked out as possessing telepathic potential—and the match was virtually exact.

Basil said, "I don't believe it."

Nadine, who had always been forced into unreasoning faith by Basil's consistent pessimism, said, sunnily. "Here he is, just the same. Male. Aged 15. Name Roland Washman. Only child. Plainview, Iowa. American Region, actually."

Basil studied Roland's genetic pattern, as delivered by Multivac, and compared it with the pattern worked out by Multivac from theoretical considerations. He muttered, again, "I don't believe it."

"It's there before you."

"Do you know the odds against this?"

"It's there before you. The Universe is billions of years old and there's been time for a great many unbelievable coincidences to happen."

"Not this unbelievable." Basil pulled himself together. "Iowa was included in one of the areas we scanned for telepathic presence and nothing ever showed up. Of course, the pattern only shows the *potential* for telepathy—"

It was Basil's plan to approach indirectly. However much the Planetary Genetic Council might post the possibility of telepathy as one of the goal-patterns to be searched for, along with musical genius, variable-gravitational endurance, cancer resistance, mathematical intuition, and several hundred other items, it remained that telepathy had an ingrained unpopularity.

However exciting the thought of "reading minds" might seem in the abstract, there was always an uneasy resistance to the thought of having one's mind read. Thought was the unassailable bastion of privacy, and it would not be surrendered without a struggle. Any controvertible claim to have discovered telepathy would, therefore, be surely controverted.

Basil, therefore, overrode Nadine's willingness to move straight to the point and to interview the young man directly, by making that very point.

"Oh, yes," he grumbled, "and we will let our eagerness lure us into announcing we have found a telepath so that the PGC will put half a dozen authorities on his track in order to disprove the claim and ruin our scientific careers. Let's find out all we can about him *first*."

The disappointed Nadine consoled herself with the obvious fact that in a computerized society, every human being left tracks of all kinds from the moment of conception, and that it could all be recovered without much trouble, and even quickly.

"Umm," said Basil, "not very bright in school."

"It could be a good sign," said Nadine. "Telepathic ability would surely take up a sizable fraction of the higher functioning of the brain and leave little over for abstract thought. That might explain why telepathy has not evolved more noticeably in the human species. The disadvantages of low intelligence would be contra-survival."

"He's not exactly an *idiot savante*. Dull-normal."

"Which might be exactly right."

"Rather withdrawn. Doesn't make friends easily. Rather a loner."

Nadine said, excitedly. "*Exactly* right. Any early evidence of telepathic ability would frighten, upset, and antagonize people.

A youngster lacking judgement would innocently expose the motives of others in his group and be beaten up for his pains. Naturally, he would withdraw into himself.''

Data was gathered for a long time, thereafter, and Basil said, finally. ''Nothing! There's nothing known about him; no reports, not one, that indicates anything that can be twisted into a sign of telepathy. There's not even any comment to the effect that he's 'peculiar.' He's almost disregarded.''

''*Absolutely* right. The reaction of others forced him, early on, to hide all telepathic ability, and that same telepathic ability guided his behavior so as to avoid all unfavorable notice. It's remarkable how it fits.''

Basil stared at her with disfavor. ''You can twist anything into supporting your romantic view of this. Look! He's fifteen and that's too old. Let's suppose he was born with a certain amount of telepathic ability and that he early learned not to display it. Surely the talent would have atrophied and be entirely gone by now. That has to be so for if he remained a full telepath, he couldn't possibly have avoided displaying it now and then, and that would have attracted attention.''

''No, Basil. At school, he's by himself and does as little work as possible—''

''He's not scapegoated, as he would be if he were a telepathic little wise-guy.''

''I told you! He knows when he would be and avoids it. Summers he works as a gardener's assistant and, again, doesn't encounter the public.''

''He encounters the gardener, and yet he keeps the job. It's his third summer there right now, and if he were a telepath, the gardener would get rid of him. No, it's close—but no cigar. It's too late. What we need is a new-born child with that same genetic pattern. Then we might have something—*maybe*.''

Nadine rumpled her fading blonde hair and looked exasperated. ''You're deliberately trying to avoid tackling the problem by denying it exists. Why don't we interview the gardener? If you're willing to go to Iowa—I tell you what, I'll pay for the plane fare, and you won't have to charge it to the project, if that's what's bothering you.''

Basil held up his hand. ''No, no, the project will bear it, but I tell *you* what. If we find no signs of telepathic ability, and we won't, you'll owe me one fancy dinner at a restaurant of my choice.''

''Done,'' said Nadine, eagerly, ''and you can even bring your wife.''

"You'll lose."

"I don't care. Just so we don't abandon the matter too soon."

The gardener was by no means enthusiastically cooperative. He viewed the two as government officials and did not approve of them for that reason. When they identified themselves as scientists, that was no better ground for approval. And when they asked after Roland, he neared the point of outright hostility.

"What do you want to know about Roland for? Done anything?"

"No, no," said Nadine, as winningly as she might. "He might qualify for special schooling, that's all."

"What kind of schooling? Gardening?"

"We're not sure."

"Gardening's all he's good for, but he's good at that. Best I've ever had. He doesn't need no schooling in gardening."

Nadine looked about appreciatively at the greenhouse and at the neat rows of plants outside as well. "He does all that?"

"Have to admit it," said the gardener. "Never this good without him. But it's all he's good for."

Basil said, "Why is that all he's good for, sir?"

"He's not very bright. But he's got this talent. He'll make anything grow."

"Is he odd in any way?"

"What do you mean, odd?"

"Funny? Peculiar? Strange?"

"Being that good a gardener is strange, but I don't complain."

"Nothing else."

"No. What you looking for, mister?"

Basil said, "I really don't know."

That evening, Nadine said, "We've got to study the boy."

"Why? What have you heard that gives you any hope?"

"Suppose you're right. Suppose it's all atrophied. Still, we might find a *trace* of the ability."

"What would we do with a trace? Small effects would not be convincing. We have had a full century of experience with that, from Rhine onward."

"Even if we don't get anything that would prove anything to the world, so what? What about *ourselves?* The important thing is that we'd satisfy ourselves that when Multivac says a particular genetic pattern has the potential for telepathy, it's right. And if it's right, that would mean your theoretical analysis—and my programming, too—was right. Don't you want to put your theories to the test and find confirmatory evidence? Or are you afraid you won't.''

"I'm not afraid of that. I *am* afraid of wasting time."

"One test is all I ask. Look, we ought to see his parents anyway, for whatever they can tell us. After all, they knew him when he was a baby and had, in full, whatever telepathic powers he might have had to begin with—and then we'll get permission to have him match random numbers. If he fails that, we go no further. We waste no more time."

Roland's parents were stolid and totally non-informative. They seemed as slow as Roland was reported to be, and as self-contained.

There had been nothing odd about their son as a baby, they said. They repeated that without guilty over-emphasis. Strong and healthy, they said, and a hard-working boy who earned good money over the summer and went to high-school the rest of the year. Never in any trouble with the law or in any other way.

"Might we test him?" asked Nadine. "A simple test?"

"What for?" asked Washman. "I don't want him bothered."

"Government survey. We're choosing fifteen-year-old boys here and there so we can study ways to improve methods of schooling."

Washman shook his head. "I don't want my boy bothered."

"Well," said Nadine, "you must understand there's two hundred fifty dollars to the family for each boy tested." (She carefully avoided looking at Basil, certain that his lips would have tightened in anger.)

"Two hundred fifty dollars?"

"Yes," said Nadine, trying hard. "After all, the test takes time and it's only fair the government pay for the time and trouble."

Washman cast a slow glance at his wife and she nodded. He said, "If the boy is willing, I guess it would be okay."

Roland Washman was tall for his age and well-built, but there seemed no danger in his muscles. He had a gentle way about him, and dark, quiet eyes looked out of his well-browned face.

He said, "What am I supposed to do, mister?"

"It's very easy," said Basil. "You have a little joy-stick with the numbers 0 to 9 on it. Every time that little red light goes on, you push one of the numbers."

"Which one, mister?"

"Whichever one you want. Just one number and the light will

go out. Then when it goes on, another number, and so on, until
the light stops shining. This lady will do the same thing. You
and I will sit opposite each other at this table, and she will sit at
this other little table with her back to us. I don't want you to think
about what number you're going to push."

"How can I do it without thinking, mister? You got to think."

"You may just have a feeling. The light goes on, and it might
seem as though you have a feeling to push an 8, or a 6, or
whatever. Just do it, then. One time you might push a 2, next
time a 3, next time a 9 or maybe another 2. Whatever you
want."

Roland thought about it a bit, then nodded. "I'll try, mister,
but I hope it don't take too long, because I don't see the sense of
it."

Basil adjusted the sensor in his left ear-canal unobtrusively
and then gazed at Roland as benignly as he could.

The tiny voice in his left ear breathed, "Seven," and Basil
thought: Seven.

And the light flashed on Roland's joystick, and on Nadine's
similar joystick and both pushed a number.

It went on and on: 6, 2, 2, 0, 4, 3, 6, 8. . . .

And finally Basil said, "That's enough, Roland."

They gave Roland's father five fifty-dollar bills, and they left.

In their motel room, Basil leaned back, disappointment fighting with the satisfaction of I-told-you-so.

"Absolutely nothing," he said. "Zero correlation. The computer generated a series of random numbers and so did Roland,
and the two did not match. He picked up absolutely nothing from
my thought processes."

"Suppose," said Nadine, with a dying hope, "he could read
your mind but was deliberately masking that fact."

Basil said, "You know better than that. If he were trying to be
wrong on purpose, he would almost certainly be *too* wrong. He
would match me less often than chance would dictate. Besides,
you were generating a series of numbers too, and you couldn't
read my thoughts either, and he couldn't read yours. He had two
sets of different numbers assailing him each time, and there was
zero correlation—neither positive *nor* negative with either. That
can't be faked. We have to accept it, he doesn't have it, now,
and we're out of luck. We'll have to keep looking, and the odds
of coming across anything like this again—"

He looked hopeless.

* * *

Roland was in the front yard, watching after Basil and Nadine, as their car drove off in the bright sunlight.

He had been frightened. First they had talked to his boss, then to his parents, and he thought that they must have found out.

How could they have found out? It was impossible to find out, but why else were they so curious?

He had worried about all that business of picking numbers, even though he didn't see how it could do any harm. Then it came to him that they thought he could hear human voices in his mind. They were trying to think the right numbers at him.

They couldn't do that. How could he know what *they* were thinking? He couldn't ever tell what people were thinking. He knew that for certain. Couldn't ever!

He laughed a little to himself, very quietly. People always thought it was only people that counted.

And then came the little voice in his mind, very thin and very shrill.

"When— When— When—?"

Roland turned his head. He knew it was a bee winging toward him. He wasn't hearing the bee, but the whole mind of the whole hive.

All his life he had heard the bees thinking, and they could hear him. It was wonderful. They pollinated his plants and they avoided eating them, so that everything he touched grew beautifully.

The only thing was they wanted more. They wanted a leader; someone to tell them how to beat back the push of humanity. Roland wondered how that could be done. The bees weren't enough but suppose he had all the animals. Suppose he learned how to blend minds with all of them. Could he?

The bees were easy, and the ants. Their minds built up in large crowds. And he could hear the crows now. He didn't used to. And he was beginning to make out something with the cattle, though they weren't worth listening to, hardly.

Cats? Dogs? All the bugs and birds?

What could be done? How far could he go?

A teacher had once said to him that he didn't live up to his potential.

"When— When— When—" thought the bee.

"Not yet—Not yet—Not yet—" thought Roland.

First, he had to reach his potential.

KNIGHT OF SHALLOWS
by Rand B. Lee

Lately we have had a lot of thought on the possibility that in infinity there may be real alternates to every decision ever made. In this unusual story, an adventure among alternate murder tracks takes us on a kaleidoscope of hairbreadth adventures.

They were not at all gentle. "You are a murderer!" they told him, whereupon he told them what they could stuff where; whereupon they said, "We can prove it." So they dragged him from his senior secretary's desk down in the bowels of Lifetimes, Inc., and dragged him up many elevators and through many security clearances to a place he had not dreamed existed. It was a room, empty except for a bean-bag chair and a wall-sized screen. "We're hooking you up," they informed him, although he neither felt any hooks nor saw to what he was being hooked up. "Now look," they said. So he looked in the screen, and saw, as they say in the Bible.

Afterwards, someone kindly cleaned him up; and they sat him down in a different room and talked it all over. "What do you know about probability mechanics, Roger Carl Shapiro?" they asked.

"Nothing," he said. "My God."

"Tell us what we showed you."

"You showed me some murders."

"Twenty-three, in fact. Did you see the murderer?"

"Yes." Dully.

"And whom did he resemble?"

"He was fat and he didn't have a beard."

"And whom did he resemble?"

"Abraham Ribicoff. Jesus, guys, what is this, some sort of psych——"

"And whom did he resemble?"

Silence. "Me. He looked like me." Pause. "Only overweight, and clean-shaven."

"Anything else?"

"And sad. He looked sad." Shapiro wept for some time.

When he was through weeping, they said, "What about his victims?"

"I don't know."

"Roger, this is important." [A consultation: "He's rejecting it. He's rejecting it." "Goddamn it, he's *got* to accept it." "Try the back door."] "Roger, where did the murders take place?"

This was easier. "A bar. It looked like a bar I knew—a long time ago. Beejay's. On Duval Street, in Key West."

"That's good. You lived in Key West for five years, didn't you?"

"Yes." Pause. "After I got out of college. I was a bartender for a little while. I didn't like it, so I left." Another pause. "But it wasn't Beejay's. Bill would never have let them put in that linoleum."

"Do you remember the bartender?"

A long silence. "Yeah."

"Yes, who, mister?" ["General, for Christ's sake." "General, please."]

"Yes, sir."

"What can you tell us about the bartender, Roger?"

"He had dark hair."

"Anything else?"

"And dark eyes. He was different in some of the pictures. In some of them he had a beard; in others he didn't."

"What about his clothes?"

"He had a tank top, once."

"And whom did he resemble, Roger?"

"Nobody." Very quickly.

"And whom did he resemble, Roger?"

"Somebody—maybe—I don't—"

"And whom did he resemble, Roger?"

"The murderer. The guy who shot him over the counter." Shapiro put his hands over his face. "They both looked like me."

Much later they took him back into the featureless room and showed him other things in the screen. This time it was not murders he saw. "Probabilities, Roger," they said to him. "Probability mechanics is a phenomenon unfathomable to anyone wedded to the old physics. Consciousness as a basic force in the universe. Or rather, multiverse. You're looking at logical spin-offs from the eventualities of your life."

They showed him a farm somewhere, with fields growing many kinds of vegetables. It was a commune. He saw himself, digging sweet potatoes. He was more muscular in the picture, although in real life he was not too bad, either. "This *is* real life," they said to him.

"I thought about joining a commune once," he admitted. "East Wind, in Tecumseh. But I didn't."

They showed him his uncle's synagogue, in Bridgeport. He was sitting in the front row with a woman he did not recognize until he noticed the necklace she was wearing. His mouth went dry. "Shirley Greenblatt," he moaned. "What in hell did I want to go and marry her for?" but the man on the screen looked happy.

["We're getting there. He's starting to accept it."]

They showed him alone in a darkened room, masturbating. "Hey," he said. One side of his face was badly scarred; he was sitting up in a chair with his legs bent queerly. The door opened; the man in the chair covered up. A woman came in with a face drained of life, bearing a tray. "That's Mom. What in hell?"

"We were going to ask you. Were you in a car accident?"

"Jesus. No, never."

"This 'you' was."

They showed him walking down a street somewhere in a shiny suit, looking prosperous. They showed him standing in front of a group of old people with a black yarmulke on his head. "The last time I wore one of those was when Dad died." The people on the screen were smiling. They showed him swinging a blonde child in the air. They showed him running from a pack of dogs in a bombed-out city. They showed him swinging from a rope, one end of which was knotted around his neck. "Charming," he said.

"But it happened, somewhere."

"Somewhere where?"

"In another sequence of probabilities. All these men are you as you might have been—as you might be—if you had made or do make a certain series of choices."

"No way would I choose to hang myself."

"Haven't you ever considered suicide?"

"I'd take pills. I'm a coward."

"If you had no pills? And were driven to desperation?"

He remembered certain August nights in Key West. "Yeah."

They showed him a woman with dark hair working at a

computer console. "Now that I like to see," he said. "Do I get to marry her?"

"Hardly. She's you."

"You guys are nuts."

"Not all probability sequences arise from human choice. Some of them arise from natural events: an extra chromosome, for instance, introduced to your biological makeup because one sperm made it to your mother's ovum first."

"That's me as I could have been if I'd been born a woman?"

"Yes. Now most sequences, like the Armageddon scenario— the dog-pack picture—are a combination of your choices, the choices of others, and natural event. You came to work here at Lifetimes, Inc., because the economy is bad and you couldn't get enough of your articles published to support yourself on your writing. God knows why we hired you; you're hardly efficient secretary material. A situation arising from many different factors, some of them dependent upon your choices."

"Bull. It was the only thing I could do. I needed work."

"You could have made it as a writer. You still can." Roger Shapiro stood up. They waited. He sat down again. "We've seen a sequence where you did stick it out and did very well. We've seen another sequence where you stuck it out, then quit, became a janitor at a grammar school, went back to writing, and won the Pulitzer Prize."

"These aren't actors, then."

"No. They live and breathe at this moment. The ones who aren't dead, of course."

"Where? Not here."

"No. In other universes."

After a very long time he said, "What about the murders?"

"What do you think?"

He thought. "If what you've been handing me is straight shit, they could be me. Could have been me. The bartenders I saw get shot. Because I did work at Beejay's for a while, and I guess I might have stayed on."

"The bartenders were you, all right."

"Then I don't get the murderer. He looks like me, too, if I'd let myself go, or gotten real depressed over a long time. Assuming these alternate universes exist, there's no way I could exist twice in the same one. Much less kill my other self. I mean, why would I want to?"

[A silent chorus of cheers from the observers behind the briefing room wall.]

"Twenty years ago, when we started this company, we would have agreed with you."

"But now?"

"We know it is possible. Not only to view our probabilities, from this screen here; but to enter them."

He laughed and laughed, and they decided it was enough for one day.

They did not let him go back to his sec desk, but they did not keep him a prisoner, either. He was given a considerable raise in salary, many security passes, and freedom to come and go between 5 P.M. and 8 A.M. The first night he did not go home at all, but sat watching dirty movies in a twenty-four hour theater. The next day they showed him more pictures, without commentary. He saw himself buried as a child in the corner of the family plot in Roxbury, Connecticut. In real life—in his base sequence, as they insisted upon calling it—he had recovered from the pneumonia. He saw himself giving blood in an Army hospital. He had never been in the service. He saw himself working bar in a Beejay's identical to the one he remembered, until he looked more carefully and saw that the napkins had **BIG RED'S** printed on them and that his other self had a mermaid leering from his right arm.

He discovered that his apartment had been cleaned in his absence and e refrigerator-freezer freshly stocked. In his bedroom he found a folder. He opened it and drew out some photographs. One was of a diploma with his name on it, issued by a university from which he had not graduated. He had transferred following his sophomore year. The second was of him with a man in a large oval bed. The third was a photograph of a page of manuscript. It was somewhat blurred, as though it had been blown up from a detail. He sat on the edge of his bed and read it; then he read it again.

The next day they said, "Well?"

"I believe you."

Suspicion. "What convinced you?"

"None of your business."

"What con——"

"I said it's none of your Goddamn business." He stood. "Now you want something from me. What is it?"

"Please calm yourself, Roger."

"Jesus." He sat, fighting back tears. "Okay. Shoot."

Carefully. "We're prepared to show you other proofs: retinal scans, hand writing comparisons, other documents we've photographed through the viewers. However, to answer your question in a nutshell: we want you to help stop this murderer.''

"Why me, if you'll excuse the cliché?''

"Because you're the only person in this universe who can enter your chain of probability-sequences. And that's what it'll take to stop him.''

"Wait, wait, wait.'' He viewed them through narrowed lids. "You people can look into my—probabilities—but you can't go into them?''

Discomfort. "I'm afraid so.''

"How come?''

"We don't have the time and you don't have the background for us to explain that satisfactorily. You must accept that we are telling you the truth. We would far rather entrust this task to a trained operative if it were at all possible. That we are asking you to take it on should be evidence enough of our sincerity.''

"Asking me to take it on?''

"Urging you.''

"Ordering me. Coercing me. Shaming me.''

"If you like.''

"Jesus.'' He pondered. "I'm not a cop. I can't fight, and I don't know how to shoot a gun. And I've never killed anyone.''

"We're not asking you to kill him.''

"You've lost me. I thought you said you wanted me to stop this guy from murdering people. Shit—from murdering me.''

"To answer that, we have to answer a question you haven't asked yet: how can this alternate 'you' travel from probability sequence to probability sequence? In fifteen years of alternate monitoring, he is the first such interfacer we've encountered.''

" 'Interfacer'?''

"Dimension-shifter. We've assumed that our probability-sequence was the only one in which probability mechanics has been developed. This may sound harsh to you, but the mere fact that you are murdered in sequence after sequence would not be enough to impel us to interfere. It is that an alternate persona is murdering your other selves—that is the crisis. So: how can he shift from sequence to sequence? We assume it's by the use of equipment similar to that which we have developed. Why do we not want you to storm into a sequence and gun him down? Because we need to know more about him. We need to know whether he is working alone or as the agent of someone else, some other-sequential person or persons. Imagine the possible danger to our universe if there exists an organization or culture of malevolent interfacers?''

"Come on," said Shapiro. "Come on, guys. Be realistic."
Smothered laughter from behind the wall. "Look who's being
murdered, will ya? Every murder you've shown me so far has
me tending bar in goddam Key West. What organization of
malevolent 'interfacers' would waste their time bumping off
nobodies?" His interrogators exchanged embarrassed looks. "I
mean, I'm important to me and maybe to God, for God's sake,
but who the hell else?"

"We think it might be a test run."

"Swell."

"We don't know. That's just it, Roger. This is new to us. We
don't know a thing. He could just be a nut. He's apparently been
connected with probability mechanics work in his own sequence;
he might even be someone important."

"Thanks for admitting the remote possibility," said Shapiro.

"It's his base sequence that we want to get to. Now we could
search among your probabilities-line for eternity and not hit on
the right sequence. Or we could send you to follow him home."

"Follow him home to his universe of malevolent interfacers?"

"That's it in a nutshell."

He sat quiet. "I have a lot of other questions."

"We'll do our best to answer them in the time we have."

"How much time do we have?"

"We don't know. That's why we'd like to get going on this
project pronto."

"Who's going to pay my rent while I'm gone?"

"It may not take long enough for that to be a problem, but we'll
support your obligations."

"My insurance payments, too?"

"Yes. Although why you need life insurance as well as major
medical eludes us. You have no dependents or close relatives to
benefit from your demise."

"There's my uncle, Sheldon."

"You hate your Uncle Sheldon."

"How convenient I'm turning out to be for all of you."

"Does that mean you'll do it?"

Silence. [Much tension behind the wall.] A grin. "Oy. And I
thought I was working for a career planning service."

[Pandemonium.]

It all had to do with brain waves and energy fields, none of
which Shapiro attempted to understand; to him it was just magic.
They implanted things in his head and put a button under the
skin of his left hand, which told them when he wanted to talk

with them. He was given a weapon and made to practice firing it. They called it a burner; he called it his raygun. To everyone's astonishment, he was not a bad shot. They tried to give him lessons in self-defense but gave it up when he objected. "I'm not a fighter," he said. "I buckle under stress." This statement made them nervous, which was his intent. He watched his probabilities in the scanner by the hour. Most of them varied little from the lives he had glimpsed already; in none did a Lifetimes, Inc. appear. This intrigued him—the company had begun to figure so hugely in his existence that he could not understand why his other lines were not dominated by it also.

"The more improbable the involvement, the less likely it is that you'll see it in the screen," they told him.

He glimpsed the Pulitzer Prize sequence they had told him about and several more in which he was female. "Are my probabilities infinite?" he asked them. They said they didn't know. "May I see into somebody else's probabilities?" he asked.

Much apology. "We don't want to risk losing our focus on your sequences. It took a lot of time and effort to lock onto them."

To which he replied: "You lied to me."

"What makes you think that, Roger?"

"Maybe 'lied' is the wrong word. Omitted some information. To whit: which came first, looking into Roger's lifelines or stumbling onto Roger-the-Murderer?"

"Uh—"

"Allow me. If you say, 'Stumbling onto Roger-the-Murderer,' I will say 'How? Were you looking through a catalog of random probabilities and chanced on little Roger's?' If you say, 'Looking into Roger's lifelines,' I will say, 'Why little Roger's? And who gave you the Goddamn right, you warped bunch of voyeurs?' "

Very pale indeed, they told him the truth: they had selected him and a number of other employees of Lifetimes, Inc., without their knowledge, to be part of their experiments in probability-viewing. They had been doing that sort of thing for many years. Each had been chosen for their single, socially unencumbered status and tagged electronically to transmit their brain-wave patterns to the viewer complex. "We lock onto those patterns," they told him, "and they access the probability-lines for us."

"Do the others know what I know?"

"No."

"Why not?"

"This is a top secret facility."

"These are very private lives."

"We're explorers, not voyeurs. We don't control what images come to us, or how long they stay on-screen."

"Liars."

"We don't—"

"Liars. You must have image-holding capacity. How else could you have been following my murdering career so closely?" They admitted it all. They admitted also that they had chosen the unencumbered against the chance that they might come across a sequence demanding personal investigation. This Shapiro heard calmly. He did not walk out. He knew that they would not let him go at this juncture. Instead he said, "I want to talk to someone who's done this before."

"Done what?"

" 'Interfaced.' "

They brought her to him. She was a woman of about sixty, iron-haired, sharp-nosed, and gruff. She had the look of some-one who had been important once and had given it all up because it had bored her. She lived, she said, in Monaco, which im-pressed him. "What do you want to know?" she asked.

"Why you went."

She was taken aback, and showed it in the flicker of her grey eyes. "For science, of course."

"Not you the professional," Shapiro said. "You alone with yourself."

She did not do him the discourtesy of evading him. "All right. There was a young man, many, many, years ago. We were lovers for a while; we planned to marry. There were career conflicts. It didn't happen. I found a probability in which it did." She shrugged. "I wanted to see him again."

He stared at her. "You're not bullshitting me?"

"I don't bullshit."

He examined his nails. "I had dreams," he said. "They showed me a photo of a page from a story I wrote. They saw me writing it in the screen and shot it from the image." He looked at her. "I never wrote that story, really. But you know something? I remember planning it. Taking the notes."

"Why didn't you write it?"

"I was afraid it would be lousy. Because so much of my stuff was."

"Was it?"

"No. It was really good." He wiped his eyes. "I don't know who you are," he said, "but I want you to tell them some things from me. Tell them I'm not a kid, and I'm not a fool, and I resent like Hell how they've tried to intimidate me into this. I know they don't give a shit about me, or any of my 'me's; I'm convenient, a handle. I'm going to do this thing they want me to do because I don't think anybody has the right to put an end to somebody's choices.''

"Fair enough.'' She rose to go.

"That includes them,'' he said. "Tell them that.''

What she told them was, ''You've got him.''

And:

They flew him to Key West at night in a plane that did not have to change at Miami. He found himself staring at the clouds outside under the moon as though he might never see clouds or moon again. The gruff woman had sent a small package along to him, which when opened proved to contain a pocket notebook and a pen with a special ink supply. Inside the notebook, on the first page, she had written:

There is a tide in the affairs of men,
Which, taken at the flood, leads on to fortune;
Omitted, all the voyage of their life
Is bound in shallows and in miseries.
On such a full sea are we now afloat,
And we must take the current when it serves,
Or lose our ventures.

It has rained three days in succession, but the air lies so thick on Duval Street that even the mosquitoes are sluggish, even the fragrance of the frangipani dampered. The tourists are few and irritable. "Worst goddam weather I ever saw,'' says a man from Ohio to a man from Michigan.

"It's a blanket bearing down,'' agrees a woman from New Jersey.

"Stay drunk; that's what I do,'' suggests a resident retiree. "Bartender? More of the same.'' The bartender comes over. His furry chest is bared and gleaming with sweat, despite the laboring of the big ceiling fan. To the woman the retiree says, "You want a pineapple colada? Roj makes the best pineapple colada in the Keys.''

"Make it a gin and tonic,'' says the woman. "How long have you been sweating down here, Roj?''

The bartender grins. "Would you believe ten years?''

"The man's insane,'' says the Michiganian.

Roj's hands move deftly among the bottles. "It's not so bad. I used to live in Connecticut. That was a place to get away from.''

"My sister lives in East Hartford," says the man from Ohio.

There are people playing pool in the adjoining game-room, and a few youths vying for a turn at Pac-Man; otherwise, the bar is empty. A stuffed flamingo stands in one corner. Above the bartender's station, Lucille Ball looks down from an autographed publicity still, as though presiding over this Friday night. "Ten o'clock," announces Roj. "Anyone want to hear the news?" No one does. Outside on Duval Street, the sign yells, **B.J.'S DEN.**

"I played Connecticut once," the woman is saying. "The old Wembley Theater in New Haven. I got the Mexicali trots from some lousy chop suey I gulped between acts. Talk about uncomfortable! It gave me eyestrain just to walk."

"Were you anybody important?" asks the Michiganian. She shrugs, then smiles.

"Nah," she replied. "But I could of been."

Roger Carl Shapiro walks out of the men's lavatory. He is wearing jeans and a loose cotton shirt, standard Key West costume. He halts near the cigarette machine and surveys the bar. At first he thinks, *It didn't work*. The same three tourists are sitting at the bar: the loud woman and the old man in the hibiscus shirt. The same flamingo stands in the corner. But the sign says **B.J.'S DEN,** not **BEEJAY'S;** and the floor has been painted ship-deck green; and the man behind the counter is himself.

ROGER-PRIME, says the wink-blink in his head. HAVE YOU ESTABLISHED VISUAL CONTACT?

He is like him, but unlike. His skin is darker; he looks almost Latino. There is a cigarette pack in the pocket of his shirt; Roger does not smoke. The greatest difference is the hardest for Roger to define: the man moves with a confidence that Roger cannot imagine possessing. *He's accepted things*, he thinks. *He's stopped running*.

All of a sudden he wants to go home. ROGER-PRIME. WE ARE HAVING DIFFICULTY WITH THE VISUALS.

He realizes that he has forgotten to engage the scanner circuit, which had to be turned off during transfer; he presses his left palm and receives, ENGAGED, in reply. He looks around, he needs a seat near the bar but not too near. In Beejay's there are booths; in B.J.'s Den there are none. He gathers his resolve and saunters up to the counter.

"Ever been to Montreal?" the man from Michigan is asking the woman from New Jersey. Roger selects a stool opposite the little group. At his back, the game-room door spills soft curses, the bartender comes over.

"What do ya need, friend?" Roj asks him. His eyes are very

brown. RETINAL SCAN CONFIRMED, says the wink-blink. THIS
IS YOUR PERSONA FOR THIS SEQUENCE, ROGER-PRIME.

"I know," says Roger.

"Pardon?"

"Sorry. I'll have a Perrier with lime, if you don't mind."

"Right." The man moves off. *He didn't notice*, wonders
Roger. *He didn't see a thing.* He is conscious of the tourists
looking him over, but his skin is light, his beard full, and the
man behind the bar is clean-shaven. *Still*, he thinks, *I would
have known*. Roj brings him the drink and asks for seventy-five
cents, which Roger pays in coin. He does not have much money
with him. He does not expect to remain for very long in each
sequence. The watchers have noticed that in each probability in
which the rogue interfacer appears, not only does he appear in
this Key West bar, but he appears about the same time, always
between 10 and 10:20 P.M. on this sultry Friday evening in June.
The murder is always committed at 10:33 P.M., whereupon the
rogue drops out of interface. Roger has asked them why; they
have admitted ignorance. "Perhaps it's some conservation law,"
they have suggested. "Perhaps some limitation in his equipment."
Or maybe, Roger has thought, *it's God saying there are limits*.

He has thought a good deal about God in recent days. ALL
TRANSMISSIONS FUNCTIONING NORMALLY, reports the light
in his head. It does not sound very excited, but Roger realizes
that his hand is shaking where it grips the Perrier. *Another
universe*, he thinks. He watches himself fiddle with the cash
register. *Me. That's me.* The days spent by the viewers have not
prepared him for the tangibility of an interface. There are no
sounds receivable through the viewers; no textures sensible. He
smooths the wood of the bar-top. It is scored beneath the polish.
It has a history; it was once a tree growing somewhere. *Was
there a Hitler here?* he wonders. *A Vietnam? Was FDR a polio
victim? Are there Key Wests where Hemingway never wrote,
where gay people never learned to flock, where women still
don't have the right to vote? Is there a best of all possible
worlds?*

His mind feels three times too big for his skull, and the
exhilaration that grips him is savagely intense.

The place begins to fill up. Roj calls out greetings ("Hey,
Rita!" "Howzit, Mr. Foley?"); Roger stares, trying to feel a
kinship with these acquaintances of his self. Beer foams; glasses
tinkle. It is a neighborhood crowd: everyone seems to know
everyone else, the tourists included. *They must be regulars*, he
thinks. *Back every year*. He finds himself assessing these people

in an unaccustomed way. It is as though his realization that there exists a multiplicity of each one of them has enhanced his appreciation of each one's individuality. He wants to let them know how important they are.

ROGER-PRIME, says the wink-blink. ROGER-PRIME, WE HAVE A NEW INTERFACE. REPEAT; A NEW INTERFACE. He starts, looks toward the street entrance, then the men's room door. It is opening hesitantly. GOING TO TELESCOPIC, mutters the base. Roger's vision does not change, but he knows that back home, the viewers are zooming in. The rogue is wearing a light nylon jacket, too hot for this island; a conservative sports shirt; and rumpled dark trousers. He is baby-faced, overweight. He stands as though on eggs, unsure of himself, although Roger cannot think why he should be, having already killed as many as he has. He does not look like a murderer. RETINALS CONFIRMED, says the light in Roger's head. THAT'S YOUR MAN, ROGER-PRIME. KEEP A LOW PROFILE.

He's here, thinks Roger. *He's actually here.* They have told him not to interfere; they do not want the rogue knowing that he is under observation. The man moves slowly toward the drinks counter. He is looking at the bartender. Roger hunches over his Perrier and watches covertly. The resemblance between killer and victim is obscenely fraternal. Roger closes his eyes. MAINTAIN VISUALS, snaps the monitor primly. He opens his eyes and panics. The rogue is gone. Then he sees him a few yard away, making for the gameroom. *Is he that cold-blooded?* he thinks. The watch they have given him adjusts to the local time in each sequence; it says 10:22. *Eleven minutes,* he thinks, and is afraid.

He is not sure what he is afraid of. It is not of being hurt; it is not of seeing the violence: he has seen it so often in the screens, often dim, it is true, but unchoreographed, uncleanly. He looks at the rogue. *You're afraid of finding out there's really no difference between him and you.*

The rogue goes into the gameroom and hovers near the pool tables. Shortly thereafter he returns to the bar. He sits on a stool four customers down from Roger. Roj goes over. "Help you?" Roger hears him say. It is 10:27.

"Perrier with lime, please," says the rogue. His voice is the voice of a shy adolescent; Roj's voice, completely drained of confidence. Roj moves to fetch the drink. Roger wants to shout, *You idiot, can't you see? Can't you feel what's coming?* He watches money exchange hands. He is struck by a sudden fancy: *Fingerprinting by and large is useless in cases of intersequential homicides.—Multiversal Policepersons's Manual.* The woman named Rita catches Roj's sleeve as he whisks by her. He bends forward, so that she can whisper in his ear. Whatever she says makes him laugh softly, showing strong throat and white teeth. Suddenly Roger remembers her. He had met her shortly before he had left Key West; she had been one of his boss Bill's significant others. She had given him a very long kiss at his going-away party. *And here she is,* he thinks. She is wearing a white peasant blouse, which will show the blood.

The rogue's face bears no expression; but he is watching her, too. Roger's nerves shriek.

More people come into the bar. At 10:30, the rogue slips his right hand into his right-hand jacket pocket. The woman from New Jersey is announcing to all and sundry that she really, really could have been somebody in Hollywood if she hadn't given it all up for love. At 10:31, Roj is lighting a cigarette under the appreciative eye of Rita. At 10:32, the telephone next to the cash register rings; the bartender puts the receiver to his ear. The rogue gets to his feet. So does Roger. PRIME, says the wink-blink. NO INTERFERENCE. WE'VE LOCKED ONTO THE SUBJECT: REMEMBER OUR OBJECTIVE.

"But," says Roger. The woman to his right gives him a curious look. Roj is grinning into the phone. The end of his cigarette flips up and down as he talks. The rogue takes his hand out of his pocket. Roger recognizes the weapon he is holding; he has seen it in the screen so many times before. It ejects a quiet red zip of needle light. Roj is facing Rita; the beam passes through him from back to front, taking most of his heart with it and spreading it over Rita's chemise. He does not even have time to look surprised.

And the rogue simply is not there.

INTERFACE, says the base in his head. WE ARE TRACKING. PREPARE FOR TRANSFER, ROGER-PRIME

My God. Rita opens her mouth.

ROGER-PRIME, PREPARE FOR TRANSFER.

"My God." A tiny voice squawks from the dangling phone, just like in the movies. Roger gets off his stool. There are too many people around the screaming woman, and Roj's body has slipped down behind the counter. He stumbles toward the lavatory. He wonders how such a narrow beam can make a mess this size. His own raygun is much less dramatic. The lavatory swims toward him in the weak bar light. The door flies open and the retiree in the hibiscus shirt rushes out and past him. The bathroom is empty. He finds the rightmost stall, goes inside, and bolts the door. He sits down on the toilet seat, then remembers, and stands up. He presses his left palm. "Transfer," he says. "For God's sake."

TRANSFERRING, says the unemotional voice of the base.

His watch says 10:33.

Everything changes. There is no men's room, no bar, no uproar. He is standing hip-deep among weeds in a vacant field. Under a cloudless, moon-heavy sky, jasmine runs rampant where coral vine has not choked it out. He can smell the sea. Hidden frogs, with exquisite unconcern for probabilities, sound their territories in concert. He is shaking again. *Base,* he thinks. *Base, is this right?*

WE'RE SORRY, ROGER-PRIME, comes the reply. WE'RE EXPERIENCING SOME DRIFT OF YOUR SIGNAL. WE'RE CORRECTING NOW. YOU'RE DOING WELL. DO NOT CHANGE POSITION; REPEAT, DO NOT CHANGE POSITION.

He does not. The moonlight gleams off blades of palmetto scrub. He hears the stir of the huge dark roaches, the "palmetto bugs" of the Keys, restless beneath the mangroves. He wonders why there are no big trees and no signs of buildings. *Maybe people have never come to this island,* he thinks. *No syphilis, no Cuban refugee "problem," no queer-bashing.* He wonders why he is not weeping. *He killed him,* he thinks. *He killed me. I killed me.* The chorus of the frogs touches his heart. All at once, he longs to remain here. *I'll welcome the Seminoles when they arrive,* he decides.

TRANSFERRING, says the base.

He is back in the toilet stall. The wall, which was green, is white where it is not scarred with graffiti. He is about to push open the stall door when it is opened for him. "Jesus, I'm sorry," says a man in a hibiscus shirt.

"No problem" says Roger-Prime. He walks past the man and washes his hands at a sink. In the mirror he observes Mr. Hibiscus go into the stall and close the door. It is the older man he has seen in the earlier sequence, but a more sober, more fit version of the older man. He looks at his watch. It says 10:04. He has half an hour before the next murder. He dries his hands and walks out into the bar.

The stuffed flamingo has become a stuffed pelican. The photograph of Lucille Ball now hangs over the cigarette machine. The floor is not painted green; it is wood left natural with sawdust sprinkled all over it. The television mutters a talk show; the picture quality is superb. No loud woman holds forth at the bar, no man from Michigan. The tourist from Ohio is there, however, and well on his way to intoxication. Of Roger's alter-egos there is no sign. The bartender is blond and very young. "What'll it be, bud?" he asks.

"Perrier with lime," Roger replies. The gameroom door is shut; a sign on it declares it closed for repairs. "When's your partner come on duty?"

"Carl? He's late now."

"Pardon me, sir," says the Ohioan, "but you're sitting in my friend's seat."

"Where do you know Carl from?" asks the young man.

"Around," says Roger-Prime. *Carl,* he thinks. His parents had struggled for three months over whether to name him Carl Roger or Roger Carl. "He might not even remember me; it's been so long."

"Sir," says the Ohioan. Roger squelches an urge to turn around and shoot the man through the throat. He gets up and moves around to the other side of the bar, taking his Perrier with him. Mr. Hibiscus comes out of the lavatory and sits down next to the Ohioan. Roger-Prime squeezes the lime into the mineral water and wonders how he can possibly sit through the experience again. He sips; bubbles feather his palate. He wants a real drink, but he does not know what it will do to the things they have put in his head. He does not like the base's silent voice; it makes him feel exposed, as though he were walking around with his fly open. He looks up, and the young man is leaning against the cash register.

"Been in town long?" the boy asks.

Wrong move, buddy, Roger thinks. *A good barkeep should be able to tell when his customers want to be left alone.* "Not long. But frequently."

"You look kinda familiar. I been workin' here six months; you see a hell of a lot of faces in six months."

"Six months is a long time to work in one place down here," says Roger.

"No shit. Bill, the owner? He says the turnover at the Casa Marina's one person out of three every six months. What do ya expect? Key West is a dead end town."

"We must take the current when it serves," murmured Roger-Prime, "or lose our ventures."

"Hey, Phil." A hand comes down on the blond's shoulder. It is the murdered man, now moustachioed, and somewhat disheveled. "Sorry I'm late. Some faggot took my parking spot."

"No problem," says Phil. "It's been slow." He leaves,

glancing at the two of them so as to catch some spark of recognition jump between them; but Carl is busying himself about the bar and Roger is busying himself with his drink. *Did I talk like that?* he thinks. *"Some faggot?"* He studies his new self. Like Roj, Carl is deeply tanned, competently muscular, confident in his movements. Nevertheless, he has a disturbing arrogance that Roj did not have. Carl glances Roger's way and smiles professionally. Roger smiles back. *What are you made of, my man?* he wonders.

CONFIRMED, reports the base. THIS IS YOUR PERSONA, ROGER.

No kidding, returns Roger. *I thought I'd been cloned in the crapper.*

On the TV, a film critic whom Roger-Prime does not recognize is discussing a new Paramount offering. The star's picture is flashed; it is the woman from New Jersey. The clock on the wall says 10:15. A couple of French sailors come in with women hanging on them. They are followed by some young men in T-shirts; the shirts bear the legend: **EAT IT RAW—KEY WEST OYSTER BAR.** They are shaved almost bald, American Marines on leave from Trumbo Point. They giggle at the red pom-poms of the sailors. The bar fills slowly at first, then rapidly. He sees a great many military persons. Carl is kept busy, and by the time he has a moment free, it is nearly 10:28. "That was sudden," says Roger-Prime, because he must say something, do something.

"No fooling." Carl lights a cigarette, head cocked like the man in the Marlboro ads. "It's the base. The duty rosters are all screwy these days. Guys get off at weird hours."

No murderer yet. "Something up at Trumbo?"

"Falklands shit."

Roger hazards it: "I thought Thatcher had things pretty much under control."

"Thatcher? Where've you been, buddy? Maggie has gone home to that great brassiere factory in the sky."

"What?"

"Last week. Argentinian terrorists blew up her car. There've been rumors of British retaliation ever since. With Fidel backing Argentina and Uncle Sam backing England, a lot of kinds of shit could hit the fan. Excuse me."

The bartender wades away into dimness. *Ten-thirty,* observes Roger. The military people are drinking hard, as though they have things they want to forget. He is feeling very detached. He does not like Carl. *Where's our rogue?* he asks the base.

SCANNING, ROGER, they reply.

There are two minutes to go before Carl will be dead. He is shocked by his own thought: *No great loss, this one.* The wedge of lime lies belly-up at the bottom of his glass. The napkin says **BIG RED'S** on it. *Where is he?* he thinks.

EMERGENCY, PRIME. EMERGENCY. IMMEDIATE TRANSFER NECESSARY.

What's happened?

IT SEEMS TO BE OUR DAY FOR MISCALCULATIONS. HURRY, PRIME.

He forgets Carl. He slips from his stool and pushes his way through the crowd toward the men's room. There are some people by the urinals. All the stalls are filled. He waits, fretting. A man comes out of the middle stall. He rushes into it and locks the door. There is a window high up; through it he can see the branches of the royal poinciana swaying, showing off their vermilion under the street lamps. *Ready,* he says. *Ready, base.*

The building shudders. The lights in the bathroom go out. Men curse, and in the next room, glass shatters. People are screaming, but he knows that this time they are not screaming because of Carl. *Hurry up, base,* he thinks. He presses his palm repeatedly. "Hurry up, base, Goddam it, it's something bad." He remembers the screen image of the ruined city. *British retaliation?* he thinks. *Cuba's only eighty miles away.* "Base, what in Hell have you gotten me into?" He looks out the window. The sky is full of sea.

TRANSFERRING, says the wink-blink cheerfully. It is 10:33.

The wall is back to spotless green. The lights are back, and the building is quiet. *What happened?* he manages to ask. On the floor of the stall, a tract that was not there a moment previously says, **CHRIST IS THE ANSWER.**

"What happened?"

SORRY, PRIME: WE PROJECTED YOU INTO A CATACLYSM-LINE.

He sits down on the toilet and laughs weakly. *Taken at the flood,* he thinks. No wonder our rogue never showed up. Little Carl gets zapped by the Commies. He has drunk too much Perrier and he finds he must urinate. The wall, he notices, is the only fixture of the stall that is spotless. There is no paper in the toilet roll, and the floor around the tract is littered with cigarette butts. *Where am I now?*

ON TARGET, UH, A LITTLE LATE. It is already 10:20. WE SCAN YOUR PERSONA NOT FAR. ALSO THE ROGUE.

I don't want to see another killing. Can't I wait out this one?

WE'RE HAVING TOO MUCH TROUBLE TRACKING HIM. YOU'RE GOING TO HAVE TO SLAP A TRACER ON HIM.

Swell. How?

WE'VE BEEN THROUGH THAT.

I do get murdered in this one, don't I? Not swallowed up in an earthquake, or kidnapped by aliens?

YOU KNOW WE CAN'T VIEW A PROBABILITY WHEN YOU'RE IN IT, SAVE THROUGH YOUR TELEMETRY. THE ROGUE IS, HOWEVER, AT INTERFACE.

Where's your sense of humor, folks? says Roger-Prime. He exits the stall. A man stands in front of him, combing his dark hair in the mirror. Roger moves past him; for an instant their reflections hang side by side. The man lowers his comb. It is the bartender. "Jesus Christ," he says. They are identical. There can be no mistake. Down to their beards, they are identical. The bartender faces Roger-Prime. He is high on something, and his skin is not deeply tanned. "Jesus, do you see that?"

"Sorry?"

"We could be twins." Roger-Prime does not know how to react. He affects mild interest.

"Huh. I guess. Didn't think anybody could match my mug for ugly." He starts to leave. The man will not let it go this easily. "Wait." The bartender sticks out his hand. "This is like what they used to call a Cosmic Experience. You know, back in the Sixties, when we all believed in that stuff? I'm Shep."

"Uh, Shifter. Charlie Shifter." They shake hands. Shep's grip is firm. *Shep from Shapiro,* thinks Roger. All of a sudden he longs to know this man. "It is pretty amazing, isn't it?"

"So it's not just me. I mean, it was good Colombian, but it wasn't *that* good." He laughs. "I can't get over it. They say everyone's got a double somewhere. Doppelgänger. When you meet him, you die." He raises his eyebrows in mock terror. *My God, the rogue,* thinks Roger. *I can't let him see us together.* "Wait till Bill sees this. You want a drink?"

"I was just leaving, actually."

"Damn. I mean, I am definitely up there, but this. Even our beards. You in town long?"

"Not long." says Roger Carl Shapiro. He goes to the sink and turns on the water. His heart is pounding. *Doppelgänger, shit!*

"I'll bet you're a writer, aren't you? Shep?"

"Jesus. Yeah. Trying, trying." Delight. "How'd you know?"

"You have the look. And you talk like one. I hear Key West is good for writers."

"I used to live here right after I got out of college." The words pour out. "I worked bar here, right in this place, and I tried to write, you know, in my spare time. Couldn't hack it. Woman troubles and shit. I hadn't set foot in the Keys till last October. Thought I'd give it another try." He is combing his hair again, unnecessarily.

"And how's it going?" Roger washes and washes.

"Well." His twin grins at him. Roger can just make out the tiny scar below Shep's left eye, where a dog bit both of them when they were four. "I just sold a story."

Envy. Excitement. "No shit?"

"Just sold one. God damn, brother; it's better than orgasm! I've been trying for years. Giving up. Maybe it'll never happen again, but it happened once. Shit." Shep peers at him. "Come on in and have a drink. Business is shit."

"Uh." He imagines the people at the base, chewing their nails. It is 10:26. "Uh, Shep, actually, there's somebody in the bar I'm trying to avoid."

"Yeah?" Shep says, with sympathy.

"Uh, money matters. I'll tell you what. When do you get off?"

"Not till three, man."

"I'd, uh, really like to sit down with you some time. Do you have a number where I can get a hold of you?"

"Hey, yeah." The bartender searches his apron. Roger-Prime remembers the pad and pen that the grim woman has given him, and digs them out of his back pocket. Shep takes them and opens the book. Roger watches his eye strike the first page. "Fantastic. *Richard the Third*."

"I wondered which one it was from."

Shep writes down his address and phone number. "Higgs Lane. It's right off Elizabeth between Eaton and Caroline. I work nights, but if I'm out when you call, my old lady'll take a message."

"Old lady, huh?"

He grins again. "Either feast or famine, isn't it? I knew her before; her name's Rita. You'll like her." They shake hands. "You can get out without going through the bar; just make a right just outside here. There's a phone by the storeroom and the back exit's marked."

"Just like a spy movie."

"Hey, man. This is Key West. Anything can happen in Key West." Shep leaves. "Give me a call," he tosses over his shoulder. The lavatory door swings shut. Alone in the front of the mirror, Roger-Prime takes out his burner. It is light in his palm, toy-like; the very very latest thing from Dow, of all places. PRIME, says the wink-blink. YOU MUST NOT INTERFERE.

"The Hell I mustn't."

WE MUST TRACK THE ROGUE TO HIS BASE SEQUENCE. MORE THAN A FEW LIVES ARE AT STAKE.

"We don't know that."

YOU HAVE FOUR MINUTES TO ATTACH THE TRACER. ROGER PRIME?

"*All right!*" he yells, mind and voice together.

He hurls himself through the door. The bar has been remodeled and it takes him a moment to recognize the old lines beneath the ugly new. The cleanliness of the bathroom is echoed in the bar. The gameroom is a disco, at the moment silent. The Pac-Man and the pool tables line the Duval Street wall. Lucille Ball is nowhere in evidence. The drinks counter has been moved against the far wall, which means that anyone sitting there has their back to the lavatory. He spots the rogue almost immediately. The fat man has not changed clothing. He is sitting pensive in the row of vacant stools. The Michiganian tourist is shooting pool with the retiree, who has exchanged his hibiscuses for palm trees.

Base, says Roger. *There's no way I'm going to be able to tag this pig without his seeing me. And once he sees me, he'll know what's what.* Shep wipes the bar-top, moving around his killer so as not to disturb him.

WE MUST HAVE A TAG.

Not by me. Or do you want a universe of malevolent interfacers crawling up your asses?

There is silence for some time, for which Roger is grateful. He has put his gun back in his pocket, but as he watches Shep work, that foolish smile on his hairy face, he struggles once more with the temptation to kill the rogue. The fat man stirs in his seat; Roger ducks right, through an open door that has always been closed before, to the telephone and the **EXIT** sign. It is 10:30. He thinks, *If the rogue has a base backing him, why haven't they picked up on my presence yet?* He looks at the phone. A notion strikes him: a way he can interfere without giving away the game. *Our voices are the same,* he thinks. *If I call the cops and say it's him, they'll never know it isn't.* He picks up the receiver.

"There's no time," says a voice. "Besides, cops don't intimidate him. He can shoot in a second and interface as quickly." So Roger turns. She has come out of the men's room; she lets the door swing shut and approaches him quickly. She wears a grey jumpsuit; her dark hair is thickly looped about her head. *Uh, base*, he thinks. "They can't read you," she tells him. "Your telemetry is somewhat limited; a convergence of four personas is a little much for it."

"You're the woman I saw in the screen. Sitting at a console."

"Quite possibly. I've been following you, I'm afraid."

"You're me, then, too." His palms sweat.

"My name is Catherine. My mother's name. Catherine Shapiro." It is his mother's name, too. "I'm here to help. Our base has been monitoring him for a long time. I'm supposed to impress upon you the historicity of this occasion: the first meeting of representatives from the two benign, interfacing cultures."

"Is that what we are? Benign?"

There is concern in her face, but it is controlled.

He feels instinctively that he is in the presence of power. "We have to stop him. He's going to kill one of us in two minutes. And this one of us is a particularly nice guy. We have to stop him."

"That will be difficult. I've tried."

He starts.

"Oh, yes. I've tracked him through eleven sequences, personally."

"Does he work alone?"

"Yes. We're in contact with his base sequence. He's a genius, Roger. He's responsible for most of their breakthroughs in probability research. What he's got is an experimental, portable interface-unit, something we've never even begun to develop. He stole it on its test-run. His people want him back."

No rogue base. A weight lifts from him, and he is freed. He takes out the burner. "What are you doing?" she whispers.

"I won't let him kill Shep."

"I won't let you kill him." Her weapon is pointed at his chest. "Be reasonable, Roger. His people want him back alive. They're prepared to exchange technical data for him."

"I thought you said you'd never met anyone from an interfacing culture before."

"We haven't. You can't enter a probability that your persona has vacated. But we've learned to communicate with them. As we're communicating with your base, now."

"There has to be a way to save Shep. There has to be a way." *He has to finish*, he thinks. *He's going somewhere. He's off the shoals.*

"There is. Put your weapon away."

He believes her. He pockets the burner. *One minute.* A few new customers have entered. They hear the woman from New Jersey and Shep's delighted greeting.

"Does he know you're after him?"

She nods. "He's seen me several times. But he has no monitoring capability. All he can do is shift. Now listen." She lowers her gun, but does not put it down. "This is the first good chance I've had to get at him when the bar wasn't crowded. I'm going to shoot for his weapon-arm. I think I'm a better shot than you are, from what I've seen. When I hit him, he's going to interface. Don't let him see you. Follow him."

"How? On foot?"

"Your base will regain control when he interfaces. They'll want you going after him whether or not they believe my people."

"What about you?"

"I'll meet you. Between us, we may be able to trap him."

It is 10:32 ½.

It has all happened too quickly, and what happens next he is not prepared for. She races into the bar. He cannot keep himself from pursuing. She falls into a crouch and fires, all at once. The rogue is on his feet, raising his burner. Shep is out from behind the counter, facing the woman from New Jersey, his left side exposed. He is grinning from ear to ear. His shoulder is three feet from the rogue's muzzle. Catherine's beam strikes the fat man's wrists; he vanishes with a scream, like a sentient balloon when pricked. His burner clatters on the filthy wood floor. Instantly, Roger's head is full of chatter. Catherine starts forward, toward the gun. Something warns her; she flings herself backwards, ripples, and fades out.

"What in hell?" says Shep. He bends down to the spot where the rogue's weapon lies glowing. It blows up in his face.

TRANSFERRING, says the wink-blink happily.

He wails in darkness. He is in a box of a room with dust and skeletons. TRANSFERRING. He is in an open meadow, and people are flying kites. TRANSFERRING. He is buried, earth pressing. TRANSFERRING, TRANSFERRING! He is up to his ears in mud, surrounded by curious, long-necked animals with eyes like dinner plates. TRANSFERRING, GODDAMIT! He is in a bar with blue walls, a bar with grey walls, a bar full of naked men gyrating to music, a bar thick with sweet pot smoke, a bar of slime and ancient rot. He wails for Shep, whom he loves. TRANSFERRING, they say.

The shadow settles and stays. He is kneeling in a deserted

room. There is no furniture, not even a drinks counter. The street windows have been boarded up. A few cracks admit anemic moonlight: no electric Duval glow. Wind whines outside. The only other creature in the room is a pregnant cat. With no place to hide, she stands with feet rigid and back arched in the center of the room, bristling with every night-fear. His watch has stopped.

The smell of the pot still clings to his clothing. He wonders who he is. *Roger Carl Shapiro,* comes the reply, but he seems to remember other names as well. He sits down, and a discomfort at his buttocks makes him rise. He draws the pen and notebook from the back of his jeans. **There is a tide,** he reads.

"Roger?"

She has materialized in the gloom. Her features are ashen, like her clothing. "Hello, Catherine," he says. "It took off his—it took—" He stops. On the second page, the name is written, in Roger's own sprawling loops, **R.C. Shapiro,** and the rest: **#8 Higgs Lane Key West Fla 33040 (Shep) Call me buddy!!! 66403.** He puts the book away. "What now?" he asks.

"I don't know." She stands peering out between some slats. "I'm not sure where we are. Rather, I know where we're not. This isn't a murder sequence. It's another cataclysm zone."

"You heard?"

"I'm afraid I was partly responsible. My following you is what's been causing the drift in your signal. My people have corrected for it now, but—"

"Where is he?"

"The rogue? Nowhere."

"Dead?"

"No. Unconnected as it is to an external power source, his shifting equipment must carry its own energy supply. He needs to recharge after every shift. He does this between probabilities."

He does not even ask her what this means. "Then why are *we* here?"

"This is where he was heading when he dropped out of interface."

"You said I could help you trap him. How?"

She takes something from a pocket. "See these? They're like the tracer chips you're carrying. We've been able to do some scans of his unit, and we think that if we can manage to get these into him, we can remove the unit from his neural control and take over his shifting-capability."

"You think."

"We think."

"At least he doesn't have a burner any longer."

"At least we managed to do that much. He won't be killing any more Shapiros." She squats beside him. "Roger, I'm sorry."

"For me?" She cannot answer his tone. The cat has crouched, still suspicious, but no longer afraid. "You say this is a cataclysm zone?"

"See for yourself." He looks out at devastation. Under the Moon, the town is dead. The stucco looks scoured. Duval Street is strangled with rubble: rusted cars; masonry; blackened, leafless trees.

"What did it?"

"We don't know. My people have never mentioned this probability before. They report no radiation or plague."

"Somehow, knowing that doesn't really comfort me." He looks at her. "You've sold out to them, haven't you? To your version of Lifetimes. You're their woman. You're sad because your lousy shot killed Shep, but not undone."

"Give me a break, you sanctimonious creep," she answers. ROGER PRIME, says base. WE HAVE RECEIVED A COMMUNICATION FROM AN ORG——

I know all about it. Be ready to transfer me out of here if the Crawling Eye shows up.

CO-OPERATE WITH THEM, ROGER.

"Roger," she says urgently. "My people say he's interfacing. Here in the building."

The rogue is there. He has a weapon in his hand. Catherine yells and grabs Roger's arm. The world flares. His head fills with a low hum. He opens his eyes. Catherine has kept a hold of him. A cocoon of opalescent light has woven itself around them; through it they can see the rogue, cowering against a wall. His mouth is open. Roger-Prime fumbles for his burner. "Don't be stupid. You'd fry us both."

The rogue vanishes. Their shield dissipates with a little sigh. The cat has managed to work its head between two slats in an effort to escape the room. Numb, he watches it wriggle, but cannot summon the interest to help it. "Who works your shield, you or your people?" he asks. *So much for our little gain.*

"There's no time for this. He's on the run now. We have to catch him. Come with me." She heads for the lavatory. It is shut tight. Roger realizes that he has not seen a women's room in any of the probabilities. This strikes him as funny, and he giggles. She gives him a sharp look and takes her gun to the locked door. It flames and sags. A stench envelopes them. "Oh, Christ," she says. "Don't look." He looks. The lavatory is packed with skeletons. Roger-Prime leaps backward with a cry. She fires the weapon a second time. Bones blacken, fall to charcoal. Heat hits their faces. The stench does not lessen. She clears a space for them and leads him into the bathroom. "Are you all right?" she asks.

"I don't like death." *They were running,* he thinks. *From what?*

"Nobody likes it. Not even our rogue."

"You could have fooled me."

She takes him by the shoulders. "Some people deal with death by ignoring it. My mother was one. For three years after Daddy died she kept his dressing-table exactly as it had been on the day of the accident. She'd talk to him when she thought I wasn't listening. Other people deal with death by embracing it. The 'my life is over' bit. And some people accept it as part of living and get past it. Which sort of person do you think we're dealing with in our alter ego?"

"Let's talk about this someplace else," Roger says. She sighs and consults her palm. READY FOR TRANSFER, his wink-blink announces. TRANSFERRING. She vanishes. He is alone among the stinking bones. *"What in Hell happened?"* he screams. ROGER-PRIME, YOU'RE NOT TRANSFERRING. Something thumps the eaves of the building. "A seagull," suggests Roger to a skull. He knows it is not a seagull. He runs to the lavatory door. A dull green light is leaking through the slats of the boarded windows. For the first time he notices that the windows are boarded up on the inside. The pregnant cat is still stuck, and her wriggling has become fevered. *"Get me out of here base,"* he says. There is an unhealthy look to the light that makes his skin crawl. *"Base!"*

"Roger." He jumps and yells. She is back. "Your signal is being jammed. It might be the rogue, or whatever's out there."

" 'Whatever'?" he says. "I love horror movies. Can I link with you?" One of the boards springs loose and clatters on the floor. He takes his gun and fires at the frantic cat. She flames briefly, then hangs still. "Can I link with you?" he asks again.

"Yes. We've never done this before, though; it might cut you off from your own people."

"I'd rather be stuck in your probability than here. Hurry up, Catherine; Jesus." Light slops from the space the board has vacated and leaks into the room. They retreat to the lavatory. Masonry groans somewhere; wood splinters and collapses. The doorway is filled with the sickly light. The stench increases. Roger cannot stop giggling; it is so much like a Lord Dunsany story he once read. The woman grips his left palm and presses her left palm to it. Base squawks in his head, then goes silent. A strange voice resonates within him: TRANSFERRING, CATHERINE-PRIME.

It does not happen. The wall to the men's room dissolves into a writhe of worms. Something rears up, not at all pleasant. *More power, base,* thinks someone. *You have five seconds.*

READY, says her base.

Then do it! they cry together. The light sucks at them. Roger does not notice the transfer; he is too busy screaming. It is 10:33.

They are falling, the three of them. It is a strange fall, more like a dance than a fall: at junctures they seem to orbit one another, and interweave, and very nearly coincide. Roger-Rogue fires his reserve weapon repeatedly. The beams exit the nozzle and spread into rainbows, and ribbons. *Catherine!* cries Roger-Prime. *Between,* she replies. He reaches for her, and finds her moving away from him. Roger-Rogue fires a spray of silver, edged with blue. *You bastard!* cries Roger-Prime. *You filthy Nazi!* His words become pillows, which strike the rogue about the ears and send him tumbling in a great cartwheel.

Catherine-Prime is at Roger-Prime's elbow. *Let it take you,* she says to him. *Don't fight.*

I've never fought, he thinks. The words string themselves out against a milk-white sky, black as beads. *Give me the chips.*

Wait till it ends, she cries. *We're between interfaces.*

I know where we are, he says. *The chips.* She gives him two of the four. He dives for the tumbling rogue.

The first thing he notices is the sound of a fountain. He is lying under a curve of concrete. He pulls himself up to sitting position; he has materialized in a messy garden. It is surrounded by a high brick wall matted with jasmine. An arbor of glory-bower spills its blood-red, white-bracted blooms into the nights, but the trusses need trimming, and several of the slat supports are broken. In the fountain bowl, a bird floats gently. He does not put his hand into the water. The sky is clear. On the other side of the wall, a royal poinciana displays its plumage. He recognizes it as the one that has grown outside the bar in most of the sequences. *Base,* he calls. His mind is empty.

Another dead zone, he thinks. He gets to his feet. He feels fatigued but not exhausted. Catherine is nowhere to be seen.

The house at the back of which he stands is something from a Key West guidebook: a two-storied, New-England-style structure with peeling white paint and gingerbread railing on its balconies. He finds a door and opens it. There is a wood-burning stove, copper pans on hooks; copper sinks with ornamented fittings that look as though they are made of brass. Noting the disrepair of the garden, he is not surprised that the metals are tarnished and dull. Things tarnish quickly in the salt air of the island. He notices no plastics or paper toweling. He roams the house rapidly, searching for the rogue. There is much wickerwork, mostly white. There are no electric outlets. One room is a Victorian fantasy of lace, velvet, and polished wood. The wood has been polished recently, and smells of honey.

Throughout the house he finds many photographs of poor quality in gilt frames. They are all of stern bearded men and unsmiling dour women, dressed in clothing similar to that which was worn in the century before his own. One he picks up and studies. The man stands behind the woman. She is seated on a white chaise. They are dressed in black. Their expressions are restrained, but not miserable. The woman could be Catherine; the man, the rogue. He finds them in another portrait, too: she is aswirl with lace and satin and he wears a top hat. The formality of the moment cannot hide their happiness. Her hand is clasped in his.

The photograph is faded, and a bit smudged, as though it has been handled many times.

In one of the upstairs bedrooms he finds a chair, and he sits in it. It is a man's room, darkened by many mauves; but there is lace at the windows. He looks out of one of them. Duval Street has been stripped of its tarmac down to hard-packed earth. The trees far outnumber the houses. There are no streetlamps, no traffic lights. Men in queer costumes stalk up and down, some in groups of three and four, most alone. The moon touches sails on the harbor. A saloon spills noise far down the street; occasionally a horse trots by. Once he sees a black woman, burdened and solitary; some sailors catch at her, and she flees from their laughter. Mosquitoes dance about his neck.

Not a dead zone, he thinks. *Just a quiet house owned by an indifferent housekeeper. Maybe he's too poor to keep servants, or too fearful to.* He begins a methodical search of the room. At the base of the big oak wardrobe he feels something give; a hidden spring uncoils, and a drawer slides open. In it lies a raygun.

The creature must have screwed up our signals. I shifted sideways, and he shifted backwards and sideways. No other explanation occurs to him. He wonders if the bride is she. There is another bedroom; he walks into it. It is a woman's room, full of bric-a-brac. The bed is turned down, the mosquito netting lovingly arranged. About the dressing table hangs a scent of rose. He traces the perfume to a small porcelain jar filled with leathery petals, topped with a perforated cover. There are more photographs. The rogue is in some of them, but most of them are of her: perched on a horse looking uncomfortable; in an ugly travelling-costume, standing with an old woman against the backdrop of Big Ben; very young, with her hair down, at a piano.

Young, and with her hair down. He looks more closely. The girl is perhaps fifteen.

There is another wardrobe. Inside it he finds a row of gowns. Most of them are silken, many faded. Some are so rotted that they fray under his fingers. *Things rot fast here,* he thinks, *but none of these have been worn in years.* He looks around again, and for the first time notices the stain on the ceiling, high up near one corner. He rushes back to the photograph of the girl. "Damn," he murmurs. "Goddam, it isn't her!" Catherine has never had a childhood here. He goes back downstairs. In the photograph in the parlor, the woman is in her forties, the man in his fifties.

She never made it here, he tells himself. *But he did. At some point sometime. His wife must have been our persona in this probability.* He does not understand the time inconsistency, and he does not care. *She died, and he left her dressing-table as it was.* It is all part of the same pattern: the ignoring of death. It is finally clear to him why the rogue has killed. *Probability sequences are choices made manifest,* he thinks. *Before shifting was brought home to us as a reality, we could dream of ourselves as we might have been, and somewhere deep down hold out to ourselves the illusion that there's still time to do that one great thing. To recoup our losses. Probability mechanics put an end to that indulgence. It told us, "Too late; you could have been this if you'd done this then, but not any more."*

The rogue has not been able to accept the reminders of his could-have-beens. Roger thinks of Catherine. *We're lucky,* he thinks. *I might be able to accept your sequence, and you might be able to accept mine. But would either of us be willing to change places with him?*

"So there you are," says Roger-Rogue. "I expected you years ago. You don't know our Amazon friend never made it here. Perhaps she did, and I killed her." He is no longer fat. There is a strange scar on his forehead, and he is whiskered. "I see you found my burner."

"You've done well for yourself," Roger says. The man laughs. There is much of Carl in him; a little of Roj. "You've been stranded, haven't you?"

"Beached," says the rogue, and jumps him.

He is strong, and he knows how to fight. He gets on top of Roger and pummels him. His face is full of glee. The burner bumps and skitters. Roger-Prime reaches up through the blood and slaps two chips against the man's neck. Then he puts the heel of his right hand under the rogue's chin and pushes hard. The grey head snaps back. They grapple, Roger biting and screaming Shep's name. He has never hit anyone as hard as he could; he does this now. The rogue sags. Roger scrambles to his feet and dives atop the burner. It is somewhat larger than his own, with a battery compartment. He points the muzzle.

The man has his face. "So get it over with, already," Roger-Rogue says.

"Where are we?"

"Somewhere to right angles of your 1982," his persona answers. "A retarded time, and quite racist. Kill me, will you?" The rogue keeps his tone light.

Roger grins, knowing better.

"You find this situation amusing?"

"Those telemetry-chips are glowing," Roger says. He grins and grins. They have not lost him. "You're about to enjoy a belated visit home." The man touches his neck. The chips have sunk into the flesh, shedding pearly light. "Beached, huh? That scar have something to do with it?"

"You're perceptive," Roger-Rogue says. "I knew you were both after me; I'd killed enough of us to feel reasonably avenged. I shifted at random. It was foolish. I shifted to—not a cataclysm zone, precisely, but a disaster sequence—an improbability. It was—" He laughs and rolls his bleeding head. "Oh, Jesus. I still dream about it. They weren't human at all. Not at all. We'd evolved into something quite different; I can't imagine what ancestry. I rather horrified them, I imagine. They attacked me."

"Sounds human enough."

"Yes. I was struck," he taps his forehead, "here. You may know that I designed the shifter to be a plate of microcircuitry, a glorified Fresnel disc, actually. I had them implant it against my skull. I had good reasons at the time: it made for a more efficient tie-in to the volitional centers. When our cousins struck me, they disrupted the circuitry. I made one more shift. I landed here."

"Was that before or after the rainbows?" demands Roger-Prime.

"What rainbows?"

"The ones in the between-place. You shot them out of your raygun."

"I'm not going home," says Roger-Rogue. He claws at his throat. "Goddam you, this is my home!"

"Calm down or I'll burn this house to the ground." It works. The man drops his hands. "Get up." He does. "Now tell me what was so Goddamn terrible that you had to kill twenty-five nebbish bartenders to avenge it."

The man looks astonished. "Don't joke with me."

"I'm asking. One of them could have been a very dear friend of mine."

"Why, to avenge this." He spreads his hands. "This. Look." There is a mirror hanging on the parlor wall. He stands before it, his lean face full of loathing. "Can't you see? It's indelible. I'll never lose their mark on me. It was always, 'Work, work,' and I was always alone. My private life? I didn't have one. They were surprised that I should even want one. I didn't look like something out of an ad campaign, you see. I was Roger the Researcher. I hope you're finding this entertaining."

"Illuminating."

"Confession is good for the soul. When people weren't there, food was. It was my only comfort for some years, that and masturbation. I tried to shed the weight; I never could. Eventually I tried to quit that Goddam research position. They wouldn't let me do that, either. Do you know what it's like to breathe air like sterile gauze day in and day out?"

"You could have left."

"Don't tell me what I could have done." The skin around his nostrils has turned pale. His fists are knotted. "*You've* made it. You got out. You've never had to wrestle night in, night out with the weight of your Goddam flesh. Don't tell me what I could have done. Her family found me when I showed up here: the Sappers. It's unwise to be Jewish in this sequence. I convinced them I was their cousin, somehow; who knows? And she," he says, the tears streaming, "she loved me. Now old man Sapper is dead; now Kathy's dead; T.B., it's still deadly here. And I'm back where I started. Alone." Suddenly he laughs. "God, what a penchant I have for melodrama. I should have written plays. At least I ended up in Key West. You know? When I was in college I wanted to be a bartender? It seemed—so sexual. And free." He holds out his hands. "Please shoot me."

"I'm sorry," says Roger-Prime. "I understand what you're saying. But it's not enough." The rogue's eyes widen; Roger hears a sound behind him. He glances over his shoulder. It is

Catherine, dressed in a blue jumpsuit, looking no older than he remembers her. "Well, hello," he says. "We've got to stop meeting like this."

"Good work, Roger." Her left hand smooths an antimacassar, and her right keeps her gun trained on the rogue's chest. "You can lower your weapon. Doctor Shapiro, if your present circumstances are as melancholy as you indicate, you're lucky we caught up with you when we did."

"It would be so simple if you'd just shoot me," says the rogue.

"What are you going to do?" Roger asks her.

"Shift him back to his home sequence. My base and his have linked equipment: our sensors isolate and amplify his signal, and they do the actual recalling. When he gets home, he'll have some minor surgery."

"I assumed that. I meant, what are you going to do with him after they've removed his portable shifter? What happens then?" She looks blank. "Catherine, he's a murderer. He has to be tried."

"Of course," she says. She is thumbing her left palm. The chips embedded in the rogue's neck have begun to glow a deeper color, an almost-peach.

"Wait," pleads Roger-Rogue. He points. Slowly Roger-Prime picks up the photograph of the happy newlyweds and hands it to the scientist. "Thank you," says the older man. He looks at the picture as though he has never seen it before. The blood trickling down his neck turns orange-red in the glow from the chips. The rogue looks at his dead wife, then at Catherine. "You're nothing alike," he pronounces. "You looked exactly alike, and you're nothing alike." Puzzled, she frowns. Roger looks again at his older persona, and sees his face begin to crumble from the forehead down, wrinkle and crumble and twist with anguish. All at once, Roger-Prime feels the way he felt facing the skeletons in the cataclysm sequence. He backs off, awash with dread. *It's me,* he thinks, knowing it with a certainty with which he has known nothing else. *It's me, dear Christ, it really is me. Everything squandered. All the richness.*

He hears Catherine say, "They're transferring him—now." The peach light spreads suddenly over the rogue and swallows him. An instant later, he is gone. "Are you all right?" the woman asks him. "I drifted; they had to recall me and send me out again after you. You're all bloody; did you know that?"

"My head's empty," he says.

"Your base lost you when I transferred you out of the cataclysm sequence. I'm afraid you're going to have to shift home with me; it'll be easier to project you to your own sequence from our base. Is that all right?''

"Sure, Company Lady." He sticks the rogue's burner into his pocket. Her eyes are narrowed, trying to fathom him. "Bravo for us, huh?" He grins. "We caught him. No more bartender-Shapiros biting the dust. He married us in this sequence, you know."

"That's sick." READY FOR TRANSFER, her base says in his head.

"I think I understand it. I think he and I are a lot more alike than you and I."

But she surprises him. "We've all been beached and set adrift, Roger," she says. "That, and hugged the coastline waiting for the perfect wind to blow. And he's by no means the worst of us. I've sat at our scanners longer than you have, I think." She pauses, then smiles back at him. "There are no safe harbors."

They both laugh. "Then we'd better get a move on," he says. "New tide's in. And I'm sick to death of the shallows." He feels the pad in his back pocket. *I'll do it for you, Shep,* he thinks. *For you and Roj and Dodger and all of us. Who knows? Now that our three bases have started to work together, maybe we'll find one of us who's a publisher. The possibilities are endless.*

When the transfer comes, he is ready.

SPENDING A DAY
AT THE LOTTERY FAIR
by Frederik Pohl

*Not too many years ago, gambling and lotteries
were outlawed in many parts of the United States
and condemned by the religious as evil. But no
sooner did the economy take a turn for the worse
than somehow lotteries ceased to be objects of sin
and became acclaimed systems for "alleviating
the condition of the poor" or whatever the excuse for raising money. Suddenly the instinct to
gamble became, if not exactly heaven-sent, at
least good for the state. So Frederik Pohl applies
this thrilling system to another of the horrendous
problems of the very near future—over-population.*

They were the Baxter family, Randolph and Millicent the parents,
with their three children, Emma and Simon and Louisa, who was
the littlest; and they didn't come to the fair in any old bus. No,
they drove up in a taxi, all the way from their home clear on the
other side of town, laughing and poking each other, and when
they got out Randolph Baxter gave the driver a really big tip. It
wasn't that he could really afford it. It was just because he felt it
was the right thing to do. When you took your whole family to
the Lottery Fair, Baxter believed, you might as well do it in
style. Besides, the fare was only money. Though Millicent Baxter pursed her lips when she saw the size of the tip, she certainly
was not angry; her eyes sparkled as brightly as the children's,
and together they stared at the facade of the Lottery Fair.

Even before you got through the gates there was a carnival
smell—buttered popcorn and cotton candy and tacos all together—
and a carnival sound of merry-go-round organs and people screaming in the roller coaster, and bands and bagpipes from far away.

A clown stalked on tall stilts through the fairgoers lining up at the ticket windows, bending down to chuck children under the chin and making believe to nibble the ears of teenage girls in bright summer shorts. Rainbow fountains splashed perfumy spray. People in cartoon-character costumes, Gus the Ghost and Mickey Mouse and Pac-Man, handed out free surprise packages to the kids: when Simon opened his it was a propeller beanie; a fan for Emma; for little Louisa, cardboard glasses with a Groucho Marx moustache. And crowded! You could hardly believe such crowds! Off to one side of the parking lot the tour buses were rolling in with their loads of foreign visitors, Chinese and Argentines and Swedes; they had special entrances and were waved through by special guards who greeted them, some of the time anyway, in their own native languages—*"Willkommen!"* and *"Bonjour!"* and *"Ey there, mate!"*—as long as they didn't speak anything like Urdu or Serbo-Croatian, anyway. For the foreign tourists didn't have to pay in the usual way; they bought their tickets in their country of origin, with valuable foreign exchange, and then everything was free for them.

Of course it wasn't like that for the regular American fairgoers. They had to pay. You could see each family group moving up toward the ticket windows. They would slow down as they got closer and finally stop, huddling together while they decided how to pay, and then one or two of them, or all of them, would move on to the window and reach into the admissions cuff for their tickets. Randolph Baxter had long before made up his mind that there would be no such wrangles on this day for his family. He said simply, "Wait here a minute," and strode up to the window by himself. He put his arm into the cuff, smiled at the ticket attendant and said grandly, "I'll take five, please."

The ticket seller looked at him admiringly. "You know," she offered, "there aren't many daddies who'll take all the little fellows in like that. Sometimes they make even tiny babies get their own tickets." Baxter gave her a modest I-do-what-I-can shrug, though he could not help that his smile was a little strained until all five tickets clicked out of the roll. He bore them proudly back to his family and led them through the turnstiles.

"My, what a crowd," sighed Millicent Baxter happily as she gazed around. "Now, what shall we do first?"

The response was immediate. "See the old automobiles," yelled Simon, and, "No, the animals!" and, "No, the stiffs!" cried his sisters.

Randolph Baxter spoke sharply to them—not angrily, but firmly. "There will be no fighting over what we do," he

commanded. "We'll *vote* on what we do, the democratic way.
No arguments, and no exceptions. Now," he added, "the first
thing we're going to do is that you kids will stay right here while
your mother and I get tickets for the job lottery." The parents
left the children arguing viciously among themselves and headed
for the nearest lottery booth. Randolph Baxter could not help a
tingle of excitement, and his wife's eyes were gleaming, as they
studied the prize list. The first prize was the management of a
whole apartment building—twenty-five thousand dollars a year
salary, and a free three-room condo thrown in!

Millicent read his thoughts as they stood in line. "Don't you
just wish!" she whispered. "But personally I'd settle for any of
the others. Look, there's even a job for an English teacher!"
Randolph shook his head wordlessly. It was just marvelous—
five full-time jobs offered in this one raffle, and that not the
biggest of the day. The last one, after the fireworks, always had
the grandest of prizes. "Aren't you glad we came?" Millicent
asked, and her husband nodded.

But in fact he wasn't, altogether, at least until they safely got
their tickets and were on their way back to the children, and then
he was quickly disconcerted to see that the kids weren't where
they had been left. "Oh, hell," groaned Randolph. It was early
in the day for them to get lost.

But they weren't very far. His wife said sharply, "There they
are. And look what they're doing!" They were at a refreshment
stand. And each one of them had a huge cone of frozen custard.
"I *told* them not to make any purchases when we weren't with
them!" Millicent cried, but in fact it was worse than that. The
children were talking to a pair of strange grown-ups, a lean, fair,
elderly woman with a sharp, stern face, and a round, dark-
skinned man with a bald head and immense tortoise-shell glasses.

As the Baxters approached, the woman turned to them
apologetically. "Oh, hullo," she said, "you must be the parents.
I do hope you'll forgive us. Mr. Katsubishi and I seem to have
lost our tour, and your children kindly helped us look for it."

"It's all right, Dad," Simon put in swiftly. "They're on this
foreign tour, see, and everything's free for them anyway. Dad?
Why can't we get on a tour and have everything free?"

"We're Americans," his father explained, smiling tentatively
at the tall English-looking woman and the tubby, cheerful
Japanese—he decided that they didn't *look* like depraved child
molesters. "You have to be an international tourist to get these
unlimited tickets. And I bet they cost quite a lot of money, don't

they?'' he appealed to the man, who smiled and shrugged and looked at the woman.

"Mr. Katsubishi doesn't speak English very well," she apologized. "I'm Rachel Millay. Mrs. Millay, that is, although me dear husband left us some years ago." She glanced about in humorous distress. "I don't suppose you've seen a tour leader carrying a green and violet flag with a cross of St. Andrew on it?"

Since Randolph Baxter had no idea what a cross of St. Andrew looked like, it was hard to say. In any case, there were at least twenty tour parties in sight, each with its own individual pennant or standard, trudging in determined merriment toward the pavilions, the rides, or the refreshment stands. "I'm afraid not," he began, and then paused as his wife clutched his arm. The P.A. system crackled, and the winners of the first drawing were announced.

Neither of the Baxters were among them. "Well, there are six more drawings," said Millicent bravely—not adding that there were also six more sets of raffle tickets to buy if they wanted any hope of winning one of them. Her husband smiled cheerfully at the children.

"What's it to be?" he asked generously. "The life exhibit? The concert—"

"We already voted, Dad," cried Emma, his elder daughter, "it's the animals!"

"No, the stiffs!" yelled her baby sister.

"The old autos," cried Simon. "Anyway, there won't be any stiffs there until later, not to speak of!"

Baxter smiled indulgently at the foreigners. "Children," he explained. "Well, I do hope you find your group." And he led the way to the first democratically selected adventure of the day, the space exhibit.

Baxter had always had a nostalgic fondness for space, and this was a pretty fine exhibit, harking back to olden, golden days when human beings could spare enough energy and resources to send their people and probes out toward the distant worlds. Even the kids liked it. It was lavish with animated 3-D displays showing a human being walking around on the surface of the Moon, and a spacecraft slipping through the rings of Saturn, and even a probe, though not an American one, hustling after Halley's Comet to take its picture.

But Randolph Baxter had some difficulty in concentrating on the pleasure of the display at first because, as they were getting their tickets, the tall, smiling black man just ahead of him in line put his arm into the admissions cuff, looked startled, withdrew his arm, started to speak and fell over on the ground, his eyes open, and staring, it seemed, right into Randolph Baxter's.

When you have a wife and three kids and no job, living on welfare, never thinking about tomorrow because you know there isn't going to be anything in tomorrow worth thinking about, then a day's outing for the whole family is an event to be treasured. No matter what the price—especially if the price isn't in money. So the Baxter family did it all. They visited six national pavilions, even the Paraguayan. They lunched grandly in the dining room at the summit of the fair's great central theme structure, the Cenotaph. And they did the rides, all the rides, from the Slosh-a-Slide water chutes through the immense Ferris wheel with the wind howling through the open car and Simon threatening to spit down on the crowds below, to the screaming, shattering roller coaster that made little Louisa wet her pants. Fortunately her mother had brought clean underwear for the child. When she sent the little girl off with her sister to change in the ladies' room, she followed them anxiously with her eyes until they were safely past the ticket collector, and then said, "Rand, honey. You paid for all those rides yourself."

He shrugged defensively. "I want everybody to have a good time."

"Now, don't talk that way. We agreed. The children and I are going to pay our own way all the rest of the day, and the subject is closed." She proved the point by changing it. "Look," she said, "there are those two foreigners who lost their tour group again." She waved, and Mrs. Millay and Mr. Katsubishi came up diffidently.

"If we're not intruding?" said Mrs. Millay. "We never did find our tour guide, you see, but actually we're getting on quite well without. But isn't it hot! It's never like this in Scotland."

Millicent fanned herself in agreement. "Do sit down, Mrs. Millay. Is that where you're from, Scotland? And you Mr. Kat—, Kats—"

"Katsubishi," he smiled, with an abrupt deep bow. Then he wrinkled his face in concentration for a moment, and managed to say: "I, too—Sukottaland."

Millicent tried not to look astonished, but evidently did not succeed. Mrs. Millay explained, "He's from around Kyle of Lochalth, you know." Since Millicent obviously didn't know, she added, "That's the Japanese colony in northern Scotland, near my own home. In fact, I teach English to Japanese schoolchildren there, since I know the language—my parents were missionaries in Honshu, you see. Didn't you know about the colony?''

Actually, Millicent and Randolph did know about the colony. Or, at least they almost did, in the way that human beings exposed to forty channels of television and with nothing much to do with their time have heard of—without really knowing much about—almost every concept, phenomenon, event, and trend in human history. In just that way, they had heard of the United Kingdom's pact with Japan, allowing large Japanese immigration into an enclave in the north of Scotland. The Japanese made the area bloom both agriculturally and economically. The United Kingdom got a useful injection of Japanese capital and energy, and the Japanese got rid of some of their surplus population without pain. "I wish we'd thought of that," Millicent observed in some envy, but her husband shook his head.

"Different countries, different ways," he said patriotically, "and actually we're doing rather well. I mean, just look at the Lottery Fair! That's American ingenuity for you." Observing that Mrs. Millay was whispering a rapid-fire translation into Mr. Katsubishi's ear, he was encouraged to go on. "Other countries, you see, have their own way of handling their problems. Compulsory sterilization of all babies born in even-numbered years in India, as I'm sure you're aware. The contraceptive drugs they put in the water supply in Mexico—and we don't even talk of what they're doing in, say, Bangladesh." Mrs. Millay shuddered sympathetically as she translated, and the Japanese beamed and bowed, then spoke rapidly.

"He says one can learn much," Mrs. Millay translated, "from what foreign countries can do. Even America."

Millicent, glancing at the expression on her husband's face, said brightly, "Well! Let's not let this day go to waste. What shall we do next?" At once she got the same answers from the children: "Old cars!" "Animals!" "No," whined Baby Louisa, "I wanna see the stiffs!"

Mr. Katsubishi whispered something in staccato Japanese to Mrs. Millay, who turned hesitantly to Millicent Baxter. "One doesn't wish to intrude," she said, "but if you are in fact going to see the Hall of Life and Death as your daughter suggests . . . well, we don't seem to be able to find the rest of our tour group, you see, and we would like to go there. After all, it is the theme center for the entire fair, as you might say—"

"Why, of course," said Millicent warmly, "we'd be real delighted to have the company of you and Mr. Kats—Kats—''

"Katsubishi!" he supplied, bowing deeply and showing all of his teeth in a smile, and they all seven set off for the Hall of Life and Death, with little Louisa delightedly leading the way.

The hall was a low, white marble structure across the green-sward from the Cenotaph, happy picnicking families on the green gay pavilions all around, ice-cream vendors chanting along the roadways, and a circus parade—horses and a giraffe and even an elephant—winding along the main avenue with a band leading them, diddley-boom, diddley-boom, diddley-bang! bang! bang! —all noise, and color, and excitement. But as soon as they were within the hall they were in another world. The Hall of Life and Death was the only free exhibit at the fair—even the rest rooms were not free. The crowds that moved through the hall were huge. But they were also reverential. As you came in you found yourself in a great domed entrance pavilion, almost bare except for seventy-five raised platforms, each spotlighted from a concealed source, each surrounded by an air curtain of gentle drafts. At the time the Baxters came in more than sixty of the platforms were already occupied with silent, lifeless forms of those who had passed on at the fair that day. A sweet-faced child here, an elderly woman there; there, side by side, a young pair of newlyweds. Randolph Baxter looked for and found the tall, smiling black man who had died in the line before him. He was smiling no longer, but his face was in repose and almost joyous, it seemed. "He's at peace now," Millicent whispered, touching her husband's arm, and he nodded. He didn't want to speak out loud in this solemn hall, where the whisper of organ music was barely audible above the gentle hiss of chilled air curtains that wafted past every deceased. Hardly anyone in the great crowd spoke. The visitors lingered at each of the occupied biers; but then, as they moved toward the back of the chamber, they didn't linger. Some didn't even look, for every tourist at the fair could not help thinking, as he passed an empty platform, that before the fair closed that night it would be occupied . . . by someone.

But the Rotunda of Those Who Have Gone Before was only the ante-room to the many inspiring displays the hall had to offer. Even the children were fascinated. Young Simon stood entranced before the great Timepiece of Living and Dying, watching the hands revolve swiftly to show how many were born and how many died in each minute, with the bottom line always showing a few more persons alive in every minute despite every-thing the government and the efforts of patriotic citizens could do—but he was more interested, really, in the mechanism of the thing than in the facts it displayed. Millicent Baxter and Mrs.

Millay were really thrilled by the display of opulent caskets and cerements, and Randolph Baxter was proud to point out to Mr. Katsubishi the working model of a crematorium, with all of its escaping gases trapped and converted into valuable organic feedstocks. And the girls, Emma and Louisa, stood hand in hand for a long time, shuddering happily as they gazed at the refrigerated display cases that showed a hideous four-month embryo next to the corpse of a fat, pretty two-year-old. Emma moved to put her arm around her mother and whispered, "Mommy, I'm *so* grateful you didn't abort me." And Millicent Baxter fought back a quick and tender tear.

"I'd never let you die looking like *that*," she assured her daughter, and they clung together for a long moment. But Randolph Baxter was becoming noticeably ill at ease. When they finally left the Hall of Life and Death, his wife took him aside and asked in concern, "Is something the matter, hon?"

He shrugged irritably at the foreigners, who were talking together in fast, low-toned Japanese. "Just look at their faces," he complained. And indeed both Mr. Katsubishi and Mrs. Millay's expressions seemed to show more revulsion than respect.

Millicent followed her husband's eyes and sighed—there was a little annoyance in the sigh, too. "They're not Americans," she reminded her husband. "I guess they just don't understand." She smiled distantly at the foreign pair, and then looked around at her offspring. "Well, children, who wants to come with me to the washrooms, so we can get ready for the big fireworks?"

They all did, even Randolph, but he felt a need stronger than the urging of his bladder. He remained behind with the foreigners. "Excuse me," he said, somewhat formally, "but may I ask what you thought of the exhibit?"

Mrs. Millay glanced at the Japanese. "Well, it was most interesting," she said vaguely. "One doesn't wish to criticize, of course—" And she stopped there.

"No, no, please go on," Randolph encouraged.

She said, "I must say it did seem odd to, well, *glorify* death in that way."

Randolph Baxter smiled, and tried to make it a forgiving smile, though he could feel that he was upset. He said, "Perhaps you miss the point of the Hall of Life and Death—in fact, of the whole Lottery Fair. You see, some of the greatest minds in America have worked on this problem of surplus population—think tanks and government agencies—why, three universities helped design this fair. Every bit of it is scientifically planned. To begin with, it's absolutely free."

Mrs. Millay left off her rapid-fire, sotto voce Japanese translation to ask, "You mean, free as far as money is concerned?"

"Yes, exactly. Of course, one takes a small chance at every ticket window, and in that sense there is a price for everything. A very carefully computed price, Mrs. Millay, for every hot dog, every show, every ride. To get into the fair in the first place, for instance, costs one decimill—that's 1% of a .0001 probability of receiving a lethal injection from the ticket cuff. Now, that's not much to risk, is it?" he smiled. "And of course it's absolutely painless, too. As you can see by just looking at the ones who have given their lives inside."

Mr. Katsubishi, listening intently to Mrs. Millay's translation in his ear, pursed his lips and nodded thoughtfully. Mrs. Millay said brightly, "Well, we all have our own little national traits, don't we?"

"Now, really, Mrs. Millay," said Randolph Baxter, smiling with an effort, "please try to understand. Everything is quite fair. Some things are practically free, like the park benches and the rest rooms and so on; why, you could use some of them as much as a million times before, you know, your number would come up. Or you can get a first-class meal in the Cenotaph for just about a whole millipoint. But even that means you can do it a thousand times, on the average."

Mr. Katsubishi listened to the end of Mrs. Millay's translation, and then struggled to get out a couple of English words. "Not—us," he managed, pointing to himself and Mrs. Millay.

"Certainly not," Baxter agreed. "you're foreign tourists. So you buy your tickets in your own countries for cash, and of course you don't have to risk your lives. It wouldn't help the American population problem much if you did, would it?" he smiled. "And your tour money helps pay the cost of the fair. But the important thing to remember is that the Lottery Fair is entirely voluntary. No one has to come. Of course," he admitted, with a self-deprecatory grin, "I have to admit that I really like the job lotteries. I guess I'm just a gambler at heart, and when you've spent as much time on welfare as Mrs. Baxter and I have, those big jobs are just hard to resist! And they're better here than at the regular city raffles."

Mrs. Millay cleared her throat. Good manners competed with obstinacy in her expression. "Really, Mr. Baxter," she said, "Mr. Katsubishi and I understand that—heavens, we've had to do things in our own countries! We certainly don't mean to criticize yours. What's hard to understand, I suppose, is, actually, that fetus." She searched his face with her eyes, looking for understanding. "It just seems strange. I mean, that you'd prefer to see a child born and then perhaps die in a lottery than to abort him ahead of time."

Mr. Baxter did his very best to maintain a pleasant expression, but knew he was failing. "It's a difference in our national philosophies, I guess." he said. "See, we don't go in for your so-called 'birth control' here. No abortion. No contraception. We accept the gift of life when it is given. We believe that every human being, from the moment of conception on, has a right to a life—although," he added, "not necessarily a *long* one." He eyed the abashed foreigners sternly for a moment, then relented. "Well," he said, glancing at his watch. "I wonder where my family can be? They'll miss the fireworks if they don't get back. I bet Mrs. Baxter's gone and let the children pick out souvenirs— the little dickenses have been after us about them all day. Anyway, Mrs. Millay, Mr. Katsubishi, it's been a real pleasure meeting the two of you and having this chance to exchange views—"

But he broke off, suddenly alarmed by the expression on Mr. Katsubishi's face as the man looked past him. "What's the matter?" he demanded roughly.

And then he turned, and did not need an answer. The answer was written on the strained, haggard, tear-streaked face of his wife as she ran despairingly toward him, carrying in her hands a plastic cap, a paperweight, and a helium-filled balloon in the shape of a pig's head, but without Emma and without Simon and even without little Louisa.

IN THE FACE
OF MY ENEMY
by Joseph H. Delaney

*Somewhere out there there may be—there must
be—intelligent beings far beyond the level of
Earth's best. If so, then this story is not impossible and merely moves the legend of the miracle
man who occasionally walks among the mortals
into the realms of the starry universe. Come then
and let us explore a new planet for exploitation—
where everything is not as reported.*

PROLOGUE

*The broken creature hung suspended on fields of force, amid
devices half matter and half energy, flung into patterns and
functions unfathomable to but a few minds in all creation.*

"It is loathesome," said one voice to the other. "Does it
live?"

"Its life force is near extinction, but now static. It is primitive,
yet I believe it truly thinks."

"It intrigues you?"

"Indeed. As it is now, so we once must have been. I will,
therefore, know this being, and ourselves of yesterday."

It probed the body of the beast, and knew it, and was saddened.
"Tragic," *it remarked.* "I have descended into its cells. What
ghastly inefficiencies. They battle; they eat one another. They
are predator and prey within the organism. Equilibrium may be
briefly achieved: never harmony."

"The damage appears complete. What will you do?"

"I shall make repair; observe it in life and function."

*The being touched the broken form. With disciplined force he
built anew according to its pattern.*

"Fascinating. It lives. For a time there is balance. It struggles to retain this, but the struggle cannot endure long against the inner conflict. It spends its energy to forestall destruction, yet it spares enough for thought."

"That is conjecture."

"No. It is fact. It is conscious of its existence. It conceives the flow of time. It questions its reason to be. This is sentience. It calls itself 'Kah-si-omah.' "

"Perhaps, in time, that will be fact. It does not appear presently probable. If it snatches only fleetingly at this sensory flood, how can it learn?"

"Perhaps it learns only small things. We may yet determine this, for I grow curious. Perhaps we shall never again pass this way, yet if by chance . . ."

"What will you do?"

"I shall change it; bring discipline, provide order. You will perceive its present lack."

"Indeed. Observe; the cells replicate, and as they replicate they drift. The process is unfaithful and unhealthy for the creature, yet the organism permits it. It is as you said; they eat each other."

"I shall adjust."

"How? The drift is cumulative. Each replication deviates a little further. Chance alone determines how far. It is the pattern that is faulty. The fidelity of replication cannot endure under purely chemical control. More is needed."

"Restraint? Yes. Brilliant."

"You set yourself an exceedingly difficult task."

"True. It will be challenging. Observe, these large cells function differently. They are the keys. They interconnect throughout the organism. They are the vehicle of its consciousness. They are subject to the being's command."

"If such it has."

"There is room within them for innovation. I shall form echelons of them, and cross-controls. Command will ascend to the being's core of consciousness."

"The endeavor seems worthwhile. I shall observe your efforts. I may, perhaps, comment."

"I would be pleased if you should do so."

Again, the boundary obscured. Matter melded with its higher state. Subtle changes followed.

"Interesting. Satisfaction must surely be yours."

"Indeed. Observe: even as we watch its wounds heal, its form

regenerates and returns to it. Control descends from its center of consciousness and seeps into the cells.''

''It is still loathsome.''

''It now need not be. Its will controls, sluggish though it is. Perhaps the creature hears you. Properly contrite, it may experiment and find a form more pleasing to you.''

''It lacks the intellect.''

''No, not the intellect; the experience. It has lived but the instant nature gave it. I have given in eons more.''

Time passed. The dalliance ended. The need which had brought visitors to this young world was satisfied. Their vehicle, having probed the bowels of the mountain, having found, extracted and refined the fissionables it sought, now rose from the blackened slag pit, where it had rested so long, and squandered the energy it had gathered in its journey between suns.

Their toy, transformed, and this time safely out of harm's way, watched, mystified. It did not comprehend the works of gods, nor now, even itself.

I am not a coward by nature, though surely there is a little cowardice in all of us. And mine surfaced as soon as I could make out the features of the man disembarking from the shuttle. It was Ivan Carmody himself, my boss.

There are men. Also, there are MEN. The difference is one of kind, not degree, and the mind perceives it instantly, unerringly, and inexplicably.

One approached whom I feared, but to whom duty demanded I explain the other. And I wondered if I could.

My months on Campbell had been filled with many strange experiences, some of which, I felt, were better left out of my report. But this, Carmody; HE, I feared; HE would demand to hear them all. And worst of all, I knew, I would tell.

I was too minor even to have met him face to face, of course, until now, but as Secretary of Extraterrestrial Affairs he was the U.N.'s most powerful figure, and its most colorful.

As he approached, I understood why, for he was imposing. Tall and gangly, he had the look of an eagle about him, from the straight white hair he wore combed back to the huge curved beak of his nose. The thick glasses perched on its bridge magnified piercing green eyes that did not blink.

If he overwhelmed me by his physical presence, it was nothing compared to the devastation created when he spoke, and I hoped I could stand the strain.

"Kimberly Ryan," the voice boomed. "Are you in charge of this mess?"

I glanced around me at the muddy street, the burned-out buildings and the crushed equipment. Some of the men who had watched the shuttle's approach had skulked away at his sight. "Yes, sir. I have assumed command under Emergency Regulation Number 309," I said, hoping I had cited the right one. I felt his stare on my body; at the rough leather clothing that Casey had made for me. "This is all I have left, Mr. Secretary. Everything burned."

"I'll want to hear your report immediately, Miss Ryan, preferably not out here in the street."

"Yes, sir. We can go to Solar Minerals H.Q., to Mr. Meyers's office. What's left of it, that is. I'll show you the way."

I turned and started off down the street, trying to stick to the dryer spots. He followed along a pace or two behind.

"Where is Meyers?"

"Dead," I told him. "He shot himself before the settlement, uh, fell, when he thought the aliens were going to fire the building. I can send for Mr. Bigelow, though. He's in charge of Solar's operations now, I guess."

"No. I want your report first. We may be filing charges against the management, including Mr. Bigelow."

I reached the stairs and started up, wondering if the flight would hold both of us in its damaged condition. It had taken a glancing hit from the catapult, which had partially destroyed the landing, but Carmody did not hesitate to risk it. He followed me up the twenty or so steps closely enough for me to hear him panting.

We entered Meyers's office and Carmody took it upon himself to sit at Meyers's desk, in Meyers's chair, despite the fact that the back rest was still spattered with dried blood and brains. He propped his chin on his hands, leaning over the desk, hunching forward and looking right at me. "Find a chair, Miss Ryan. I don't like looking up at people."

I pulled one of the rough-hewn chairs closer to the desk and sat down carefully, mindful that it contained splinters, and when I was as comfortable as I could be in the presence of such awesome power, I asked him where he wanted me to start.

"At the beginning, Miss Ryan; from the time you set foot on Campbell. And you will omit nothing; is that clear?"

"Very. But actually, it really started before I ever got here. I found that out later; Mr. Bigelow told me."

Carmody slapped the fingers of one hand against his chin. "Whatever," he said.

"Well, evidently he—that is, Captain Corsetti—he was the master of the *Wilmington*, had orders to buy a little time for Meyers before I got here. He called Meyers on the radio as soon as we were in orbit and warned them I was coming. That's an indication to me that Solar management back on Earth knew about the cairn, and meant to conceal it from . . ."

"Forget that part. I'll take care of them. I want to hear about this Indian; what's his name?"

"Kah-Sih-Omah. But we called him Casey. How did you hear about him?"

"Never mind. Get on with it."

"Yes, sir. Well, here again, some of this is second-hand from Bigelow, and it was much later when I found out about it, but to begin with, I certainly didn't hit it off with Mr. Meyers. He knew why I was here, or thought he did, and he saw his job about to be snatched out from under him. He'd be through if I learned of the cairn."

"Without comments, please, Miss Ryan. Stick to what's relevent."

"I'm only trying to show his attitude, Mr. Carmody."

Carmody seemed to give up at this point. He didn't respond, and I felt safe in going ahead, repeating as much as I could remember, verbatim.

And it had started out innocently enough; I'd merely thanked Meyers for meeting me at the dock. His reply had been harsh.

"I didn't come down here for that, lady. I came down here to check cargo. As far as I'm concerned, you can go back on the next barge. What do you want here, anyway?"

"You know why I'm here, Mr. Meyers. I'm here to make the ecological survey. That's the law. No planet can be opened to colonization or exploitation until the U.N. Ecological Committee has approved it and imposed the necessary restrictions. That's my job, okay? I'm not looking for a fight."

"Nor am I. But I've got enough work to do now without looking after you, and without wasting time leading you around."

"I don't need looking after. I don't need leading. I can find my own way around. You won't even know I'm here."

I started to leave, and that was when he grabbed me by the arm. It hurt, and I suspect this was his intention. I couldn't shake loose. "Get your hands off me," I demanded. "I'm an officer of the United Nations. You could go to jail for this."

He let go, but left big red marks. "Have it your own way, lady, but keep this in mind: there are 450 healthy construction men on this planet, and no women. Some of them have been

here two years without a woman. Maybe I won't know you're here, but every one of them will before you're off this dock."
He'd have been all right if he'd stopped there, but he didn't. "Course, maybe that's the way you like it. A girl like you could get rich in the four months you'll be here."

I knew it was a mistake when I did it. I lunged and threw a punch.

He stopped me easily with one hamlike hand. "There'll be none of that, lady. On Campbell I'm the law: judge, jury, and all the rest of it. Assaulting me ought to be worth ninety days in the brig, at least. Bigelow," he called.

A big, sleepy-eyed man came over. Meyers called him Scotty. I didn't know it then, but he wasn't quite as harmless as he looked. Bigelow was the project architect. He was responsible for erecting the landing web, but he had a sideline too. He was a part-time assassin.

I went with him to the operations building, where Meyers had told him to take me immediately. Meyers hadn't been subtle about that, although he did try to mask his real purpose. I heard him tell Bigelow to find somebody big, ugly, and stupid to be my bodyguard.

Bigelow had seemed nice enough at the time, though he too gave me to understand I was in the way; they had deadlines to meet, that any delay, however slight, cost the company and the consortium to which it belonged great sums of money, all of which had to be made up to the investors who would bid on the minerals when the web was finished. He, personally, feared for his bonuses, which field management would not get if they didn't make the deadlines. And he told me all about the expensive family he was supporting on Earth.

I stood there, locked in a back room feeling sorry for him, and even for Meyers, although I still didn't like Meyers. I was a problem to them, and maybe in their place I'd have felt the same way, guarding against 450 potential rapists.

It seemed like hours before he returned. I amused myself by staring out the one window the room contained. It overlooked a muddy street remarkable for its complete lack of traffic. Then Bigelow came back into view followed by a hulking, shambling figure dressed in bib overalls and a hard hat. He wore no shirt, and from beneath his hat fell long black braids, which lay on coppery-skinned shoulders. He was as massive as he was brawny. Bigelow had followed orders in one respect; the man was big. At the time I hoped he was not too dumb, though he gawked around like a tourist. He was not ugly; he was simply ordinary.

Bigelow introduced him as K.C. Oma.

"Hello, Mr. Oma." I said.

"I am called Casey," he replied, somewhat shyly. "I am pleased to meet you. Are you ready?"

I thanked Bigelow and followed Casey down the stairs and into the street, walking slightly behind him, watching him. He moved like a shadow, without effort or urgency, and I found myself admiring him for the graceful way he managed that massive form. I had known Indians before, and that was no doubt what he was, considering the prominent nose and high cheekbones, which seemed to highlight the copperish cast of his skin. He was tall enough and light-skinned enough to have been a Northern Sioux, but they were rarely as heavy.

We did not speak until we were inside the suite: a foyer, a kitchen, and two bedrooms, all of rough-sawn native timber and sparsely furnished with articles of the same material. "Not the Ritz," I said, "but adequate." Then I realized how dumb that sounded.

I looked around. There was my luggage in the larger bedroom. I peeked into the other one. In it was a beat-up military-style duffle bag.

Before I could ask the question, Casey answered it. "Mine," he said, "I am to guard you every moment." He said it like he really meant it.

I felt the words of protest rise in my throat. But there they stopped, unuttered, and I thought, *It does seem reasonable*. Who could menace me with him nearby? And he did seem nice enough. So I said instead, "Fine, I'll try not to be any trouble."

And then, with great innocence, he remarked, "You do not trouble me at all, Miss Ryan. Tell me, what is it you will do here?"

"I'm a busybody, Casey. Haven't they told you?"

He shook his head gravely and grunted a cautious "No."

I realized I was behaving defensively; making this simple man the object of my revenge for the hostile reception at the dock. "Forgive me," I said, "I meant to say I'm here on an ecological survey of the planet, to see if the presence of men will harm it: hurt the local life forms, or create hazards for future colonists, that sort of thing. Understand?"

"Yes, Miss Ryan."

"I'll need to go out in the field, perhaps for days at a time, and I assume that means you'll go too."

"Yes, Miss Ryan. I shall go."

"Have you been out there before?"

"Only near the station, never far in."

At first, this answer disturbed me, and I was angered that Meyers had not furnished me with an experienced guide; but then, after thinking it over, I liked this better. This way I could choose where to go, and this simple man seemed so sincere in his assurances that I believed he could and would protect me, even from Meyers.

"Fine, we'll get started in the morning. We'll need a skimmer. I assume you can arrange that, and that you can drive one."

"Yes, Miss Ryan, I can."

My next question was redundant, in the light of what I later learned, but at the time it seemed appropriate, and Casey took no offense. "We'll be camping out for several days, Casey. You'll need to collect equipment and food. I assume you know a little something about camping and cooking."

"I can manage, Miss Ryan. I will obtain what we need and be ready by morning."

He got me settled in, then left me behind locked doors to make preparations. I did not know at the time what a foment I had caused, or what drastic preparations Meyers and Bigelow were making to insure I did not leave Campbell with word of the cairn. Though it lay far away in dense woods, and the odds I would find it were astronomically high, they were unwilling to risk even that, fearing that if its existence were known their operation would be halted until we had determined what it represented. Perhaps they thought we could consider it the mark of some other race's claim to Campbell and order the planet abandoned.

They had already tried to destroy it, with no success whatever, and the effect of modern explosives upon it was nil. Man could not have built it, and he could not demolish it either. Later I learned that Meyers had considered burying it under a mound of dirt but my unexpected arrival had left him no time for that. So they decided instead to destroy Casey, the big, dumb, expendable Indian, and me.

We did not know that then, the morning we left the station aboard a skimmer loaded with death.

At first the day was pleasant, though we were cool to start with, both in shorts, but this area of Campbell was tropical and soon it grew hot, even with the blast of the skimmer's fans to cool us. We headed inland, across the coastal plain where protograsses flourished, but these gave way to a cycad-like growth, which was evidently a survivor of the planet's earlier plant evolution. Farther in in the uplands, they were rare, supplanted by larger organisms closely resembling terrestrial trees.

There was much of interest to see, and we flew low, just high enough to avoid obstacles, while I drank it in. We spoke little, beyond what was necessary to call each other's attention to some new curiosity. I was too excited to risk missing something, and he too taciturn.

Our course was leisurely, and we followed the streams that flowed down from the highlands to the sea. Here life teemed, and we stopped many times to observe and photograph it, hanging on the skimmer's fans, and hovering silently over small herds of little animals which gathered at the streams to drink.

Campbell was made for skimmers. Its sun was bright and poured its energy into the cells that covered our hull, from which it flowed into the plastic batteries built into it, thence into the motors which drove the fans. Riding in one made me feel detached, as though it was the magic carpet of old Arabian Nights.

Nightfall found us in the highlands, where the air was cooler. Casey set up a tent for me, there among the trees, and we ate from supplies brought from the settlement. Casey, whether out of shyness or out of some unspoken preference, refused to occupy the tent, but instead rolled up in a blanket outside.

By then he had demonstrated he was no stranger to the woods. He had laid out the camp in an expert manner, with the tent rigidly erect on taut ropes, and perched for drainage on a little hummock. His fire blazed brightly and cleanly, fed with dry, dead wood, and banked carefully to last the night. Whatever doubts, whatever reservations I had about the man disappeared that night. I slept as soundly in my tent as I ever had on Earth.

The morning brought the smell of fresh coffee into the tent, borne on a gentle breeze. I rose to find Casey bent over the fire, cooking breakfast. Around us there was a heavy fog, which swathed the tops of the trees and blotted out the half-risen sun.

I took the steaming mug from him and tasted it, while he divided the contents of the skillet onto stainless steel plates. It, too, smelled wonderful, and I found myself drawing deep breaths of Campbell's morning air into my lungs. And I said to him, "Casey, this is why I'm here. Smell that air. Nothing like it exists on Earth—anywhere. All that, man spoiled long ago. But I mean to see that no one spoils this."

He handed me a plate, which I took gratefully, but he said nothing. Instead he met my gaze, pausing a brief moment before resuming his task. Had that been a tear in his eye? From the smoke, perhaps. Surely not because of what I'd said. But then, of course, I did not know that Casey had seen it all before.

We ate, struck camp, wiped the condensate from the skimmer's cells, and started off again. More and bigger trees appeared, growing in clumps, not yet numerous enough to become continuous forest. They yielded a kind of nut, on which fed little beasts about the size of cats. We saw the first sizable group of them that morning. They were quadrupedal, but had good manipulative ability in their front paws, and scurried about gathering and crunching nuts despite our approach.

I did not know a great deal about Campbell's life forms. What I did know came from survey reports which were made by the first scout teams to visit here, and like all survey reports they covered only the obvious.

They had, to their own satisfaction, ruled out the existence of intelligent life; a fairly safe bet, since Campbell appeared to be geologically younger than Earth, and its life consequently less highly organized. There were evolutionary confluences, of course, but on this land mass, at least, these did not extend to large grazing forms or to large predators.

Campbellian protein was organized slightly differently from the terrestrial norm, and utilized different amino groups in its structure. Most of it was simply useless as food for human beings, who couldn't metabolize it, but some of it was poisonous as well.

We observed and photographed animals for a while, then began to follow a stream which wound its way through the foothills of the still-distant mountains. Here again we saw teeming life, this time in a pool. The creatures which threw their shadows on its sandy bottom were not fish, of course, but occupied the same ecological position as fish, and had the same problems; they were hunted.

The predator beast had fangs in his jaws and claws on his feet. He was only as large as the nut grazers, though small as he was he managed to look ferocious, even leonine, as he growled at us. We left him to his fishing and continued.

That night we camped in the foothills. Once again Casey pitched the tent. This time I was not content to bury myself in notebooks as I had the night before and retire early from the weariness of the journey. I had become acclimated to outdoor life and caught up in the spirit of the adventure. I was resolved to leave the recording of trivia to another day, and instead enjoy those things that made this journey personally memorable.

And so it was that I took over the task of cooking while Casey went to the stream for water. I sat by the fire and drank in the aroma of the food and the still, calm pleasure of Campbell's star-studded night.

Casey returned, looking troubled. At first he refused to tell me why. But I pestered him without mercy, and then he explained.

"It may mean nothing," he said. "But I found the remains of a fire."

He took me to it, and we examined it in torchlight, along the banks of the stream: charred lumps of wood, so tiny I could barely see them, scattered around and half-buried in the sand, meant something to him. I would never have noticed them, much less equated them with the presence of men, and did not understand his concern.

"So," I said, "other men have been here, made a fire. Why should this disturb you?"

"Because now I must search for their bones." He reached down and took an object from the sand, where it had been shallowly buried. He brushed away debris. It was the skull of one of the fishlike creatures, and it looked charred. "The creatures of this world are different from those of Earth. Some can be safely eaten, though they provide little nourishment and taste foul. Most are not safe. These are poisonous, yet it appears that they have been roasted and the flesh eaten."

"By whom? Surely if you know this, others do as well."

"Yes. It is common knowledge—now. So this must have been done by an early exploration party, dead before I came here. I know of no one missing from the station since then, and the signs are old. I will search again in the morning."

He did, but found nothing except more fishbones. That day I saw the grim side of Casey, for he was morose and troubled, as though he took this as a sign. And in truth it was, for us, as the first of the disasters struck us.

Suddenly our dead reckoner became a dead dead reckoner. It refused to show our position on the console display, but meandered from one side of the screen to the other. We could get nothing but a feeble, anemic-looking blip that rolled around on the bottom of the screen.

"Can you repair it, Casey?"

His glance answered even before his words. "It is beyond my skill, even if I had parts and tools. We will have to work; use the satellite beacon and calculate our position from its next pass. I suggest we do not move until we have done that." He switched on the radio and punched the red button for the navigation channel.

We waited. The time came and went, but the beacon did not

register as it overflew. Casey removed the cowling from the receiver; no easy task without proper tools. He looked into the works and sighed. "Fused. The tuner will not move. There has been a surge of some kind; an arc across the plates. They have been welded together. If I force them, the tuner will break. If I do not, we cannot match the satellite's frequency."

"What else do we have?" I asked him. I felt peculiarly helpless, since my education did not extend to such technical things, and I lacked the knowledge even to fully appreciate our predicament.

"Nothing. Not even a compass. Modern science replaced such things long ago with the contemptible gadgetry. I'm afraid we will have to resort to even more primitive methods."

"Can you find our way back to the station?"

"Certainly. To the east is the sea. We could hardly miss that, and once there we can follow the shoreline to the station. We are not in any danger of becoming lost, but I suggest we do not risk further problems by continuing inland. We should return at once."

Reluctantly I agreed. I was disappointed, but then, there was still plenty of time. We could get another skimmer and go out again, and this time we'd check it out carefully before we left.

Casey changed course, headed east, and carefully watched the skimmer's shadow on the ground below. He took what he hoped was the proper heading to get us near the station, holding a slight angle to the right and trying to compensate mentally for the passage of time. It was tedious work.

I left him alone, partly because I realized he was very busy and partly in reflection of my own disgust with this unhappy turn of events. I sat there, feeling the rush of the wind through my hair and listening to the steady hum of the fans.

I began hearing a click, at first barely audible, which grew louder as time went one.

Casey noticed it too, and cocked an ear to listen. There was a look of concern on his face, as though he anticipated more mechanical problems. Then the sound vanished, and Casey's look went with it.

After that we flew on at a steady speed of about forty-five knots for nearly two hours without a hint of what the mysterious noise had been. With their simple construction and controls, there was little that could go wrong with a skimmer, and neither of us then suspected the click represented anything more than a twig lodged in one of the fan grilles.

Then the escarpment appeared. It threatened to run for miles perpendicular to our path. To go around meant risking the loss of our orientation, human senses being as fallible as they are. Casey, therefore, decided to increase our altitude and climb it, and then to camp on the high plains for the night, which was rapidly approaching.

But as he increased power to gain the necessary lift, the click abruptly returned. It grew into a loud knock, and then a squeal joined it. Together they lapsed into a pounding vibration. I clung to the seat, fearful of being thrown out, for the skimmer had begun to list and pitch. Casey fought to control it, but could not stabilize us. In desperation, he cut the power and we dropped like a stone, our lifting surfaces inadequate to support us without the help of the fans.

Trees, in the path of our steep and rapid glide, plunged toward us. I could see Casey straining with the stick, trying to guide us toward the small clearing near the bend of the stream, but I knew we'd never make it. I was still watching in horror when the ground came up and we struck it with a glancing blow that jolted every bone in my body. We were sliding along the ground, striking bushes and rocks, a cloud of dust and debris rising around us. Then I felt myself being flung forward and knew I would hit the windscreen. Desperately I tried to duck.

Then I saw the stars and briefly tasted blood. After that came darkness.

I do not know how long my personal night lasted. I awoke to the real night, staring upward into Campbell's star-strewn sky and feeling wet and cold. There was pain, in my face and in my arms and legs. I could still taste blood, and a couple of my front teeth felt loose. But testing, I found my arms and legs seemed to work.

I strained to raise my head, felt a wave of pain, and dropped back into the coarse sand beneath me. I would have to try that a little slower. In the meantime, I looked around again, into the darkness, turning my head from side to side. There was little to be seen in the darkness except a glow on my right toward a distant hilltop. As I watched, I could see it was creeping up the slope, and the realization came, aided by the acrid smell of smoke in the air, that it was a fire. And then it dawned on me that I didn't know where Casey was.

Ignoring the pain this time, I struggled to my feet, took an experimental step or two, and stumbled over something. I strained to see in the darkness of Campbell's moonless night. Below was a shapeless mass. Our tent? No, the satchel of supplies; some of it, anyway. It smelled funny, and I realized it had been burnt.

I groped at it, trying to find the opening and get a flashlight. That was when I heard Casey moan. He was underneath the bag, holding it with both arms. It was they, not the bag, which had been burnt.

I struggled with the bag, pulling it downward toward his feet, until at last it slipped off him. I opened it and searched frantically through its contents, until at last I found a shape that was right.

Pushing the switch brought forth a stabbing beam of light. In it I could see the burned stumps of trees, and the ground, covered with blackened ash. Grasses, still holding their living form, but now consisting only of fragile ash, disintegrated into little puffs as eddies of wind hit them.

I turned the light on Casey and gasped in horror. His fingers, at the ends of arms which still encircled the space the bag had occupied, were charred stumps. Above them, his arms were blistered horribly, and while the bag apparently had protected his upper chest and face, his hair hung loosely around his head, the braids singed off. There was a deep gash in his forehead, from which he'd apparently bled profusely. The blood had run down his neck and puddled darkly beneath his head.

The moan had told me Casey lived, and the sight told me how badly off he really was. There are few things more painful than burns, and fewer still more difficult to treat. And I knew that, in time, when the protective shock wore off, he would be suffering horribly, and I must then be ready to give him what help I could.

There was precious little in our bag of medical supplies. I searched through it and found nothing even remotely adequate. There was a tube of antiseptic jelly with which I coated the worst parts of his burnt arms and hands. But there were no large dressings, no unguents, and only three ampules of morphine sulfate to relieve his pain. These would not help for long. I decided to wait until his need was greatest before using this. I covered him with a blanket and sat down beside him to consider my own situation.

I was not badly hurt. I had only small bumps, cuts, and abrasions, and I had not been touched by the fire. From the looks of the front of my blouse, I had bled profusely from the nose, and while this was sore, it did not seem to be broken.

Alone, with the shock wearing off, I tried to piece things together. I knew what must have happened: the crash of the skimmer, into a rock or large tree, must have ruptured cells in its hull, shorting them out and setting fire to the underbrush. This would have melted other portions of the hull and started more fires.

I did not see the remains of the skimmer nearby; therefore I
had been removed from the site, dunked in the stream, then
placed here on the sand. Casey would have been all right then.
And the fact that I had not been burned, or even singed, meant I
had not come through the fire. That meant Casey had returned to
the wreck to get the bag, and by that time the fire must have
been fierce. He'd gotten his injuries retrieving the bag; but, I
asked myself, why did he risk it?

Then I remembered: the native foods would not sustain human
life. We needed terrestrial food. Without the skimmer, return to
the settlement would take weeks; long enough so that we'd have
risked starvation on the way. Casey knew we needed the bag to
get back, that we were isolated and lost, with no expectancy of
rescue. That's why he'd gone back.

I felt brief anger at him then, for sacrificing both of us. His
male mind had told him he must save me by getting the food, but
not that without him I had no hope whatsoever of making it. I
knew that, and strangely enough it didn't bother me to know; not
like it bothered me to have the responsibility for comforting
Casey in what I realized would be his last hours.

As I sat there, all alone in the darkness, I realized I had
absolutely no way of coping with a situation like this. I could
only huddle here, wrapped in a blanket, and watch Casey's life
pass away along with Campbell's night.

The shock wore off, fatigue marched in and took me away. For
a time I slept. Then the rising sun woke me. It flooded in in all
its brilliance through my closed eyelids. Opening them, I could
see it was already at least an hour past dawn. I must be up, to
see to Casey. I strained again to rise, and found that slumber had
brought me stiffness to go with my pain. Every joint ached,
every movement was agony; nevertheless I did gain my feet.

Around me, the blackened landscape loomed starkly. A hundred yards away the skimmer hung, its bow perched on the bole
of a still-smouldering tree. Its skin had melted off in the fire,
exposing the steel skeleton, now buckled and bent in the middle
so that the stern rested flat on the ground.

Casey had not moved, and still lay arms aloft, beneath the
blanket. I could not tell if he was alive, and hesitated long
moments before taking up the challenge and raising the blanket
to look.

It would have shocked me less to find him dead, with his eyes
closed. They were open. Incredibly, they moved. He was
conscious, and remarkably, composed, and he seemed to have
been waiting for me.

I gasped at the sight, and it was a moment before I found my voice. "Casey, I have the morphine. I'll give you some."

"No." His voice was strong. It was not consistent with the terrible pain I knew he must be experiencing. "Save it," he said. "I am in control." Then he closed his eyes.

He's delirious, I remember telling myself. I broke. I was not in control. "Casey! Your hands," I shouted. "There's nothing left of them. What are we going to do?"

The eyes opened again calmly, to reassure me. Again he spoke strange words. "We will wait."

"Casey. We're lost, hundreds of miles from the station. Nobody knows we're here. I can't get us back. I can't even get myself back, much less move you."

"We will wait." His voice fairly boomed at me. "Set up the tent around me, then let me sleep. And wash that blood off your face. You look awful."

Again he closed his eyes, and again I was terrified. Was this merely the product of delirium, or was Casey some kind of superman, immune to pain? He looked so bad; yet he sounded so strong, so positive. For long moments I knelt there, bent over him, watching his chest rise and fall with deep, even breaths. Then I covered him again and went to do as he asked.

I washed away the blood, soaking a bandana in the cool water of the stream, so that I could go back and do the same for him.

I could not tell whether or not the strain was playing tricks with my imagination or whether I really saw what I thought I saw. But at the time he seemed a little more gaunt, a little thinner, than he had the day before. When I went to clean the dried blood from his face, the gash that had gaped at me so malignantly the night before now seemed tiny and insignificant.

I had to get hold of myself, curb my imagination; and nothing helps do that quite so well as work. So I pitched the tent: not so well as Casey would have, but adequately, then gathered wood and built a fire. I cooked and ate a light meal, then took the dishes to the stream to wash them, terrifying, in the process, the fish creatures which swarm there, trapped in this oxbow pond.

Casey slumbered on inside the tent, oblivious of the awesome destruction his body had endured. He did not waken again, though I feared he would at any moment; that he would find his control gone and fearsome pain present, and I would need the morphine.

I pondered now his recovery, where short hours ago I had pondered his death. If he survived he would be helpless for weeks. I looked at the bag of supplies, which was by no means full, and wondered how we could stretch them out. We'd planned six days in the skimmer. On foot, it would be more like six weeks, if we could make it at all.

Time passed. I waited silently in the shade just inside the tent flap, and adjusted it from time to time to keep the sun off Casey. Campbell rotated in slightly more than nineteen standard hours. With next to no axial tilt there were roughly ten hours of daylight. As light began to ebb, I resolved the night would not be dark, and that this time the fire would be friendly.

Because of the destruction of vegetation in the area I had to go rather farther than usual to find wood, but I returned just as the light was about to fail, intending to check once more on Casey before it did. I dumped the wood on the ground and brushed off pieces of bark, then entered the tent and raised the blanket.

He did not stir, but appeared to be sleeping peacefully. Sometime during the day his arms had descended, and now rested across his chest beneath the blanket. Is it the light, I asked myself, or does he look yet thinner than he did before?

Over the bones of his face the skin stretched tight, and his cheeks seemed hollow. Then I glanced at his forehead. The gash had dwindled; shrunk, the way a healing cut does, to a fraction of its former size, as if days had passed instead of hours. This, I knew, was real. It was not a product of my mind. And I knew that what was real was in no way natural either, but I found my attitude about Casey's situation changing. It was not a question of if he recovered, but when.

Troubled by this perplexing fact and many others, I went outside and looked up into the night. Ahead and low on the horizon was the escarpment, which was probably the best reason I had to be pessimistic. We would have to climb it to reach the sea, and though Casey's miraculous slumber might eventually mend what was left of him, he might survive it merely to join me in starvation. The escarpment was our greatest obstacle, and we had met it at the worst time.

It seemed to stretch out endlessly in both directions. It was both steep and high. And what was nothing to a skimmer was unsurmountable to us now. No doubt along its course there existed breaches in its face, where a healthy person could climb up, and I could imagine myself struggling up some steep ravine, slipping on fallen rock and tearing at creepers for handholds. But Casey? No. His battered stumps of hands would be useless, and I simply lacked the strength to get him to the top.

I caught myself thinking, if only there was help; somebody else near that we could go to. A useless plea that flashed across my mind about the time I saw, or thought I saw, the fire up on top of the escarpment. Fire? Did I see it or did my need create its image? It was but a flicker, a pinpoint, that flashed across my retinas, then was gone.

I grew cold, and wrapped myself in a blanket. And creeping inside the tent, I lay at Casey's feet, staring at the flickering embers of our own fire. It had not occurred to me, as I fell asleep, that this, too, might be seen from far away.

Morning came. I rose with the sun, feeling somewhat less achey than I had the day before, and now resigned to what was to be. Casey slumbered on, looking even more skeletal, eyes now sunken in their sockets beneath dark lids. But the gash! The gash was gone! Not just diminished, but gone, without scab, without scar; not even a discoloration. I felt my blood run cold.

With shaking hands I grasped the blanket and drew it down, past his now-bony neck and across his chest. Through the unbuttoned shirt it, too, looked shallow, and where before thick muscles laced across it, ribs now pushed prominently through his skin.

And then I looked at his arms, which rested across his abdomen, expecting to see devastation, perhaps gangrene. Burnt skin had sloughed off and lay in flakes beneath them. Blisters had drained. In place of blackened ruin now appeared smooth pink skin, devoid of any scarring.

Reason told me this could not be; that it was in my mind the fantasy lay. But even as I gazed in disbelief my eyes dropped to his hands, no longer charred and cracking, oozing fluid and dripping life away, bare stumps of useless tortured flesh. A scream rose in my throat, which at the last minute I stifled, while blood thumped a fierce tattoo and went pounding across my temples.

The hands were whole, smooth and pink, lacking only nails, and at the fingertips these, too, were budding. I dropped the blanket and knelt there, over this strange new Casey, reflecting on what I'd just seen, convinced it was not real. Then I wondered: did fantasy deceive touch, as it did the eyes? And some insane curiosity impelled me to reach out. I felt, not charred and hardened ruin, but firm warm flesh, and a pulse, faint, but regular. This time the scream came, shrill and piercing, and echoed down the valley.

Casey stirred. He opened his eyes and smiled weakly, totally obliterating the demonic picture of him that had been forming in my mind, becoming once again only a man. I lost my fear and again I knelt beside him, holding his hand, waiting for him to gain the strength to speak. Whatever sort of miracle was taking place, I was now grateful.

Presently his lips began to move. At first no sound came out, but I bent near and strained to hear, and at last he became audible.

"I have control," he said. "I have rebuilt; replaced the damaged tissue. But my body's reserves are gone; used up. They now must be replaced. Help me."

He referred, of course, to his emaciated condition. Somehow he had moved tissue into the wounded parts, perhaps at great peril to his system as a whole, and it was this he wanted to protect now. But what was it he wanted me to do?

"How, Casey? Tell me how."

"I need protein; lots of it. I must eat meat."

I started to rise. "I'll get it for you, Casey."

But he held tightly to my hand. "No," he said, "Not from the supplies. Those are for you. You need them."

"Where, then?"

"From the stream. There is food in the stream."

"The fish? But you said they were poisonous." I knelt again, still holding his hand.

"To you; not to me. I can metabolize them; make the poisons harmless. You cannot. Listen to me; you have seen that I am different. Now, do as I ask."

Weak though his voice was, its tone was commanding, and I went down to the stream, to trap the fish creatures imprisoned in the pond. Some spare clothing and a length of springy root became a net, with which I hurled the helpless creatures up on shore until I had all of them the pool contained. Then, with my hands, I dug a passage through the soft mud and sand, so more could enter from the stream.

They smelled terrible, cooking on the spit. I did not know how to clean them. Casey seemed not to mind but ate every bit I fed him. Throughout the day he ate all I could catch, interrupting his disgusting repast with catnaps in between.

By nightfall he had gained strength to the point where he could sit up. "Tomorrow," he said, "I shall hunt."

I had not troubled him with questions throughout the long day. In truth, I lacked sufficient insight to ask anything meaningful. I knew only that he was a most extraordinary man, if that was in fact his nature; that the experience I was having was unique to human memory. When the sun set, I fell asleep, still wondering whether this was real or a dream.

I rose late, with the sun high outside the tent and Casey gone.

I found him outside, transformed. Still thin, still gaunt, but looking fit and now whole, he stood there, moccasins of deerskin on his feet, a deerskin loincloth spanning lithe hips. His hair, now too short to braid, was bound with a strip of cloth. These had come, no doubt, from the depths of the battered duffle bag, along with the curious necklace that now hung across his chest.

He saw me look at that.

"Serpents' teeth," he said, "for luck. One of my talismans. We can use some good luck for a change."

"I hope so," I said. "So far, it's all been bad."

Casey was fashioning a javelin of sorts, using a stick and a sharpened tent peg. "Luck," he said, "had nothing to do with our misfortunes. It was sabotage."

I stared at him for long moments, finally finding voice. "But how, and who?"

"As to the instruments, I cannot say for sure. The fire left little trace of them. But I found the fan-bearing housings full of emery, and that is why they failed."

"But who? Who would want us dead?"

"Not us; you. I am nothing to them, whoever they are. You menace someone at the station. Compelled to guess, I would say they fear your mission here is to discover something which will deny them this world."

"What? Certainly I've yet found nothing which would require that, unless . . . ." The thought came to me. "Casey, how long have you been on Campbell?"

"About three years; since the first crews came."

"And you've traveled about?"

"Some, though never this far from the sea."

"Have you seen, or heard rumors of, any advanced life forms here?"

"No, I never have. Why do you ask?"

"Because," I said, still not sure I had not dreamed it, "the other night I thought I saw a fire, out on the escarpment."

"Perhaps you did. Maybe it was a search party, looking for us."

"But they don't know we're lost. We're not overdue yet. And why, if they were men, have they not yet come to us? Perhaps they are not men. This is a big world. And, unlikely though it seems, considering the low order of life the planet seems to support, it is not impossible that intelligence arose here. Making, even using, fire requires intelligence of a relatively high order. Certainly well beyond anything we've yet encountered. And," I added, "the existence of native intelligent life is an eminently good reason to kill me. The planet would belong to them. Solar Minerals would be out on its neck.''

"Show me where you saw the fire, Kim."

I pointed with reasonable certainty toward the escarpment. *Had he used my first name?* "It's there," I said, "where the dark streak is."

"Then we shall go that way. Now, eat, while I prepare packs. I am afraid we must abandon the tent and the less useful equipment, to travel light."

All day we trekked across the scrublands, which lay between the foothills and the escarpment. Our goal was the escarpment's base, and it was deceptively distant. The going was difficult; our passage was hindered by heavy brush and gulleys strewn with rocks. When at last we stopped, to camp by a small stream, Casey would not allow a fire. We ate cold food, and after that Casey went to work, fashioning snares of tent cordage and setting them by the water.

When the sun set we lay in darkness, huddled together under blankets. Though exhausted, I could not sleep, but lay there wondering if, even with his marvelous skill at woodsmanship, we'd ever make it back to the sea. More than that, I believed that now I could summon the nerve to ask the question which had nagged at me since the crash; a question I had been afraid to ask, because I did not know if I could live with the answer if I got one.

So, following my impulse and without further reflection, I blurted it out, and it raced past my lips too fast for anything to stop it. "What are you, Casey?" *There, I'd done it.*

He did not answer at once, but paused, and sighed. "I am Kah-si-omah; He Who Waits, in the tongue of my fathers."

I rose on my left elbow, and faced him. "No," I said. "Not who; *what* are you, Casey? You know what I mean. You owe me a truthful answer."

Again he paused, as if deliberating whether or not to say anything at all. Again came the sign. "This is true, Kim. I do indeed owe you that. But I fear what you ask is unanswerable. I have myself asked the same question too often to remember."

I was becoming angry now, finding courage in my impatience. "Don't try riddles with me, Casey. You aren't, and never were, the dumb Indian you pretend to be, though you play the part to perfection. Admit it: you're more than human; now tell me truthfully: what are you?"

He protested my anger. His answer rang with sadness all the same, and there was a curious cracking in his voice. "In truth, I do not know what I am, or even exactly how I came to be. I can only tell you this; if I am no longer a man, I once was, long ago. I have lived a very long time already. I may never be able to die, however much I may wish to."

A horrible thought struck me. "The fish, Casey! Did you eat them to poison yourself, so you could die?" I pictured myself alone, beside his rotting corpse.

"No, Kim. I ate them for strength, knowing they could not harm me. I desperately wanted to live because you needed me."

I felt ashamed at this and spoke no more, but Casey, having started, was constrained to continue, as though it meant something special to him to explain; to have someone share.

"I have done this before," he said. "Some believed me and some did not. I have shared this tale of grief with other friends, only to watch them age and wither away; to leave me in death, all alone, separated from all others by the cruelest of all barriers: time. I am trapped in an eternal present."

His voice took on plaintive tones. There was a great sorrow in it, and a touch of frustration he tried very hard to subdue. "I have tried many lives, and been many things in the time I have already lived. In the beginning I was most assuredly a man, with all a man's infirmities. I grew old as a man, then suddenly I was young again, and have remained so ever since, though I can take the appearance of age or any other feature of man whenever it suits me.

"I was a shaman of the *people*; a medicine man. This I remember, as I remember all that happened before, and all that happened since the vision which changed me. I had gone to the mountaintop to fast, in hopes that the spirits would speak to me. For many days and nights I waited, and they were silent. Then I took the cup; the spirit of the sacred mushroom steeped in water. It is hallucinogenic, which compounds the mystery of my transformation, since I could not tell what was fact and what was fantasy. I have a memory of an awesome flame and terrible burning pain, then of a satisfying inner peace such as no other I have ever known. I believed at the time that I had been with God.

"When the vision began, I was an old man, perhaps sixty, or older. The *people* had no accurate way of reckoning time, but in my calling age was much revered. When I awoke I was much as you see me now, and the *people* did not know me, though I told them I was Kah-sih-omah. My wife and children denied me. To them I was a stranger who had come upon cherished family secrets through magic and overcome Kah-sih-omah. I had his medicine bundle, therefore I was more powerful than he, potent though he was. And in superstitious fear they drove me away with threats of death.

"I did not know then of my immortality. I still feared death.

"I wandered the land as an outcast, perhaps for millennia, certainly for many centuries. I found that within certain relatively broad limits I could control both my form and my features, though radical charges were onerous and required enormous concentration to hold. Minor changes became habitual and required next to no effort; therefore I could adapt to any tribe and live among them, learn their tongue and customs and be as they were, until they noticed I did not grow old. I rarely remained that long in any one place, and so, in time, I had no identity. And as time changes men, so also does it change cultures. Even the *people* lost their identity in the time I had lived.

"When I was young, mammoths roamed the Americas. By the time they passed, I was already intimate with both continents and with those who lived upon them. I conversed with each in his own tongue and believed at the time this was all there was to the world.

"Then I learned of great, fierce strangers who visited the far north. Great hulking Vikings with pale skin and hair on their faces, who used weapons and implements of iron brought from lands beyond the eastern sea. I went north, becoming as they were, and lived among them. But they found the land too harsh and the distance too great. When they sailed away, I went with them.

"It was in Europe where I began to really understand my plight, for the Europeans possessed a true conception of the passage of time. Here too, I made my first acquaintance with the messianic redemptionist religions of the Middle East. It was an era of foment. Islam and Christendom fought each other on the battlefields, each claiming true insight into the destiny of man.

"I had to know my reason to be. For a time I believed the answer lay in the East, and I went there, seeking to find the purpose my existence served, to end the boredom of useless existence. Still none could, or would, tell me. I began to regard what answers they gave as purely parochial. They were seers, such as I had been, whose movements had acquired the trappings of cults and mired themselves in mindless dogma. I knew well the ways of the wizards. I understood their motives and how wily, indolent men sometimes corrupt a noble concept, using knowledge to acquire wealth and power.

"I wanted none of these, so I abandoned them and traveled

on, to India. There, despite more mountains of superstitious nonsense, I remained a century or two and sifted through it, finding much which was good. I found, not an answer, but an aid: a truly realistic concept of the vastness of time, that contemplated both a beginning and an end.

"And then I knew I was not truly immortal; that I would someday end, if not with death of Earth, then with the death of the universe. I knew also that, while life was finite after all, it would yet seem infinite to me, and yet, in that infinity—somewhere, out of sight and understanding, to be revealed to me someday—I had a purpose.

"So I wait, as I have for centuries, for my sign, preparing myself as best I can for what must come. Now I know my destiny approaches, but it is a lonely wait."

Then, Casey spoke no more. I huddled near him, to comfort him. Though I was but an infinitesimal fraction of what he was, he took it, and for a while the loneliness we both felt ebbed, and was for a time forgotten.

With daylight we could risk a fire. I was kindling one when Casey returned from checking snares. He carried one of the nut creatures, and the head of his javelin was stained with its blood.

He plunged the javelin into the ground, where it would be handy, and set about skinning the animal with one of the mess kit's knives. Though he had talked a great deal the night before, he was strangely silent now. He finished the flaying, spitted the carcass over the fire, and took its entrails down to the stream to wash them. At the time I thought perhaps he now regretted baring his soul to me.

He returned, bearing a glazed mass, which he stuffed into a plastic jar and liberally salted. Then he took the spit from me, turning it slowly until the meat turned uniformly brown and began to crackle, dripping melted fat into the fire.

I watched him tear off a small fragment and chew it carefully. Then he swallowed it and said, "You may safely eat this. Your body will make use of little of it, but it will not harm you, and it is filling. We must now use all the land will give us, if we are ever to reach the station."

Strange words, I thought. His voice carried foreboding, but I did not pry. I knew now that Casey revealed himself in his own good time and at his own pace. I ate what he gave me, and it was good.

Then, while I broke camp, Casey scraped and salted the animal's hide. He rolled it up and tied it with a thong. "Come," he said, picking up his pack and javelin. Then he walked off in the direction of the wrecked skimmer.

"Casey! That's the wrong direction." I was mystified.

"I know, but come with me. I must show you something."

I followed him, sensing his disturbance, all the way to the stream, where we came to an area of packed sand.

He stopped and pointed down. "Look," he said, pointing to tracks in the sand. "Something stalks us."

Fear washed over me. "What—who?"

"I do not know. It is not human, but it is not a beast, either. I had four snares. All caught game, but three were raided. Only that closest to our fire was undisturbed."

"Maybe another animal . . ."

"No. Animals bite or break the cord. They do not untie the knots. They kill with teeth or claws, not clubs. The thief had a stone ax. He put in on the ground while he took our game. He stepped on it, leaving its impression on the sand. There are the thongs binding head to haft. Observe this footprint, this foot was not bare. It was covered. When the creature knelt on one knee, it did not mark the ground with toes."

I tried my best to see what he saw, but even with his explanation this was not easy. But then, he had been here before and had had time to think about an explanation, and if he thought the thief had not been human, I wanted to know why.

"There are other tracks, farther along. They are in soft mud and bear impressions well. And the shape and size of the foot is wrong. So is its articulation. There is no arch, and the foot that made the tracks did not bend in the manner of the human foot. The creature's strides are impossibly long, suggesting a giant, yet it is also impossibly light. There are other signs, less visible but equally informative. We are fortunate that there was only one of them."

"So Campbell has sapients. And Solar Minerals knew it. You were right about them wanting me dead."

"It would seem so. But now we face new danger; more enemies. That is why I must now make weapons and why I may again have to kill, loath as I am to do so. But come, we must travel. We can learn nothing more here."

Throughout the day we walked steadily. I found myself taking frequent nervous glances behind, searching the underbrush for signs of the tall creature. Once or twice I thought I saw something, but Casey assured me there was no cause for alarm.

From time to time he stopped and picked rocks from the ground, slipping them into his pack. Once, while I rested, he went off into the brush and cut a stave. Later, as we walked, he whittled on it, and I wondered why. The stave took on form and symmetry, becoming a bow before my eyes.

We camped that night at the base of the escarpment, taking shelter in a shallow cave, from whose entrance Casey labored long to erase our spoor. Again we ate cold food, afraid to risk a fire. "Tomorrow," Casey said, "we shall be armed, and make preparation for the climb."

I lolled around the next day watching Casey's wizardry with the rocks he had collected. Pressing shards against a bit of bone, he fractured and shaped them with consummate skill into dozens of exquisitely formed arrowheads. Then, with enough of these, he ventured out to cut quills, which peeled, split, and notched, and winged with bits of plastic, became the shafts of his arrows. Their heads he bound on with twisted strips of wet gut taken from the animal in the snare. Other strips, tightly twisted, became the bowstring, and sewed the seams of the quiver he made from the salted hide. As the thong dried, it bound tightly whatever it encircled; such was Casey's skill in the wild.

That night I fell asleep in his arms, confident, as the light died, that I was safe with a protector far better armed than any enemy who stalked us.

Later on we met the enemy, there in the dark hollowness of the cavern. I was thrown suddenly aside, awakened by a scream never uttered through a human throat. I crawled away from thrashing feet and grabbed a torch from my pack; then flashed its light around the cave.

Casey struggled with a gangling giant, who reached nearly to the top of the cavern. In one of the creature's hands was a stone ax; in the other, Casey's throat.

Casey held back the ax arm with one hand. With the other he lashed out. His enemy was mighty and determined, and was pushing Casey back toward the wall, though Casey's muscles strained and knotted in resistance. His feet left furrows in the cave's sandy floor as he was forced to give way.

I jumped to my feet, side-stepping them, and they struggled past me. I flashed the light around the cave, fearing other enemies might be about to enter and trying to think of something I could do to help. Casey was no weakling, but he had not yet recovered his full strength.

There in the corner stood the bow and quiver, which I lacked the skill to use. But there also, stuck in the sand, was the javelin. I ran to it and pulled it free just as a strange sound struck my ears. I flashed the light at the wall. Casey's opponent had kicked his feet from under him, and the sound had come from his head hitting the wall.

The light momentarily distracted the creature. It turned to look at me. For the instant I froze in my tracks as that face inspired pure terror in me, but when it turned its attention back on Casey I knew what I had to do; I brought up the javelin and thrust its head deep into the middle of the creature's back.

There was another blood-curdling scream, but it lasted only an instant. Before my eyes and in the torchlight the being literally wilted. A torrent of orange-pink fluid poured from its wound onto the cave floor. It seemed to collapse in sections, like a beach toy deflating. The ax clattered to the ground.

Casey scrambled to his feet. He seized the torch from me and held it on the dying alien, now curiously flattened on the floor of the cave and growing even flatter with each passing moment. My nerve broke. I sank to my knees and broke into tears. Casey moved to console me. I struggled for a time to speak, and found words difficult to come by. When they did come they were in broken gasps. "Casey—uh—what is that thing?"

"It is the being who raided our snares, I would guess. It has been tracking us, presumably with this." He pointed to its long snout. "Such noses are found on all earthly creatures with acute sense of smell. I wish you had not killed it."

I suddenly felt hurt; defensive. "But you were losing, Casey. I had to do something."

"Its anatomy was strange to me. I needed time to find its vulnerabilities, so I retreated to the wall to explore it. Despite its size, it is far weaker than a man. You will perceive it has no bones."

"No bones," I screamed in disbelief.

"It lacks a rigid skeleton on which to anchor muscles, therefore it has great resilience but little strength. That is the reason it died so swiftly once punctured with a deep wound. The fluids expelled were under considerable pressure to hold it rigid, but once released, its form collapsed. Probably it suffocated. I will know in the morning when light permits dissection. That should be facinating."

I was horrified. "Dissection! I can't stand to look at it now. How can you be so morbid?"

He placed his hand on my shoulder and helped me to my feet. "I have been many things in my long past, Kim, including on many occasions a physician. I was at Waterloo, for instance, and at Gettysburg and Iwo Jima. I was there because while I could not confer my own invulnerability, I could ease pain. I learned from those experiences as I will from this. Perhaps I may even learn how to avoid killing any more of these creatures, should we be attacked again.''

"I don't want to meet any more of them." I shuddered at the thought.

Casey's answer was firm and resolute. "Nor do I," he said. "But if we do, I do not intend to take another life. My own may be safe, but that of others is so transitory it is by comparison that much more sacred to me.''

I slept no more that night, but huddled in my blanket waiting for dawn. When it came, I avoided Casey. This was illogical, and I knew it. What he said had been true, and his grisly work was necessary, but I waited outside the cave while he did it.

When finally he joined me he was grim and he seemed puzzled, though not disposed to explain why. I packed, while he buried the creature's body in the woods beneath a pile of stones and marked the spot with the stone ax.

We started out, walking silently along the base of the escarpment, searching for a path to the top. Presently we came upon a promising ravine, through which trickled the waters of a small stream. We climbed its slippery rocks as far as the cataract, which fell near its summit. There we rested, and drank. I bathed my aching feet in the cool waters of the cataract's pool while Casey kept his bow ready and his eyes on the rim.

Finally I could endure silence no longer, and I asked him, point blank: "What disturbs you, Casey? What did you find?"

"I found many things, Kim. All of them strange, most unfathomable. The alien's limbs bore marks on what would be wrists and ankles were it human. I have seen such marks before, on the bodies of slaves. Manacles and leg irons make them. These were fresh.''

I pondered this remark. Casey seemed so sure. "Slavery," I said, "is not new to human culture. It existed on Earth into the last century. I am shocked to find such evidence here on Campbell, where higher life is supposed not to exist at all, but what bothers me more is the possibility that Solar Minerals . . .''

"No." Casey had never interrupted me before. He did now. "Solar Minerals has no slaves. They may know of the creatures' existence; they may have suppressed that knowledge, but nothing more. That I know for sure.

"The alien you killed was not a native form. It did not evolve here. There are no anatomical parallels with Campbell's other life. It is grossly unrelated to them. It is, like us, an alien.''

He paused a moment to let that sink in, then continued. "There is more. That creature, at least, has been here very briefly. I examined its dentation. In the past it has had caries, and these have been repaired with skill few human dentists could match. I found a stainless steel bridge, which implies a very high order of technology, yet the creature was armed with a stone ax *Homo erectus* would have been ashamed to carry. Why?"

I did not know, but the implication sent shivers through me. Suddenly I felt cold and pulled my feet from the water. But the chill was not in the water, it was in my mind. I felt uncomfortable here. "Can we go, casey?"

He was willing, and we started out. At the top of the escarpment we found flat land, thickly forested. The protograsses grew profusely between the clumps of trees, but the bushes were sparse, which made easy travel. The grass was high enough to almost conceal herds of the little grazers, and from time to time we would flush a group of them by stumbling into their hiding places. Toward the end of the day Casey shot two of them: more than we really needed for food, but as he pointed out, I was rapidly tearing my clothing to tatters, struggling through the bush. And while not deerskin, and though it promised to be malodorous for want of adequate curing, it was all we had.

I was reassured, watching this demonstration of his skill with the bow: sure, swift shots that never missed. Less reassuring was the fact that now he kept it always at the ready, while I fell heir to the less complicated javelin, and held it ever tighter.

We stopped well before sundown that night, so that we could have a fire and cook the meat before darkness fell.

Casey picked a thorny thicket and plugged its entrances with branches. "If we have visitors tonight," he said, "they will have to pass slowly through this. I only hope the wood is too green for them to burn us out. The spoor I have seen nearby is old, but it is best to use care."

Spoor, I thought. So there was more alien activity in the area. He knew but hadn't told me. Again I spent an uncomfortable night, awaking to a dawn that promised even more danger.

Again we set out in the direction of the rising sun. Long shadows shrank like the dew as the sun cleared the tree tops and pounded down on us, bringing us yet another enigma.

Casey noticed it first, of course. His impulse was to give it wide berth and hope I missed it. I didn't. "What is it, Casey?"

Caught at deception, he owned up. "A building, I think. I cannot see it all. Parts are hidden by the trees, though it is, undoubtedly, artificial. I am reasonably certain men did not put

it there. That leaves the aliens, whose signs abound.'' Then, as
if to forestall alarm in me, he added, ''Old signs, though. None
have passed this way in recent days.''

It lay across our course, and there no longer being any reason
not to approach it, we did so carefully, stopping about 500 yards
away. At this distance its surface was clearly visible. It gleamed
in off-white brilliance, standing about three times man-height,
with a base of about the same diameter. Concentric stone disks
about a foot thick made up its layers, the largest at the bottom. A
man would have been hard pressed to stand on the tiny disc at
the apex. We could not tell if these were molded or stacked. But
if stacked, the seams were undetectable.

We went nearer and circled it. Casey studied the ground,
found nothing recent enough to bother him, then motioned me to
come closer.

''It's just a stack of stone steps, Casey. Out here in the middle
of nowhere. Why?''

''I cannot even make a conjecture. I can tell you more aliens
exist; perhaps more than one kind. I can detect impressions of
three distinct shapes and sizes of feet. One fits our dead alien,
one is hooflike, and the third is human. All are old and faint.''

''Human! Then Solar does know there is a connection.''

''They know of the structure.'' He bent down and walked
around it, surveying its base, then picked something up. ''Paper
fragments, charred and faded. Very old.'' He stopped again.

This time the retrieved object was larger. He held it to his
nose and sniffed.

''What have you found, Casey?''

''Men have been here. One of them smoked cigars. This is
tobacco leaf. The paper fragments came from the wrapping of
half-pound blocks of nitrostarch, such as we use for blasting.
They have tested the strength of this edifice, or perhaps tried to
obtain a sample of it. The blast discolored it, nothing more, but
the grass and ground yielded though the stone did not.'' He
pointed.

''Newer growth, though still weeks old, perhaps a couple of
months old. They knew long before you came. I think this area
merits further exploration.''

He turned and started off, eyes on the ground, stepping carefully.
I walked behind and waited for him to tell me what I saw. None
of it meant anything to me, but I knew he was following tracks
of some sort. They led out of one grove and into another.
Casey's paced quickened.

Once within it he again bent down; began picking up bones,

dried and bleached, which looked to me to be the same as those from animals we ate. Farther in there was a firepit, edged with stones and littered with more bones.

"The remains of feasts, Kim. Some old, some relatively recent. Some of the parties were large. The last consisted of ten or twelve individuals."

"Men or aliens?" I asked.

"Aliens. I can find no useful tracks among these leaves, but men would leave distinctive signs. And men have mental implements. What ate here had not even flint knives, but only axes, crudely made of stone. Observe the fragments in the fire: seasoned wood was broken, green wood only was cut, because stone blades can handle that. Bones were smashed at the joints, then twisted loose, a somewhat messy, inefficient process compared to cutting.

"And I have noticed something else about this place. I did not climb the structure, therefore I missed it before, but look at this."

He led me to a large, flat, oblong stone set in the ground, obscured by grass. Behind it, in a line leading to the structure, were others. "A marked path, visible from the top of the structure, but barely noticeable from the ground. Note the stones are not dressed, but natural, though carefully selected. The builders of the structure did not lay them; the diners did. Neither work has been here very long."

"How do you know?"

"The bushes tell me. Outside a fifty-or-so-foot circle many large ones grow, but few grow inside and they are small. And the grasses within are thinner. They grow in soil recently disturbed to a considerable depth, and therefore poor in nutrients. But come, let us continue."

I followed him around, while he searched for obscure things I would not have dreamed bore information. The signs led him to another stone. Again it was flat, and very large, sunk deep into the ground and partially covered with leaves. On its face, crudely scratched in the soft limestone, were several lines of symbols, each rubbed with some kind of clay to give it contrast with the rest of the rock.

"Writing," Casey said. "Several different languages, too, I'd say. And far from primitive."

"You can read it?" I asked incredulously.

"Of course not. Even so, there is much it tells me. I am familiar with most human script. Writing begins with pictograms. Stylized symbols follow, then true alphabets. Alphabets are refined.

Their use demands extreme abstraction of thought. Being so fundamental, their symbols are repetitious; economical. Alphabets do not occur in non-technical civilizations. Certainly no human writing system predates the use of metals."

"Which means?" I wondered if he himself really knew.

"The primitive tools are an expedient to the people who carved this stone, used because better ones demand technology they don't have. They cannot even shape flint decently."

"Perhaps they did not come here purposely, Casey, but were shipwrecked. Perhaps the structure is for signalling."

He did not agree. "I think not, but I have no better explanation. However, the writing clearly conveys a message; the intention of the writers is also clear: it is to be seen by someone on top of the structure. The writer intends that the reader first ascend. What intrigues me is why."

"Perhaps the structure is a monument."

"If so, it is poorly placed, hidden in the grove."

For the rest of the morning we explored the area around the structure. Casey found much to indicate heavy past traffic through the woods, but nothing that would tell him why. But from the signs he saw he concluded the beings came and went from some location to the east. There was a fairly well worn path in that direction.

We, too, set off to the east, but kept to a nearby ridge which ran parallel, not wishing chance encounters. The difficult ground and the need for stealth made the traveling slower, so we had gotten only about a quarter of a mile when Casey suddenly stopped.

His reason was not apparent to me. "What is it, Casey?" I asked.

"A strange sensation. I feel peculiar." He looked down at his arm. His sparse hairs were twitching. Then I saw the hair on his head beneath the band move and stand out. I felt my own hair rise like a wreath around my head.

"Some kind of electrostatic field," Casey said. "Let's get off this ridge."

I looked up at the sky. It was cloudless, so it was not an electrical storm that was producing the effect. Nevertheless I followed Casey to lower ground. A noise began: a hiss, then a crackle. It came from behind us, in the direction of the structure. We could see only the top of this. It was glowing.

Soon it was brighter than the sun. The air around it shimmered and the noise rose in both amplitude and pitch. An object, dark by comparison, appeared atop the structure, at first indistinct but rapidly gathering form. It became a great cross; then, as we watched, the image changed, and became a figure with outstretched arms. Abruptly the hissing died down, and the figure dropped its arms to its sides. Then it ran down the tiers and disappeared from sight.

Again the hiss grew; the structure glowed. In the same manner as before a being appeared, then fled the pinnacle. Six more times the episode was repeated. Then the glow died.

I broke our long silence. "Well," I said. "Now we know how they got here. It's some kind of matter transmitter. The next question is why. How can we reconcile this with stone axes?

"We can't, Kim," he answered gravely. "Not without revising our previous speculation. I have the beginning of a hypothesis, but I want to see what happens next before explaining. Let's get up on the ridge where we can watch the trail. Be very quiet."

I followed him to the crest, where we could see in both directions for nearly five hundred yards.

He took note of the direction of the wind and notched an arrow to his bow. "We are downwind," he said, "and thus may not be noticed."

About ten minutes later forms appeared, heading west. There were four of them, all carrying axes. The two in front were the tall boneless kind. Those behind, and having difficulty keeping up, were short, thick, heavily muscled creatures with hoofed feet. They passed without noticing us.

Twenty minutes or so later six of each passed in the opposite direction, but the newcomers had no weapons.

Casey waited until they were well ahead of us, then motioned me to follow him along the ridge. "I think I know now where we are," he said.

"Another riddle, Casey? Where are we?"

"This is Devil's Island; a penal colony, like the one the French used to have in South America. I believe this is where the aliens send criminals, and I think that is what those creatures are. Whoever sends them doesn't know humans have come here. Probably they never visit. There would be no reason for it."

I didn't understand, and said so.

Casey explained his theory. "It fits the facts we have. Consider: these beings possess nothing not obtainable here; not even clothing, if they wear it. This is not compatible with a colonizing or commercial venture, nor with an invasion force, given the means they have of transporting material things of great size.

"Also, note the condition of arrival. The subjects are restrained on crosses. Released, they run and disappear. This may, of course, be necessary to transmission, but I find another possibility more likely; they are restrained because they would otherwise resist. They are freed only when safely trapped here. And they are not slaves as I once supposed, since slaves are useful only when they can be worked.

"But the best support of the convict theory was found on the dead one. He got adequate but cheap dental care; stainless steel instead of gold, porcelain, or silver alloy. It smacks of institutional dentistry; the sort, perhaps, that he'd get from another inmate who had lots of time on his hands and who employed great skill and patience in the job, but who couldn't get his hands on really first-class materials. The convict dentist's talent shows in the humbler medium, just as the skill of early American goldsmiths showed in the pewter they sometimes substituted when gold was too scarce and too dear.

"Then there are the old signs of turmoil I found at the structure. The first arrivals probably battled one another, then gradually saw that this was foolish and began cooperating. Later they probably organized into some loose form of government and made the guide marker and stone plaque. I think the feasts took place at an earlier time, when they stayed near the structure. Then, as their numbers increased, they hunted the area bare, and had to leave. They probably made the plaque then."

"It sounds reasonable, Casey," I said. "But then, so does everything else you say. I am amazed you learn so much from a few simple signs that I don't even notice. Tell me, what have you thought it means for us?"

Casey looked at me and smiled. He was obviously proud of his powers of observation and deduction. "Some look," he said, "others see. If asked to speculate—and I have been—I would conclude, as I have said, the makers do not suspect the presence of men here. Perhaps long ago they sent a ship here to build this station, and possibly others elsewhere on the planet, though I think this unlikely. Perhaps they send only a few convicts here, and it may therefore have been a long time since they built the structure.

"In the interim, humans came, and the convicts have not molested them, though I believe they know of us. Perhaps promiscuous attack is discouraged by our relatively great numbers and their knowledge that we possess better arms and explosives.

"In any event, I have heard no rumors among the men concerning aliens. It may be therefore that, while management knows of the structure, they think it is sessile."

The impact of that settled on me. It meant we would now be hunted by both groups.

But Casey reassured me. "I think the alien you killed was a scout, who did not get back to report. Perhaps he saw the forest fire and surmised a skimmer crash. The fire would have been visible for great distances, particularly from atop the escarpment, and the wreck would have represented a valuable source of metal for making tools and weapons.

"He arrived, perhaps, the day we left the site, but dared not attack us then. Instead he followed us to the cave, assuming we would be taken more easily while asleep. He was, therefore, alone at that time, though others may have followed. That, too, is unlikely, since we had much of value to him, and he took nothing. If he were part of a group he would have selected choice objects for himself. Since he did not, he counted on retrieving them later. Therefore, he was alone."

"That," I said, "is bad enough, even with only half the planetary population against me. I have a real talent for finding trouble, don't I? What am I going to do?"

"The situation would seem to call for skillful diplomacy, Kim. I was about to ask you that question."

"Well, this is obviously going to change Campbell's whole history. I'll have to report the situation as soon as I can, whether Solar Minerals like it or not, and let the U.N. handle it."

"That is plainly the proper course. The method, however, is critical. This is not a situation of indigenous life having a primary claim; it is a question of who has a better discovery claim. Solar will adopt that position if discovered. I would: and I know something of law, having been a lawyer at various times during my existence.

"However, I have been a human being for longer and, I hope, a sensible one. It does not seem sensible to me for you to mention any of this to Solar's local management. Remember, we are 114 light years from Earth. The *Wilmington* is our only contact, and it is under their charter. You have a four-month wait until the ship returns, and fifty-two days in space."

"I don't think I can keep the secret that long, Casey."

"You must. Meyers condoned, if he did not order, one attempt to kill you. When they discover their failure there will be another try, unless in the meantime you prove yourself innocuous."

"Why can't we just hide out in the woods until the ship comes?"

"You would starve. I can exist on native foods; you can't.

You need Earthly nourishment, and what we brought will not last you.''

"So I have to cook up a story, leaving the part about the beasties out of it?''

"It is the only way. You may not succeed in convincing Meyers you are not a danger to him, but it is less likely he will try to harm you at the station with so many others around. And he will have no way of knowing for sure that you have knowledge of the aliens.''

I deliberated.

Casey went on. "You have certainly seen enough to make a judgment and complete your survey; you will not have to go out again.''

That was true enough, I thought. But I said, "What about you, Casey? You're in it, too. And you can't run like I will.''

"Do not worry,'' he told me. "I'm just a dumb Indian, with more luck than brains. They know I'm too slow-witted to be trouble. Besides, you have seen what my body can do. I cannot count the times I have been killed in the past. As long as a single cell lives, so does He Who Waits; though it may take as long as a century to regenerate, my body will rebuild.''

That, I thought to myself, is something else I have to figure out how to handle.

In twenty-seven days we reached the sea. I had gained muscle, but lost weight, and was feeling very fit despite the lack of certain nutrients in my diet. But for the red hair and light eyes, I might have been Casey's tribesman, tanned as I was and sporting a set of leather clothing he'd made from the skins of our food animals. They smelled a little ripe, but wore better than what I'd started out in.

There we rested for a day, playing in the surf and sand of the nearly tideless seashore. I felt a certain sorrow fill me. To leave this life, and make the transformation back to a civilized being, would not be easy after tasting this. True, life in the wilderness was not easy either, but it was strangely fulfilling. It satisfied my psychological need to find out what was really in me. I was satisfied with what I found. I had the stuff of pioneers. In bygone days I might have been one, seeking fate and fortune in the wild American west or in the harsh beauty of Herschel.

In part, that was my reason for joining the Ecological Service; to see how much of that I could take, without risking all. Now, the work seemed tame. The U.N. was a stodgy bureaucracy, an extension of the old U.S.A, which now dominated planetary government on Earth.

The Earth, poor now in resources, horribly overpopulated, was still man-home. And Earth assumed that the space around her was hers to control, particularly as man had met no challengers as yet. Mudron didn't count. It was a fluke, an old system which experts felt was not really a part of local stellar evolution; its inhabitants were backward, and didn't and never would represent any threat to human supremacy.

The beings who'd built that matter transmitter did. That scared me. They were far and away our technological superiors. They might greet our discovery with resentment, perhaps extermination; who knew?

Casey said they could do something worse: ignore us, as they had his people; pen us up on reservations, leaving us to starve and stagnate. And Casey knew what that was all about.

I found myself feeling a little fear of him, too. Not of the man, but the idea behind the man. Before as we traveled, it had seemed natural for me to be with him, but what of the end of the journey? What would happen then?

To Casey, all other men were as children. He, who had already lived throughout ages eternal, would still be alive and vital when I was dust. He treated me as an equal, knowing that I wasn't, any more than all the others. He trusted me with his secret, speaking freely of his past, concealing nothing. Perhaps this was the greatest wisdom of all. I understand, yet the secret was still safe. Who would I tell? Who would believe a story so fantastic? He could deny everything without saying a word. Silence would suffice, and the rest of the world would assume I was deranged.

I hoped he would never do that to me; that somehow I would find a way to join him in his destiny, here among the stars, if only for a little while. A dream taunted me. In it, we were together. I knew that he had done such things before with other partners, now long gone, and come away each time again a lonely man, without a purpose or the solace of a kindred soul to share his misery. Of all the creatures in the universe only he was unique, lacking both siblings and descendants.

"My creator gave me wondrous powers," he told me once, "and many gifts are mine. But that which made me truly a man, he took from me."

It didn't matter. I decided, on that last night on the beach, that the rest of the dream was worth it.

We started south in the morning, this time following a trail of a different sort: the *Wilmington*'s. It was as clear as any path could be, even to me. Until the cradle of the landing web was finished she came down on her spacedrive; a process enormously destructive to the offshore island which served as landing site. The drivefields were tame in space, where matter was scarce, but in an atmosphere their inertial force churned the sky and raised cubic miles of seawater into the air. Each takeoff or landing resembled a small hurricane, but beyond that, as the vessel settled, these forces went to work on soil and crustal rock, fracturing it into powder, which fell to the ground in concentric rings according to its density.

We followed these, taking into account the distance the island lay beyond the great promontory, which itself extended fifty miles to sea. Near its seaward end, on a bay, lay the settlement.

When the net was finished, ships would come down on it, and an array of twenty banks of continuously firing lasers dumping power into the system would lower them slowly into the cradle Solar's crews were building.

One more night was spent out under the stars, there on the sandy lowland. I tried to get back to reality, sifting mental notes of what I had seen so that I could compile a report. I had no written notes or photographs, of course, but I was satisfied I knew what was here; that, except for the aliens, I could have passed this world for colonization. I intended to do so.

"I still do." Suddenly, I found myself burst from reminiscence into reality, and shouting at the boss.

Carmody looked at me critically. He had listened politely while I rambled on. He had not interrupted. He did now, though somehow his manner was softened. "I am here to make that choice, Miss Ryan, though I'll take your recommendation into consideration. Actually, it's become more political than technical now, in view of your discovery of the aliens. Would it surprise you to hear that we'll probably follow it?"

I was surprised, and showed it.

Carmody smiled. "This may be just the break the human race needed: a chance to get a free lunch, to learn from willing teachers. The government'll probably give you a medal, and Casey, too, if they can find him."

"Casey's not likely to be very impressed," I answered. "Now if they made that a necklace of prime serpent's teeth . . . ."

"I want to hear the rest of it, Miss Ryan, including all you can tell me about him. Maybe it'll help us find him."

"Okay. Let's see, where was I? Well, needless to say, there

was quite a ruckus at camp when we turned up. We walked out of the bush looking like Tarzan and Jane; scared the pants off two guys who were goofing off behind a piling at the construction site. We went back to the settlement in their truck, riding in the back because we smelled bad. Meyers himself met us when we got in . . .

"We thought you were dead," he told us, probably wondering where he'd failed. "I sent search parties out when you didn't return. They found a burned skimmer and we just naturally assumed you'd been in it."

I did the talking. Casey went back to being the dumb Indian. "Well, as you can see, we're all right. All I need is a bath and some real food. We've been eating what Casey shot with his bow."

Meyers had been watching Casey with new respect. "Oh, so that's what it's for." He examined one of the arrows. "Certainly looks deadly." He turned to Casey. "I guess you'd better get back to your regular work."

No, you don't. I wasn't about to let myself out of Casey's sight and protection. "Uh—if you don't mind, Mr. Meyers, I'd like to keep him for a while, if you can spare him. I need him to help me with my report."

"Him? What can he do?"

"I want to pick his brains. I lost all my samples and photographs, and I couldn't take notes on the trail, so my report will have to be composed from memory—mine and his. And as you can see, he's a woodsman. He must have noticed thousands of things I didn't."

There was no credible way Meyers could refuse, though I doubt he bought my explanation, so Casey stayed, and we went back to our old quarters together.

"You shouldn't have done that, Kim."

"Why not? I do need the benefit of your observations. And I need your protection. Did you see the way he looked at your bow?"

"I noticed. But a man like Meyers wouldn't be afraid of a savage, and it's difficult to play Dumb Indian when you make me party to scientific studies. I'd be more effective in the field, where I could keep an eye on things."

"Quit worrying, Casey. Human nature will take care of the problem. We can trust Meyers's prurient mind if nothing else. He'll figure I wanted to hang on to my stud. I'll bet that rumor's all over the settlement by now."

Casey didn't say another word about it. In spite of his vast experience, I guess he still didn't understand women. He settled in with me, and went to work on a report.

We still needed some information we didn't have, mostly about marine life on Campbell. This provided an excuse for short local field trips, and gave us a chance to reminisce. We spent many days on Campbell's broad beaches or out in a motorboat.

I loved Campbell's mild climate and its friendly sun. "I think," I told Casey, "that I could stay here forever. I really like this."

"Have you forgotten that night in the cave," he replied, "or what we saw in the interior?"

"No, Casey, but I can dream, can't I? It will end soon enough, when my report hits. Then the government will tell us we can't have Campbell."

He was compassionate, and he let me have it a while longer, but there came a day when the dream, too, died. He came back from a sojourn; they had flooded him with innuendos about "his squaw," but he had learned useful things.

"It has begun, Kim. Great care must be taken now."

Casey always had a penchant to talk in riddles. It irritated me more than anything else he did. I guess it showed. "What has started?" I demanded.

"Men have begun to vanish. They disappear into the bush around the cradle site."

I was appalled. "If the aliens now existed in sufficient numbers, this might be the beginning of an attack."

"None have been seen," Casey said grimly. "Management has an official explanation, so that the workers do not know. They say that with the web near completion, the missing men have simply taken off, to get the jump on the colonists who will come later. But Meyers knows the real reason."

"How do you know that?"

"The machine shop is making weapons. Lathes turn gun barrels; the smith is making pike heads and short swords. There are armed skimmers patrolling the periphery."

"War, with the aliens?" I saw myself trapped here, perhaps, imprisoned or killed, to keep word from getting back to Earth.

"Perhaps. Perhaps not." Casey pondered each phrase. "Meyers may believe he can quietly exterminate the aliens or drive them deep into the bush where they will not be rediscovered. He may bring mercenaries here to hunt them. Certainly he will station marksmen at the transmitter to pick off new arrivals."

"What are we going to do, Casey?"

"For the meantime, nothing. Everything depends on getting

you out, unsuspected, when the *Wilmington* returns. I now believe the government must be told, even if we lose Campbell. This is better than interstellar war, which man would surely lose.''

We waited, and hoped.

I learned later that Meyers and Bigelow had, in fact, tried extermination; had placed a garrison at the alien transmitter. They succeeded for a while in preventing the formation of large concentrations of aliens, but this did not last. Men still disappeared; amusingly enough, some had run off voluntarily, believing Meyers's explanation for the disappearance of others and determined to get in on a good thing.

Not so amusing were the discussions they'd had about Casey and me, which Bigelow admitted to later; to his credit, he balked at murder, but Meyers thought they could blame it on the aliens if they ever got caught.

I was getting packed to leave while this was going on and didn't suspect a thing, not even when landing day arrived. How Meyers talked Corsetti into doing what he did, I'll never know. Casey and I discussed it later and agreed that even a moron should have known it wouldn't work. But some things are just destined to happen, and I guess it was one of them.

We were on the back porch looking at the sky, watching the great bulk of the ship descend. On the first down-orbit pass she was just a gleaming point of light which moved rapidly over the station. The second pass would bring her down, and we waited for her to reappear in the western sky. She did not.

''Something's wrong, Kim,'' Casey told me. He pointed westward.

The air shimmered, and an enormous dust cloud had risen from the ground to race to the top of the atmosphere and flattened out. Then the planet itself started to shake, and there came a series of sonic shocks, followed by a great wind. In the dust cloud appeared blazing halos.

Both of us had seen these things before. It was the awful tumult which accompanies a ship's descent on Aschenbrenner drive, but it belonged on the island, not in the bush to the west.

Casey's eyes blazed. He grabbed my arm and shoved me to the door. ''Get inside, quickly,'' he warned. ''Those fools have turned *Wilmington*'s drive on the alien transmitter.''

I found myself on the rough floor with Casey on top of me, and started to protest his rough treatment. I stopped when I saw the flash, brilliant like a thousand suns. The fireball singed the settlement as it rose, despite the vast distance; then it dimmed. Through the top of the window I could see it rise toward space.

More shock waves followed; more howling wind. The building shook and rattled but it held together.

One, maybe both of them, went; either the ship's engines went critical or the transmitter did. There might be nothing left of either. Casey let me up.

"What now, Casey? What do we do now?"

This time he didn't have an answer.

Outside, men could be heard shouting, screaming; vehicles roared wildly through the streets, racing engines and squealing tires. We knew that there must have been casualties.

A few minutes later Meyers came and brought two men, both armed with crude, but lethal-looking guns. "Your time has come, Miss Busybody," he said to me.

They herded us off to the brig. The cell looked adequate even to hold Casey.

I sat there on the edge of my bunk, crying. Casey paced.

"I have experience with prisons, too," he said. "There is a way out of all of them."

I was pessimistic. Our cell was essentially a steel box, with walls perforated for ventilation. Its seams were welded, and it was barred and locked from outside, with no openings large enough even to pass a hand. It was also guarded by one of Meyers's gunmen, who sat in a chair outside the door.

After a while Casey came over and sat beside me. "Kim," he said. "I want you to stop that; get control of yourself. That is what I am going to do; understand?"

I hiccuped, and nodded my head. I didn't, really.

"Good," he whispered. "I will need three or four hours, and the result may be quite frightening. Do not allow it to upset you."

"Okay," I whispered.

"In the meantime, keep me covered, but try not to distract me. If anyone comes you must warn me. Is that clear?"

"Clear."

"I am just going to rearrange a few things."

Then he left me and climbed into the other bunk, covering himself with a blanket.

A new guard relieved the first one. He came to the door to talk to me, but I told him to let Casey sleep. Soon he, too, settled into the chair by the door.

About sundown, Casey stirred. I watched an arm snake out from under the blanket and rise to grasp its edge. The arm was pink and covered with a light brown fuzz. It rolled the blanket down, revealing a face: one I knew; one I hated. A hand rose to its lips, and Fritz Meyers stood up.

"Rankin." Even the voice was the same. "Get over here."

"Mr. Meyers? How? . . ."

"Never mind; get this door open."

"Yes sir, only . . . what are you doing in there?"

"None of your business, Rankin; the lady and I made a deal. Get the door open."

The lock clicked and the bar slid back. Casey hit the door like a battering ram, driving it into Rankin's face, smashing flesh and bone alike. He crumpled to the floor.

"Come on out, Kim."

I left the cell, still not completely convinced I was looking at Casey.

He shoved Rankin inside, flipping him onto my bunk, and covered him up. Then he reached into his own and withdrew a clump of black substance.

"My own hair," he said. "I can't reconstitute dead tissue. I had to get rid of it and start over. We'll hide this somewhere outside."

"Where are we going?"

"Back to our quarters first, to get our equipment and some food for you. Then into the bush. We'll hide there until contact with Earth is re-established. Meyers has to try to kill us now if we stay, and in your case, death's permanent."

We started out into the compound. It was strangely empty. Then I heard a faint popping, and in the south there was a glow in the sky. It looked like a fire, and I thought I smelled smoke, too. For an instant I was afraid it was our quarters that were burning, but the fire seemed to be farther away. We hurried off in that direction.

Others appeared in the street, scurrying about, some moving equipment in the direction of the fire. Casey called to one of them. The man stopped running and came over.

"What's happening out there, Barker?"

"Mr. Meyers. How—I just talked to you on the phone. How did you get way over here?"

"Never mind. Fill me in."

"Well, okay—you mean the fire? Them things set it, we think. I ain't seen none myself, but they're supposed to be all over. There's gonna be a fight, I think."

"What are we doing about it?"

Barker looked at him as if to say, *Don't you know?* He didn't say that, though. "We got the guys with guns on rooftops, and some in a skimmer. The rest of the men got axes and machetes. We ain't gonna beat fire, though. If they decide to burn us out, we can't stop them."

"You're doing the right thing, Barker. Get back to work."

Barker took off.

"General foreman," Casey explained. "One of the dumber ones. We'd better hurry before the battle really gets started. Barker's right: they can't stop a fire, though I doubt the aliens want to burn up what they themselves hope to get from this raid. Most likely the fire is just a diversion."

We reached our rooms, got what we needed, and left again. I noticed the Meyers form was fading, and commented.

"It takes too much concentration to hold a new pattern, Kim. At least until I really get used to it. On occasion, I've held them for years, the Comte de Rochambeau, for instance. Now there was a role where I had everybody guessing."

I had not seen the mischievous side of Casey before, but this proved he had one.

We made our way out of the settlement, heading west in the direction of the cradle site. Once or twice we stopped and Casey listened for sounds of others moving in the bush, but we encountered neither men nor alien. Casey led us across the lowlands into higher country, and by morning we were high on the spine of the promontory about twenty miles west of the station. He selected a campsite where there was both water and cover, and we rested. That is, I rested. Casey climbed a tree and examined the surrounding countryside with field glasses.

I awoke and ate, while Casey explained our situation. "I see little groups of aliens converging on the station. All are poorly armed. As of now, there are probably not enough of them to overcome the men, but more arrive hourly. Soon they can start a siege, if they can find enough food to maintain one. Still, if the men narrow their perimeter and defend it well they may yet prevail. I think last night's raid was simply a test of human strength."

"Maybe they don't know how many men there are."

"A good point. But neither do the men know the aliens' strength. If the transmitter has ceased to function, their numbers will not grow, but I regard that as a particularly disastrous possibility."

"Why? I should think that would be better for us."

"In the short run, perhaps. But for the race, devastating. If the aliens can detect its malfunction, they may return to investigate and find us. Discovery, I think, is something best postponed as long as possible. In the interim perhaps we will be rescued and obliterate our traces from Campbell.''

"Do you think we'll have to go that far?''

"I cannot see the future, Kim.''

"We could have a long wait, Casey. It'll be almost two months before the *Wilmington* is even overdue. More time will be wasted deciding what to do, and still more will pass before another ship can get here. What happens to us in the meantime?''

"Nothing, I hope. We will survive it and do what we can to find solutions. There was a time when I thought we might simply get you back to Earth and let the government handle things. Now that won't work. We're out of time. But I wish I had a better insight into this.''

I had thought he did, but something apparently still bothered him. I asked him what it was.

"The aliens are inept. That's not typical criminal behavior, at least not for the human criminals I've known. They're not nearly aggressive enough. Even allowing for cultural differences they ought to show more resourcefulness, particularly in weaponry. We ought to be seeing some spears along with the clubs, and some concerted effort to get hold of human materials for weapons. The one thing they do seem to rely on is fire; otherwise, they behave like amateurs.''

We moved again, farther into the interior, to find a place which, as Casey said, "You and I can defend by ourselves for long enough to bring this business to an end.''

He didn't tell me what he meant by that, but he found our redoubt: a cavern halfway up a cliff face overlooking a broad stream. We had brought much food, and the shrubs from the narrow pathway would provide fuel. Inside the cavern was a pool containing more water than we could drink in years. But farther down the valley was a ford, where aliens sometimes crossed, headed for the settlement.

Casey got me settled in, then told me to rest. "Tonight,'' he said, "you will not close your eyes at all, but you will be safe here until I return. Even you, alone, could hold this place against an army with nothing more than a few rocks and a knife.''

When darkness fell he sallied forth, armed only with a staff. I waited in darkness all alone for his return, and all the while fought off the savage creatures my imagination conjured up. Once or twice I felt the bow and wondered, if the need arose, if I could summon the strength to draw it or the skill to find the mark.

With the first light of dawn I heard a noise on the trail below me, and I felt a fright. Casey would move more silently than that. And Casey did. But the lanky prisoner he led, bound tightly and stumbling, had no wish to cooperate.

I stood, watching from the cave's mouth, as Casey dragged it in, and it seemed to me to be in life even uglier and more menacing than the dead one at the other cave, though it was much smaller.

"I chose it for its size," Casey said. "In time, you will understand why. Now I must get to work and learn yet another tongue, so I may speak with it."

And in the days that followed he struggled to master the grunts, the hisses and squeals that made up the alien's speech. I despaired of matching his resolve and left the two alone, preferring to speculate on what was happening to the settlement.

Later, when it was over, I learned that these had been desperate times for Meyers, and had finally driven him to self-destruction. By that time most of the outer buildings had been leveled to provide a clear field of fire for what was left, huddled behind barriers of barbed wire. In two months he had lost four hundred men; not simply killed, but gone, their bodies dragged away by the aliens.

The cairn had not been destroyed, and the *Wilmington* was sacrificed in vain. Aliens still came through, to be cut down by human sharp-shooters mounted in skimmers. Then the aliens ended that; they fired the motor pool. Immobilized, Meyers had sat within his reduced perimeter, along with fifty men who remained, and waited for the end. By that time, Casey had been ready.

Again the secretary broke into my narrative.

"That's the part I understand the least," Carmody said. By this time he seemed far more mellow; almost human. His haughtiness was gone. "Perhaps if we could find Kah-sih-omah . . . ."

"Casey doesn't want to be found, Mr. Carmody. Don't you see—if he doesn't, he won't be. And until he does turn up this is only a story; a myth, both to us and the aliens." *But he was more than that to me*, I thought. And the thought was painful.

"I want to hear the rest of it, Miss Ryan, especially the ending."

"I suppose that's the part that really matters most of all," I replied.

"I wasn't in on much of it. All I really know was pieced together later, from people I talked to. A lot of my information comes from Bigelow, and has to be considered less than reliable. And I'm sure the aliens don't suspect a thing.

"It all started one morning when I woke to find the message, scratched in the sand at the cave mouth. Casey and the alien were gone. By that time, of course, Casey was fluent in the alien speech and . . ."

"What was the message?" Carmody interrupted.

"It didn't make sense, Mr. Carmody. It was only three words. I couldn't really make it out." I lied. "Anyway, Casey was gone, and after that things started happening at the settlement.

"Meyers had succeeded in holding on as long as the aliens simply besieged him, and he was able to fight off their night raids with superior tactics and weapons. The aliens couldn't mount a direct assault.

"Then, suddenly, the aliens brought up trebuchet and used them to reduce the buildings. Meyers shot himself and Bigelow took over. He had guts; I'll give him that, going out to parley with the aliens. You pretty well know the rest."

Carmody did, though he wasn't quite sure how to handle it from there. I wasn't either, and I said so. I found it awkward, but didn't say so.

"I'm leaving you in charge, Miss Ryan, while I go back to report all this. Somehow, I can't see the government abandoning Campbell over this; not with all this knowledge available for exploitation. I think we'll get the landing web finished in record time now. There'll be all kinds of people coming in. In the meantime you'll have to keep things stable here. I hope you get along all right with the native leader."

"Yes," I said. "We understand one another. His English seems to be pretty good."

"Fine. Then I won't worry about a thing." He rose from the chair and motioned for me to follow him down to the dock. "This'll mean a promotion for you, you know. Maybe even to an advance scout team. Would you like that?" He had my written report in his hand, and patted it lovingly.

"Yes, if I could get the right partner; yes, I think I would."

He climbed into the launch and I watched it leave, until at last the image became too small, and disappeared over the horizon.

He hadn't had time to read the report, that I knew. When he did, he would find no reference in it to the extraordinary powers Casey had displayed. So far as that part of the story was concerned, it would remain a myth.

EPILOGUE

The alien entered the room and sat down in the chair beside me, it legs bent awkwardly, arms resting in its lap. I looked no more than necessary at its face, which appealed to me not at all, though I knew what lay behind it. Instead, I looked away and said, "When, Casey. How much longer?"

"Shh. Not so loud." He raised an arm, but I retreated. I would not allow it to touch me.

"There are," he said, "grave disadvantages to my present form, but until the job is done it is necessary. I grow used to it and it has become easier to hold. Tell me, Kim, how did your interview go?"

"Better than expected, I think. Carmody appears to be a very prudent man. He will have my report and read it as he travels back to Earth. He believes the aliens can be exploited."

"So do I, and I believe that they will permit this willingly, in the hope that we can someday aid their fellows."

"For all we know, they may really be criminals."

"No. Not in the sense you mean. And we do know, in general, where they originate: from farther in on the spiral arm. Their home systems are in ferment. They are what they claim to be: political refugees. They are politicians, philosophers, scientists, writers, artists, and the like; anything but criminals, and certainly not soldiers. This is why I had to lead them and teach them to make war. They could not even bring themselves to kill, but simply captured humans and dragged them off, often with heavy casualties to their own.

"And they don't want Campbell; at least, not in the sense we do. Their government simply dumped them here with nothing, to fend for themselves on what they thought was a vacant world. These people embarrassed them.

"To us, they can be partners. We can trade them sustenance for knowledge. The matter transmitter alone is worth that. Spaceships will always be needed for exploration, but commerce needs something better to be really worthwhile. It will make colonization really practical too, and you know what that means."

"We will need many more new worlds."

This time I did not avoid his touch. I knew also what the message meant, that still I pictured scratched in the sand. He Who Waits had found a companion "For A Time."

THE NANNY
by Thomas Wylde

With the world seemingly on the verge of blowing itself up, the idea of seeding human life elsewhere in the galaxy appeals to a lot of scientific minds. But it is never that simple, and this slightly hysterical story of such a seeding may give some idea of what could possibly occur in such an attempt.

I

Eismann woke up eighteen years too early.

He woke up panting, and the lights were on already. There was something wrong with the gravity; there wasn't any.

Surely, he thought, there ought to be *some* gravity.

The lid on his sleepbox was open and he heard two things: a high whistling sound like the air running out, and a faint clicking sound like an alarm bell tired of ringing.

Eismann's mouth was crackling dry, as evil tasting as a mummy's cigar. His headache was increasing, but from somewhere deep inside, where his training was stored, came an urgent warning about the air pressure. . . .

He thought: the world is destroyed, or I wouldn't be here now.

It was an odd thought, and he searched his memory for help.

The last day. There had to be a Last Day. And a last *minute*, when they came for him, when his luck ran out—when everybody's luck ran out—but he couldn't find it.

He looked around. The room was familiar and anonymous—merely a small compartment, softly lighted. A jail cell, probably (he thought). There was a meal slot—not yet used—and another hole (he suddenly remembered) that would take his wastes and send them indirectly back to the meal slot. Tidy, but disgusting. Part of the game. (What game? he wondered.)

132

The alarm bell was still ringing—clicking, anyway—and Eismann figured it was about time to look into the matter.

He rolled painfully out of the sleepbox and floated free. He followed the whistling sound to a hole in the corner, down at deck level. Air was escaping through the hole at supersonic speed, passing out into intersetellar space.

Space. I'm in space. Therefore the world is destroyed. . . .

The leak was small. Apparently something had hit the ship at the bulkhead. He guessed most of the damage was "below" him in the evacuated compartment where the eggs were stored.

The eggs . . . ?

Damn it, he thought. Why the hell didn't they leave him something to remind him what the hell was going on? A simple comic book, anything to jog his sleepy brain cells.

So—he was in interstellar space with the eggs, therefore the world was destroyed.

"And I only am escaped alone to—"

Job's messengers, he thought. But there were *four* of them. There are supposed to be two of *us*.

The other sleepbox was less accessible—the cramped shuttle didn't allow side-by-side arrangements. Eismann ignored for the moment the airleak—God knew how long it had already been leaking—and dove across the compartment for the second sleepbox.

There was the desiccated body of a man inside. The face was gone, but the name on the jumpsuit was familiar. It was Mackay, one of the meditechs at the orbital station—

Eismann suddenly remembered the station, how the ten of them had been in readiness, working the spy cameras and the laser downlinks, evaluating data, waiting suspensively for the Big Blowup.

—Mackay, the man everyone thought was a nark or a NASA spy. He must have been the one who put Eismann in the sleepbox and hooked him up. Then he'd tried to get himself set. And failed.

Things must have been pretty hectic at the end. A mutiny, maybe, or sabotage—anything to get free of the station and on the way. They had been pretty vulnerable up there, drifting along in the center of several laser cannon sights.

Eismann lowered the lid on the sleepbox. So much for his partner. Fine. Nobody liked the guy anyway.

You saved my life, he thought. Excuse me if I don't thank you right away.

He wanted to find out how bad things were first.

Eismann got busy.

He sealed the leak with some plastic gunk from a repair locker. In ten minutes the oxygen was steady at .3 atmospheres. It was too late for his head or his raw throat. He went looking for the medicine dispenser and got some aspirin and something sour to suck on.

The alarm bell continued to click, so he checked the mission status board. It was then he found out he had awakened eighteen years too early.

There was no gravity because the deceleration burn was sixteen years away. He was still in the long coasting part of the trip.

Things were starting to drift back to him.

The mission—his crushing responsibility: in the event the world is destroyed, he and his ship were to leave the solar system on the small but not insignificant chance he could locate a habitable planet where the specially created and fertilized eggs could be brought into adulthood. A new race of Man, preserved and safe to start again.

It was Eismann's duty to raise the fortunate members of this new race, to nurture and teach them, to protect and parent them—he was their Nanny. And he didn't even *like* children.

Now he was awake eighteen years too early, eighteen years before the first planet checkouts. Unless he could get his sleepbox working again, he'd have to hang around those eighteen years, losing his vitality all the while, waiting for the ship to reach the star system and analyze the first stinking, long-shot planet. And *if* it were habitable, he'd pop the eggs—twenty at a time—into the mechanical wombs.

A new generation every nine months—and there were twenty generations of eggs aboard. Enough colonists to go up against whatever a hostile planet could hit them with, enough warm bodies to survive the inevitable setbacks. Enough, maybe, to reestablish Man in the galaxy.

It wasn't going to be that easy.

Eismann found out why he was awake eighteen years early: whatever collided with the ship had damaged the liquid gas tanks. He came awake because his sleepbox had run low of coolant and triggered emergency revival procedures. There was no going back.

The same system supplied coolant for zygote storage.

Twenty generations of the last hope of Man were going to rot in the next compartment. The world *was* destroyed now, utterly.

(And I only am escaped alone to tell thee. . . .)

All right, Eismann. Heads up. There has to be *something* you can do.

He wedged himself in front of the computer terminal and began typing.

In ten minutes he'd transferred twenty eggs—ten each male and female—into the twenty wombs. As each zygote was encapsulated and monitored, he learned if it was alive or dead.

He had to go through a hundred eggs to find his twenty.

But they were the best twenty on the DNA lists, the most able-to-survive of an already impressively talented collection of genetically manipulated zygotes.

The cream of the crop, he thought.

(The proud Nanny . . .)

My twenty babies—you've got the Iceman on your side. We'll make it yet.

When he began asking some tougher questions, the computer kicked out an alarming message apparently left for him:

How do you like that, Eismann? You bastard sinner! How many more bombs are there? You're so smart—you know what Man needs to survive—you figure it out!

So it hadn't been a collision after all. A bomb.

There had been fanatical opposition to the so-called Egg Trip. (Who says Man may survive God's wrath?)

On the other hand, there were those who just hated Eismann—the Iceman—as they watched him move up the Last Man Alive List. Maybe they thought he moved up too fast, especially after Kathy's death.

Eismann shook his head slightly, more like a shiver. It had been an accident, but half of them thought he'd done it on purpose. In any case, the result of that midnight car crash was obvious: when Kathy died his stock rose. Now he was free, unattached (and unscratched)—a bona fide One Way Man. Kathy had been on that list too. . . .

Eismann cleared the message on the computer screen. There would be plenty of time to hash over the Good Ol' Days.

Back to work, sinner.

The ship's course had been thrown off by the explosion, but corrective burns had already been made. They were back on course, coasting at .2 speed of light.

Food was plentiful—some five years' worth for 135 persons of varying ages and requirements, enough surely to maintain 22 souls for eighteen extra shipboard years. No problem, except . . . except the food was all dehydrated. Of course.

Any planet capable of supporting humans *had* to have *some* water. That was basic. And the children were not to be born until such a planet was already underfoot.

He checked the life-support systems, checked the crucial water supply. . . .

It was this way: the water recycled through the food/waste systems, and though the original plan called for Eismann to be up and about for only a few months prior to a landing, there was enough reserve water to make his stay quite comfortable.

But twenty children? Ultimately twenty-two adults?

No way.

Too damned much protoplasm, that's all.

Eismann looked at the computer screen readout, pondering the twenty numbers arranged in two neat columns.

"Some of you guys," he said—the Iceman Cometh—"have got to go. Sorry."

Which ones? Easy: let the computer decide. The big question: *how many*?

Eismann asked.

Eighteen.

Well, hell . . . there was no point in arguing. He had to jettison eighteen eggs. He said, "Adam and Eve time."

Then he thought: Why one each? Why not two females?

He could nearly double the chances of Man's survival if he grew himself a couple wives.

He asked the computer to list the two best females. Hmmmm. No hurry, really.

Three-hundred-eighty eggs were dead or dying in the ruptured storage compartment. Nothing he could do about that. It's true he had a water shortage, but that problem wouldn't become acute for years, really.

Oh, God . . .

He had a vision: twenty nervous little girls, all lined up, a shadow passing overhead—the Iceman, brother—touching eighteen blonde heads, one by one, yanking them out of line and over to the waste disposal maw, which was so small he'd be forced to butcher . . .

No! The decision had to be made *now*, while the eggs were still microscopic abstractions. He took a deep breath and let it out slowly.

Two females, then. Or one of each . . .

Then it occurred to him that by the time he'd have to report for stud duty he'd be over sixty.

What if I'm not fertile?

Fertile . . . infertile . . . that thought set off an old memory. Something they said during the long, boring pre-mission discussions . . . those cold men (the real Icemen) . . . a solution to an old cultural problem . . . uncles and nieces . . . the question of ostensible incest . . .

They had supposed he'd be among the young population in better, younger shape, his aging severely retarded by the sleepbox.

They wanted a clean start with this population—his filthy, contaminating genes were not allowed. He was, after all, just the bus driver.

So they sterilized him, even *before* Kathy's death.

God, he really moved up the list *that time*. The staff admired (and hated) him for his decision. Boy, they said, you really *do* wanna be the Last Man, don't you? He just smiled coldly—the Iceman—then they hated (and envied) him all the more. At that cynical time nobody considered the possibility Eismann really *cared* about the future of Man. Oh, well . . . ancient history.

Okay, back to square one: Adam and Eve. It was a story he could tell Adam when he was old enough to appreciate it.

On second thought, better not. By that time the dude might be willing—and certainly able—to deck his old Nanny. . . .

Eismann selected the two eggs, designated one of the pair of emergency water tanks for their use, then prepared to empty the remaining wombs. He hesitated again.

He knew (*damn it!*) that success of his mission demanded he wait as long as possible. Any birth defect could be disastrous. One sudden infant death (if there were only two in the running) would mean defeat; utter, hopeless defeat.

He *had* to let *twenty* fetuses come to term. He *had* to wait at least until their first birthday before selecting the fortunate two. One-year-old babies would not be conscious of his intent. They would not suffer. . . .

He *knew* what must be done.

This was why they'd chosen him (the Iceman). Hard decisions had to be made. Hadn't he demonstrated he was up to it? (That accident with Kathy worked—horribly—to his advantage. He knew it—and it made him wonder.) They needed a hard-core *survivor* to run this mission, and that's what they got. Congratulations, suckers. . . .

Yeah, he knew what had to be done. But he could not face the horror of that delayed selection. It was simply too gruesome.

Eismann the Iceman. *My ass* . . .

He reached out and dumped the eighteen eggs.

Now there are just the three of us.

Three of us, plus two each one-hundred-liter water tanks. He called up a water-inventory display. There was only one code on the screen. He fiddled with the computer, asking after the second water tank.

It took several minutes to find out—then more minutes to check and confirm—that the second tank was empty. Apparently he'd dumped it with the eighteen zygotes.

Babies and bathwater . . .

He stared at the computer screen. No question about it: there was now only enough water for two full-grown adults, plus a little extra for emergencies. Case closed.

It was clear that before the eighteen years were up there would only be two humans aboard the ship.

Eismann wouldn't be one of them.

Did I do that? he wondered. Or was that another of the "bombs" they promised? Does it matter now?

He and the computer got together on a little calculation. Assuming the two kids grew at the optimum rate, there'd come a time when the three of them would have to say their goodbyes. Say seven or eight years after birth . . .

Eismann sighed and went on with his chores. He had to do something about Mackay's mummified body, so he bagged it in plastic and shoved it into the trash compactor.

His finger hesitated above the RUN switch.

"Well, Mackay, you did your job. And you almost made it yourself. Maybe I'd have got to like you after a few years. And maybe not. As for thanking you—well, let's just say I'm still thinking about it." Then he pushed the button and drifted away.

"See you in nine years. More or less."

Eismann slipped into the webbing of the inoperative sleepbox, his day's work done. He investigated his personal locker (which some NASA joker had named *Eisbox*) and found a desiccated cigar. Felicitations & Bon Voyage, sucker. He unwrapped the cigar, broke it in two, and began to chew on one stale end. He knew he couldn't light it, but this was better than nothing.

After a minute he realized he felt pretty good. The Big Trip was underway—and under control. The Earth was—well, screw the Earth. *He* was the Earth now. Man still had a chance. NASA would have been proud . . . not that he cared. He was the Iceman, right? He didn't need anybody to *approve* his actions, right? Isn't that right (damn it)?

Settle down, Eismann. You done good. Now shut up.

He stretched out and thought a long time about the kind of

tapes he'd leave behind for the benefit of Mankind. Instructions on how to start up a new human colony . . .

If only he *knew* how.

II

Eismann had plenty of time to reacquaint himself with the particulars of the mission.

He was on his way to Alpha Centauri.

There had been a lot of discussion during the planning stages of the mission, a lot of rather bitter argument. The mission was obviously a one-shot deal—all or nothing.

From the start, though, Alpha Centauri was the logical choice. Not only was it the closest—and hence the shortest trip—but the star system contained one extremely close copy of Sol, plus a lesser star of some possibilities. The chances of finding an Earth-type planet in this area was estimated as high as ten percent. Virtually the best bet going.

Man's lifeboat was a hastily thrown together patch-up job, a reworked third-generation space shuttle. For years they'd been siphoning off anti-matter from the busy weapons labs, putting together enough for the deceleration burn. Then they used every resource—huge chemical rocket drop-off boosters, matter/anti-matter reactors, and a close-solar whip orbit—to get the shuttle on its way.

They'd set him going at .2 cee. The deceleration burn would be a slow, matter/anti-matter burn at about one-tenth gee. Two years of deceleration. Total trip time: twenty-two years.

With luck.

Eismann spent a few hours exploring what parts of the shuttle he could get into.

Most of the cavernous payload bay was filled with electromagnetic matter/anti-matter fuel tanks. The rest was food—with automatic retrieval—then seed, nitrogen-fixing soil bacteria, fertilizer, and too little water. This whole area was sealed off.

The cockpit was crammed with extra life-support equipment and the planetary analysis experiments, but there was still enough room to pull himself into the one pilot seat left. He looked out the window.

The shuttle still faced forward—to be turned around before the deceleration burn—and Alpha Centauri was a visual binary dead ahead. At .2 cee the spectrum of the orange B star was shifted to blue, the yellow A star to blue-violet. Visually the change was not nearly so dramatic, since normally invisible infro-red light blue-shifted into the visual to make up for the lost reds and oranges. The stars seemed tinged with blue-green, but he gave up trying to make sure when his eyes began to water.

Though planetary entry would be automatic, the actual landing of the shuttle was too problematical for total computer control. There'd be oceans—not much reason to land if there weren't— and he'd try to put the ship down in a shallow, protected bay.

It was going to be tricky. Space shuttles, because of their ambivalent natures, always seemed to land too damn fast. He touched the controls and picked up a static charge of stage fright, as though the landing were coming up in *minutes* instead of—

He laughed suddenly, spraying out soggy flakes of his chewed-up cigar.

The landing was eighteen years off; plenty of time to—

He stopped laughing.

Well, it was not *his* problem, the landing . . . but how would *they* handle it, his kids? How the hell could they spend the last ten years of the trip without him—and then know how to make the landing?

He had spent years learning to pilot the beast, and there was no guarantee *he'd* remember enough, despite programmed rehearsals.

What the hell chance would *they* have?

He began to wonder if he was even *supposed* to succeed. Had they picked him in order to *make sure* the mission failed? He'd been the Iceman all his life—forced into the role by the accident of his name. Was that a clue? Had they seen some flaw, smoothed over by his unconscious role-playing, that they *expected* to break him apart?

He'd already *failed* to meet the egg-selection problem head on. Now here he was thinking up excuses to stay alive (the essential pilot)—at the expense of the entire mission.

Was he acting out his fatal weakness, just as someone high up in mission planning suspected he would?

The note had threatened him with more bombs. Maybe they meant *him*.

The ultimate doomsday device—all he had to do was reach out and caress the control board, flicking a few inappropriate switches, and the mission would be over. Mankind would be dead. All very sanitary.

It would save a *lot* of trouble.

Eismann suddenly reached out and snapped on the VHF radio. He'd never even thought to check. What if the Earth was *not* destroyed? What if this was all just a . . . a what? A joke? A prank? A damned expensive prank.

The speaker hissed uniformly as the radio scanned for signals. Nothing.

Let's see, he thought. I've been on my way four years—or so the computer says—at .2 speed of light. Earth is directly behind me (more or less) about eight-tenths of a light-year away. Commlink delay time 19 months and change—that's a strain on snappy conversation.

Tuning in a *specific* channel would require some calculation. The red shift of a 50 MHZ signal coming out of a rapidly receding Earth would be about ten megahertz. If he tried to broadcast—but no, there was no point in that. He was too far away; it was too late.

So, he was alone. Probably. There'd been rumors about another shuttle headed in another direction. And the Soviets might have set something up—if there'd been time. It was all speculation. *He* was alone, at least, And the radio was silent. (He declined to aim his directional antenna at anything but the Solar System. For the moment he didn't want any big surprises.)

Better not to think too hard about any part of this. Not now, not yet. He'd have years to brood about this mission, to decide if he really wanted to go through with it.

Eismann climbed out of the cockpit and drifted back to the sleepbox.

In the two activated wombs the bodies formed, without hope and without despair, cell upon cell, the heirs of Man.

III

Eismann sweated in the elastic bicycle, nearing the end of his second exercise hour.

"How's that?" he said, shaking sweat out of his eyes.

The twins—the mechanical wombs had disgorged them precisely ten minutes apart—clung to the webbing of the sleepbox and watched quietly.

Ten months old, naked—as was Eismann nowadays—and already attentive, already clinging like bald monkeys to the webbing, swaying in zero gee. They seemed amused.

The only time they cried was just *before* fouling themselves. He decided they were afraid of the whining hand vacuum he chased them with, collecting their wastes. He'd *conditioned* a pre-evacuation fear. He wondered what Freud would have made of it. He hoped it wouldn't scar their psyches too badly.

He came out of his exercise corner and floated through the cool air toward them. He jammed the green hunk of soft plastic in his mouth (the lone cigar had long since been chewed to pieces).

He decelerated on the webbing and poked the boy in the gut. "How ya doing, guy?"

He couldn't bring himself to name the children. It was simply too *momentous*. He'd let the kids name themselves when they were old enough to know what names were for.

"You too, girl," he said, fingering her head.

The twins were tiny, very frail.

In zero gee they got no exercise just hanging around. And they were too young to learn any of the special zero gee routines that he performed so religiously.

He stared at them, and they back at him, their eyes large and trusting. They never complained.

He shook his head at them and smiled sadly.

Every day he had an impulse to strangle them.

"What am I getting you into?"

They looked ordinary enough, despite zero gee frailty. Eismann kept expecting to see signs of their genetic superiority. The eggs and sperm cells that produced the frozen zygotes were rumored to be illegally manipulated—super clean, recessive gene weeded, piggy-backed, quadruple stranded DNA—it was never clear exactly what had been done. The idea was to compensate for the colony's severely limited gene pool. The mission planners couldn't have known *how* limited it was going to be. These kids, and their children—there was no telling what might develop.

Anyway, it was not his problem.

He held out his forefinger and the little boy took it, floating away from the webbing.

"You're light as a feather, my friend. You know that?"

The little guy reached back as his "sister" reached out. Now both babies floated free from the sleepbox webbing, hand in hand.

Eismann pulled his finger away, and the twins floated before his face, watching.

He felt the sweat going off his body, going into the air, going ultimately into the water retrieval system and back into the reservoir.

He thought a lot about the water in that reservoir.

Every gram the babies gained came from that reservoir, water permanently removed from the cycle.

"How long before you're on your own, hunh?"

And then what will you do?

The twins refused to exercise.

They'd whine and complain (*now* they complained) and bounce off the ceiling a few times. It was easy to catch them, the room was so small, but he hated to force them into the elastic bike if they were so set against it.

Five years old, and heavy into anarchy. Same old story.

The girl was Kathy, a name she insisted had to come from him. He regretted it now. Maybe she'd change it later.

The boy was Ice. He had insisted on taking Eismann's name, calling himself variously "Eismann II" and "Eismann too."

Eismann urged him to change it, but the kid would have at least part of his name. (*Nobody* wanted his first name: Horace.) Eismann thought calling him *Mann* was too pretentious, so they settled on *Ice*. He hoped that, too, would change with time.

Time . . .

At the rate they were growing—*slowly*—the damned deadline kept moving back.

He brooded about it, but it was not something they discussed, though the kids seemed emotionally and mentally ready to take on any load. It was phenomenal, really, how quickly they developed in that area.

They both spend hours before the computer screen: Q&A.

Eismann spent a lot of time querying the computer himself, trying to find out exactly what had happened on Earth. But there was nothing, no current history readout to augment his vague memories of heightened tension in the world. He so utterly failed to remember the final day—the moment when they actually came for him—that he wondered if perhaps they didn't fiddle with his mind. Maybe there was something built into the sleepbox to blank his memories. Did that make sense?

He had a theory. The events leading up to the Last Day of the Earth—pathetic, outrageous, prideful and greedy as they must have been—were likely to cast doubt on the worthiness of Man to continue as a species in the universe. Maybe they wanted to prevent him from pre-judging Man. They probably cursed the flimsy technology that kept them from eliminating him altogether. They had to trust him completely. Too bad.

Now they counted on him to—

"That's not right," he said, wedged in front of the computer keyboard.

"They" no longer counted on him. "They" were long gone. If "they" existed still on Earth, if there was any bombed-out remnant of human life on that diseased, dying planet, Eismann doubted any of them even knew of this mission—or would care. "They" had their own problems.

No, the only people who counted on him now were the twins. They required his help, *demanded* it. And for now, they got it.

The artificial "day/night" cycles continued to pile up as the years drifted past. They settled into an unending series of routines: the bedtime routine, when Eismann tried to remember stories to tell them, invariably choosing something too childish or too adult for them—the twins were alternately bored or baffled; the "work" routine, when he tried to get them to help with the housekeeping of the shuttle, vacuuming and filter cleaning and checking the status of life support systems. The computer kept up a steady drizzle of preventative maintenance jobs for them, but the twins only worked hard on things they'd never done before, like calibrating the instruments that analyzed the waste/food cycle for impurities. And finally, there was the "play" routine, when Eismann tried to sneak in some organized exercise for the twins—a plan they saw through from the earliest attempts, escaping with zestful ease and generally causing more work for Eismann than it was all worth.

And what, exactly, was it all worth? He didn't know. The "importance" of the mission waxed and waned on its own routine schedule, as if tied to some remnant of tidal force in Eismann's mind. Some days the responsibility squashed him flat, on others it exhilarated him. Most of the time it meant nothing at all; the "mission" floated high above his consciousness, like a wispy cloud in a clear blue sky—it could safely be ignored because there would be plenty of time to think about it later. He was surprised, every now and then, to remember he hadn't yet come to a conclusion: was human life worth preserving?

There were adventures to mark the passage of time. When the twins were six or so, Eismann woke up with a toothache. After weeks of enduring the throbbing pain he decided he'd have to pull the tooth. He searched through the shuttle tool kit and found a pair of pliers, but they looked awfully unwieldy. Consulting the computer he located an excellent set of dentist's tools—complete with crash-course cheat sheet instruction manual—but the storage code indicated the pack was stashed deep within the cargo hold and not available to him. It would be the pliers or nothing.

The twins floated nearby, amused and interested in this novel activity. "Whatcha going to do, Eismann?"

"This is serious medical business," he said.

"We know."

Ice nudged Kathy and reached for a bulkhead gripbar, grinning. Anything to break up the routine, even "serious medical business."

Eismann wedged himself into the vanity before the stainless steel mirror. He probed awkwardly with the pliers. Somewhere somebody was giggling.

There was no trouble finding the right tooth—he had only to tap it gently to send a ghost-nail through his lower jaw—but figuring out how best to grip the thing was a problem. The pliers weren't shaped right for a smooth yank outward. He'd have to pull the tooth upward.

Kathy clung to his forearm, her mood locked into his, now dark and gloomy. He positioned the pliers over the tooth and gently squeezed. He pinched his gum and involuntarily jerked his arm, his eyes blinking tears. Kathy hung onto his elbow. "Push off!" he told her, but it must not have sounded right with a pair of pliers in his mouth. She held on, looking concerned. A moment later the pliers' grip was right and he yanked hard.

The tooth broke in two and the pliers slipped, smacking his upper molars at the gumline. He yelled and jerked his hand away, accidentally biting his knuckles. The pliers swung out and smacked Kathy on the arm, sending her flying across the compartment where she smashed into the cockpit ladder.

Eismann roared in pain and regret and pushed off after her, trailing small globules of bright red blood. Kathy had bounced by then, and Ice—who had stayed clear throughout—pushed off in a trajectory to intercept. Eismann got to her first. Her eyes were wide with fright and pain, and he cursed himself as he assessed her injuries: a broken left ulna where his pliers had struck, and a broken right femur where she'd hit the ladder. He felt small hands tighten painfully about his throat. "Leave her alone!" screamed Ice.

"Leave *me* alone, goddamn it!" he yelled back, sending a necklace of darkening blood over his shoulder. He finally had to put Ice in the Place, an area in the center of the compartment, out of reach of bulkhead or handhold. Ice would be stranded there until Eismann came for him.

Eismann consulted the computer Medifax file, then gave Kathy a half-ampule of Demeraid before setting the fractures. She cried slowly as he worked, mumbling her apologies for getting in his way. Ice struggled and twisted in the Place, screaming to be set free. Eismann ignored him. Ice was naked, of course, so he had nothing to throw, nothing to use as reaction mass. He was stuck good and he knew it, and his frustration was a torment to them all. He made sure of that.

After he'd put Kathy to bed—and after assuring her he didn't blame her for any of this—Eismann went to talk to Ice. "It was an accident, damn it," he said, slurring his words a little as he worked his tongue around an aching mouth. The bleeding had stopped, but the pain was more real than the steel in the shuttle's superstructure. And he had yet to face the other half of that broken tooth, still anchored in his throbbing jaw.

Ice stared at him sullenly. "Let me go."

Eismann took a breath. "*She* forgives me."

"She can if she wants."

"My tooth hurts."

"That's too bad."

Eismann stayed by the wall, out of reach. Ice floated motionless in the Place, hands on his hips.

God, he's pissed, thought Eismann. And not afraid to show it. Not like me.

"You want to protect her," Eismann said.

"Of course."

"She's not your *sister*, you know."

"Yes she is!"

Eismann looked away. It was too early to go into *that*. He said, "It doesn't matter. You should protect her. But not against *me*. You have to know I'll never want to hurt her. Never."

And he thought: but I haven't decided yet, have I? I may even *kill* her, kill *both* of them. Isn't that right? Isn't that still a possibility?

His hand whipped out and grabbed Ice by the ankle. He spun him around and aimed him at the sleepbox where Kathy floated, her frail limbs splinted and gunked in fast-setting plastic. He pushed him—gently. "Go to bed, Ice. And don't worry. But don't forget, either. Something's bound to happen someday. I want you to be ready."

Then he squirmed into the cockpit to brood. Every few seconds, in a motion he seemed powerless to control, his tongue dragged across the jagged fragment of his broken tooth and probed its soft, ultra-sensitive center. And every time he did this his head shivered with a pain of almost stunning intensity. And each time he felt that exquisite pain he vowed never to do it again. But he couldn't stop himself, no matter how hard he tried, no matter how bad the pain got. Amazing, he thought.

Absolutely amazing.

About a year later they had a little party. The computer had said: ten years to go.

"Ten years till *what?*" asked Ice, teasing.

The twins were seven-and-a-half—a pair of loud-mouthed *runts*. That day Eismann told them about the journey to Alpha Centauri. But they'd known all along (computer Q&A).

They knew about *everything*.

Ice said, "Got the latest update, Eis*mann*. At our present rate of growth, the water reserve will become critical in five-and-a-half to six years."

"I can hardly wait."

Kathy wouldn't talk about it, but neither would she cry.

Ice said, "Me and Kathy are supposed to keep Mankind alive."

"It's a big responsibility."

Ice laughed, echoing Eismann's short, ironic chirp. "Maybe not."

"What do you mean "

Ice toyed with one of the spherical "cupcakes" Eismann had struggled to bake for the celebration. The sugar-coated globe wobbled as it spun, a bite out of one side. "The thing is," said Ice, "nobody asked *us*. What if we don't want to?"

Eismann shrugged. This was not the time to argue about it. So the kid had doubts.

Welcome to the club.

They spent a lot of time, singly and in groups, watching TV and movies on the monitor. Nearly a quarter of the inventory was available to them, the rest in "deep storage" (a phrase that continued to infuriate Eismann every time it appeared on the computer screen).

The twins liked the old movies best—westerns like *Red River* and *The Wild Bunch,* war flicks like *Casablanca* and *A Guy Named Joe,* comedies like *The Philadelphia Story* and *The Awful Truth.* These were Eismann's favorites, the ones he always used to watch on the late show on TV back in the World. The twins took to them automatically.

They had little interest in the more modern stuff, the porno snuff comedies of the '90s, or the early made-in-space spectaculars from the turn of the century.

Their TV selections were likewise vintage: "Leave It To Beaver," "The Mary Tyler Moore Show," and "Spuds Pozo!"—

all shows that were already in reruns when Eismann was a kid. The newer stuff just didn't captivate them.

Maybe the twins were getting a biased notion of what the world had been like; maybe they were learning it was a better place than it had been. So what? They'd need all the optimism they could get when they set out to build a new world.

If, thought Eismann, this little experiment lasts that long.

He understood now that the sleepbox had been designed to do more than preserve his vitality and conserve the consumables. According to the flight plan he'd have come awake with very little time left and a hell of a lot to do. He was supposed to be far too busy to think. Too busy to *doubt*.

But the landing was still eight years off.

One "game" they played was called Shuttle Landing. They took turns going through the computer simulations, responding to mock emergencies, scoping out hypothetical landing sites, gaining points toward a goal of "Safe Landing."

Kathy was the best "pilot"—a fearless barnstormer. It even began to look as if the twins *could* handle the landing by themselves.

Of course the transition to "real" time was a killer, but Eismann knew that there was precedent. Ninety years earlier, when aircraft were single-seaters, would-be pilots packed what advice they could carry and went up to solo on the first try. If they crashed, they flunked.

If Kathy crashed the shuttle . . . Man flunked out forever.

Still, it was the only chance. . . .

When he was ten-and-a-half, Ice came to him and said: "You screwed up, Eis*mann*."

"That right?"

"Kathy and me should never have been born."

"Don't be pessimistic," said Eismann dryly. But how could they *not* be, living with him. "All the eggs were spoiling. I had to do something."

"You could have opened the egg storage compartment to vacuum and kept it in the shade. They'd have kept frozen, you know."

Eismann just stared at him.

"You could've kept *all* the eggs frozen until we got to Alpha Centauri. That way we wouldn't have the water problem, you know?"

Eismann knew, and his face grew hot with realization of what he'd done. He'd doomed them all—almost certainly—by setting up this train of events. Sure, there'd been a bombing—that wasn't his fault. But his first reaction at that moment of crisis was wrong. He'd had other options. Christ, it might even have been possible to reactivate his sleepbox.

There was no point in trying now. It was too late, and he had the twins to look after. His children. His doomed children. Some goddamn Nanny he'd turned out to be.

He didn't have to say a thing. He could tell by the amused expression on Ice's young face that he'd been caught. One more thing to think about in the horrible years to come.

Ice floated away. He never mentioned it again.

On their fourteenth birthday the twins came to him with a plan.

Eismann was edgy. He exercised one hour three times a day, checked the water level *four*. Soon, soon . . .

There'd been no more of the promised "bombs" in the system. Maybe the threat was an exercise in psychological warfare.

He stayed alert. The next critical phase was coming . . .

"Listen to this," Ice said. "In fifteen months or so we'll begin our deceleration burn, right?"

"I told you not to use that word," Eismann said. "There is no moon; there are no *months!*"

Ice looked at Kathy and smiled. "If I say one and a quarter *years* he'll just say—"

"Get on with it!" Eismann said. He was nervous.

Ice explained slowly. They—the twins—were afraid of the coming deceleration. Afraid of the one-tenth gee bogey man that had been coming to get them all of their lives. Nothing they had read or dreamed about gravity, real or artificial, had made them eager to experience its unrelenting grip. They wanted no part of it.

"You can handle it."

"We can *learn* to," said Ice, "if we must. But we'll never make it on a planet, Eis*mann*. Never."

But they had a plan.

And the Iceman wept when he heard it.

"You have to promise," said Ice, staring hard at him, staring right through him to where the heart of doubt and fear stirred miserably.

Kathy nodded. "You have to."

Eismann felt himself dwindling beneath the force of their

commitment and the somber weight of their sacrifice. There was no way out. He whispered, "I promise."

IV

It was close, but they made it. And Eismann got to keep both his legs. Ice was right; he'd need them.

The shuttle was already within the orbit of Alpha Centauri B and closing in on the A star, the heavier of the two. B had passed apastron before the mission was launched, and now was still poking along the slow side of its eighty-year orbit.

(The C star, also called Proxima Centauri, was way the hell off somewhere, and in any case was not under consideration as a suitable star.)

Alpha Centauri A got picked mainly because it was currently closer. It was also pure yellow again, now that the ship had lost nearly all of its wavelength-shifting speed.

Eismann turned forward in the observation bubble and looked back along the way he'd come.

Sol was the brightest star in Cassiopeia.

Eismann dropped down into the main room. He was well used to the one-tenth gee thrust (used even to living on the back wall), and he was anxious to get even heavier. His muscle tone was good (he'd worked long enough getting it), and his bone calcium was fair.

He was sixty-two—a skinny, bald old man. He felt great.

His brood looked up as he hit the wall (floor).

A dozen babies, ranging in age from one month to one year.

All the children of Ice and Kathy—and twenty more in the wombs.

All parentless now, except for their aging Nanny.

Ice's plan was simple and inevitable.

The twins would never live to walk the new planet—should one be discovered—but their children could. Their children, most of them, would be born in the planet's gravitational field. A dozen more would be brought there at a very early age—and out of an already one-tenth gee inertia field. Most would adapt easily.

And Eismann must be ready to land and attempt the adaptation to full gravity. It was—after all—his job, his mission.

Ice and Kathy matured and supplied the fertilized eggs for the twenty wombs. (Eismann never discussed sex with either of the twins, but he agreed—gratefully—to Kathy's request for a private corner. Ice took full charge of the tricky egg gathering phase, acting quite dispassionately. The Iceman saw his unconscious tutoring at work here—and it scared him . . . but in other areas the twins proved remarkably warm and generous. Eismann hoped he'd contributed some part of this, too.)

The twins were of slight build, Kathy too frail even to bear her own children. It was probably a miracle she matured sexually at all. But then, she *had* to.

They both suffered quietly in the one-tenth gee deceleration field. Kathy, especially—her broken femur had not set properly. When Eismann watched her limping and saw the unconscious grimace of pain that tightened her pretty face, he wanted to cry.

Have I done *any*thing right? he asked himself. Anything at all?

"Here comes old Gimpy," she'd say, bouncing off the floor. She'd laugh and Eismann would think of Kathy, his Kathy. They looked the same in his mind now, indistinguishable, equally loved, equally mourned.

I'm haunted by a trillion trillion ghosts, he thought. The ghost of every creature that leapt, swam, or crawled on a dead planet once called, briefly, Earth.

There are a million ghosts in orbit around every cell of my body. I am aswarm with the dead.

On some days he felt very . . . *thick*.

Before the end, as the water level sank below the minimum, sacrifices had to be made. It was agreed both that Eismann should remain whole and that the fetuses be given priority in the fight for protoplasm. The twins gave up their almost useless legs.

Then, the final egg implanted, they gave up everything else. They went together.

Eismann was three AUs from Alpha Centauri A when he spotted the planet.

Automatic equipment monitored A and B and predicted planets by orbital perturbations. Eismann looked where the computer told him and there it was—1.04 AUs from the A star, moving in a rather complicated series of precessing ellipses. Eccentricity of the orbits varied, but even the worst-case prediction from the computer was acceptable.

Besides: green forests and blue oceans under cloudy but transparent skies. And oxygen . . . yes, it would do.

The ten-to-one longshot had paid off.

*   *   *

Eismann made a slight course change—the third in as many days—then held his breath and shut down the main drive. He spent several nervous hours manipulating the remaining plasma of anti-matter fuel (using the remotes, of course). The ejection capsule used the fuel to power the electro-magnetic bubble that kept the anti-matter isolated. When the fuel ran out, the field would collapse—but by then there should be little anti-matter left. Just enough to blow the capsule to pieces.

Eismann watched the beaconed capsule accelerate away from the shuttle. He hoped nobody would come across it before the anti-matter was gone—it was a hell of a discourteous package to leave drifting about.

Far too dangerous to risk bringing to the planet with him. Unless—

That would be funny, he thought. If the whole damned planet was made of anti-matter—what a great joke on me!

Rather unlikely now: if the planet were anti-matter it would be almost certain the suns were too. But the shuttle was already caught in the swirl of their stellar winds. If those particles were anti-matter, his ship would have been eaten away by micro-detonations by now.

So—not to worry. Plenty of other problems to keep him occupied.

The planet was coming up rapidly. There was only going to be one landing attempt, anti-matter or no. There wasn't enough fuel left to orbit the planet—the bomb-induced course corrections eighteen years ago had seen to that—no time to scour the planet for safe landing sites. Or airports . . .

On the last day Eismann lit off the main chemical engines and emptied the propellant tanks in less than three minutes. After that there was barely enough time to get the shuttle turned for a head-first entry. He was coming in too damned fast, but there was nothing he could do about that now. He'd have to dive right into the atmosphere and skip his momentum away.

Too deep a bite, and that would be it—meteor time. Too shallow and he'd skip right back out, on his merry way to nowhere. Eismann gnawed nervously on his plastic teething ring. Then he grinned.

Here's where I earn all that back flight-pay.

Well, not quite yet—computers were still running the show. The shuttle pitched slowly upward until Eismann could no longer see the planet out his cockpit window. The sky was black and sprinkled with constellations, their patterns familiar, yet slightly distorted. He was not so *very* far from home.

It was peaceful up there. The only sounds were those of air fans and the hiss of an ink-jet printer making hard-copy log entries. Eismann tightened his harness straps, eager for something to do. There was still no sense of motion, save the flickering read-outs of the radar altimeters. The radios were quiet, so far.

All the Space Traffic Controllers must be on strike, he thought.

He started to laugh, then stopped.

I'm an old man, he thought suddenly. Too old to start something like this.

The shuttle quivered, and a ripple of fear swept his body. A row of white and green status lights flickered amber for a moment, then settled down.

Eismann shut his eyes and listened to the rush of surging blood in his ears. I *am* too old for this.

In fact, he thought, I am the oldest living astronaut.

Hell, I'm the oldest living *any*thing.

And I don't want to die. Not now, not after—

The shuttle shook and bounced, porpoising on the invisible, almost nonexistent air. Alarms gonged softly; again the board lit up red. Two control computers overloaded and shut down; they tried to reset, failed, and put themselves on hold.

That's the plan, he thought abruptly and with horrible certainty. The final "bomb" in the system. They'd rigged the shuttle computers to blow the landing. So close and yet—

Eismann reached out and took the stick.

The shuttle reacted badly to his touch, yawing immediately to port and beginning a slow clockwise roll. By the time he'd corrected the ship's attitude his whole body shook with every thudding heartbeat.

My God, I am going to die. We are all going to die.

I should not be in this pilot's seat, he thought desperately. Kathy was twice the pilot I was.

Which Kathy? Either one, damn it.

Both dead now, what does it matter?

(And I am escaped alone to tell thee.)

Christ, I *am* the survivor-type all right. But the best man doesn't always win, brother. There are other factors.

(They couldn't take the chance drugs or poisons would contaminate the water supply as their tiny legless bodies entered the system. "There is no other way," said Kathy, turning her back, offering her frail neck to his muscular hands. It was worse than he could have imagined. And afterward . . .)

The best Men he'd ever known—Kathy and Ice—were dead. He'd seen to it. The hell with logic. *He'd* killed them, just as he'd killed Kathy, his Kathy.

And now he'd finish the job, wreck the shuttle, and kill them all. Kill himself, kill the babies, kill Man.

All he had to do was nudge the stick downward a half centimeter.

Is this why they chose me?

If the babies knew, if they understood.

(The babies were strapped each-to-each like link sausages and tucked into his sleepbox. If they cried he couldn't hear them. They trusted him.)

We could die now and no one would ever know, he thought.

But the shuttle steadied up and straddled its imaginary flight line. He was still in control—for the moment. No "bombs," just nerves.

The atmosphere was thicker up there than expected. Maybe there'd been a lot of stellar activity lately, warming up the air and pumping it higher. The first of how many surprises?

He began to torture himself with a litany of possible disasters.

What if there's no ozone layer? The ultra-violet will cut me to pieces. Or what if the soil kills all my seeds? And what if the native plants are inedible or poisonous? Or what if the air is crowded with lethal bacteria or viruses? Or the forests thick with ravenous beasts? What if I trip over my shoelaces and bust my skull?

The shuttle vibrated harshly in the thickening air. The sky was blue-black, the stars hazy. Daylight failed quickly as the shuttle raced into the nightside of the planet. The red-orange glow of the heatshield tiles blossomed ominously around the windows.

Within minutes he was in the shadow of the planet, and all he could see was the ship on fire. His hand tensed on the stick.

I used to like this part, he thought. Flying . . .

Flying the shuttle, flying *any*thing. But that's all over now. This will be the last time, the last flight.

For twenty-two years Man had been an interstellar race—for the duration of this one voyage. Man at his apex.

In half an hour the Space Age would be over, the Dark Ages re-begun. Or maybe there'd be . . . nothing.

The final flight.

All those years of training—of playing the Game with Ice and Kathy—they would all pay off in the next few minutes. Or not.

He saw their faces, their smiling, determined faces. They wanted this to happen. They'd given up everything for this to happen, sacrificed everything so Eismann could put his cargo safely on the ground of this new planet. Why?

What did they know about Man? How could they care about His preservation? The only man they ever knew was Eismann. What about him convinced them Man was worthy of staying alive?

Nothing, he thought. Not a damned thing.

No, they did it for *me*. So *I* could live. So I could pace the fresh earth of this new planet, chomping on my silly plastic pacifier, watching their children grow up.

They did it for their old Nanny.

It was *personal*.

Then Eismann realized why he couldn't waggle the stick and end the Final Flight in a futile blaze of light. It was personal. He had a cargo to deliver, the precious children of his oldest friends. He had *promised* them, and now he'd have to keep his promise— even if no one would ever know.

Especially if no one ever knew.

It was something Men did.

Eismann wiped his eyes. The fiery glow of the shuttle's nose and belly flared brightly and the cockpit groaned and muttered. Cooling fans picked up the pace. They were still fifty miles high.

"I'll do my job," he said. "I'll make you proud, or rip my guts out trying."

I'm one hell of a meteor, he thought suddenly, as he blazed across the night sky.

I wonder who's watching? I wonder what they think?

Invaders from Earth, coming to *get'cha*. One bald old Nanny and his vicious gang of Earth babies.

God help you, here we come.

THE LEAVES OF OCTOBER
by Don Sakers

> *Have you ever read a story told by a tree? Can
> you conceive of trees, rooted deep in the soil,
> wise for their long years, yet prepared to make a
> small effort on behalf of the quick hot life scam-
> pering about among their roots? It's only natural
> to love trees . . . but considering what civiliza-
> tion is doing to the great forests, could they love
> us?*

I

I am but a sapling, yet already I have become proficient in the
reading of the First Language, in the rustles and whispers of the
Second Language, and even a bit in the vast soundless waves of
the Inner Voice with its meanings from beyond the sky.

I am also skilled in relations with the other orders of life,
although this world has circled its sun but a dozen times since I
broke soil. You may find it strange to hear a Hlut speak of
relations with other orders—these are the Hlutr, you may say to
yourselves, who stand so far above the others that they touch the
clouds, who live so long that they watch mountains change, who
talk among themselves in their two languages (for what can you
know of the Inner Voice?) all oblivious to the world. How, you
may ask, can they even be aware of others?

And your thoughts are partly right, Little Ones—but only
partly. True, the Elders . . . those who are old even as the Hlutr
count time . . . do not pay that much attention to others. True,
they live so slowly that your lives are but a flicker, and to them
you are less than goats are to a mountain. Yet you must not
make mountains of us, Little Ones, for we are alive (even as are
you) and we know the pains and beauties of living. We feel kin
to all life.

Let me assure you that the Hlutr *do* care, tiny and ephemeral as you are. We know you and feel you and cherish you, although you may not think so; for truly, we do not speak with you and seldom acknowledge you. We are aware of the flying creatures who perch upon us; of the land beings who jump, walk, and creep around us; of the grubs and many-legged crawlers who live on us and in us and within the ground beneath our roots. We appreciate, we feel for, we cherish all Little Ones—down to the tiny, primal bits of pulsing, growing, mindless life within you and their dull feeling for the Inner Voice, their dull awareness of the great world about them.

I have been taught to be even more conscious of you, Littles, than are my brethren Hlutr. I have been taught by Elders and normal Hlutr alike, living so fast that I have fit many of your lifetimes into my scant dozen years. With each day I grow better with the First and Second Languages, the expressions of my people; with each day I become more attuned to the waves of the Inner Voice . . . not only that I might communicate with my brethren of far-off worlds, but also that I might talk with you, Little Ones.

Why, you may ask, have I been created this way, why have I been bred and trained into such a non-Hlutr type of Hlut? You may wonder what need the Elders have of a Hlut like me. I wonder too, my Littles. I have some idea. There are whispers in the wind, and pulses in the Inner Voice, that bear news across the galaxy and around the world to me. There is news from the Ancients of Nephestal, whose culture is almost as old as the Hlutr.

The Daamin, the Ancients, tell us that there is a new race ready to come forth and join the Scattered Worlds of the Galaxy. We will all have company soon, dear Little Ones, and I believe the Elders wish to be ready for these new ones.

There are strange stories about them, stories which I do not quite understand. The Daamin tell of these new ones, these Humans, and of their distant planet and their odd ways. We have learned of our stunted relatives the Redwoods of Terra; we have been told of Animals and Dolphins and some of the Humans' strange societal customs (some of them a little like the many-legged crawlers and some of the grubs). In their own way they have studied the Universal Song and learned some of its principles. Enough, at least, to harness some of the power of the First Cause. And they are coming, Little Ones; already their seeds flash outward from their world at speeds as fast as the Inner Voice can move, and soon they will be here among us.

Little Ones, we must prepare for the Humans.

You are afraid of them, Little Ones. Their silver seed sits in the clearing, and it frightens you. Their odd alien smell hangs over the wood, and you are alarmed. They have come among you with boxes-that-make-noise, and you have run from them. And now you seek sanctuary among us.

Do not be afraid. The Hlutr will care for you. As we *have* cared for you, for your mothers and their mothers, back beyond the memory of the Eldest of us all. Ever have the Hlutr cared for all innocent Little Ones. Ever have we delighted in you. Ever.

Look with me, Littles, at these new creatures. Try to hear the Inner Voice as it sings in them. For truly they are alive, and they are children of the stars as are we all, Hlutr and Flyers and Crawlers and Grubs alike.

They move among us now, as you tremble and scurry into your burrows and caves, frightened by their noise and their odor and their strangeness. Only the Hlutr stand, unafraid.

Let me help you to know them, that you may not fear them. My brethren Hlutr speak to me, asking me to explain the Humans—let me explain to you as well. Those harsh sounds are like unto the Second Language, although clearly they lack the quiet soughing beauty of Hlutr speech. Listen to me, Little Ones, and you may grasp something of what they say. The smaller one speaks.

"It's the trees, Karl. Listen—no wind, and yet they seem to be making noise at one another."

"Talking trees. Right."

"What else? Look at the color changes in those trunks. There's some sort of pattern there, I'm sure of it. That's communication on some primitive level."

She feels wonder, Little Ones, the same wonder that all feeling creatures experience when they contemplate the mystery and majesty of the Hlutr.

But the other . . . it sends discord in the Inner Voice. Listen:

"They're plants. How would they even sense the color changes?" He listens to his boxes; they seem to speak to him in some bizarre form of the First Language. "Ship's instruments misread. There's no ore concentration here. Lousy site for a settlement. Let's get back."

"No, Karl. Look—the leaves are multicolored. Maybe each one absorbs a different shade. Or maybe the black ones are sensory apparatus. This needs more study."

"Two more worlds to check on, and you want to study trees."

"We can take a specimen back to Terra."

"Sure, you're going to bring back a fifty-meter tree. I can see Captain's face now."

"Look at this one—it can't be more than three meters tall. It would fit in a corner of the starboard cargo hold." (Surely you have noticed, Little Ones, that the Elders have not allowed me to grow to but a fraction of my potential.)

"Fight it out with Captain. I want lunch. Here, mark it on the map so you can find it again."

They wander off in the direction of their silver seed. Yes, I can see that you did not understand more than a little of what they said. I must confess that *I* understood all too little of myself.

But the rustles in the wind convey meaning to me, meaning of the Elders' plan, and I am afraid that I understand far too much. Fear stirs in me, just a bit. I ask if there is no other way, and they remind me of the story of the Redwoods. We cannot allow that to happen to the Hlutr; for where would the other orders be without the Hlutr to protect and guide them?

Perhaps Humans acted with ignorance, with the Redwoods. We must see that it does not happen again. We must understand why it was allowed to happen in the first place. A Hlut must go with them, back to their world.

For the last time I listen to the wind of my home world; for the last time I feel the coolness of my home soil.

A Hlut must go to Terra.

Remember me, faithful Little Ones, when I am gone.

II

Such a different world! And yet, in some ways, not so unfamiliar. *You* are here, my precious ones; true, you are not the Littles of the world I have learned to call Amny—but all Little Ones are the same for all their infinite diversity. Already there are flyers and crawlers about me, already I can feel some grubs tentatively testing the new-scattered dirt at my roots. Welcome, Little Ones, welcome.

It is good to feel fresh air, fresh soil, fresh light again. They have been kind to me, these Humans . . . and the voyage was not a long one. I lived slowly, more slowly than I have ever lived before, and it seemed no more than the merest flicker before we were on Terra.

I have shouted with the Second Language until my leaves hurt from quivering, and all the answer I have received is the meaningless murmur of wind, and the rhythmic whisper of waves on far-off shores. It is lonely—although we have these sounds on

Amny, there is also the rustle of intelligent conversation from my brethren.

Here on Terra, though, all the plants are nonsentient. However much they may resemble Hlutr form, they lack the Hlutr mind. The Redwoods, perhaps, were intelligent (although they never communicated by Inner Voice with the rest of the Hlutr. Perhaps they were deaf in that sense). Some form of Hlut, no matter how primitive, must have existed on Terra to guide the long march of animal evolution from Pylistroph seeds into customary channels—for the Humans are of the same biochemistry and general structure as so many other races in the Scattered Worlds. It saddens me that none of these ur-Hlutr are left to perchance answer my calls.

No matter, though—there is enough else to keep me busy for a long time.

Those who watch me, for example. I have an honored place in the middle of a botanical garden and many Humans come to stand before me, looking at a tiny metal rectangle and gazing at me. I greet them with the First Language (which is not as much of a strain as the Second) and they watch. Some even respond with flickers of glee.

Terra has spun six times since I arrived here; and although the first five turns were spent in isolation to make sure I was rid of all Amny's Little Ones, the watchers came. I have learned much about those-who-watch.

Most are full-grown Humans (how strange to call ''full-grown'' creatures who cannot be three-seventieths the height of a mature Hlut!) making the unending noises they call speech, their minds filled with distortions of the Inner Voice concerned with time and rush and ever, ever with movement. With a few, there is curiosity and even a healthy appreciation of me. (My brethren are delighted to learn that Humans can be awed by the sight of a Hlut, but all too often my brethren think too highly of the Hlutr place in the Universal Song.) But none of these adult Humans, not one, is ever content. Their thoughts and feelings, when they can be read at all, are fastened upon something else. Always they have little regard for the Universal Song of which everything is a part—Humans, Hlutr, botanicalgarden, and Terra too. Always they have even less regard for the magic and beauty of themselves.

There are others, however, who come to look . . . and I find them much more pleasing. These are the Human seedlings, who are always in the care of the mature Humans (you need only think of the many-legged crawlers who protect their eggs and larvae). The seedlings make noise too—and their noise is more raucous and less soothing, even, than the speech of the adults. Despite that, my Little Ones, if you will look at them with the eyes of the Inner Voice you will see that they are simpler than the adults. These children are more like *you*, Littles, the way they happily watch as the colors of the First Language race across my trunk and through my leaves. Sometimes I feel that I can talk to the Human children, as I can talk to you, my dears.

Some come who are upset—as you are often upset, when you are hungry or your young are threatened, or when your mate has died. For some of them, those who will listen, I can work a twist of the Inner Voice and they go away happier, more peaceful. I do not mind this work—indeed, when has a Hlut ever minded helping the Littles?

But I feel that there is more important work I should be doing. The Elders have not expressed themselves well in the eddies of the Inner Voice—and those eddies are hard to read across the parsecs, with all the interference of all the Hlutr on other worlds. I shall think hard, and consider deeply, and perhaps it will come to me. Following the orders of the Elders, I shall try to talk with the Humans—although I have been here six days, and have had little if any success in making them realize that I can speak. However, we must not expect Humans to be as fast as a Hlut would be; I shall give them time.

Meanwhile, I have those-who-watch, especially the children. And I have *you*, Little Ones.

III

There are parades, there is joy and cheer all around. The Botanical Garden is hung with bright holos and flags and signs, and the children skip about shouting and laughing at my colors; I am shouting in the First Language to produce pretty patterns for them.

You must be careful, Little Ones, not to get hurt on this day of joy. The Humans are often forgetful of you, and you are all too used to the careful attention of a Hlut. So scurry when you see the Humans coming, and watch their feet lest you are tromped on. The children are the most careless. You must not think ill of them—for if you could but see the Inner Voice within them as I do, you would know that they are filled with joy and not malice. Their minds are small, though, and they can only pay attention to a few things at a time. And some of you are so little that you cannot take much of their joy.

Why, you may ask, are the Humans so exuberant? You have

seen before parades and fairs and celebrations, but none in your experience match the reckless joy of this day. Gather around me, Little Ones, and I shall try to explain. Although I do not fully understand.

You see, Humans love one another with powerful feeling. You may understand this, tiny crawlers, but the others may not be able to see it. And Humans have a strange desire to see themselves in many places in the Universal Song. The more places, more Humans to love. (Yes, birds, you may rest upon my branches.)

Well, my Littles, this day we see the declaration of much love for many Humans in the Galaxy. This day, there has been the proclamation of an Empire. (Come, squirrels, and sit with me.) This day, starships will begin to sweep across the Scattered Worlds and unite all the colonies of Humanity. There will be much pain and much joy and ever so much glory. It will be a beautiful and tragic addition to the Universal Song.

Yes, I know it is a difficult thing to explain. I must admit, now that you are all confused by my explanation, that we Hlutr do not grasp the Human drive for Empire any better than you do. We have received some conception of it from the Daamin, and even more from the sons of Metrin, who have a similar drive. And there have been many examples in the distant past, from the sad Iaranor to grand Avethell and all her daughter worlds.

It must be a very animal thing, not known to plants. It is but one of the mysteries about the Human race. They will lose themselves in this power-and-glory struggle, lose themselves to the most evident joy and the strongest emotions.

Why Humans should wish to lose themselves is another question entirely.

It has been almost sixty years, my Little Ones, since I have been on Terra. I have grown, as all Hlutr grow (either slow or fast as they wish) . . . can you believe that there was once a time when I was only as tall as a Human, I who now stand as high as ten Humans one atop the other? I have seen many things: I have watched children grow and adults die, and I have seen new ones born. (They are truly delightful when they are born, so very vegetable, just like tiny seedlings pushing their heads into the light for the first time.) Still I do not understand them. I have been living very quickly, as quick or quicker than Humans themselves live, and I have been thinking very much.

I suffered, Littles, across Human light years with the rape of the ecologies of nearby Laxus and Leikeis and other worlds. I have watched thousands of red and beautiful sunsets, and have rejoiced with all the creatures at the stinging freshness of Terra's clean rain. I have sung with the Whales, greatest of my Little Ones, once I found the way to pick up their own Second Language from the world-seas.

Humans have not talked with me. My brethren on Amny and other worlds tell me that Humans ignore them as well. After a few regrettable murders, the Human colonists have left the Hlutr alone. Every once in a while someone wonders about our color changes (although to my knowledge, not one has ever suspected the existence of the whispers of the Second Language—mayhap because it sounds so much like the wind . . . but they have never quite realized that the First Language *is* language.)

That is why I am so happy today, Little Ones. I have great hopes for this Empire of theirs. I sense a new spirit in the Inner Voice of these creatures; they are taking a good look at the Universal Song, and it is possible that they will begin to discern the place of the Hlutr in that Song.

Ah, here comes a child. No, my Little Ones, don't flee from him. Stay, and see how innocent he is. Mind, now, don't get stepped on.

Welcome, child. You children, sometimes, watch my colors with curiosity—perhaps *you*, lad, will grow up and retain your wonder at the pretty colors you watch so absorbedly, and will discover that the Hlutr actually talk.

Run along, now; my leaves quiver to the sound of your parents' voices, you must return to them. But . . . perhaps you will be back.

IV

A terrible thing has happened, Little Ones, something which has shocked the Elders and the Hlutr of all the Galaxy.

Could I intercede for the Humans, I would. But I do not understand. Elders, Stars, Universal Song . . . *why?*

I of course never saw Credix, grand world that has now become one of the Provincial Capitals and a major military base for the Empire. Yet I have seen images of it still burning in the minds of those who visited. And I have sung the melodies of the Inner Voice with the ancient community of Hlutr who lived there.

Gone, gone. Not one Hlut remains on Credix. Few enough died directly from Human bombings—perhaps twenty times seventy. More Hlutr than that die naturally all over the Scattered Worlds each Terran year. But oh, twenty times seventy Hlutr in the middle of their lives, living fast or slow or in between, growing and sheltering—and all the Little Ones that dwelled with them. The backlash of the Inner Voice killed every other Hlut on the planet. Even on Amny, eight hundred parsecs distant, some of the frailer Hlutr died.

Why? you Little Ones ask. And why, ask my brethren from beyond the sky. Why?

Can I explain how important this Empire has become to these Humans of Terra? Can I explain how they have invested all their being into its realization, so much so that they are willing to deforest whole subcontinents to build spaceports? Stars and Music, how can I explain when I do not understand?

There are those of my brethren who wish me to take revenge. The way is clear . . . we Hlutr have taken it before. We alone of all the creatures in the Universal Song, we possess the ability to manufacture those helices of matter that are the very stuff and foundation of life.

I could . . . I could.

You, my Littles, could provide the basic materials upon which I could work. The Hlutr have guided evolution on seventy-times-itself-seven-times worlds, large and small. We possess the control to make you over, Littles, into beings that would have the means to kill every Human on this world. A plague, one of my brothers suggests to me—your little pulsing bits could be converted into other little bits that would spell the end of Humanity.

I could do it. It would require my death—that death-detonation which is the ultimate meaning of the Hlutr race, that last gasp that so few of us have ever really undergone—to spread the synthesized substances far.

I could. I will not.

Listen to me, brethren. I plead for the Humans. They did not know what they did. It is *my* failing, for I have not yet been able to make them realize that we are sentient. Just as a Hlut does not hesitate to destroy a nonsentient plant that is in his way—so these Humans did not hesitate to destroy what they imagined to be nonsentient Hlutr on Credix.

Let me work harder, brethren, and let me make them see what we are. And And then . . . then they will hurt us no more.

The Elders answer with a sigh that is both dirge and decision. Until I can do a better job, until I can convince the Humans that we are sentient . . . they will be spared.

A terrible thing has happened, Little Ones. Now the sap of all those Hlutr, all the forests of Credix and all the dead Hlutr beyond . . . are my responsibility. Ever in the Universal Song will my failure be noted, and ever will I be linked with Credix in the tales that will follow.

Ever.

V

Winter comes . . . as it has come over three-times-seventy-times since I have been here. I have watched the leaves of the trees with which I share the Imperial Botanical Garden turn color and fall many times, and I shall never grow tired of the sight. It is a joyful vision, which we do not have on Amny; for Amny has no winter, only eternal spring.

The Humans also like to watch the leaves. They cannot guess that within those colors is preserved a genetic memory of the Hlutr spores from which these trees' ancestors of millions of years ago sprang. For the yellow-red-orange pattern of the leaves is the same pattern seen on a Hlut deep in communion with the Inner Voice, listening contently to the ebb and flow of tides from brethren Hlutr and from life the Galaxy round. It is the sigh of a Hlut experiencing the profound joy without which the Universal Song is toneless and without purpose.

These last few winters have been even more delightful for me. There are few of you about, with the snow gathering—and nowadays you tend to come near me less and less, for the Research Station's new building was put up less than five man-lengths from me, and many of you still fear to approach it.

I am left with the company of crawlers and grubs, and a few brave birds. You, birds, no longer nest in my upper branches—thirty man-lengths is a bit high for a nest—but I cherish your homes in my lower branches. I have cared for your young, as much as I am able; for the Hlutr *do* love you, Little Ones. Yet you feel that I am more distant from you than I have been in the past.

True, I have not spoken with you much. I have been very busy.

I have been living faster than I have ever lived, save for the hectic days of my saplinghood on Amny. It is necessary, you see, to live quite fast to keep up with Doctor Rubashov and the others of the Research Station. It is important to me, Little Ones, and important to the Hlutr as a race, that Doctor Rubashov be given all the evidence he needs to prove the Hlutr sentient in Human terms.

I do the bidding of the Elders, in this and in all things. For this I was sent to Terra, for this I have stood in this Botanical Garden for Human centuries.

Now young Doctor Rubashov approaches, and I must concentrate all my energies on the seedlings' talk which we have managed to improvise in the First Language. His apparatus is all set up; I greet him.

"Good day, Doctor. Are you understanding me?"

A televisor screen flashes color-patterns at me. Were he to shout, I could understand his speech—in my time I have become quite good at reading Human speech—but it is easier to use the First Language.

"I am reading you. Good morning. Are you ready for the day's experiments?"

"Certainly." To tell the truth, Littles, the prospect of another day of numbers and simple concepts, as if I were a seedling being taught by the Elders, is abhorrent. I don't mind living fast to talk with things, but I dislike doing it simply for numbers.

Before he starts the day's trials, Doctor Rubashov adjusts some of the leads which monitor my biochemical states. When his hand touches my trunk I have a sudden flash of Inner Voice clarity.

"Doctor, you are disturbed. Why?"

"I've been working for two years to show that you are intelligent. I've convinced myself time and again, but the (something) are not yet convinced. With such slim evidence we won't ever be able to get the (something else) to recognize you as sentient. And that'll be the end of my career."

"Have you noticed how beautiful yon city looks all covered with snow? Does not appreciation of that beauty qualify me as sentient?" (You may wonder why we include appreciation of beauty and wonder in our definition of what constitutes sentience. Why, certainly one of the most important things we share with other sentients, Iaranori and Avethellans, Dophins and Metrinaire, even the poor children of Nepehestal—surely it is this ability to be profoundly stilled by the simple miracles of the Universal Song.)

"Well now, you may think so. And I may think so. But I don't think the (something) agrees. Now let's get started."

"But are the hills not beautiful?"

"I suppose so." He is still disturbed, and I cannot read his feelings well enough to do more than guess. I live more quickly and try to match my own chorus of the Inner Voice with his cacophony. There are shattered images—a Human woman, and unpleasant scenes of anger, and—but it all fades back into the private reaches of his mind.

"We have a lot to do today," Doctor Rubashov continues, "for we won't be able to work the next few days."

"Yes, of course. Let me wish you a joyful Solstice, Quen Rubashov."

"Where did you learn that?" He sends a quick wave of surprise in the Inner Voice out toward the stars.

"I have been here a long time. I have observed much of your race and your customs. Oh, and I have an important matter to discuss with you—in the spirit of Solstice."

"Go on."

"My brethren and I have noticed the new center for emotionally disturbed children that was built a few kilometers from here. Disturbances in the Inner Voice have made it difficult for me to communicate with my brethren Hlutr beyond the sky."

"There's no way to have that center moved further away. How do you know about it? Has one of the techs . . . ?"

"You misunderstand, Doctor. No, I don't want the center moved away. If you will move the youngsters closer, I believe I can help heal them with the Inner Voice."

There was a long pause. "We'll see." Then Doctor Rubashov started flashing numbers at me. I settled down to a long day's work.

Little Ones, Little Ones, come close to me. How the wind rushes through my branches, how it shakes me to the roots!

How could he do it? No, Littles, I am not asking a literal question. I *know* how he could do it. He took a dropshaft to the top floor of the Imperial State Building and threw himself off. And after long seconds of freefall, Quen Rubashov was no more.

How? Why? Because his work was going badly? Because that woman left him? Because, because, because . . . a thousand so-called reasons beat in the minds of those on the research team. They have not told me yet—but there is no hiding it. I was attuned to his own theme of the Inner Voice. There was no mistaking his cry on Solstice Eve.

How could a sentient being do that? Littles, I fear I will never understand Humans. How can any living being embrace nonlife? How can it hate itself so much as to wish to be not-self? Make no mistake, my faithful simple Little Ones . . . what I felt in Quen Rubashov's mind that night was not only anguish, not only dread, but a feeling of welcome for the fate he had chosen.

How can an individual be able to perform such a supremely unsane act? How, when faced by all the wonders and mysteries of existence, can he choose to embrace its opposite?

One tiny voice in the Universal Song was stilled that night, Little Ones, stilled by its own hand because it preferred silence to the Song.

I do not understand.

Come closer, Littles, please. Feel the wind. . . .

VI

Children are delightful, my Little Ones . . . their minds are almost as simple as yours, yet so very complicated at times. Through it all, though, they have an awareness of the Inner Voice like none I have seen in other Humans. The others call these seedlings disturbed. They cannot be aware that the disturbance stems in many cases from a talent for understanding the Inner Voice. They come to the Center, in the buildings of Rubashov's old Research Station, and they play with their blocks and toy trains and dolls; and all the time I soothe the raucous noise of the Inner Voice that they project. In time, many are cured and they leave.

The ones I like best, Littles, are those who are never cured. The ones who sit and stare deeply into my trunk and the patterns that race there, and who listen to the Second Language as if they could understand. Oh, they are bothersome, with their rages and hatreds and deep depressions. But there are times when the Inner Voice is at peace in them. Those times, I can almost get through. I send waves of the Inner Voice after them and they strain to hear.

Lately, I think a few have even begun to answer.

I must tell my brethren Hlutr. The Elders will be very interested. Maybe, even, the time will come when these children can cast ripples of the Inner Voice outward to other Hlutr.

Perhaps the nurses think that *they* are caring for the children, perhaps the programmers think that they have worked miracles. I know better. And more and more lately, I believe that the children know better too. When they look at me their eyes are bright and aware, and the Inner Voice sings. I am on the brink of communication.

In addition I have you, my Little Ones. For you must never imagine that I have forgotten you. Birds and ants and spiders and squirrels and worms beneath my roots, I remember and feel and cherish you one and all.

And I live for October each year, when the beautiful colors sweep through leaves around me, when I am reminded of my sapling days on Amny, and of other Hlutr.

I have not seen any of my brethren since Amny; had I stayed,

I would have been surrounded by a forest of them. It saddens me a little, my friends. I have a mission, and I content myself with the sight of autumn and the remembered whisper of the Second Language. Humans have yet to find me sentient, and I have lately been much more content with autumn than with my mission. And, of course, with the children.

I think little Chari Anne is trying to talk with me.

VII

Chari Anne comes now, my Little Ones—I can feel her vibrations in the Inner Voice. You mustn't be afraid of her, nor of the tiny one she brings with her. She has learned much, in eight decades, of the way of the Hlutr and their concern for the other orders of life. Chari Anne cherishes you, Littles, as do I.

You see, she walks among you without harming even the smallest, projecting peace with the Inner Voice. She moves to the equipment that once belonged to Quen Rubashov, in the abandoned building of the Center for Disturbed Children. The children have been moved away, over the years, as Human psychologists learned more about the Human mind and began more and more to distrust this alien creature. I have felt loneliness, but I have at least been able to live a good deal more slowly. That is a good thing, for I am coming near the end of my span. I have always lived fast, however, when I am visited by some of the children from the old Center: Chari Anne, Staven, Daris, Kaavin, and the few others.

Chari Anne sits before the communication screen, holding a Human boychild on her knee, and switches on the equipment. Since adulthood her command of the Inner Voice has been fading, and meaningful talk is now difficult without the equipment.

"Good morning," she says.

"Good morning, Chari Anne. Thank you for coming to see me. Are the leaves not beautiful?"

Her Inner Voice radiates warmth that I have learned to associate with her smiles. "Yes, they are. You always did love to see autumn leaves."

"I always did." She waits. I think she is tired, and I fear it will not be much longer before she passes out of the Universal Song. Once, Little Ones, I would have told you that this is the way of all creatures, except the Hlutr, who are so old they live hundreds of your lifetimes. Now, as I near the end of *my* time in the Song, I am not too sure.

"Chari Anne, who is the Little One you have brought with you? His mind is delightfully sharp."

"This is Elsu; he is my first great-grandchild. Elsu is Liene's son." Chari Anne is the progenitor of many Humans; she always brings the infants to me, and while they grow they are much in my company. As adults, they return every so often. I remember Liene as a child, Littles, and now Elsu gives me the same wondering look, coos in delight as I race patterns of the First Language up and down my trunk for him.

All my children from the Center—they all bring me their young ones. Were we to gather every one here on this hill, we could fill the old building to overflowing.

"What news do you bring of the others?" I ask.

"Daris has finished her major composition at last, and her troupe is touring with it. The show is very popular."

"Daris dances well." I do not tell her what I have seen in Daris's mind when she dances, for it cannot be put into words. It is a feeling of the Inner Voice, when all harmonies are matched and one is in union with the Universal Song. Daris feels it when she dances . . . and in Daris's children and grandchildren I have caught the same joyful melodies.

"Kaavin sent me a long holotape just the other day. He's at work in some far-off system, testing some theories he has about stellar formation or some such. I didn't completely understand what he said—but then, few enough of us ever understood Kaavin."

"He is happy."

"He certainly seems to be." Elsu imitates his great-grandmother and hits keys on the board; the equipment transmits a raucous squawk. Chari Anne feels my glee, and she laughs. Elsu chuckles as well. "Oh, Staven has some good news. Do you remember the problem he had with those Kaanese?"

I thought. Yes, Staven had told me just a while ago. Half a hundred nonhumans were trapped on a Human world, because their home was far across the border and a war was going on. Staven made it his lifework to study and help nonhumans. He'd been trying to find a way to get these Kaanese primitives home.

"He succeeded?"

"Yes. More than we hoped. Both governments made a truce across that border long enough to get the Kaanese back where they belonged. It's the first truce ever between Patala and the Empire."

"I am proud of Staven."

"We all are."

For a while neither of us says anything. This is fine, Little

Ones, for I can feel Chari Anne's Inner Voice melodies, and I listen busily to and sing with the innocent song of Elsu.

Finally Chari Anne puts hands back on the keyboard. "I have news. I just learned yesterday. The Empress is going to sign the bill declaring Hlutr legally sentient. The Imperial Council passed it along with all the attendant protection laws. Staven's data and my own experiments convinced them at last." With the Inner Voice I can hear her listening. "What's wrong, aren't you excited?"

"I sigh, Chari Anne. Yes, I am excited. My brethren will be pleased to hear it. And yet . . . well, Chari Anne, I am not long for this world."

She is very concerned. "What's the matter? I thought that Hlutr lived . . . well, if not forever, at least a very long time."

"Again I sigh. How long we live depends upon how fast we live. The Elders, who are as old as my world, live very very slowly. Here on Terra, I have been forced to live very quickly. And I am nearing the end."

"I am distressed."

"Don't be. All that is mortal passes from the Universal Song. We must accept its passing."

The Inner Voice is disturbed with her rage, and it drowns out the background murmur of all the life around us. Even Elsu feels it. "Damn it, how can you be so philosophical?"

"A tender smile, Chari Anne. There is no other way. I have watched Humans die for four hundred years and more, and it has not upset me. I have watched the other orders live and die countless times since I arrived on Terra. The life is important, Chari Anne . . . but more important is the way it is lived. I have lived mine well." Again we say nothing for a time, while I use the Inner Voice to calm the seething storm of Chari Anne's mind. Littles, this is one of the jobs of the Hlutr. Being masters of the Inner Voice, we naturally try to use it to help others when we can. "Chari Anne, I would like it very much if you could do something for me. Now that the Empress is declaring us sentient, I will not be needed for study."

"I suppose not."

"Do you think that you and the other children—" (for I still think of Chari Anne and the others as the children they once were. The important part of them never did grow up and become lost) "—could arrange to have me shipped back to Amny, so that I may die among my own kind?"

Again her Inner Voice is in turmoil. "If that's what you want . . . except . . . Staven pulled a lot of strings to get those

Kaanese home. Especially after Patala attacked Karphos. I don't
know if he could get another truce so soon. He doesn't want to
push things. If Amny is anywhere near the war zone—''

I am not ignorant of galactography, Little Ones, and I calm
her fears. "Amny is near Credix, Chari Anne, across the galaxy
from Karphos." The Elders are deeply disturbed by the destruction of Karphos and the progress of the Human war. There have
been Hlutr killed, and their pain echoes yet on crests of the Inner
Voice around the galaxy. And Humans have died by the millions,
at the hands of their brethren . . .

"We'll do it. We'll have you taken back to Amny."

There is another long pause, and I look at the brilliant, joyful
leaves of October. Soon I will leave you, Little Ones, birds and
squirrels and insects and worms; I shall remember you fondly,
and I hope you will remember me until your little lives are over.
"One more thing, Chari Anne. Before I go, do you think
it would be possible . . . for me to say goodbye to all the others,
and their children and grandchildren?"

VIII

Again I feel the soil of Amny below my roots, and again I am
among creatures of my own type. True, Amny has the smell of
Humans now; their city dominates the clearing where once a
grassland stood in happy golden awareness. True, their airships
drift through the sky bearing cargo, and their starships arrive and
depart on a daily schedule from the spaceport. These changes
cannot overcome the feeling of my home world.

For the first while, Little Ones, the world seemed wrong. I
was too heavy, the air was too cold, the sun was not the right
color. I learned to forget these minor differences. Amny, at least,
has something Terra never did—the intelligible rustles of the
Second Language, the colors of the First.

At my request the Terrans placed me in the middle of a group
of Elders. They were impatient (insofar as an Elder can be said
to be impatient) to learn of Earth and Humans, and I knew they
would use the First Language. Had I been placed in my original
spot, out of sight of the Elders, they would have been obliged to
use the Second with its much lower information density.

I live slowly now, Littles, almost as slowly as an Elder. I tell
them all I saw and felt and heard.

They debate; the sun moves against the stars. A message
comes through the waves of the Inner Voice, a message from the
Hlutr ambassador to New York. Chari Anne has died. So, my
Little One, I have outlived you. I am saddened, as no Hlut

should be for the passing of a lesser order. I shall remember you joyfully and with wonderment, Chari Anne.

The Elders debate for seven years; near the end they are living almost as fast as normal Hlutr, and I am living almost as slowly as the crystalline Talebba. Finally one of them lives slowly enough to talk with me; he is the Elder who trained me, a lifetime ago.

"Brother Hlut," he says with the First Language across seasons, "we have debated with ourselves and with Hlutr on the other Scattered Worlds. The Inner Voice has been in turmoil with our discussions. And we have reached a decision." More of the Elders join us; and in slow pulsations of the Inner Voice I am aware that Hlutr Elders from all over the galaxy are joining this conclave. "I shall repeat our decision to you."

"Thank you, Brother Elder." I have trouble with the First Language . . . age is telling upon me. Is the sun shining? I feel so cold.

"You were sent to Terra, you know, for a mission. The Humans investigated you, and finally they judged you and the Hlutr sentient. That was not the purpose of your mission."

"This I have suspected, Elder."

"From what you learned about Humans, we must needs rule on their own sentience. We must rule on whether they present a menace to the Hlutr and other orders of life in the Scattered Worlds."

"Let it be so, Elder. For the Hlutr must protect life and the Inner Voice. So has it been since the first seed vessel of the Pylistroph (blessed be!) set forth into the Scattered Worlds, so shall it be when the last star dies." I am so cold. Chari Anne, will I see you when I die? Do Hlutr and Humans go to the same place when we pass on? Chari Anne, do we go anywhere?

"Then hear the decision of the Hlutr Elders. You have watched Mankind slaughter Hlutr. You have watched him slaughter other orders. You have watched him turn his back on the miracle of existence and slaughter his brethren and himself."

"This I have watched."

"You have seen that most Humans are nonsentient. You have seen that they do not appreciate the wonder of the Universal Song and do not even delight in their own lives."

"I have seen cases of this, Brother Elder. Many cases. But—"

"Hear then the answer of the Elders. Man is fundamentally a beast, we proclaim. He grew up on a world with barely any supervision of Hlutr. He destroyed the last vestiges of Hlutr control on his planet. And now he spreads through the stars with

his strange unsane ways. Man is a beast—and a beast with too
much power. He *does* represent a threat to the Hlutr and to life.
And so Mankind will be destroyed.''

Living slowly as I am, it is hard to feel strong emotions
quickly. Yet the blast of impatience I sent out on the Inner Voice
must rock all Hlutr on Amny. ''Elders, you do wrong to decide
this way. Let me be heard.''

''Speak.''

''Humans all start out as wonderers, as children delighted with
every segment of the Universal Song. A few do not lose these
qualities into adulthood. Whatever their ultimate fate, all men
begin as sentients. On the basis of the potential that Humans
show as children, and on the basis of those few who never lose
that potential, I beg that Humanity be spared.''

I feel no agreement from the Elders—only astonishment that I
should speak this way. The one closest to me projects feelings
that, in Humans, are associated with a sad shake of the head.

''Brother Hlut, you are blinded to the danger of Mankind.
Look with me.'' He sings in the Inner Voice, a terrible song that
I had almost forgotten.

Credix. A thriving planetful of Hlutr, and then came the
bombs. To clear a spaceport, in the name of all the gods! The
Elder sings me the deathsong of all those Hlutr, and it shakes me
to the core.

Another Elder sings, sings of Laxus and Leikeis and a hundred
billion Little Ones destroyed, fast or slow, by Human ecological
meddling. And he sings to me the song of the Humans who did
it—not even criminal, they were totally unconcerned.

And another Elder sings to me of Karphos, of great naval
battles and of Humans killed, Humans suffering, Humans fighting Humans and glorying in the task. Of Human colonists on a
thousand planets, colonists who delight in stripping whole forests,
in slaughtering herds of animals, in hunting for the sheer pleasure of cruel destruction.

My teacher projects sadness. ''*This* is the beast that you want
us to spare, Brother Hlut? Because of a potential that may never
be realized? How many more times does Credix have to happen,
how many more Battles of Karphos must there be, how many
Little Ones must die before you are convinced that we do right?''
He addressed the other Elders. ''The way is simple. We know
Human biochemistry. We can construct diseases that will kill all
Humans but spare other Little Ones. There are enough of us on
Human worlds that we can strike before they even become aware
of the danger. And then the threat of Humanity will be finished.''

All that is mortal passes from the Universal Song, Chari Anne. There is no need to be saddened about that. Then why am I so unquiet? I am glad that you died, Chari Anne, before we could destroy your race. I only wish Staven and Daris and Kaavin, and all their children and yours, could die first as well.

I wish I could cry, Chari Anne, for the passing of Humanity.

I wish the Elders could have seen the wondering sparkle in your eyes.

"NO!" This time my Inner Voice roar shakes all life on the planet. Even the Humans feel it touch the edges of their minds. "Elders, hear me."

They sigh. "Speak," my teacher tells me.

What to say? "You tell me that Human potential may never be realized. That too few ever retain their original wonder and delight in the Universal Song. I say that you are wrong, Elders.

"I know Humans, Human men and women, who are entities worthy of Hlutr friendship. One of them, who just recently passed out of the Universal Song, was so alive with the glory of existence that she spent her entire life working so that Hlutr could be declared sentient."

"That is one case, Brother Hlut."

"Yes, Chari Anne was one woman. But when she succeeded, and Human beings realized we were sentient . . . then all of them ceased hurting us. One Hlut now stands in New York as ambassador to Humanity. Laws have been passed, Elders, laws which protect Hlutr in the future." I quivered. "For four centuries Humans thought us unintelligent, and so our deaths were to them little more than the passing of a grassland. I grant you that very few ever wondered, in that four centuries, whether we were intelligent. Yet when Chari Anne *did* wonder, when she and Staven proved us sentient—all other Humans agreed. Credix and Karphos cannot be erased, cannot be forgotten . . .. but they will not happen again. And these are the creatures you call beasts?"

Another Elder sings, from kiloparsecs away. "Not just Hlutr are endangered by Humans. They fight among themselves, showing total disregard for life. Many of the lesser orders will be hurt, have been hurt already."

"Let me tell you of Human attitudes toward the lesser orders, Elders. The Kaanese are surely one of the least progressed races in the Galaxy. They can barely be said to have self-awareness and language. Yet my Little One Staven convinced Human governments to stop their war long enough to bring some Kaanese home. Staven is one man, one very exceptional man who has kept his own wonder and respect for other orders—but what of the diplomats, Navy officers, the Empress and the Patalanian President? They still have flickers of the innate and original goodness of the Human being.''

This has been a long speech, Little Ones, and I am living far faster than I should. I cannot feel my upper limbs. Elders, Stars, Universal Song . . . do not let me die before I have pled my case.

''Let me tell you, Elders, of the wonderment that Humans retain for the Universal Song.'' I sing with the Inner Voice—I sing as Daris does when she is dancing. ''This melody is one that is Hult-flavored in all respects. Yet it originates in a Human mind. Do we have the right to destroy the mind that can produce that song?''

''Brother Hlut, you yourself guided that individual in her development. If she sings glorious melodies, it is because you taught her. Ordinary adult Humans cannot learn to sing such songs.''

''No? Then listen with me, Elders, as Daris dances.'' I cast out with the Inner Voice, seeking a pattern I know so well. In a little while as we Hlutr count time, I find Daris and her troupe dancing before an audience of two thousand. ''Listen, Elders, to Daris's Inner Voice. Then listen to the Inner Voice of those who dance with her. And listen to the Inner Voice of those who watch. Do you not hear the same theme repeated over and over? You say that I taught Daris to sing . . . who taught her audience?''

They listen, and they hear what I have described. And the tides of the Inner Voice that flow through this conclave begin to change.

My teacher tries one more time. ''Brother Hlut, all the arguments you have used depend upon the fact that you, a Hlut, taught these Humans while they were children. You could go through all the descendants of these Humans, and the answer would be the same: they are what they are because a Hlut taught them. Not because they live up to their potential on their own. In the four centuries you spent on Terra, you have managed to change only a small number of Humans. The vast majority of them are still a threat to the Universal Song.''

Now I am saddened in a new way. One has respect for one's teachers, one always thinks that they are intelligent and worthy. It is a terrible thing to be shown otherwise.

''Brother Elders, can the Hlutr *not* try to help Humans more? Must we turn our backs on them and destroy them, when with time and teaching we might be able to help them alter themselves? The few Humans I have helped—who are now helping change others of their kind—show that progress is possible. Are we now to close our senses to that possibility, are we to deny to this order of Little Ones the help that they so plainly need, and so plainly can profit from?

"They had no Hlutr to help them when they were growing on their planet—now, when the job is more difficult, are we to put aside our ancient obligations and consign this entire order to nonexistence? Elders, I believe that the Hlutr are better than that. I ask that Mankind be spared."

Cold, I am so cold. I cannot see beyond this grove—I would have liked one more sight of the stars.

My teacher speaks slowly. "The Elders have made their decision, Brother Hlut. Hear it now. Man is a beast . . . but a beast with the potential to become sentient. Hlutr can help him to realize that potential. Therefore, Man will be spared, and the Hlutr will take up their obligation to work with him, that he may become more fully what he *could* be. Let it be so."

"Let it be so, Brother Elders. Brother Hlutr." I am cold, so cold. Chari Anne, are you there? It must be autumn, Chari Anne; look how my leaves are red and orange and yellow. Are they not beautiful, my Little One? Is not the Universal Song a grand and glorious thing, to have contained two such as we?

I always did love the leaves of October.

AS TIME GOES BY
by Tanith Lee

The twists and tricks of time are the stuff of mathematics speculation, but only after space is conquered and the problems of faster-than-light travel is directly challenged will the permutations of time show themselves. Here is a work of such science fiction from the vivid and boundless imagination of a very talented author.

We had half a crew in here two twenties ago, swore they passed the *Napoleon*, coming up into the Parameter. But you know what spacers are, particularly when they're in a Static Zone. Two-thousand-plus time streams colliding in space, and a white ironex wheel, fragile as a leaf, spinning round at the centre of it all. You're bound to get time-ghosts, and superstitions of all sorts.

The wheel here at Tempi was the first way station ever created, in the first Parameter they ever hit when they finally figured how Time operates out in deep space. You'll know most, if not all of it, of course. How every star system functions in a different time sphere, everything out of kilter with everything else, and that the universe is composed of a million strands of time, of which only two thousand have as yet been definitely charted and made navigable. And you know too that Tempi, and her sister Zones—what they jokingly call the *white* holes in space—are the safe houses where time is, forever and always, itself at a stop. And that, though wheelers reckon in twenty-hour units, and though, like anywhere else, we have a jargon of past, present and future—yestertwenty, today, tomorrow—temporal stasis actually obtains all around a wheel. *We* move all right, but over the face of a frozen clock, over the face of a clock without any hands at all. Which means that whatever ship blows in, out of whichever of those two thousand odd time continuums, can re-align here, or in another of the white holes, docked against a white ironex wheel, having come back, as it where, to square one. It's here they wipe the slate clean before flying out again into chaos. A tract of firm ground in the boiling seas. In scientific terms: a Parameter, one constant sphere in a differential Infinity. In common parlance, just another way of keeping sane.

But sanity, like time, is relative. As I say, Tempi has its share of 'ghosts'; like the Lyran wild flowers that are sometimes supposed to manifest on the Sixth Level. Not that I ever saw those. I did see the *Napoleon*, once.

It was back in the twenties when they still had that bar here on the Third Level—Rouelle Etoile, Star Alley. Maybe you've heard of it. It owed quite a lot to early twentieth century celluloid, you know those old movies, like thin acidulous slices of lemon. The Rouelle had that square-shouldered furniture, and the glass chunk ashtrays. The walls had rose and black satin poured down them. And some of the women would get out of their coveralls, and come into the Rouelle with satin poured down them too, and those long, dark scarlet nails, and those long earrings like chandeliers. There was also a chandelier in the roof. You should have seen it. Like ice on fire. And under the chandelier there was a real piano, and a real pianist, a Sirtian, blue as coal, with the face of a prince, and hands like sea waves. The sounds that came out of the piano were the shape and colour of the blades of light snowing off the chandelier. You should have seen that chandelier.

But I was telling you about the time I saw the *Napoleon*.

I was up on the Fourth Walk, one level over the Rouelle Etoile, where you can watch the ships explode in out of nothing, leaving the Warp Lanes at zero 50. Space was blind-clear as a pool of ink, without stars obviously, since you never see stars inside a Parameter. Incoming traffic was listed as over for that twenty. When I saw this great bottle-nosed dolphin surging up out of nowhere, I started to run for the Alert panel. Then something made me look back when I was two thirds along the gantry. And the ship just wasn't there any more.

I'm not given to hallucinations, and besides, I have a pretty good Recall. I remember sitting down on the gantry, and putting that ship together again on the blackboard of my mind, and taking a hard long look at her. And I realized, inside a second, she couldn't be any crate left on the listings. The numerals and date-codings, you see, were Cycles—out about nineteen years or more, by Confederation reckoning. With the time-tangle out here, every code gets changed once every Cycle. Naturally, there's the occasional tin can comes careering out of Warp, with its dating markers legally a few points overdue. But they're little ships, freelance clippers nobody makes much fuss over. This was a big ship, a cool, pale giant. She had the old-fashioned diesel-pod at her stern, too, burning like a ruby. But there was something else. My Recall was showing me enough to know her markings weren't just out of date, they were *wrong*. And she had a device. Anyone who's ever heard of the Trade War knows about the pirate ships, and the blazons they used to carry. Quite a few people know what the device of the *Napoleon* was: An eagle over a sunburst. And that's precisely what this ship had on her bow.

I didn't report anything. Just hinted around, you know the kind of thing. Then I began to get comparison sightings, and there were quite a lot. To my knowledge, nobody's ever come face to face with Day Curtis himself. Except, there is one story.

Curtis had a reputation all his own, something of a legend going for him, even before *Napoleon* disappeared with almost all hands. The Trade War had broken the Confederation in three neat pieces, and there were plenty of captains running through the guns on all three sides, taking cargo to wherever it was meant, or not meant, to go, for a suitable fee, and not averse to accumulating extra merchandize if they came across it in the Warp Lanes. Curtis was unique in that he'd hire out to any side at any time, and simultaneously commit acts of piracy against the very side he was running for. The reason he still got paid was he could make *Napoleon* play games with the time streams and the Warp that are technically impossible, even today. If you could outbid everyone else and buy him, he'd get whatever it was that had to be got to wherever it was it had to go. No matter what was in the way: Sonic barriers, radiation strips, a flotilla of fully-armed attack vessels. More than once he split a fleet in two, led one half away through the Warps, now visible and now not, eventually bringing them back by the hand straight into the cannon of the second half who were still waiting for him. He would slip between like a coin through a slot, while they, reacting to pre-primed targets, inadvertently blasted hell out of each other. But you'll have heard the stories about Curtis and his ship, everyone has.

Tempi Parameter was a truce zone then, because it had to be. There were only two wheels spinning in those days, and everybody needed them, whichever part of the Confederation owned you. There was every kind of craft passing in and out: Patrol runners, battle cruisers, destroyers, merchantmen, smugglers and privateers. And the crews knew better than not to keep quiet when they met each other in the corridors, the diners and the bars. With ships diving in and out of time like fish through water, and only a couple of safe places to go between, you bowed to the rule and you left your gun at the entry port. Some of the most notorious desperadoes that ever took to space came through here, time and time again, on their way to and from mayhem. But even in that kind of company, Day Curtis stood out.

A slight dark man, with the sombre pallor most spacers get, a type of moon-tan, and those thick-fringed Roman-Byzantine eyes you find in frescoes on Earth. You may have seen news-video of him. There was some, the Cycle *Napoleon* towed that shelled liner, the *Aurigos*, through her enemy lines into harbour on Lyra—for the bounty, of course. Or the occasion the entire three segments of the split Confederation each put a price on his head, and most of his brother pirates went out to get him and never got him. He was even finer-made then he looks in those old videos, but the expression was the same. He never joked, he never even smiled. It wasn't any act, anything he'd lost or become. Whatever it is that smooths the edges of human isolation, that was the item he'd come into life without. His crew treated him like a stone king. They knew he could run the show, and with something extra, a sort of cold genius, and they trusted him to do it. But they hated him in about the same measure as they respected him, which was plenty. He had a tongue like a razor blade. You got cut once, and that was enough. Since he was handsome, women liked him all right, until they learned they couldn't get anywhere with him. The ones that kept trying were usually sorry. All that being the case, the story, this last story I ever heard about Day Curtis, is probably apocryphal. The man who told it me didn't claim it wasn't.

I heard that last story two years after I saw the *Napoleon* from the Fourth Walk. I heard it on the twenty that they closed up the Rouelle Etoile. It was the ninth Cycle, and the day after the tempest smashed those fifteen ships to tinder between Sirtis and the Dagon Strip. I can remember it very well, even without Recall. The bar despoiled, naked and hollow, seeming to echo, the way a dying venue does, with all the voices, the music, the colours that have ever existed in it. A team of men were portioning up that huge glissade of a chandelier, lifting it on to dollys, and carrying it away. The piano was long gone, but there were the dim sheer notes of a girl quietly sobbing to herself, somewhere nearby. I never knew the reason; someone on one of those ships, maybe, had belonged to her. . . . The man and I were finishing the last flask of Noira brandy, at the counter in the midst of the suspirating desolation. And we grew warm and sad, and he told me the story.

And outside the oval ports, innocent and terrible, the field of space and timelessness hung on the rim of the vignette, a starless winter night.

The Rouelle Etoile was almost deserted, that twenty. There was some big action out at zero 98, and the ships had lifted off like vultures, to join in or to scavenge. The tall marble clock against the wall said nineteen fifteen, but the blue pianist was still rolling the tide of his hands up and down the keys. About four or five customers were sitting around chewing trouble, or playing Shot over on the indigo baize. And in one of the corner booths was Day Curtis. *Napoleon* was in dock, had come in two twenties before with a hole in her flank, and the crew were going all out to patch her over well enough to take her out into 98 and see what was left worth mopping up. But it didn't look as if the repairs were going to make it in time, and at eighteen hundred Curtis had walked into the Rouelle with a look like dead lightning in the backs of his eyes. Curtis seldom showed when he was angry, but he could drink like dry sand, and that's what he was doing, steadily and coldly drinking the soul out of the bar, when the woman came in.

She looked late twenties, with hair black as the blackest thing you ever saw, which might be space, or an afterimage of some sun, cropped short across the crown, but growing out into one long free-slung black comma across her neck and shoulders. She had the spacer's tawny paleness otherwise, and one of the poured dresses that went with the Rouelle, almost the same colour as she was. She was off one of the ships that had stayed in dock, an artisan's shuttle that had no quarrel with anyone in particular, but she walked in as if she'd come on a dare, ready to fight, or to run. She went straight to the bar counter and ordered one of the speciality cocktails, which she drank straight down, not looking at anyone or anything. Then she ordered another, and holding it poised in the long stems of her fingers, she turned and confronted the room. She moved like a dancer, and she had the unique magic which comes with a beauty that surpasses its name, a glamour that doesn't fit in any niche or under any label. Four or five of the men in the bar were staring at her, but her gaze passed on over them with a raking indifference. She was obviously searching for something and, the impression was, hoping not to find it. Then her eyes reached the corner booth, and Curtis.

It's possible he may have noticed her when she came in, or he may not. But implacable scrutiny, even in a truce zone, is frequently the prologue to trouble. After a second or so, he lifted his head slowly, and looked back at her. Her face didn't change, but the glass dropped through her fingers and smashed on the polished floor.

For about a quarter of a minute she kept still, but there was a sort of electricity playing all around her, the invisible kind a wire exudes when there's a storm working up in the stratosphere. Then, she kicked the broken glass lightly out of her way, and she walked very fast and direct, over to Curtis' table. He'd kept on watching her, they all had, even the Sirtian pianist, though his hands never missed the up and down flow of the piano keys. The woman had the appearance of being capable of anything, up to and including the slinging of a fine-honed stiletto right across the bar into Curtis' throat. Only a blind man would have ignored her. Maybe not even a blind man.

When she reached the table, the slim hand that had let go the glass flared out like a cobra and slashed Curtis across the face.

"Well," she said, "you win the bet. What am I supposed to pay you?"

He'd had these one-sided scenes with women before, and supposedly assumed this was only another, one more girl he had forgotten. He said to her, matter-of-factly, "I'm sure you can find your own way out of here."

"Yes," she said, "I remember now. You warned me. Last time."

"I probably warned you you were a fool, too. Either get out of the bar. Or I will."

"Fifteen years is a long time," she said. Her eyes were like scorched freckled topaz, and there were white flowers enamelled on her crimson nails. "I presume I've changed. Even if you haven't. Oh, but I don't expect you to recollect me. How could you? I just wanted to see, to understand—"

Curtis got up. He was moving by her when she caught at his arms. Her face was stark with the genuine terror the anger had been all along, and she said flatly: "Suddenly I've worked it out. I do understand. I've been afraid for years, and now I know why. You're dead, Curtis. Or you will be. Tomorrow—soon—"

She'd started to retreat from him even while she said it, in a dazed, bewildered glide, but of course now he reached out and caught her back. A threat was a threat, and even a woman off an artisan's vessel could be in Confederation pay.

"All right," he said, holding her pinned. "I'm interested. Tell me more about my death."

"I'm sorry," she said. "Please let go."

"I let go when I hear what you have to say. Perhaps."

"I don't, after all, have anything to say."

"What a shame. Let me prompt you. You're dead, Curtis. Or you will be."

"We all could be," she said with an attempt at sombre lightness. "There's a war going on out there."

"There's a war going on in here," he said. "You just started it."

"You're hurting me."

"Not yet."

She went on looking at him and he went on holding her. The room was full of piano currents and utter listening silence.

"I'll tell you," she said. "Let me sit down, and I'll tell you."

He nodded, and she slid into the booth, but he kept a grip on her wrist. They sat facing each other, almost holding hands, almost like lovers, ignoring the rest of the room, and he said to her gentle,

"In case you forget this is a truce zone, you'd better bear it in mind I can break your wrist in two seconds flat."

She smiled dismally.

"I believe you would."

"What's more important, I believe it."

She looked at the table-top between them.

"This is going to be difficult."

"Only for you."

She said bitterly, "you know, you're almost funny."

"The word funeral," he said, "also begins with the word fun. Think about it."

"All right." Her eyelids tensed like two pale golden wings pasted across her eyes. Then her face smoothed out, relaxed, lost every trace of character. She might have been a doll, and her voice might have been a tape. "When I was sixteen, around half my lifetime ago, I was here in Tempi. I was travelling in my grandfather's ship, the *Hawk*, before the war really hotted up. We'd come from Sirtis and we were heading for Syracuse. The ship was just a little cargo runner, completely legitimate and authorised up to the hilt. He wasn't expecting any trouble—the cargo was safe and dull—and he'd brought me along to get me out of military school for a few months. I was so glad to be away, glad to be playing female and adult, and not just guns. He brought me in here, and gave me my first sunburst in a tall narrow glass. About seventeen hundred all the Alert panels started going off. An unscheduled life-boat had blown into the Parameter. The markings were scalded off, and when they got the casings open, there was only one man in it. There was quite a squall then, because the name of the vessel he claimed to have come from wasn't down on any of the listings. Besides, he was talking about a tempest out on zero 98, a time gale that cost him his ship, and there was no gale registering anywhere. Even so, he kept insisting there must be other survivors to be pulled in, but no one came, and when they used the sonar to scan, they picked up nothing, just as they weren't picking up the gale. They questioned the man from the life-boat until about nineteen hundred, and then they let him come into the Rouelle Etoile, with an official escort. He went over to the bar counter, and then he turned and looked right round the room. There was quite a crowd. My granddaddy was playing Shot over on the baize, and I was sitting exactly where you are now, in my grown-up frock, with one of the young helmsmen off the *Hawk*. The man who'd come in out of space looked at everyone until he got to me. Then he walked across. He dragged me to my feet and held me by my shoulders, and he swore at me. Jove, my helmsman, landed out at him, and the stranger thunked poor Jove across the head. Granddaddy came running with the official escort, and there was something of a fight. When somebody finally laid the stranger out with one of those chunk ashtrays from the bar, I took stock of my feelings. I was scared, horrified, and very flattered. It was all crazy. But I looked at the crazy stranger on the floor, with blood running through his hair, and he was the most beautiful man I'd ever seen, and, for whatever reason, I was the one he'd singled out. Quite logically, though I didn't know it at the time, I fell in love with him. And it was you, Day Curtis.'' She raised her eyes again, and gazed at him again. ''You. Exactly as you are now. And I was sixteen.''

There was a pause. Curtis appeared bored, and simultaneously very dangerous. When she didn't continue, he said:

''If I let you go on, I imagine you'll eventually reveal why you're giving me this time cliché myth.''

''The nature of time,'' she said, as coldly as he. ''What do we really know about it? Two thousand streams, and us playing about in them like salmon.''

''The kind of time paradox you're doling out is the sort of

junk a Parameter is there to invalidate. Assuming it could even happen. You should change your brand of dream pills.''

"All right, mister,'' she said. "Do I go on, or do I get out?''

He sat and studied her. He said,

"You can tell it to the end.''

"Thank you,'' she said icily.

"It'll be interesting, seeing you hit the rotten wood and fall right through it.''

"Damn you,'' she said.

"It takes more than you to do that.''

She stared at the table-top again. She said:

"They put you—it *was* you, Curtis—in the Medical centre on the Second Level. Guess what I did?'' She glanced at him, and away. "I was sixteen, and I was in love. I went to your room. You were sitting staring out of the port at that blind-black Parameter sky, and your eyes looked just as black. . . . though they're not black at all, are they? Never mind. You said: What the hell do you want? Wasn't that a tender greeting? I didn't know what to do, whether to fight you or surrender, or go away, or stay. I stayed. I stayed, Curtis. And gradually you started to tell me. About the time storm, about the number of the Cycle— fifteen years on from where it really was. You told me how I'd be when I was thirty-one, and how I'd walk into the Rouelle in the last hours of this twenty, and I'd see you, and drop my glass on the floor. . . . I had to come in here tonight, to act it out. I didn't think you'd be here. No. I did think you would. But if you were, it had to be some joke. You'd be in your forties. You'd laugh at me. But you're not in your forties, and, my God, you're not laughing. You're just the way you told me, warned me, you'd be, that night I was sixteen and you told me not to come to Tempi ever again. But I had to. You can see that. Anyway, my ship came through Tempi, I didn't have any choice this time. I could hardly have avoided it.''

She stopped, and detached one of the long white cigarettes from the dispenser. She drew on it and the ignition crystal broke, and the end glowed a pale, dull rose. The smoke made a design round her words as she said: "Tomorrow you take your ship out and you meet the storm. Your ship dies out there in the Warp Lanes. So do you. It's just some part of you that's left wandering there, lost, unaligned. And somehow, I draw you back, to the wrong Cycle, the wrong time, back to that night I was sixteen and I sat here in the Rouelle Etoile. I said, some part of you. Much more than that. You. It had to be because—'' she faltered remotely, as if reading from a board abruptly obscured. Then, "I made you come back out of nowhere, and you hated me for it. It was the first intense emotion you'd ever felt for any human being. I think you wanted to kill me more than anything. And I think I'd have let you kill me. My own first really intense emotion, too."

"So," he said, "you got laid to the sound of discordant violins."

She smiled tightly.

"You should know. Unfortunately, you can't. It's my past, your future."

"There are two alternatives," he said. "Either you're insane, or someone paid you to spook me about the next flight I take. Which is it?"

"No one paid me."

"Which means you were paid. I hope you kept the money. You may need it for medical expenses."

"Even if you kill me tonight, which you don't, I'd still be waiting for you, in my yesterday. Tomorrow you'll come out of space, and I'll be there." She finished the cigarette, and let it die in the glass ashtray. "I don't think," she said, "you had any right to come back out of death and time and space and haunt me, and ruin my life. I don't think you have any right to be here, in my future, and ruin it again. I shouldn't have tried to find you. But how could I resist?"

Curtis was no longer touching her, just his eyes, fixed on her, long lids blinking now and then, that was all. The rest of the room hadn't been able to hear their conversation once it was trapped inside the booth, a low, coldly-impassioned murmur of two voices, but mostly her voice, saying what she claimed to be the truth to him, as if it were a poem, the monologue from some play. So the room cast a look at them now and then, but nothing else. The two Shot players had even finished up and left the bar. And the pianist kept the dark blue tides coming and going on the piano keys, and the chandelier snowed its lights.

"I don't want you to die," she said finally.

"I can make you deliriously happy then," he said, "because I don't intend to."

"I wish," she said, "I could show you the proof of what happened. If I could prove it to you—if I could convince you— But I was sixteen, and the proof got lost, snatched and swept away, like everything else." She met his eyes again, for a long, long time, and then she said, "I don't think you have a soul anyway. Not this Cycle. I gave you a soul. It grew inside you, like the hate you felt for me, unless it wasn't hate at all. And in the end, it looked back at me out of your eyes. But your eyes tonight are like the flat discs of sunglasses.''

He said: "If it meant so much, why didn't I stay with you?"

It was the first, and the only admission, that he accepted what she said—not as factual or possible, certainly neither of those—but as a fiction worthy of analysis. But he said it with an edge to his voice that could have skinned an apple.

She said softly, "you couldn't or wouldn't, or weren't allowed to. Or maybe, if you were some extraordinary kind of ghost, the power to survive in time is limited. Like light-cells. Or an echo. Except—" she put her hands together as if examining some element caught between them. "Next twenty you were gone. They searched. The theory was you'd stolen one of the Wheel's own life-boats. I suppose one might have been missing. My grandfather said none was. But that was the theory. The wreck you'd come in on had disintegrated under the tests they'd been subjecting it to. They'd been careful, and that surprised them, but it can happen. As I say, you'd vanished without trace. Almost. Almost." She waited, long enough for seven or eight bars of piano melody to fill the gap between them. At last she said: "You're not going to ask me what, if anything, you left behind. Are you?"

The piano shivered like silver leaves, and he was no longer watching her. Two tears, like silken streamers, unravelled from her eyes. They didn't spoil either her looks or her make-up, and presently they dried and might never have been.

The glow dawned through the Rouelle's marble clock that showed one twenty was folding over into another.

The woman got up. She walked to the bar counter and bought a triple Noira brandy, and took it to the piano, setting the black-gold glass where the Sirtian could reach it. He bowed to her, like the prince he was, and she leaned forward and said something in his ear. He let the waves roll on over the keys while he thought, searching back through the storerooms of his brain to look out what she'd asked for, then, not breaking the rhythm, he tipped the tides of the music over into it. It was one of those old songs the Rouelle Etoile was so adept at conjuring. One of the songs from the celluloid era of twentieth century Earth. In those same years, on Sirtis, they'd been raising temples of cloudy fire, like blue winter suns. But on the screens of Earth, the black and white flickering women, in their high-shouldered dresses that clung to them like snakes, the thin, bruised-eyed men, burning smokily out like the cigarettes in their mouths, had danced and fought and wise-cracked and loved. And all the while the wild pure stars had been waiting, and the Nature of Time, and, two hundred years away another era, of looking back, full circle, amazed, into recognisable eyes and hearts and minds. Everything changes, people, never. No, they never do.

The woman leaned by the piano, listening to the Sirtian play the song, her head averted from the booth. When the song ended, she turned, and Curtis was gone.

About five hours later, her own ship pulled off from the wheel. Nothing happened to the ship, she got wherever she was going, and so did the woman who had sat in the bar with Curtis. Afterwards, no one knew her name. The artisan ship's listing had ten female crew aboard, three female passengers. She could have been anyone of those. She became a beautiful strange event, a story that got told around. Because nobody in the bar heard much of the conversation between her and Curtis, guess-work calcified round it, staled it, defused it, and, at length, changed it into just another anecdote, which probably isn't true.

What happened with Day Curtis himself, of course, is known pretty precisely.

At one-o-seven of the new twenty, he walked along the gantry to the bay where *Napoleon* lay in her repair webbing like a vast wounded whale. Despite earlier predictions, her crew had got her patched, welded and in fair shape. Certainly she looked sound enough to take the trip out to 98. Sonic reports were still coming in on that one, and a couple of liners were reportedly adrift, split wide open, and treasure-trove swirling out of them as if from cornucopia. Some of the little lazy ships were even sneaking out now into Warp; the lions and the jackals would be feeding together.

Curtis' crew were eager to be part of the show, and they hadn't anticipated he would be any different in his reaction. Then Curtis knocked the walkway from under them by cancelling the drive order and grounding the ship.

He didn't give any reason, but that wasn't uncommon. Generally the reason for anything he did would have been self-explanatory. Not now, of course.

If you credit the story of the black-haired woman, obviously you can figure out what the reason may have been. Curtis didn't credit her, but he did credit she was working on him, and for a larger stake than a fifteen-year-old love-affair. Whoever was really behind the scene in the Rouelle, had made particular deductions based on Curtis' presumed psychological patterns. Warned off going back into Warp that twenty, Curtis would, contradictorily, throw himself and his ship into immediate action. Or so somebody might have supposed. And if that was what they had predicted and wanted him to do, there must be some excellent reason also for their desires. Perhaps some very special welcome had been rigged for him, out in the Warp. Or the ship herself might have received some extra-special attention. . . . If the girl in the Rouelle had been meant to push him into some type of contrary and precipitate heroism, she had failed. Though not believing her warning, he could act as if he did. Intended to race *Napoleon* away into space, he could stay put, and watch for what new developments occurred. And for which individuals, or which organisation, was revealed by them.

Curtis gave his grounding order, and walked back along the gantry.

He had a crew who respected him totally, and, in most cases, hated him in equal measure. Up until then, their wants and their ambitions had run concurrently with his own. Now they'd been slaving on the tall white hip of *Napoleon*, in a blaze of sweat, steam and laserburn, and he strolled over from the bar and killed their hopes of loot and blood, the reward they always needed to have from him in lucre or kind, because he never offered it any other way.

Half an hour after Curtis walked off the gantry, *Napoleon's* Second Officer, a man named Doyeneau, led a ten minute mutiny. By two thirty, *Napoleon* was free of the Parameter and scorching out towards zero 98.

At two thirty-five, a message was sent back to Curtis at Tempi. He'd made the one immortal mistake of his career, and the message showed it. They were angry enough, that crew of his, to steal his ship, but much too afraid of him to sue for pardon. They would never be back. He must have known he'd lost everything, and when the second message came in, the automatic tracker on sonic, it was only the second most terrible error that twenty.

An hour out into the Warp, a little storm came up. It was so small it could have passed like the blow of a child's fist striking the hull. But Doyeneau, already in a kind of panic, panicked himself into an avoidance manoeuvre Curtis had contrived maybe a hundred times. Doyeneau dove the ship at the eye of the storm, to break the barriers and get through, but there was no eye in this storm, only a centre of spurling matter. And when, caught up in that, Doyeneau gave his order to jump the stream, one continuum to another, *Napoleon's* patched casing blew, and took out most of the side of the ship.

There is no sound in space, we all know that. No sound, no air, no stopping place. A long fall that never ends, the bottomless pit. Picture a great white fish, cloven in one curving side, shrivelling away and away down those empty rivers, her diesel-pod fluttering like a scarlet ember, dying.

At least, that's how it goes. No one was ever entirely sure, since no one ever got back from *Napoleon*. They pieced a few fragments together from sounds picked up, a whole Cycle after, on the delay play-back of the sonar here at Tempi. Her death is surmise. Like a lot of things.

Curtis lit off somewhere, at sometime. The scenario and the characterisation grow vague from the moment that his ship vanished, as if he had lost his soul. The last salient fact is that, one seven-mooned night on Syracuse, in an alley near the space-dock, someone, who is supposed to have resembled Curtis closely, negotiated a deal to run an unspecified cargo out beyond Andromeda, in a merchantman whose name has not survived. This may or may not have been Curtis, but the far stars are pretty far away. Legends burn out there, good and bad, and reputations dwindle. And there was never anything to stop him altering his name, beyond a touch of legal wrangling. Whatever caused it, you lose him like a echo, out somewhere among the rumours and the cold green suns.

As for the story about the woman in the Rouelle Etoile, as I said before, it's probably apocryphal. If it weren't, that sort of time paradox is too absurd to handle. It would be crazy enough for a man to get free of an exploding ship, take off in a life-boat, and then home in on a timeless zone—in the wrong time. And to arrive Cycles out of synchronization, because a girl had drawn him there simply by forewarning him that she would—for that, actually, is what her warning entails. . . . Yes, all that's crazy enough. But then to add this other, crazier, time paradox on top of it: He ducked. The one thing the time cliché can't take, that was what he did. He *avoided* it. He wasn't *on* the *Napoleon* when she perished. So how could he home in, a magnetised time-ghost, to this whirling ironex wheel, outside of which, in the cool pool of the Parameter, time stands irreparably static?

Clever of you to spot I'm heading somewhere. There is a sort of epilogue. Take it as you find it.

Remember, I said the story was told me on the twenty that they closed the Rouelle Etoile for keeps, the twenty after the tempest. The girl was softly crying her little lost piano notes in the background, the dead chandelier had been trundled away, and the brandy flask was almost dry. Remember, too, I said no

one here had ever come face to face with the ghost of Day Curtis
on the wheel at Tempi. Except, there is one story. It's mine. I
came face to face with that ghost, and all through that sombre
twenty, I sat in the Rouelle with him, drinking brandy. Listening
to what he had to say. It truly was Curtis, at least to look at, the
elegant build, the moon-tan skin, the dark hair, the Roman eyes.
But he was about thirty-five years of age, and Curtis wasn't his
name. And he wasn't a ghost.

You may have wondered how I knew, or how he knew to tell
me, what their conversation was, the woman and Curtis, in the
booth, which had been so low the rest of the room couldn't hear
it. But maybe she told someone. Found them and told them.
Remember what she said to Curtis? About proof, and how it had
been snatched away? Or perhaps my-Curtis-who-wasn't made it
up. Perhaps he'd seen the old videos and a freak likeness to
another man, and it took his fancy to pretend, and that's all he
was doing. Playing pirates. Sons of pirates.

But if you accept the story, only for a moment, she was
sixteen, and very likely quite innocent. She could have had a
child, although how, in any one's book, can a time-ghost convey
biological life?

The place where the Rouelle used to be is a storage bay now.
But sometimes, when you're alone up there with black nothing
crowding against the ports, you can hear the Sirtian's piano still
playing, far away. It's the stutter of the sonar link-pipes in the
walls, it has to be. There's no time in a white hole, and no true
past, and no true future, no matter what the future brings. As for
lovers, they come and go, welcome or not. And as for time,
outside the Confederation's thirty-eight Parameters, and the thirty-
six spinning ironex wheels, it's there. It goes by.

THE HARVEST OF WOLVES
by Mary Gentle

This is a "1984" sort of story and what is described may be coming to pass not too long after 1984. This sort of thing has happened already in certain instances; it may become the life our immediate descendants will know—if we don't watch out.

Flix sat in the old sagging armchair, leaned forward, and tore another page from the *Encyclopaedia Brittanica*. The fire took it, flickering in the grate.

"What the—" the boy, closing the door as he entered, strode across the room and slapped the book out of her hand. "What's the matter with you? You could *sell* that for—"

"For money to buy fuel?" Flix suggested. Adrenalin made her dizzy. She looked down at her liver-spotted hands, where the veins stood up with age; they were shaking. "Thank you, I prefer to cut out the middle man. Self sufficiency."

He glared; she doubted he recognized irony.

"You're crazy, you know that?"

"If you know it, that ought to be enough. Have you put in your report yet?" She shot the question at him.

He was still young enough to blush. Angry because of it, he snarled, "You keep your mouth shut, citizen. You hear me?"

"I hear you." Age makes you afraid, Flix thought. Pacifying him, she said "Well, what have you brought me?"

"Bread. Milk's out. Can't deliver, there's no transport. I got you some water, though. It's clean."

You wouldn't know clean water if it bit you. Flix thought bitterly. She watched the boy unpacking the plastic bag he carried, throwing the goods into the nearest cupboard. He was growing taller by the week, this one; broad-shouldered with close-cropped black hair, and the changing voice of adolescence.

"Marlow," she said, "what makes you choose community service?"

"Didn't choose it, did I? Got given it, didn't I?"

He straightened, stuffed the bag in the pocket of his uniform jacket, and came over to squat beside the open fire. Though he never admitted it, it attracted him. Probably because he'd never before been in a house old enough to have a grate, she thought.

" 'Community service'," she repeated, unable to keep the edge out of her voice. "Snooping under cover of charity; you call that service? Bringing Welfare rations, weighing me up . . . and all the time new laws, and cutting it closer every time, eh? If they've got as far as these slums, Marlow boy, then pretty soon we'll all be gone."

Resentment glared out of him. "Think I want to come here? Crazy old house, crazy old bitch—"

"That's 'citizen' to you, if you can't manage 'Flix'." She offered him a crumpled pack of cigarettes, forcing a smile. "Only tobacco, I'm afraid."

The Pavlovian response: "Filthy things'll give you cancer."

"Ah, who'll get me first, then: lung cancer, hypothermia, starvation—or you and your bloody Youth Corps?"

"You got no room to talk—it was your lot got us in this mess in the first place." He stood up. "You think we want to live like this, no jobs, nothing? You got no idea. If it weren't for the Corps I'd be—"

"You'd be waiting out your time on Welfare," Flix said, very carefully. "Seeing the deadline come up. You'd be being tested— like I am now—to see how fit you are to survive. To qualify for government food. To get government water, so you don't die of cholera. Government housing, so you don't die of cold. Instead you're here, waiting for me to—"

"That's the way it is," Marlow said. He lowered his head, glaring at her from dark, hollowed eyes. (Why, she thought, he's been losing sleep.) "You got to produce. You got to work. You got to be worth keeping on Welfare. Or else—and don't tell me it ain't fair. I know it ain't fair, but that's the way it is."

"Ah," she said, on a rising inflection, "is that the way it is."

"*Look* at you!" He swung his arm round, taking in the single-room flat. The wallpaper was covered by old posters, garish with the slogans of halcyon '90s (that final, brief economic flowering) when protest was easy. Planks propped up on bricks served as shelves for old books and pamphlets and magazines. Some had sat so long in the same place that the damp had made of them an inseparable mass. A long-disconnected computer terminal gathered dust, ancient access codes scratched on the casing. Cracking china lay side by side on the drainer with incongruously new plastic dishes, and a saucepan full of something brown and long-burned sat on the stove. A thin film of plaster from the ceiling had drifted down onto the expanse of worn linoleum, left empty by the clustering of table, chair, and bed round the open fire.

Flix poked the ashes with a burnt slat, and glanced up at the windows. Beyond the wire-mesh, the sky was gray.

"You could fix those boards," she said. "There's a wind whips through there could take the barnacles off a ship's hull, since your friends left me with no glass in the windows. . . . What, no reaction?"

"You can't blame them." The boy sounded tired, and very adult. "Thinking of you in here. Eating, sleeping. Doing nothing to earn it."

"Christ!" Flix exploded, and saw him flinch at the word as he always did. But now she wasn't goading him for her amusement. "There was a time you didn't have to *earn* the right to live! You had it—as a human being!"

"Yeah," he said wearily, "I know. I heard about that. I hear about it all the time from my old man. Free this, free that, free the other; holidays in the sun, cars for everybody, everybody working—yeah, I heard. And what happens? What do you leave for *us?* You let the niggers come in and steal your jobs, you let the Yanks put their missiles here! You let kids grow up wild 'cause their mothers were never home; you sell us out to the Reds—"

"Oh, spare me. If you're going to be bigoted, at least be original!"

"Citizen," Marlow said, "shut up."

Not quite under her breath she said, "Ignorant pig."

He yelled, "Why don't you clean this place up? *You* live like a pig!"

"I was never one for housework—and besides, I've got you to do it for me, haven't I? Courtesy of the Welfare state. Until such time as the state decides I'm not worth keeping alive."

His would not be the first report made on her (though the first under this name), but time and purges had culled the number of officials willing to turn a blind eye on changes of code, name, and location.

I am, Flix thought, too old for this fugitive life.

"Pig," Marlow repeated absently. He rummaged around in

the toolbox by the window, and began nailing the slats back over the lower windowsill.

"There's coffee in the cupboard." Flix made a peace-offering of it. "Have some if you want it. You'll have to boil the kettle. I think the power's still on."

"Where'd you get *coffee?*"

"I still have friends," Flix observed sententiously. "They can't do much, being as they're old like me; but what they can do, they will. The old network's still there."

"Subversive," he accused.

Lord Brahma! I can't seem to keep off it today, Flix thought. What is it with me—do I *want* to die? Well, maybe. But not to suit their convenience.

"Do you ever listen to anything except what they tell you?"

Marlow whacked the last nail in viciously, threw down the hammer, and stalked over to the sink. Filling the kettle, his back to her, he said, "I know what's right. I know what's true."

"I am sick to death of people who *know*. I want people who aren't sure. I want people who're willing to admit there's another side to the argument—or even that there is an argument, for Christ's sake! Marlow, will you bloody look at me!"

He plugged the kettle in. Turning, and leaning back against the chipped unit: "What?"

"You don't believe all that bullshit." Again, he flinched. They are abnormally sensitive, she thought. "You can't believe it, you're not the age. Sixteen's when you go round questioning everything."

"Maybe in your day. It's different now. We got to grow up quick or not at all." He shrugged. "Listen, I'm looking back at it, what it was like—I can see what you can't. While you sat round talking, the commies were taking over the unions; and if it hadn't been for Foster we'd be a satellite state today—"

Flix groaned. "Jesus. Marlow, tell me all the shit you like, tell me we were all commie pinko perverts, tell me we were capitalist running dogs who brought the world to ruin—" she was laughing, an old woman's high cackle "—but in the name of God, don't tell me about your precious Foster! I knew all I needed to know about dictators before you were born!"

His mouth twisted. She could see him lose patience with her.

"You don't know what it's like," Marlow said. "Five of us in a two-room flat, and the power not on, and never enough food, and for why? Because there's no work, and if there was, there's nothing to buy with the money! At least he's making it better. At least there's less of that."

"Where do you go when there's nowhere to go?" Flix asked rhetorically. "I'd OD if you could get the stuff, but that's another thing banned in your bloody utopia. Fetch us the coffee, Marlow, and hand me that half-bottle in the top cupboard."

He was as disapproving as any Youth Cadet, but he did what she asked. Whiskey, and coffee (the last now, the very last) bit into her gut. I am fighting, she reminded herself sourly, I am fighting—God knows why—for my life.

"I suppose it's no good offering you a drink? No, I thought not. Hell, Marlow, loosen up, will you?"

She had, over the weeks, gained some small amusement from tormenting him. Like all of Foster's New Puritans, the Corps strongly disapproved of drugs, blasphemy, lechery—and there, she thought, is a fine old-fashioned word. Not that I've quite got round to that . . . but wouldn't he react beautifully! Or is it that I'm afraid of him laughing? Or afraid of him? For all his 'community service', he's still a thug.

She tore a few more pages from the thick book, crumpled them, and poked them into the fire where they flared briefly. "What about coal, Marlow?"

"Reconstituted."

"Christ, that stuff doesn't burn. Still, what the hell. Come and sit down." She watched him kneel by the flames. In the dim cold room, the light made lines on his face; he looked older.

"In the nineties," she said speculatively, "there were, for example, parties without supervisors—supervisors!—and music without propaganda—"

"Without whose propaganda?"

"Bravo, Marlow!" She clapped gently. "Without theirs, of course. With ours. Now it's the other way round. Do you realize, I wouldn't *mind* if he had the grace to be original? But it's the same old thing; no free press, no free speech, no unions; food shortages, rabid patriotic nationalism—"

"You were traitors! Was that any better?"

No way out, she thought, no way in; God preserve us from the voice of invincible ignorance.

"One thing we didn't do," she said. "We didn't weigh people up as to how useful they were to the state—and let them die when they got sick and old."

He was quiet. "Didn't you?"

"We didn't *plan* it."

"There's less poverty now. Less misery. It's a hard world," he said. "They're starving in Asia. Dying. That's not going to

happen here. You used it up, this world. So you got yourselves
to blame if you don't like what's happening now.''

"Marlow," Flix said, "what are you going to say in your
report?''

Now there was no evading the question. He looked up with
clear puzzled eyes. "I don't want to do it.''

"I know, or it wouldn't be nearly a month overdue, would it?
No, don't ask me how I know. Like I said, the old grapevine's
still there. When are they going to start wondering, Marlow?
When are they going to start making reports on *you?*''

He stared into the fire. She got up slowly, taking her weight
on her wrists, and went across to pull on her old (now much
cracked) leather jacket. The cold got into her bones. Now would I
be so weak if there was proper food? she thought. Christ, my
mother lived to be eighty, and I'm not within twenty years of
that!

"I've got family," Marlow said. "The old man, Macy and
the baby. We got to eat.''

She could see herself reflected in the speckled wall mirror,
lost in sepia depths. An old woman, lean and straight, with spiky
cropped hair that needed washing from grey to silver. Marlow,
out of focus, was a dark uniform and the glint of insignia.

Flix looked straight at him, solemnly; and when his eyes were
fixed on her, she smiled. She had always had one of those faces,
naturally somber and sardonic, that are transformed when they
smile. Vanity doesn't go with age, she thought, savoring the
boy's unwilling reponsive grin.

"I could have shown you so much—so much. You haven't
got the guts to run wild,'' she said, "you haven't got the guts to
question.''

The implication of promise was there. He watched her. The
light dimmed, scummy and cold; and the fire glowed down to
red embers. The ever-present smell of the room, overlain for a
while by coffee and spirits, reasserted itself.

"You're a drunk," Marlow said. "D'you think I haven't seen
the bottles you throw out—and the ones you hide? Yeah, your
friends keep you supplied, all right! I've come in here when you
were dead drunk on the bed, place stinking of shit; I've listened
to you maundering on about the old days—I don't want to know!
If this is where it leaves you, I don't want to know!''

"Is that right?'' Tears stung behind her eyes, her voice thinned.
"You'll never live the life I lived, and you'll never know how I
regret it passing—ah, Jesus, it tears you up, to know it's gone
and gone for good. *You* were the people we wanted to help. I

mean you, Marlow! And when it came to actually thinking—
God knows how difficult that is—you didn't want to know.
You'd sooner march with your mobs. You'd sooner smash places
up on your witch-hunts. You'd sooner cheer the tanks when they
roll by. And God help you, that's not enough, you've got to
think you're *right!*''

The boy crossed the room and pushed her. She fell back on
the bed with an ugly sound. He stamped back and forth, sweeping the cracked cups crashing to the floor. Violently he kicked at
the piles of old books and pamphlets. They scattered in soggy
lumps.

"This!" he shouted. "You preach about your precious books
and you burn them to keep warm! You talk about your 'subversive
network' but what is it really? Old men and women hoarding
food and drink, keeping it from us who need it!"

She, breathing heavily and conscious of pain, didn't answer.
His first energy spent, he came back and helped her into the
chair; and made up the fire until it blazed. The cold wind blew
belches of gray smoke back into the room.

Flix felt down into the side of the chair for the hidden bottle
there; fist knotted about it, letting the alcohol sting her back to
life. When she looked up again he was putting on his coat.

As if nothing had happened, she said, "Books aren't sacred.
Ideas are, and I've got those up here." She touched her lank
hair. "Whatever else we are, we subversives, I'll tell you this—we
care about each other. That's more than your Corps will do for
you when you're old."

"I'll come in again tomorrow." He was all boy now; gangling,
uncertain, sullen.

"I don't care if you don't agree with me! Just think about
what you're doing—for once, *think* about it!"

At the door he turned back and said "*Will* they look after
you?"

After she heard the door slam, she plugged the power outlet
into the antique stereo equipment, and played old and much-
mended '90s revival-rock cassettes, blasting the small room full
of sound. It served to stop the treadmill-turning of her mind.

"You've got a letter!" Taz yelled down the stairs after her the
next morning. She grunted, not taking any notice; the old man
(occupier of the building's only other inhabitable room) was
given to delusions, to happenings that were years after their time.

But when she crossed the hallway it lay there in the crepuscu-
lar light: a thin rough-paper envelope folded and addressed to

Citizen Felicity Vance. Flix picked it up, wincing at the pain in her back. An immature hand, the letters mostly printed. So she knew.

She took it into her room, closing the door and resting her old bones on the bed.

Where is there anyone I can tell? she thought. That's another one of the boy's taunts—'if you had a husband, citizen.' Ah, but I could never live in anyone's company but my own.

Now it came to it she was afraid. Shaking, sweating; the old cold symptoms. She opened the letter.

"Citizen—

"I have to tell the truth. They check up on me too. It is the truth. You drink too much and your alone and cant take care. I have to live. If your friends are good friends you better tell them I sent my report in. Its not your fault things are like this. Im sorry I said it was. Sometimes I wisht I lived in the old days it might have been good. But I dont think so not for most of us.

"Peter Marlow"

She dressed slowly; fashions once adopted from a mythical past and previous revolutions: old jeans and sweater and the ancient leather jacket—the smell took her back, with the abruptness of illusion, to boys and bikes and books; to bright libraries, computer networks; to Xerox and duplicators, to faxsheets in brilliant colors that had been going to change the world.

He believes I'm a drunken old woman, alone, friends no more than geriatrics; he has to report me or be reported himself—and does he hope that it's more than an illusion, that some secret subversive organization still exists to whisk me off to—what? Safety? Where?

Things are bad all over, kid.

But at least he's sent in the report.

She left, locking the door behind her. It was a long time and a long walk to where she could borrow a working telephone. When she called the number, it was a while before it was answered; and a while before he remembered her name.

"Well," Flix said, "you'll have had the report by now."

"You're a fool," the man said. "You won't last a week in the Welfare camps! Flix—"

"I'll last long enough to tell what I know," Flix said. "About you—and who your father was—and what 'societies' you used to belong to. I'll do it, Simon. Maybe it won't make much difference, maybe it won't even lose you your job. But you won't have much of a career afterwards."

After a pause he said, "What do you want?"

"I want somewhere decent to live. I want to be warm. I want enough to eat, I want to play my music and read my books in peace. That's all. I'm tired of living like a pig! I want a place like the one you've got put by for yourself when *you* get old. No Welfare camps for Foster's boys, right? Now they'll put me in one—they can't ignore that report—and when they do, you know what I'm going to say!"

She could feel his uncertainty over the line, knew she had to weight things in her favor.

"Would it help," she said, "if you could turn in a few of the old subversive cells, by way of a sweetener? Those that didn't know you, those that can't give us away."

" 'Us'." His tone reluctantly agreed complicity, barely masked contempt. "Names?"

"Names after, not before."

And he agreed.

Flix grinned to herself, a fox-grin full of teeth and no humor. You and me both, Marlow, she thought; you and me both. . . .

"Like someone once told me," she said, "I have to live."

HOMEFARING
by Robert Silverberg

*Glimpses of the farthest future are always tan-
talizing. Here, the master hand of a master of the
imagination takes us beyond the age of mammals,
beyond the age of cities and machines, across a
billion years to an Earth very different from this
one where an intelligence abides that is both
familiar and unfamiliar.*

McCulloch was beginning to molt. The sensation, inescapable
and unarguable, horrified him—it felt exactly as though his body
was going to split apart, which it was—and yet it was also
completely familiar, expected, welcome. Wave after wave of
keen and dizzying pain swept through him. Burrowing down deep
in the sandy bed, he waved his great claws about, lashed his flat
tail against the pure white sand, scratched frantically with quick
worried gestures of his eight walking-legs.

He was frightened. He was calm. He had no idea what was
about to happen to him. He had done this a hundred times
before.

The molting prodrome had overwhelming power. It blotted
from his mind all questions, and, after a moment, all fear. A
white line of heat ran down his back—no, down the top of his
carapace—from a point just back of his head to the first flaring
segments of his tail-fan. He imagined that all the sun's force,
concentrated through some giant glass lens, was being inscribed
in a single track along his shell. And his soft inner body was
straining, squirming, expanding, filling the carapace to overflowing. But still that rigid shell contained him, refusing to yield
to the pressure. To McCulloch it was much like being inside a
wet-suit that was suddenly five times too small.

—*What is the sun? What is glass? What is a lens? What is a
wet-suit?*

202

The questions swarmed suddenly upward in his mind like little busy many-legged creatures springing out of the sand. But he had no time for providing answers. The molting prodrome was developing with astounding swiftness, carrying him along. The strain was becoming intolerable. In another moment he would surely burst. He was writhing in short angular convulsions. Within his claws, his tissues now were shrinking, shriveling, drawing back within the ferocious shell-hulls, but the rest of him was continuing inexorably to grow larger.

He had to escape from this shell, or it would kill him. He had to expel himself somehow from this impossibly constricting container. Digging his front claws and most of his legs into the sand, he heaved, twisted, stretched, pushed. He thought of himself as being pregnant with himself, struggling fiercely to deliver himself of himself.

Ah. The carapace suddenly began to split.

The crack was only a small one, high up near his shoulders—*shoulders?*—but the imprisoned substance of him surged swiftly toward it, widening and lengthening it, and in another moment the hard horny covering was cracked from end to end. *Ah. Ah.* That felt so good, that release from constraint! Yet McCulloch still had to free himself. Delicately he drew himself backward, withdrawing leg after leg from its covering in a precise, almost fussy way, as though he were pulling his arms from the sleeves of some incredibly ancient and frail garment.

Until he had his huge main claws free, though, he knew he could not extricate himself from the sundered shell. And freeing the claws took extreme care. The front limbs still were shrinking, and the limy joints of the shell seemed to be dissolving and softening, but nevertheless he had to pull each claw through a passage much narrower than itself. It was easy to see how a hasty move might break a limb off altogether.

He centered his attention on the task. It was a little like telling his wrists to make themselves small, so he could slide them out of handcuffs.

—Wrists? Handcuffs? What are those?

McCulloch paid no attention to that baffling inner voice. Easy, easy, there—ah—yes, there, like that! One claw was free. Then the other, slowly, carefully. Done. Both of them retracted. The rest was simple: some shrugging and wiggling, exhausting but not really challenging, and he succeeded in extending the breach in the carapace until he could crawl backward out of it. Then he lay on the sand beside it, weary, drained, naked, soft, terribly vulnerable. He wanted only to return to the sleep out of which he had emerged into this nightmare of shellsplitting.

But some force within him would not let him slacken off. A moment to rest, only a moment. He looked to his left, toward the discarded shell. Vision was difficult—there were peculiar, incomprehensible refraction effects that broke every image into thousands of tiny fragments—but despite that, and despite the dimness of the light, he was able to see that the shell, golden-hued with broad arrow-shaped red markings, was something like a lobster's, yet even more intricate, even more bizarre. McCulloch did not understand why he had been inhabiting a lobster's shell. Obviously because he was a lobster; but he was not a lobster. That was so, was it not? Yet he was underwater. He lay on fine white sand, at a depth so great he could not make out any hint of sunlight overhead. The water was warm, gentle, rich with tiny tasty creatures and with a swirling welter of sensory data that swept across his receptors in bewildering abundance.

He sought to learn more. But there was no further time for resting and thinking now. He was unprotected. Any passing enemy could destroy him while he was like this. Up, up, seek a hiding-place: that was the requirement of the moment.

First, though, he paused to devour his old shell. That too seemed to be the requirement of the moment; so he fell upon it with determination, seizing it with his clumsy-looking but curiously versatile front claws, drawing it toward his busy, efficient mandibles. When that was accomplished—no doubt to recycle the lime it contained, which he needed for the growth of his new shell—he forced himself up and began a slow scuttle, somehow knowing that the direction he had taken was the right one.

Soon came the vibrations of something large and solid against his sensors—a wall, a stone mass rising before him—and then, as he continued, he made out with his foggy vision the sloping flank of a dark broad cliff rising vertically from the ocean floor. Festoons of thick, swaying red and yellow water plants clung to it, and a dense stippling of rubbery-looking finger-shaped sponges, and a crawling, gaping, slithering host of crabs and mollusks and worms, which vastly stirred McCulloch's appetite. But this was not a time to pause to eat, lest he be eaten. Two enormous green anemones yawned nearby, ruffling their voluptuous membranes seductively, hopefully. A dark shape passed overhead, huge, tubular, tentacular, menacing. Ignoring the thronging populations of the rock, McCulloch picked his way over and around them until he came to the small cave, the McCulloch-sized cave, that was his goal.

Gingerly he backed through its narrow mouth, knowing there would be no room for turning around once he was inside. He filled the opening nicely, with a little space left over. Taking up a position just within the entrance, he blocked the cave-mouth with his claws. No enemy could enter now. Naked though he was, he would be safe during his vulnerable period.

For the first time since his agonizing awakening, McCulloch had a chance to halt: rest, regroup, consider.

It seemed a wise idea to be monitoring the waters just outside the cave even while he was resting, though. He extended his antennae a short distance into the swarming waters, and felt at once the impact, again, of a myriad sensory inputs, all the astounding complexity of the reef-world. Most of the creatures that moved slowly about on the face of the reef were simple ones, but McCulloch could feel, also, the sharp pulsations of intelligence coming from several points not far away: the anemones, so it seemed, and that enormous squid-like thing hovering overhead. Not intelligence of a kind that he understood, but that did not trouble him: for the moment, understanding could wait, while he dealt with the task of recovery from the exhausting struggles of his molting. Keeping the antennae moving steadily in slow sweeping circles of surveillance, he began systematically to shut down the rest of his nervous system, until he had attained the rest state that he knew—how?—was optimum for the rebuilding of his shell. Already his soft new carapace was beginning to grow rigid as it absorbed water, swelled, filtered out and utilized the lime. But he would have to sit quietly a long while before he was fully armored once more.

He rested. He waited. He did not think at all.

After a time his repose was broken by that inner voice, the one that had been trying to question him during the wildest moments of his molting. It spoke without sound, from a point somewhere within the core of his torpid consciousness.

—*Are you awake?*

—*I am now*, McCulloch answered irritably.

—*I need definitions. You are a mystery to me. What is a McCulloch?*

—*A man.*

—*That does not help.*

—*A male human being.*

—*That also has no meaning.*

—*Look, I'm tired. Can we discuss these things some other time?*

—This is a good time. While we rest, while we replenish ourself.

—Ourselves, McCulloch corrected.

—Ourself is more accurate.

—But there are two of us.

—Are there? Where is the other?

McCulloch faltered. He had no perspective on his situation, none that made any sense. *—One inside the other, I think. Two of us in the same body. But definitely two of us. McCulloch and not-McCulloch.*

—I concede the point. There are two of us. You are within me. Who are you?

—McCulloch.

—So you have said. But what does that mean?

—I don't know.

The voice left him alone again. He felt its presence nearby, as a kind of warm node somewhere along his spine, or whatever was the equivalent of his spine, since he did not think invertebrates had spines. And it was fairly clear to him that he was an invertebrate.

He had become, it seemed, a lobster, or, at any rate, something lobster-like. Implied in that was transition: *he had become.* He had once been something else. Blurred, tantalizing memories of the something else that he once had been danced in his consciousness. He remembered hair, fingers, fingernails, flesh. Clothing: a kind of removable exoskeleton. Eyelids, ears, lips: shadowy concepts all, names without substance, but there was a certain elusive reality to them, a volatile, tricky plausibility. Each time he tried to apply one of those concepts to himself— "fingers," "hair," "man," "McCulloch"—it slid away, it would not stick. Yet all the same those terms had some sort of relevance to him.

The harder he pushed to isolate that relevance, though, the harder it was to maintain his focus on any part of that soup of half-glimpsed notions in which his mind seemed to be swimming. The thing to do, McCulloch decided, was to go slow, try not to force understanding, wait for comprehension to seep back into his mind. Obviously he had had a bad shock, some major trauma, a total disorientation. It might be days before he achieved any sort of useful integration.

A gentle voice from outside his cave said, "I hope that your Growing has gone well."

Not a voice. He remembered voice: vibration of the air against the eardrums. No air here, maybe no eardrums. This was a stream of minute chemical messengers spurting through the mouth of the little cave and rebounding off the thousands of sensory filaments on his legs, tentacles, antennae, carapace, and tail. But the effect was one of words having been spoken. And it was distinctly different from that other voice, the internal one, that had been questioning him so assiduously a little while ago.

"It goes extremely well," McCulloch replied: or was it the other inhabitant of his body that had framed the answer? "I grow. I heal. I stiffen. Soon I will come forth."

"We feared for you." The presence outside the cave emanated concern, warmth, intelligence. Kinship. "In the first moments of your Growing, a strangeness came from you."

"Strangeness is within me. I am invaded."

"Invaded? By what?"

"A McCulloch. It is a man, which is a human being."

"Ah. A great strangeness indeed. Do you need help?"

McCulloch answered, "No. I will accommodate to it."

And he knew that it was the other within himself who was making these answers, though the boundary between their identities was so indistinct that he had a definite sense of being the one who shaped these words. But how could that be? He had no idea how one shaped words by sending squirts of body-fluid into the all-surrounding ocean-fluid. That was not his language. His language was—

—words—

—English words—

He trembled in sudden understanding. His antennae thrashed wildly, his many legs jerked and quivered. Images churned in his suddenly boiling mind: bright lights, elaborate equipment, faces, walls, ceilings. People moving about him, speaking in low tones, occasionally addressing words to him, English words—

—*Is English what all McCullochs speak?*

—*Yes.*

—*So English is human-language?*

—*Yes. But not the only one,* said McCulloch. *I speak English, and also German and a little—French. But other humans speak other languages.*

—*Very interesting. Why do you have so many languages?*

—*Because—because—we are different from one another, we live in different countries, we have different cultures—*

—*This is without meaning again. There are many creatures, but only one language, which all speak with greater or lesser skill, according to their destinies.*

McCulloch pondered that. After a time he replied:

—*Lobster is what you are. Long body, claws and antennae in front, many legs, flat tail in back. Different from, say, a clam. Clams have shell on top, shell on bottom, soft flesh in between, hinge connecting. You are not like that. You have lobster body. So you are lobster.*

Now there was silence from the other.

Then—after a long pause—

—*Very well. I accept the term. I am lobster. You are human. They are clams.*

—*What do you call yourselves in your own language?*

Silence.

—*What's your own name for yourself? Your individual self, the way my individual name is McCulloch and my species-name is human being?*

Silence.

—*Where am I, anyway?*

Silence, still, so prolonged and utter that McCulloch wondered if the other being had withdrawn itself from his consciousness entirely. Perhaps days went by in this unending silence, perhaps weeks: he had no way of measuring the passing of time. He realized that such units as days or weeks were without meaning now. One moment succeeded the next, but they did not aggregate into anything continuous.

At last came a reply.

—*You are in the world, human McCulloch.*

Silence came again, intense, clinging, a dark warm garment. McCulloch made no attempt to reach the other mind. He lay motionless, feeling his carapace thicken. From outside the cave came a flow of impressions of passing beings, now differentiating themselves very sharply: he felt the thick fleshy pulses of the two anemones, the sharp stabbing presence of the squid, the slow ponderous broadcast of something dark and winged, and, again and again, the bright, comforting, unmistakable output of other lobster-creatures. It was a busy, complex world out there. The McCulloch part of him longed to leave the cave and explore it. The lobster part of him rested, content within its tight shelter.

He formed hypotheses. He had journeyed from his own place to this place, damaging his mind in the process, though now his mind seemed to be reconstructing itself steadily, if erratically. What sort of voyage? To another world? No: that seemed wrong. He did not believe that conditions so much like the ocean-floor of Earth would be found on another—

Earth.

All right: significant datum. He was human, he came from Earth. And he was still on Earth. In the ocean. He was—what?—a land-dweller, an air-breather, a biped, a flesh-creature, a human. And now he was within the body of a lobster. Was that it? The entire human race, he thought, has migrated into the bodies of lobsters, and here we are on the ocean floor, scuttling about, waving our claws and feelers, going through difficult and dangerous moltings—

Or maybe I'm the only one. A scientific experiment, with me as the subject: man into lobster. That brightly lit room that he remembered, the intricate gleaming equipment all about him—that was the laboratory, that was where they had prepared him for his transmigration, and then they had thrown the switch and hurled him into the body of—

No. No. Makes no sense. Lobsters, McCulloch reflected, are low-phylum creatures with simple nervous systems, limited intelligence. Plainly the mind he had entered was a complex one. It asked thoughtful questions. It carried on civilized conversations with its friends, who came calling like ceremonious Japanese gentlemen, offering expressions of solicitude and good will.

New hypothesis: that lobsters and other low-phylum animals are actually quite intelligent, with minds roomy enough to accept the sudden insertion of a human being's entire neural structure, but we in our foolish anthropocentric way have up till now been too blind to perceive—

No. Too facile. You could postulate the secretly lofty intelligence of the world's humble creatures, all right: you could postulate anything you wanted. But that didn't make it so. Lobsters did not ask questions. Lobsters did not come calling like ceremonious Japanese gentlemen. At least, not the lobsters of the world he remembered.

Improved lobsters? Evolved lobsters? Super-lobsters of the future?

—*When am I?*

Into his dizzied broodings came the quiet disembodied internal voice of not-McCulloch, his companion:

—*Is your displacement then one of time rather than space?*

—*I don't know. Probably both. I'm a land creature.*

—*That has no meaning.*

—*I don't live in the ocean. I breathe air.*

From the other consciousness came an expression of deep astonishment tinged with skepticism.

—*Truly? That is very hard to believe. When you are in your own body you breathe no water at all?*

—*None. Not for long, or I would die.*

—*But there is so little land! And no creatures live upon it. Some make short visits there. But nothing can dwell there very long. So it has always been. And so will it be, until the time of the Molting of the World.*

McCulloch considered that. Once again he found himself doubting that he was still on Earth. A world of water? Well, that could fit into his hypothesis of having journeyed forward in time, though it seemed to add a layer of implausibility upon implausibility. How many millions of years, he wondered, would it take for nearly all the Earth to have become covered with water? And he answered himself: In about as many as it would take to evolve a species of intelligent invertebrates.

Suddenly, terribly, it all fit together. Things crystallized and clarified in his mind, and he found access to another segment of his injured and redistributed memory; and he began to comprehend what had befallen him, or, rather, what he had willingly allowed himself to undergo. With that comprehension came a swift stinging sense of total displacement and utter loss, as though he were drowning and desperately tugging at strands of seaweed in a futile attempt to pull himself back to the surface. All that was real to him, all that he was part of, everything that made sense—gone, gone, perhaps irretrievably gone, buried under the weight of uncountable millennia, vanished, drowned, forgotten, reduced to mere geology—it was unthinkable, it was unacceptable, it was impossible, and as the truth of it bore in on him he found himself choking on the frightful vastness of time past.

But that bleak sensation lasted only a moment and was gone. In its place came excitement, delight, confusion, and a feverish throbbing curiosity about this place he had entered. He was here. That miraculous thing that they had strived so fiercely to achieve had been achieved—rather too well, perhaps, but it had been achieved, and he was launched on the greatest adventure he would ever have, that anyone would ever have. This was not the moment for submitting to grief and confusion. Out of that world lost and all but forgotten to him came a scrap of verse that gleamed and blazed in his soul: *Only through time time is conquered.*

McCulloch reached toward the mind that was so close to his within this strange body.

—*When will it be safe for us to leave this cave?* he asked.

—*It is safe any time, now. Do you wish to go outside?*
—*Yes. Please.*

The creature stirred, flexed its front claws, slapped its flat tail against the floor of the cave, and in a slow ungraceful way began to clamber through the narrow opening, pausing more than once to search the waters outside for lurking enemies. McCulloch felt a quick hot burst of terror, as though he were about to enter some important meeting and had discovered too late that he was naked. Was the shell truly ready? Was he safely armored against the unknown foes outside, or would they fall upon him and tear him apart like furious shrikes? But his host did not seem to share those fears. It went plodding on and out, and in a moment more it emerged on an algae-encrusted tongue of the reef wall, a short distance below the two anemones. From each of those twin masses of rippling flesh came the same sullen pouting hungry murmurs: "Ah, come closer, why don't you come closer?"

"Another time," said the lobster, sounding almost playful, and turned away from them.

McCulloch looked outward over the landscape. Earlier, in the turmoil of his bewildering arrival and the pain and chaos of the molting prodrome, he had not had time to assemble any clear and coherent view of it. But now—despite the handicap of seeing everything with the alien perspective of the lobster's many-faceted eyes—he was able to put together an image of the terrain.

His view was a shortened one, because the sky was like a dark lid, through which came only enough light to create a cone-shaped arena spreading just a little way. Behind him was the face of the huge cliff, occupied by plant and animal life over virtually every square inch, and stretching upward until its higher reaches were lost in the dimness far overhead. Just a short way down from the ledge where he rested was the ocean floor, a broad expanse of gentle, undulating white sand streaked here and there with long widening gores of some darker material. Here and there bottom-growing plants arose in elegant billowy clumps, and McCulloch spotted occasional creatures moving among them over the sand that there were much like lobsters and crabs, though with some differences. He saw also some starfish and snails and sea urchins that did not look at all unfamiliar. At higher levels he could make out a few swimming creatures: a couple of the squid-like animals—they were hulking-looking ropy-armed things, and he disliked them instinctively—and what seemed to be large jellyfish. But something was missing, and after a moment McCulloch realized what it was: fishes. There was a rich population of invertebrate life wherever he looked, but no fishes as far as he could see.

Not that he could see very far. The darkness clamped down like a curtain perhaps two or three hundred yards away. But even so, it was odd that not one fish had entered his field of vision in all this time. He wished he knew more about marine biology. Were there zones on Earth where no sea animals more complex than lobsters and crabs existed? Perhaps, but he doubted it.

Two disturbing new hypotheses blossomed in his mind. One was that he had landed in some remote future era where nothing out of his own time survived except low-phylum sea-creatures. The other was that he had not traveled to the future at all, but had arrived by mischance in some primordial geological epoch in which vertebrate life had not yet evolved. That seemed unlikely to him, though. This place did not have a prehistoric feel to him. He saw no trilobites; surely there ought to be trilobites everywhere about, and not these oversized lobsters, which he did not remember at all from his childhood visits to the natural history museum's prehistory displays.

But if this was truly the future—and the future belonged to the lobsters and squids—

That was hard to accept. Only invertebrates? What could invertebrates accomplish, what kind of civilization could lobsters build, with their hard unsupple bodies and great clumsy claws? Concepts, half-remembered or less than that, rushed through his mind: the Taj Mahal, the Gutenberg Bible, the Sistine Chapel, the Madonna of the Rocks, the great window at Chartres. Could lobsters create those? Could squids? What a poor place this world must be, McCulloch thought sadly, how gray, how narrow, how tightly bounded by the ocean above the endless sandy floor.

—*Tell me,* he said to his host. *Are there any fishes in this sea?*

The response was what he was coming to recognize as a sigh.

—*Fishes? That is another word without meaning.*

—*A form of marine life, with an internal bony structure*—

—*With its shell* inside?

—*That's one way of putting it,* said McCulloch.

—*There are no such creatures. Such creatures have never existed. There is no room for the shell within the soft parts of the body. I can barely comprehend such an arrangement: surely there is no need for it!*

—*It can be useful, I assure you. In the former world it was quite common.*

—*The world of human beings?*

—*Yes. My world,* McCulloch said.

—*Anything might have been possible in a former world, human McCulloch. Perhaps indeed before the world's last Molting shells were worn inside. And perhaps after the next one they will be worn there again. But in the world I know, human McCulloch, it is not the practice.*

—*Ah*, McCulloch said. *Then I am even farther from home than I thought.*

—*Yes*, said the host. *I think you are very far from home indeed. Does that cause you sorrow?*

—*Among other things.*

—*If it causes you sorrow, I grieve for your grief, because we are companions now.*

—*You are very kind*, said McCulloch to his host.

The lobster asked McCulloch if he was ready to begin their journey; and when McCulloch indicated that he was, his host serenely kicked itself free of the ledge with a single powerful stroke of its tail. For an instant it hung suspended; then it glided toward the sandy bottom as gracefully as though it were floating through air. When it landed, it was with all its many legs poised delicately *en pointe*, and it stood that way, motionless, a long moment.

Then it suddenly set out with great haste over the ocean floor, running so lightfootedly that it scarcely raised a puff of sand wherever it touched down. More than once it ran right across some bottom-grubbing creature, some slug or scallop, without appearing to disturb it at all. McCulloch thought the lobster was capering in sheer exuberance, after its long internment in the cave; but some growing sense of awareness of his companion's mind told him after a time that this was no casual frolic, that the lobster was not in fact dancing but fleeing.

—*Is there an enemy?* McCulloch asked.

—*Yes. Above.*

The lobster's antennae stabbed upward at a sharp angle, and McCulloch, seeing through the other's eyes, perceived now a large looming cylindrical shape swimming in slow circles near the upper border of their range of vision. It might have been a shark, or even a whale. McCulloch felt deceived and betrayed; for the lobster had told him this was an invertebrate world, and surely that creature above him—

—*No*, said the lobster, without slowing its manic sprint. *That animal has no shell of the sort you described within its body. It is only a bag of flesh. But it is very dangerous.*

—*How will we escape it?*

—We will not escape it.

The lobster sounded calm, but whether it was the calm of fatalism or mere expressionlessness, McCulloch could not say: the lobster had been calm even in the first moments of McCulloch's arrival in its mind, which must surely have been alarming and even terrifying to it.

It had begun to move now in ever-widening circles. This seemed not so much an evasive tactic as a ritualistic one, now, a dance indeed. A farewell to life? The swimming creature had descended until it was only a few lobster-lengths above them, and McCulloch had a clear view of it. No, not a fish or a shark or any type of vertebrate at all, he realized, but an animal of a kind wholly unfamiliar to him, a kind of enormous worm-like thing whose meaty yellow body was reinforced externally by some sort of chitinous struts running its entire length. Fleshy vane-like fins rippled along its sides, but their purpose seemed to be more one of guidance than propulsion, for it appeared to move by guzzling in great quantities of water and expelling them through an anal siphon. Its mouth was vast, with a row of dim little green eyes ringing the scarlet lips. When the creature yawned, it revealed itself to be toothless, but capable of swallowing the lobster easily at a gulp.

Looking upward into the yawning mouth, McCulloch had a sudden image of himself elsewhere, spreadeagled under an inverted pyramid of shining machinery as the countdown reached its final moments, as the technicians made ready to—

—to hurl him—

—to hurl him forward in time—

Yes. An experiment. Definitely an experiment. He could remember it now. Bleier, Caldwell, Rodrigues, Mortenson. And all the others. Gathered around him, faces tight, forced smiles. The lights. The colors. The bizarre coils of equipment. And the volunteer. The volunteer. First human subject to be sent forward in time. The various rabbits and mice of the previous experiments, though they had apparently survived the round trip unharmed, had not been capable of delivering much of a report on their adventures. "I'm smarter than any rabbit," McCulloch had said. "Send me. I'll tell you what it's like up there." The volunteer. All that was coming back to him in great swatches now, as he crouched here within the mind of something much like a lobster, waiting for a vast yawning predator to pounce. The project, the controversies, his coworkers, the debate over risking a human mind under the machine, the drawing of lots. McCulloch had not been the only volunteer. He was just the lucky one. "Here you go, Jim-boy. A hundred years down the time-line."

Or fifty, or eighty, or a hundred and twenty. They didn't have really precise trajectory control. They thought he might go as much as a hundred twenty years. But beyond much doubt they had overshot by a few hundred million. Was that within the permissible parameters of error?

He wondered what would happen to him if his host here were to perish. Would he die also? Would he find himself instantly transferred to some other being of this epoch? Or would he simply be hurled back instead to his own time? He was not ready to go back. He had just begun to observe, to understand, to explore—

McCulloch's host had halted its running, now, and stood quite still in what was obviously a defensive mode, body cocked and upreared, claws extended, with the huge crusher claw erect and the long narrow cutting claw opening and closing in a steady rhythm. It was a threatening pose, but the swimming thing did not appear to be greatly troubled by it. Did the lobster mean to let itself be swallowed, and then to carve an exit for itself with those awesome weapons, before the alimentary juices could go to work on its armor?

"You choose your prey foolishly," said McCulloch's host to its enemy.

The swimming creature made a reply that was unintelligible to McCulloch: vague blurry words, the clotted outspew of a feeble intelligence. It continued its unhurried downward spiral.

"You are warned," said the lobster. "You are not selecting your victim wisely."

Again came a muddled response, sluggish and incoherent, the speech of an entity for whom verbal communication was a heavy, all but impossible effort.

Its enormous mouth gaped. Its fins rippled fiercely as it siphoned itself downward the last few yards to engulf the lobster. McCulloch prepared himself for transition to some new and even more unimaginable state when his host met its death. But suddenly the ocean floor was swarming with lobsters. They must have been arriving from all sides—summoned by his host's frantic dance, McCulloch wondered?—while McCulloch, intent on the descent of the swimmer, had not noticed. Ten, twenty, possibly fifty of them arrayed themselves now beside McCulloch's host, and as the swimmer, tail on high, mouth wide, lowered itself like some gigantic suction-hose toward them, the lobsters coolly and implacably seized its lips in their claws. Caught and helpless, it began at once to thrash, and from the pores through which it spoke came bleating incoherent cries of dismay and torment.

There was no mercy for it. It had been warned. It dangled tail upward while the pack of lobsters methodically devoured it from below, pausing occasionally to strip away and discard the rigid rods of chitin that formed its superstructure. Swiftly they reduced it to a faintly visible cloud of shreds oscillating in the water, and then small scavenging creatures came to fall upon those, and there was nothing at all left but the scattered rods of chitin on the sand.

The entire episode had taken only a few moments: the coming of the predator, the dance of McCulloch's host, the arrival of the other lobsters, the destruction of the enemy. Now the lobsters were gathered in a sort of convocation about McCulloch's host, wordlessly manifesting a commonality of spirit, a warmth of fellowship after feasting, that seemed quite comprehensible to McCulloch. For a short while they had been uninhibited savage carnivores consuming convenient meat; now once again they were courteous, refined, cultured—Japanese gentlemen, Oxford dons, gentle Benedictine monks.

McCulloch studied them closely. They were definitely more like lobsters than like any other creature he had even seen, very much like lobsters, and yet there were differences. They were larger. How much larger, he could not tell, for he had no real way of judging distance and size in this undersea world; but he supposed they must be at least three feet long, and he doubted that lobsters of his time, even the biggest, were anything like that in length. Their bodies were wider than those of lobsters, and their heads were larger. The two largest claws looked like those of the lobsters he remembered, but the ones just behind them seemed more elaborate, as if adapted for more delicate procedures than mere rending of food and stuffing it into the mouth. There was an odd little hump, almost a dome, midway down the lobster's back—the center of the expanded nervous system, perhaps.

The lobsters clustered solemnly about McCulloch's host and each lightly tapped its claws against those of the adjoining lobster in a sort of handshake, a process that seemed to take quite some time. McCulloch became aware also that a conversation was under way.

What they were talking about, he realized, was him.

"It is not painful to have a McCulloch within one," his host was explaining. "It came upon me at molting time, and that gave me a moment of difficulty, molting being what it is. But it was only a moment. After that my only concern was for the McCulloch's comfort."

"And it is comfortable now?"

"It is becoming more comfortable."

"When will you show it to us?"

"Ah, that cannot be done. It has no real existence, and therefore I cannot bring it forth."

"What is it, then? A wanderer? A revenant?"

"A revenant, yes. So I think. And a wanderer. It says it is a human being."

"And what is that? Is a human being a kind of McCulloch?"

"I think a McCulloch is a kind of human being."

"Which is a revenant."

"Yes, I think so."

"This is an Omen!"

"Where is its world?"

"Its world is lost to it."

"Yes, definitely an Omen."

"It lived on dry land."

"It breathed air."

"It wore its shell within its body."

"What a strange revenant!"

"What a strange world its world must have been."

"It is the former world, would you not say?"

"So I surely believe. And therefore this is an Omen."

"Ah, we shall Molt. We shall Molt."

McCulloch was altogether lost. He was not even sure when his own host was the speaker.

"Is it the Time?"

"We have an Omen, do we not?"

"The McCulloch surely was sent as a herald."

"There is no precedent."

"Each Molting, though, is without precedent. We cannot conceive what came before. We cannot imagine what comes after. We learn by learning. The McCulloch is the herald. The McCulloch is the Omen."

"I think not. I think it is unreal and unimportant."

"Unreal, yes. But not unimportant."

"The Time is not at hand. The Molting of the World is not yet due. The human is a wanderer and a revenant, but not a herald and certainly not an Omen."

"It comes from the former world."

"It says it does. Can we believe that?"

"It breathed air. In the former world, perhaps there were creatures that breathed air."

"It says it breathed air. I think it is neither herald nor Omen, neither wanderer nor revenant. I think it is a myth and a fugue. I think it betokens nothing. It is an accident. It is an interruption."

"That is an uncivil attitude. We have much to learn from the McCulloch. And if it is an Omen, we have immediate responsibilities that must be fulfilled."

"But how can we be certain of what it is?"

—*May I speak?* said McCulloch to his host.

—*Of course.*

—*How can I make myself heard?*

—*Speak through me.*

"The McCulloch wishes to be heard!"

"Hear it! Hear it!"

"Let it speak!"

McCulloch said, and the host spoke the words aloud for him, "I am a stranger here, and your guest, and so I ask you to forgive me if I give offense, for I have little understanding of your ways. Nor do I know if I am a herald or an Omen. But I tell you in all truth that I am a wanderer, and that I am sent from the former world, where there are many creatures of my kind, who breathe air and live upon the land and carry their—shells—inside their body."

"An Omen, certainly," said several of the lobsters at once. "A herald, beyond doubt."

McCulloch continued, "It was our hope to discover something of the worlds that are to come after ours. And therefore I was sent forward—"

"A herald—certainly a herald!"

"—to come to you, to go among you, to learn to know you, and then to return to my own people, the air-people, the human people, and bring the word of what is to come. But I think that I am not the herald you expect. I carry no message for you. We could not have known that you were here. Out of the former world I bring you the blessing of those that have gone before, however, and when I go back to that world I will bear tidings of your life, of your thought, of your ways—"

"Then our kind is unknown to your world?"

McCulloch hesitated. "Creatures somewhat like you do exist in the seas of the former world. But they are smaller and simpler than you, and I think their civilization, if they have one, is not a great one."

"You have no discourse with them, then?" one of the lobsters asked.

"Very little," he said. A miserable evasion, cowardly, vile. McCulloch shivered. He imagined himself crying out, "We eat them!" and the water turning black with their shocked outbursts—and saw them instantly falling upon him, swiftly and efficiently slicing him to scraps with their claws. Through his mind ran monstrous images of lobsters in tanks, lobsters boiling alive, lobsters smothered in rich sauces, lobsters shelled, lobsters minced, lobsters rendered into bisques—he could not halt the torrent of dreadful visions. Such was our discourse with your ancestors. Such was our mode of interspecies communication. He felt himself drowning in guilt and shame and fear.

The spasm passed. The lobsters had not stirred. They continued to regard him with patience: impassive, unmoving, remote. McCulloch wondered if all that had passed through his mind just then had been transmitted to his host. Very likely; the host earlier had seemed to have access to all of his thoughts, though McCulloch did not have the same entree to the host's. And if the host knew, did all the others? What then, what then?

Perhaps they did not even care. Lobsters, he recalled, were said to be callous cannibals, who might attack one another in the very tanks where they were awaiting their turns in the chef's pot. It was hard to view these detached and aloof beings, these dons, these monks, as having that sort of ferocity: but yet he had seen them go to work on that swimming mouth-creature without any show of embarrassment, and perhaps some atavistic echo of their ancestors' appetites lingered in them, so that they would think it only natural that McCullochs and other humans had fed on such things as lobsters. Why should they be shocked? Perhaps they thought that humans fed on humans, too. It was all in the former world, was it not? And in any event it was foolish to fear that they would exact some revenge on him for Lobster Thermidor, no matter how appalled they might be. He wasn't here. He was nothing more than a figment, a revenant, a wanderer, a set of intrusive neural networks within their companion's brain. The worst they could do to him, he supposed, was to exorcise him, and send him back to the former world.

Even so, he could not entirely shake the guilt and the shame. Or the fear.

Bleier said, "Of course, you aren't the only one who's going to be in jeopardy when we throw the switch. There's your host to consider. One entire human ego slamming into his mind out of nowhere like a brick falling off a building—what's it going to do to him?''

"Flip him out, is my guess," said Jake Ybarra. "You'll land on him and he'll announce he's Napoleon, or Joan of Arc, and they'll hustle him off to the nearest asylum. Are you prepared for the possibility, Jim, that you're going to spend your entire time in the future sitting in a loony-bin undergoing therapy?''

"Or exorcism," Mortenson suggested. "If there's been some kind of reversion to barbarism. Christ, you might even get your host burned at the stake!''

"I don't think so," McCulloch said quietly. "I'm a lot more optimistic than you guys. I don't expect to land in a world of witch-doctors and mumbo-jumbo, and I don't expect to find myself in a place that locks people up in Bedlam because they suddenly start acting a little strange. The chances are that I *am* going to unsettle my host when I enter him, but that he'll simply get two sanity-stabilizer pills from his medicine chest and take them with a glass of water and feel better in five minutes. And then I'll explain what's happening to him.''

"More than likely no explanations will be necessary," said Maggie Caldwell. "By the time you arrive, time travel will have been a going proposition for three or four generations, after all. Having a traveler from the past turn up in your head will be old stuff to them. Your host will probably know exactly what's going on from the moment you hit him.''

"Let's hope so," Bleier said. He looked across the laboratory to Rodrigues. "What's the count, Bob?''

"T minus eighteen minutes.''

"I'm not worried about a thing," McCulloch said.

Caldwell took his hand in hers. "Neither am I, Jim.''

"Then why is your hand so cold?" he asked.

"So I'm a *little* worried," she said.

McCulloch grinned. "So am I. A little. Only a little.''

"You're human, Jim. No one's ever done this before.''

"It'll be a can of corn!" Ybarra said.

Bleier looked at him blankly. "What the hell does that mean, Jake?''

Ybarra said, "Archaic twentieth-century slang. It means it's going to be a lot easier than we think.''

"I told you," said McCulloch, "I'm not worried.''

"I'm still worried about the impact on the host," said Bleier.

"All those Napoleons and Joans of Arc that have been cluttering the asylums for the last few hundred years," Maggie Caldwell said. "Could it be that they're really hosts for time-travelers going backward in time?"

"You can't go backward," said Mortenson. "You know that. The round trip has to begin with a forward leap."

"Under present theory," Caldwell said. "But present theory's only five years old. It may turn out to be incomplete. We may have had all sorts of travelers out of the future jumping through history, and never even knew it. All the nuts, lunatics, inexplicable geniuses, idiot-savants—"

"Save it, Maggie," Bleier said. "Let's stick to what we understand right now."

"Oh? Do we understand anything?" McCulloch asked.

Bleier gave him a sour look. "I thought you said you weren't worried."

"I'm not. Not much. But I'd be a fool if I thought we really had a firm handle on what we're doing. We're shooting in the dark, and let's never kid ourselves about it."

"T minus fifteen," Rodrigues called.

"Try to make the landing easy on your host, Jim," Bleier said.

"I've got no reason not to want to," said McCulloch.

He realized that he had been wandering. Bleier, Maggie, Mortenson, Ybarra—for a moment they had been more real to him than the congregation of lobsters. He had heard their voices, he had seen their faces, Bleier plump and perspiring and serious, Ybarra dark and lean, Maggie with her crown of short upswept red hair blazing in the laboratory light—and yet they were all dead, a hundred million years dead, two hundred million, back there with the triceratops and the trilobite in the drowned former world, and here he was among the lobster-people. How futile all those discussions of what the world of the early twenty-second century was going to be like! Those speculations on population density, religious belief, attitudes toward science, level of technological achievement, all those late-night sessions in the final months of the project, designed to prepare him for any eventuality he might encounter while he was visiting the future—what a waste, what a needless exercise. As was all that fretting about upsetting the mental stability of the person who would receive his transtemporalized consciousness. Such qualms, such moral delicacy—all unnecessary, McCulloch knew now.

But of course they had not anticipated sending him so eerily far across the dark abysm of time, into a world in which humankind and all its works were not even legendary memories, and the host who would receive him was a calm and thoughtful crustacean capable of taking him in with only the most mild and brief disruption of its serenity.

The lobsters, he noticed now, had reconfigured themselves while his mind had been drifting. They had broken up their circle and were arrayed in a long line stretching over the ocean floor, with his host at the end of the procession. The queue was a close one, each lobster so close to the one before it that it could touch it with the tips of its antennae, which from time to time they seemed to be doing; and they all were moving in a weird kind of quasi-military lockstep, every lobster swinging the same set of walking-legs forward at the same time.

—*Where are we going?* McCulloch asked his host.

—*The pilgrimage has begun.*

—*What pilgrimage is that?*

—*To the dry place,* said the host. *To the place of no water. To the land.*

—*Why?*

—*It is the custom. We have decided that the time of the Molting, of the World is soon to come; and therefore we must make the pilgrimage. It is the end of all things. It is the coming of a newer world. You are the herald: so we have agreed.*

—*Will you explain? I have a thousand questions. I need to know more about all this,* McCulloch said.

—*Soon. Soon. This is not a time for explanations.*

McCulloch felt a firm and unequivocal closing of contact, an emphatic withdrawal. He sensed a hard ringing silence that was almost an absence of the host, and knew it would be inappropriate to transgress against it. That was painful, for he brimmed now with an overwhelming rush of curiosity. The Molting of the World? The end of all things? A pilgrimage to the land? *What* land? Where? But he did not ask. He could not ask. The host seemed to have vanished from him, disappearing utterly into this pilgrimage, this migration, moving in its lockstep way with total concentration and a kind of mystic intensity. McCulloch did not intrude. He felt as though he had been left alone in the body they shared.

As they marched, he concentrated on observing, since he could not interrogate. And there was much to see; for the longer he dwelled within his host, the more accustomed he grew to the lobster's sensory mechanisms. The compound eyes, for instance. Enough of his former life had returned to him now so that he remembered human eyes clearly, those two large gleaming ovals, so keen, so subtle of focus, set beneath protecting ridges of bone. His host's eyes were nothing like that: they were two clusters of tiny lenses rising on jointed, movable stalks, and what they showed was an intricately dissected view, a mosaic of isolated points of light. But he was learning somehow to translate those complex and baffling images into a single clear one, just as, no doubt, a creature accustomed to compound-lens vision would sooner or later learn to see through human eyes, if need be. And McCulloch found now that he could not only make more sense out of the views he received through his host's eyes, but that he was seeing farther, into quite distant dim recesses of this sunless undersea realm.

Not that the stalked eyes seemed to be a very important part of the lobster's perceptive apparatus. They provided nothing more than a certain crude awareness of the immediate terrain. But apparently the real work of perceiving was done mainly by the thousands of fine bristles, so minute that they were all but invisible, that sprouted on every surface of his host's body. These seemed to send a constant stream of messages to the lobster's brain: information on the texture and topography of the ocean floor, on tiny shifts in the flow and temperture of the water, of the proximity of obstacles, and much else. Some of the small hairlike filaments were sensitive to touch and others, it appeared, to chemicals; for whenever the lobster approached some other life-form, it received data on its scent—or the underwater equivalent—long before the creature itself was within visual range. The quantity and richness of these inputs astonished McCulloch. At every moment came a torrent of data corresponding to the landslide senses he remembered, smell, taste, touch; and some central processing unit within the lobster's brain handled everything in the most effortless fashion.

But there was no sound. The ocean world appeared to be wholly silent. McCulloch knew that that was untrue, that sound waves propagated through water as persistently as through air; indeed, faster. Yet the lobster seemed neither to possess nor to need any sort of auditory equipment. The sensory bristles brought in all the data it required. The "speech" of these creatures, McCulloch had long ago realized, was effected not by voice but by means of spurts of chemicals released into the water, hormones, perhaps, or amino acids, something of a distinct and readily recognizable identity, emitted in some high-redundancy pattern that permitted easy recognition and decoding despite the difficulties caused by currents and eddies. It was, McCulloch thought, like trying to communicate by printing individual letters on scraps of paper and hurling them into the wind. But it did somehow seem to work, however clumsy a concept it might be, because of the extreme sensitivity of the lobster's myriad chemoreceptors.

The antennae played some significant role also. There were two sets of them, a pair of three-branched ones just behind the eyes and a much longer single-branched pair behind those. The long ones restlessly twitched and probed inquisitively and most likely, he suspected, served as simple balancing and coordination devices much like the whiskers of a cat. The purpose of the smaller antennae eluded him, but it was his guess that they were involved in the process of communication between one lobster and another, either by some semaphore system or in a deeper communion beyond his still awkward comprehension.

McCulloch regretted not knowing more about the lobsters of his own era. But he had only a broad general knowledge of natural history, extensive, fairly deep, yet not good enough to tell him whether these elaborate sensory functions were characteristic of all lobsters or had evolved during the millions of years it had taken to create the waterworld. Probably some of each, he decided. Very likely even the lobsters of the former world had had much of this scanning equipment, enough to allow them to locate their prey, to find their way around in the dark suboceanic depths, to undertake their long and unerring migrations. But he found it hard to believe that they could have had much "speech" capacity, that they gathered in solemn sessions to discuss abstruse questions of theology and mythology, to argue gently about omens and heralds and the end of all things. That was something that the patient and ceaseless unfoldings of time must have wrought.

The lobsters marched without show of fatigue: not scampering in that dancelike way that his host had adopted while summoning its comrades to save it from the swimming creature, but moving nevertheless in an elegant and graceful fashion, barely touching the ground with the tips of their legs, going onward, step by step by step, steadily and fairly swiftly.

McCulloch noticed that new lobsters frequently joined the procession, cutting in from left or right just ahead of his host, who always remained at the rear of the line; that line now was so long, hundreds of lobsters long, that it was impossible to see its beginning. Now and again one would reach out with its bigger claw to seize some passing animal, a starfish or urchin or small crab, and without missing a step would shred and devour it, tossing the unwanted husk to the cloud of planktonic scavengers that always hovered nearby. This foraging on the march was done with utter lack of self-consciousness; it was almost by reflex that these creatures snatched and gobbled as they journeyed.

And yet all the same they did not seem like mere marauding mouths. From this long line of crustaceans there emanated, McCulloch realized, a mysterious sense of community, a wholeness of society, that he did not understand but quite sharply sensed. This was plainly not a mere migration but a true pilgrimage. He thought ruefully of his earlier condescending view of these people, incapable of achieving the Taj Mahal or the Sistine Chapel, and felt abashed: for he was beginning to see that they had other accomplishments of a less tangible sort that were only barely apparent to his displaced and struggling mind.

"When you come back," Maggie said, "you'll be someone else. There's no escaping that. It's the one thing I'm frightened of. Not that you'll die making the hop, or that you'll get into some sort of terrible trouble in the future, or that we won't be able to bring you back at all, or anything like that. But that you'll have become someone else."

"I feel pretty secure in my identity," McCulloch told her.

"I know you do. God knows, you're the most stable person in the group, and that's why you're going. But even so. Nobody's ever done anything like this before. It can't help but change you. When you return, you're going to be unique among the human race."

"That sounds very awesome. But I'm not sure it'll matter that much, Mag. I'm just taking a little trip. If I were going to Paris, or Istanbul, or even Antarctica, would I come back totally transformed? I'd have had some new experiences, but—"

"It isn't the same," she said. "It isn't even remotely the same." She came across the room to him and put her hands on his shoulders, and stared deep into his eyes, which sent a little chill through him, as it always did; for when she looked at him that way there was a sudden flow of energy between them, a powerful warm rapport rushing from her to him and from him to her as though through a huge conduit, that delighted and frightened him both at once. He could lose himself in her. He had never let himself feel that way about anyone before. And this was not the moment to begin. There was no room in him for such feelings, not now, not when he was within a couple of hours of leaping off into the most unknown of unknowns. When he returned—if he returned—he might risk allowing something at last to develop with Maggie. But not on the eve of departure, when everything in his universe was tentative and conditional. "Can I tell you a little story, Jim?" she asked.

"Sure."

"When my father was on the faculty at Cal, he was invited to a reception to meet a couple of the early astronauts, two of the Apollo men—I don't remember which ones, but they were from the second or third voyage to the Moon. When he showed up at the faculty club, there were two or three hundred people there, milling around having cocktails, and most of them were people he didn't know. He walked in and looked around and within ten seconds he had found the astronauts. He didn't have to be told. He just *knew*. And this is my father, remember, who doesn't believe in ESP or anything like that. But he said they were impossible to miss, even in that crowd. You could see it one their faces, you could feel the radiance coming from them, there was an aura, there was something about their eyes. Something that said, *I have walked on the Moon, I have been to that place which is not of our world and I have come back, and now I am someone else. I am who I was before, but I am someone else also.*"

"But they went to the *Moon*, Mag!"

"And you're going to the *future*, Jim. That's even weirder. You're going to a place that doesn't exist. And you may meet yourself there—ninety-nine years old, and waiting to shake hands with you—or you might meet me, or your grandson, or find out that everyone on Earth is dead, or that everyone has turned into a disembodied spirit, or that they're all immortal superbeings, or—or—Christ, I don't know. You'll see a world that nobody alive today is supposed to see. And when you come back, you'll have that aura. You'll be transformed."

"Is that so frightening?"

"To me it is," she said.

"Why is that?"

"Dummy," she said. "Dope. How explicit do I have to be, anyway? I thought I was being obvious enough."

He could not meet her eyes. "This isn't the best moment to talk about—"

"I know. I'm sorry, Jim. But you're important to me, and you're going somewhere and you're going to become someone else, and I'm scared. Selfish and scared."

"Are you telling me not to go?"

"Don't be absurd. You'd go no matter what I told you, and I'd despise you if you didn't. There's no turning back now."

"No."

"I shouldn't have dumped any of this on you today. You don't need it right this moment."

"It's okay," he said softly. He turned until he was looking straight at her, and for a long moment he simply stared into her eyes and did not speak, and then at last he said, "Listen, I'm going to take a big fantastic improbable insane voyage, and I'm going to be a witness to God knows what, and then I'm going to come back and yes, I'll be changed—only an ox wouldn't be changed, or maybe only a block of stone—but I'll still be me, whoever *me* is. Don't worry, okay? I'll still be me. And we'll still be us."

"Whoever *us* is."

"Whoever. Jesus, I wish you were going with me, Mag!"

"That's the silliest schoolboy thing I've ever heard you say."

"True, though."

"Well, I can't go. Only one at a time can go, and it's you. I'm not even sure I'd want to go. I'm not as crazy as you are, I suspect. You go, Jim, and come back and tell me all about it."

"Yes."

"And then we'll see what there is to see about you and me."

"Yes," he said.

She smiled. "Let me show you a poem, okay? You must know it, because it's Eliot, and you know all the Eliot there is. But I was reading him last night—thinking of you, reading him—and I found this, and it seemed to be the right words, and I wrote them down. From one of the *Quartets*."

"I think I know," he said:

" *'Time past and time future*
Allow but a little consciousness—' "

"That's a good one too," Maggie said. "But it's not the one I had in mind." She unfolded a piece of paper. "It's this:

" *'We shall not cease from exploration*
And the end of all our exploring
Will be to arrive where we started—' "

" *'—And know the place for the first time,'* " he completed. "Yes. Exactly. To arrive where we started. And know the place for the first time."

The lobsters were singing as they marched. That was the only word, McCulloch thought, that seemed to apply. The line of pilgrims now was immensely long—there must have been thousands in the procession by this time, and more were joining constantly—and from them arose an outpouring of chemical signals, within the narrowest of tonal ranges, that mingled in a close harmony and amounted to a kind of sustained chant on a few notes, swelling, filling all the ocean with its powerful and intense presence. Once again he had an image of them as monks, but not Benedictines, now: these were Buddhist, rather, an endless line of yellow-robed holy men singing a great Om as they made their way up some Tibetan slope. He was awed and humbled by it—by the intensity, and by the wholeheartedness of the devotion. It was getting hard for him to remember that these were crustaceans, no more than ragged claws scuttling across the floors of silent seas; he sensed minds all about him, whole and elaborate minds arising out of some rich cultural matrix, and it was coming to seem quite natural to him that these people should have armored exoskeletons and jointed eye-stalks and a dozen busy legs.

His host had still not broken its silence, which must have extended now over a considerable period. Just how long a period, McCulloch had no idea, for there were no significant alternations of light and dark down here to indicate the passing of time, nor did the marchers ever seem to sleep, and they took their food, as he had seen, in a casual and random way without breaking step. But it seemed to McCulloch that he had been effectively alone in the host's body for many days.

He was not minded to try to re-enter contact with the other just yet—not until he received some sort of signal from it. Plainly the host had withdrawn into some inner sanctuary to undertake a profound meditation; and McCulloch, now that the early bewilderment and anguish of his journey through time had begun to wear off, did not feel so dependent upon the host that he needed to blurt his queries constantly into his companion's consciousness. He would watch, and wait, and attempt to fathom the mysteries of this place unaided.

The landscape had undergone a great many changes since the beginning of the march. That gentle bottom of fine white sand had yielded to a terrain of rough dark gravel, and that to one of a pale sedimentary stuff made up of tiny shells, the mortal remains, no doubt, of vast hordes of diatoms and foraminifera, that rose like clouds of snowflakes at the lobsters' lightest steps. Then came a zone where a stratum of thick red clay spread in all directions. The clay held embedded in it an odd assortment of rounded rocks and clamshells and bits of chitin, so that it had the look of some complex paving material from a fashionable terrace. And after that they entered a region where slender spires of a sharp black stone, faceted like worked flint, sprouted stalagmite-fashion at their feet. Through all of this the lobster-pilgrims marched unperturbed, never halting, never breaking their file, moving in a straight line whenever possible and making only the slightest of deviations when compelled to it by the harshness of the topography.

Now they were in a district of coarse yellow sandy globules, out of which two types of coral grew: thin angular strands of deep jet, and supple, almost mobile fingers of a rich lovely salmon hue. McCulloch wondered where on Earth such stuff might be found, and chided himself at once for the foolishness of the thought: the seas he knew had been swallowed long ago in the great all-encompassing ocean that swathed the world, and the familiar continents, he supposed, had broken from their moorings and slipped to strange parts of the globe well before the rising of the waters. He had no landmarks. There was an equator somewhere, and there were two poles, but down here beyond the reach of direct sunlight, in this warm changeless uterine sea, neither north nor south nor east held any meaning. He remembered other lines:

> *Sand-strewn caverns, cool and deep*
> *Where the winds are all asleep;*
> *Where the spent lights quiver and gleam;*
> *Where the salt weed sways in the stream;*
> *Where the sea-beasts rang'd all round*
> *Feed in the ooze of their pasture-ground . . .*

What was the next line? Something about great whales coming sailing by, sail and sail with unshut eye, round the world for ever and aye. Yes, but there were no great whales here, if he understood his host correctly, no dolphins, no sharks, no minnows; there were only these swarming lower creatures, mysteriously raised on high, lords of the world. And mankind? Birds and bats, horses and bears? Gone. Gone. And the valleys and meadows? The lakes and streams? Taken by the sea. The world lay before him like a land of dreams, transformed. But was it, as the poet had said, a place which hath really neither joy, nor love, nor light, nor certitude, nor peace, nor help for pain? It did not seem that way. For light there was merely that diffuse faint glow, so obscure it was close to nonexistent, that filtered down through unknown fathoms. But what was that lobster-song, that everswelling crescendo, if not some hymn to love and certitude and peace, and help for pain? He was overwhelmed by peace, surprised by joy, and he did not understand what was happening to

him. He was part of the march, that was all. He was a member
of the pilgrimage.

He had wanted to know if there was any way he could signal
to be pulled back home: a panic button, so to speak. Bleier was
the one he asked, and the question seemed to drive the man into
an agony of uneasiness. He scowled, he tugged at his jowls, he
ran his hands through his sparse strands of hair.

"No," he said finally. "We weren't able to solve that one,
Jim. There's simply no way of propagating a signal backward in
time."

"I didn't think so," McCulloch said. "I just wondered."

"Since we're not actually sending your physical body, you
shouldn't find yourself in any real trouble. Psychic discomfort,
at the worst—disorientation, emotional upheaval, at the worst a
sort of terminal homesickness. But I think you're strong enough
to pull your way through any of that. And you'll always know
that we're going to be yanking you back to us at the end of the
experiment."

"How long am I going to be gone?"

"Elapsed time will be virtually nil. We'll throw the switch,
off you'll go, you'll do your jaunt, we'll grab you back, and it'll
seem like no time at all, perhaps a thousandth of a second. We
aren't going to believe that you went anywhere at all, until you
start telling us about it."

McCulloch sensed that Bleier was being deliberately evasive,
not for the first time since McCulloch had been selected as the
time-traveler. "It'll seem like no time at all to the people watching in the lab," he said. "But what about for me?"

"Well, of course for you it'll be a little different, because
you'll have had a subjective experience in another time-frame."

"That's what I'm getting at. How long are you planning to
leave me in the future? An hour? A week?"

"That's really hard to determine, Jim."

"What does that mean?"

"You know, we've sent only rabbits and stuff. They've come
back okay, beyond much doubt—"

"Sure. They still munch on lettuce when they're hungry, and
they don't tie their ears together in knots before they hop. So I
suppose they're none the worsè for wear."

"Obviously we can't get much of a report from a rabbit."

"Obviously."

"You're sounding awfully goddamned hostile today, Jim. Are

you sure you don't want us to scrub the mission and start training another volunteer?'' Bleier asked.

"I'm just trying to elicit a little hard info," McCulloch said. "I'm not trying to back out. And if I sound hostile, it's only because you're dancing all around my questions, which is becoming a considerable pain in the ass."

Bleir looked squarely at him and glowered. "All right. I'll tell you anything you want to know that I'm capable of answering. Which is what I think I've been doing all along. When the rabbits come back, we test them and we observe no physiological changes, no trace of ill effects as a result of having separated the psyche from the body for the duration of a time-jaunt. Christ, we can't even tell the rabbits *have* been on a time-jaunt, except that our instruments indicate the right sort of thermodynamic drain and entropic reversal, and for all we know we're kidding ourselves about that, which is why we're risking our reputations and your neck to send a human being who can tell us what the heck happens when we throw the switch. But you've seen the rabbits jaunting. You know as well as I do that they come back okay."

Patiently McCulloch said, "Yes. As okay as a rabbit ever is, I guess. But what I'm trying to find out from you, and what you seem unwilling to tell me, is how long I'm going to be up there in subjective time."

"We don't know, Jim," Bleier said.

"You don't *know?* What if it's ten years? What if it's a thousand? What if I'm going to live out an entire life-span, or whatever is considered a life-span a hundred years from now, and grow old and wise and wither away and die and then wake up a thousandth of a second later on your lab table?"

"We don't know. That's why we have to send a human subject."

"There's no way to measure subjective jaunt-time?"

"Our instruments are here. They aren't *there*. You're the only instrument we'll have there. For all we know, we're sending you off for a million years, and when you come back here you'll have turned into something out of H. G. Wells. Is that straightforward enough for you, Jim? But I don't think it's going to happen that way, and Mortenson doesn't think so either, or Ybarra for that matter. What we think is that you'll spend something between a day and a couple of months in the future, with the outside possibility of a year. And when we give you the hook, you'll be back here with virtually nil elapsed time. But to answer your first question again, there's no way you can instruct us to yank you back. You'll just have to sweat it out, however long it may be. I thought you knew that. The hook, when it comes, will be virtually automatic, a function of the thermodynamic homeostasis, like the recoil of a gun. An equal and opposite reaction: or maybe more like the snapping back of a rubber band. Pick whatever metaphor you want. But if you don't like the way any of this sounds, it's not too late for you to back out, and nobody will say a word against you. It's never too late to back out. Remember that, Jim.''

McCulloch shrugged. "Thanks for leveling with me. I appreciate that. And no, I don't want to drop out. The only thing I wonder about is whether my stay in the future is going to seem too long or too goddamned short. But I won't know that until I get there, will I? And then the time I have to wait before coming home is going to be entirely out of my hands. And out of yours too, is how it seems. But that's all right. I'll take my chances. I just wondered what I'd do if I got there and found that I didn't much like it there.''

"My bet is that you'll have the opposite problem," said Bleier. "You'll like it so much you won't want to come back.''

Again and again, while the pilgrims traveled onward, McCulloch detected bright flares of intelligence gleaming like brilliant pinpoints of light in the darkness of the sea. Each creature seemed to have a characteristic emanation, a glow of neural energy. The simple ones—worms, urchins, starfish, sponges—emitted dim gentle signals; but there were others as dazzling as beacons. The lobster-folk were not the only sentient life-forms down here.

Occasionally he saw, as he had in the early muddled moments of the jaunt, isolated colonies of the giant sea anemones: great flowery-looking things, rising on thick pedestals. From them came a soft alluring lustful purr, a siren crooning calculated to bring unwary animals within reach of their swaying tentacles and the eager mouths hidden within the fleshy petals. Cemented to the floor on their swaying stalks, they seemed like somber philosophers, lost in the intervals between meals in deep reflections on the purpose of the cosmos. McCulloch longed to pause and try to speak with them, for their powerful emanation appeared plainly to indicate that they possessed a strong intelligence, but the lobsters moved past the anemones without halting.

The squid-like beings that frequently passed in flotillas overhead seemed even keener of mind: large animals, sleek and arrogant of motion, with long turquoise bodies that terminated in hawser-like arms, and enormous bulging eyes of a startling scarlet color. He found them ugly and repugnant, and did not quite know why. Perhaps it was some attitude of his host's that carried over subliminally to him; for there was an unmistakable chill among the lobsters whenever the squids appeared, and the chanting of the marchers grew more vehement, as though betokening a warning.

That some kind of frosty detente existed between the two kinds of life-forms was apparent from the regard they showed one another and from the distances they maintained. Never did the squids descend into the ocean-floor zone that was the chief domain of the lobsters, but for long spans of time they would soar above, in a kind of patient aerial surveillance, while the lobsters, striving ostentatiously to ignore them, betrayed discomfort by quickened movements of their antennae.

Still other kinds of high-order intelligence manifested themselves as the pilgrimage proceeded. In a zone of hard and rocky terrain McCulloch felt a new and distinctive mental pulsation, coming from some creature that he must not have encountered before. But he saw nothing unusual: merely a rough grayish landscape pockmarked by dense clumps of oysters and barnacles, some shaggy outcroppings of sponges and yellow seaweeds, a couple of torpid anemones. Yet out of the midst of all that unremarkable clutter came clear strong signals, produced by minds of considerable force. Whose? Not the oysters and barnacles, surely. The mystery intensified as the lobsters, without pausing in their march, interrupted their chant to utter words of greeting, and had greetings in return, drifting toward them from that tangle of marine underbrush.

"Why do you march?" the unseen speakers asked, in a voice that rose in the water like a deep slow groaning.

"We have had an Omen," answered the lobsters.

"Ah, is it the Time?"

"The Time will surely be here," the lobsters replied.

"Where is the herald, then?"

"The herald is within me," said McCulloch's host, breaking its long silence at last.

—*To whom do you speak?* McCulloch asked.

—*Can you not see? There. Before us.*

McCulloch saw only algae, barnacles, sponges, oysters.

—*Where?*

—*In a moment you will see,* said the host.

The column of pilgrims had continued all the while to move forward, until now it was within the thick groves of seaweed. And now McCulloch saw who the other speakers were. Huge crabs were crouched at the bases of many of the larger rock formations, creatures far greater in size than the largest of the lobsters; but they were camouflaged so well that they were virtually invisible except at the closest range. On their broad arching backs whole gardens grew: brilliantly colored sponges, algae in somber reds and browns, fluffy many-branched crimson things, odd complex feathery growths, even a small anemone or two, all jammed together in such profusion that nothing of the underlying crab showed except beady long-stalked eyes and glinting claws. Why beings, that signalled their presence with potent telepathic outputs should choose to cloak themselves in such elaborate concealments, McCulloch could not guess: perhaps it was to deceive a prey so simple that it was unable to detect the emanations of these crabs' minds.

As the lobsters approached, the crabs heaved themselves up a little way from the rocky bottom, and shifted themselves ponderously from side to side, causing the intricate streamers and filaments and branches of the creatures growing on them to stir and wave about. It was like a forest agitated by a sudden hard gust of wind from the north.

"Why do you march, why do you march?" called the crabs. "Surely it is not yet the Time. Surely!"

"Surely it is," the lobsters replied. "So we all agree. Will you march with us?"

"Show us your herald!" the crabs cried. "Let us see the Omen!"

—*Speak to them,* said McCulloch's host.

—*But what am I to say?*

—*The truth. What else can you say?*

—*I know nothing. Everything here is a mystery to me.*

—*I will explain all things afterward. Speak to them now.*

—*Without understanding?*

—*Tell them what you told us.*

Baffled, McCulloch said, speaking through the host, "I have come from the former world as an emissary. Whether I am a herald, whether I bring an Omen, is not for me to say. In my own world I breathed air and carried my shell within my body."

"Unmistakably a herald," said the lobsters.

To which the crabs replied, "That is not so unmistakable to us. We sense a wanderer and a revenant among you. But what does that mean? The Molting of the World is not a small thing, good friends. Shall we march, just because this strangeness is come upon you? It is not enough evidence. And to march is not a small thing either, at least for us."

"We have chosen to march," the lobsters said, and indeed they had not halted at all throughout this colloquy; the vanguard of their procession was far out of sight in a black-walled canyon, and McCulloch's host, still at the end of the line, was passing now through the last few crouching-places of the great crabs. "If you mean to join us, come now."

From the crabs came a heavy outpouring of regret. "Alas, alas, we are large, we are slow, the way is long, the path is dangerous."

"Then we will leave you."

"If it is the Time, we know that you will perform the offices on our behalf. If it is not the Time, it is just as well that we do not make the pilgrimage. We are—not—certain. We—cannot—be—sure—it—is—an—Omen—"

McCulloch's host was far beyond the last of the crabs. Their words were faint and indistinct, and the final few were lost in the gentle surgings of the water.

—*They make a great error*, said McCulloch's host to him. *If it is truly the Time, and they do not join the march, it might happen that their souls will be lost. That is a severe risk: but they are a lazy folk. Well, we will perform the offices on their behalf.*

And to the crabs the host called, "We will do all that is required, have no fear!" But it was impossible, McCulloch thought, that the words could have reached the crabs across such a distance.

He and the host now were entering the mouth of the black canyon. With the host awake and talkative once again, McCulloch meant to seize the moment at last to have some answers to his questions.

—*Tell me now*—he began.

But before he could complete the thought, he felt the sea roil and surge about him as though he had been swept up in a monstrous wave. That could not be, not at this depth; but yet that irresistible force, booming toward him out of the dark canyon and catching him up, hurled him into a chaos as desperate as that of his moment of arrival. He sought to cling, to grasp, but there was no purchase; he was loose of his moorings; he was tossed and flung like a bubble on the winds.

—*Help me!* he called. *What's happening to us?*

—*To you, friend human McCulloch. To you alone. Can I aid you?*

What was that? Happening only to him? But certainly he and

the lobster both were caught in this undersea tempest, both being thrown about, both whirled in the same maelstrom—

Faces danced around him. Charlie Bleier, pudgy, earnest-looking. Maggie, tender-eyed, troubled. Bleier had his hand on McCulloch's right wrist, Maggie on the other, and they were tugging, tugging—

But he had no wrists. He was a lobster.

"Come, Jim—"

"No! Not yet!"

"Jim—Jim—"

"Stop—pulling—you're hurting—"

"Jim—"

McCulloch struggled to free himself from their grasp. As he swung his arms in wild circles, Maggie and Bleier, still clinging to them, went whipping about like tethered balloons. "Let go," he shouted. "You aren't here! There's nothing for you to hold on to! You're just hallucinations! Let—go—!"

And then, as suddenly as they had come, they were gone.

The sea was calm. He was in his accustomed place, seated somewhere deep within his host's consciousness. The lobster was moving forward, steady as ever, into the black canyon, following the long line of its companions.

McCulloch was too stunned and dazed to attempt contact for a long while. Finally, when he felt some measure of composure return, he reached his mind into his host's:

—*What happened?*

—*I cannot say. What did it seem like to you?*

—*The water grew wild and stormy. I saw faces out of the former world. Friends of mine. They were pulling at my arms. You felt nothing?*

—*Nothing*, said the host, *except a sense of your own turmoil. We are deep here: beyond the reach of storms.*

—*Evidently I'm not.*

—*Perhaps your homefaring-time is coming. Your world is summoning you.*

Of course! The faces, the pulling at his arms—the plausibility of the host's suggestion left McCulloch trembling with dismay. Homefaring-time! Back there in the lost and inconceivable past, they had begun angling for him, casting their line into the vast gulf of time—

—*I'm not ready*, he protested. *I've only just arrived here! I know nothing yet! How can they call me so soon?*

—*Resist them, if you would remain.*

—Will you help me?

—How would that be possible?

—I'm not sure, McCulloch said. *But it's too early for me to go back. If they pull on me again, hold me! Can you?*

—I can try, friend human McCulloch.

—And you have to keep your promise to me now.

—What promise is that?

—You said you would explain things to me. Why you've undertaken this pilgrimage. What it is I'm supposed to be the Omen of. What happens when the Time comes. The Molting of the World.

—Ah, said the host.

But that was all it said. In silence it scrabbled with busy legs over a sharply creviced terrain. McCulloch felt a fierce impatience growing in him. What if they yanked him again, now, and this time they succeeded? There was so much yet to learn! But he hesitated to prod the host again, feeling abashed. Long moments passed. Two more squids appeared: the radiance of their probing minds was like twin searchlights overhead. The ocean floor is sloped downward gradually but perceptibly here. The squids vanished, and another of the predatory big-mouthed swimming-things, looking as immense as a whale and, McCulloch supposed, filling the same ecological niche, came cruising down into the level where the lobsters marched, considered their numbers in what appeared to be some surprise, and swam slowly upward again and out of sight. Something else of great size, flapping enormous wings somewhat like those of a stingray but clearly just a boneless mass of chitin-strutted flesh, appeared next, surveyed the pilgrims with equally bland curiosity, and flew to the front of the line of lobsters, where McCulloch lost it in the darkness. While all of this was happening the host was quiet and inaccessible, and McCulloch did not dare attempt to penetrate its privacy. But then, as the pilgrims were moving through a region where huge, dim-witted scallops with great bright eyes nestled everywhere, waving gaudy pink and blue mantles, the host unexpectedly resumed the conversation as though there had been no interruption, saying:

—What we call the Time of the Molting of the World is the time when the world undergoes a change of nature, and is purified and reborn. At such a time, we journey to the place of dry land, and perform certain holy rites.

—And these rites bring about the Molting of the World? McCulloch asked.

—Not at all. The Molting is an event wholly beyond our

control. The rites are performed for our own sakes, not for the world's.

—*I'm not sure I understand.*

—*We wish to survive the Molting, to travel onward into the world to come. For this reason, at a Time of Molting, we must make our observances, we must demonstrate our worth. It is the responsibility of my people. We bear the duty for all the peoples of the world.*

—*A priestly caste, is that it?* McCulloch said. *When this cataclysm comes, the lobsters go forth to say the prayers for everyone, so that everyone's soul will survive?*

The host was silent again: pondering McCulloch's terms, perhaps, translating them into more appropriate equivalents. Eventually it replied:

—*That is essentially correct.*

—*But other peoples can join the pilgrimage if they want. Those crabs. The anemones. The squids, even?*

—*We invite all to come. But we do not expect anyone but ourselves actually to do it.*

—*How often has there been such a ceremony?* McCulloch asked.

—*I cannot say. Never, perhaps.*

—*Never?*

—*The Molting of the World is not a common event. We think it has happened only twice since the beginning of time.*

In amazement McCulloch said:

—*Twice since the world began, and you think it's going to happen again in your own lifetimes?*

—*Of course we cannot be sure of that. But we have had an Omen, or so we think, and we must abide by that. It was foretold that when the end is near, an emissary from the former world would come among us. And so it has come to pass. Is that not so?*

—*Indeed.*

—*Then we must make the pilgrimage, for if you have not brought the Omen we have merely wasted some effort, but if you are the true herald we will have forfeited all of eternity if we let your message go unheeded.*

It sounded eerily familiar to McCulloch: a messianic prophecy, a cult of the millennium, an apocalyptic transfiguration. He felt for a moment as though he had landed in the ninth century instead of in some impossibly remote future epoch. And yet the host's tone was so calm and rational, the sense of spiritual obligation that the lobster conveyed was so profound, that

McCulloch found nothing absurd in these beliefs. Perhaps the world *did* end from time to time, and the performing of certain rituals did in fact permit its inhabitants to transfer their souls onward into whatever unimaginable environment was to succeed the present one. Perhaps.

—*Tell me*, said McCulloch. *What were the former worlds like, and what will the next one be?*

—*You should know more about the former worlds than I, friend human McCulloch. And as for the world to come, we may only speculate.*

—*But what are your traditions about those worlds?*

—*The first world*, the lobster said, *was a world of fire.*

—*You can understand fire, living in the sea?*

—*We have heard tales of it from those who have been to the dry place. Above the water there is air, and in the air there hangs a ball of fire, which gives the world warmth. Is this not the case?*

McCulloch, hearing a creature of the ocean floor speak of things so far beyond its scope and comprehension, felt a warm burst of delight and admiration.

—*Yes! We call that ball of fire the sun.*

—*Ah, so that is what you mean, when you think of the sun! The word was a mystery to me, when first you used it. But I understand you much better now, do you not agree?*

—*You amaze me.*

—*The first world, so we think, was fire: it was like the sun. And when we dwelled upon that world, we were fire also. It is the fire that we carry within us to this day, that glow, that brightness, which is our life, and which goes from us when we die. After a span of time so long that we could never describe its length, the Time of the Molting came upon the fire-world and it grew hard, and gathered a cloak of air about itself, and creatures lived upon the land and breathed the air. I find that harder to comprehend in truth, than I do the fire-world. But that was the first Molting, when the air-world emerged: that world from which you have come to us. I hope you will tell me of your world, friend human Mcculloch, when there is time.*

—*So I will*, said McCulloch. *But there is so much more I need to hear from you first!*

—*Ask it.*

—*The second Molting—the disappearance of my world, the coming of yours—*

—*The tradition is that the sea existed, even in the former world, and that it was not small. At the Time of the Molting it rose and devoured the land and all that was upon it, except for one place that was not devoured, which is sacred. And then all the world was covered by water, and that was the second Molting, which brought forth the third world.*

—*How long ago was that?*

—*How can I speak of the passing of time? There is no way to speak of that. Time passes, and lives end, and worlds are transformed. But we have no words for that. If every grain of sand in the sea were one lifetime, then it would be as many lifetimes ago as there are grains of sand in the sea. But does that help you? Does that tell you anything? It happened. It was very long ago. And now our world's turn has come, or so we think.*

—*And the next world? What will that be like?* McCulloch asked.

—*There are those who claim to know such things, but I am not one of them. We will know the next world when we have entered it, and I am content to wait until then for the knowledge.*

McCulloch had a sense then that the host had wearied of this sustained contact, and was withdrawing once again from it; and, though his own thirst for knowledge was far from sated, he chose once again not to attempt to resist that withdrawal.

All this while the pilgrims had continued down a gentle incline into the great bowl of a sunken valley. Once again now the ocean floor was level, but the water was notably deeper here, and the diffused light from above was so dim that only the most rugged of algae could grow, making the landscape bleak and sparse. There were no sponges here, and little coral, and the enemones were pale and small, giving little sign of the potent intelligence that infused their larger cousins in the shallower zones of the sea.

But there were other creatures at this level that McCulloch had not seen before. Platoons of alert, mobile oysters skipped over the bottom, leaping in agile bounds on columns of water that they squirted like jets from tubes in their dark green mantles: now and again they paused in mid-leap and their shells quickly opened and closed, snapping shut, no doubt, on some hapless larval thing of the plankton too small for McCulloch, via the lobster's imperfect vision, to detect. From these oysters came bright darting blurts of mental activity, sharp and probing: they must be as intelligent, he thought, as cats or dogs. Yet from time to time a lobster, swooping with an astonishingly swift claw, would seize one of these oysters and deftly, almost instantaneously, shuck and devour it. Appetite was no respecter of intelligence in this world of needful carnivores, McCulloch realized.

Intelligent, too, in their way, were the hordes of nearly invisible little crustaceans—shrimp of some sort, he imagined—that danced in shining clouds just above the line of march. They were ghostly things perhaps an inch long, virtually transparent, colorless, lovely, graceful. Their heads bore two huge glistening black eyes; their intestines, glowing coils running the length of their bodies, were tinged with green; the tips of their tails were an elegant crimson. They swam with the aid of a horde of busy finlike legs, and seemed almost to be mocking their stolid, plodding cousins as they marched; but these sparkling little creatures also occasionally fell victim to the lobsters' inexorable claws, and each time it was like the extinguishing of a tiny brilliant candle.

An emanation of intelligence of a different sort came from bulky animals that McCulloch noticed roaming through the gravelly foothills flanking the line of march. These seemed at first glance to be another sort of lobster, larger even than McCulloch's companions: heavily armored things with many-segmented abdomens and thick paddle-shaped arms. But then, as one of them drew nearer, McCulloch saw the curved tapering tail with its sinister spike, and realized he was in the presence of the scorpions of the sea.

They gave off a deep, almost somnolent mental wave: slow thinkers but not light ones, Teutonic ponderers, grapplers with the abstruse. There were perhaps two dozen of them, who advanced upon the pilgrims and in quick one-sided struggles pounced, stung, slew. McCulloch watched in amazement as each of the scorpions dragged away a victim and, no more than a dozen feet from the line of march, began to gouge into its armor to draw forth tender chunks of pale flesh, without drawing the slightest response from the impassive, steadily marching column of lobsters.

They had not been so complacent when the great-mouthed swimming thing had menaced McCulloch's host; then, the lobsters had come in hordes to tear the attacker apart. And whenever one of the big squids came by, the edgy hostility of the lobsters, their willingness to do battle if necessary, was manifest. But they seemed indifferent to the scorpions. The lobsters accepted their onslaught as placidly as though it were merely a toll they must pay in order to pass through this district. Perhaps it was. McCulloch was only beginning to perceive how dense and intricate a fabric of ritual bound this submarine world together.

The lobsters marched onward, chanting in unfailing rhythm as though nothing untoward had happened. The scorpions, their hungers evidently gratified, withdrew and congregated a short distance off, watching without much show of interest as the procession went by them. By the time McCulloch's host, bringing up the rear, had gone past the scorpions, they were fighting among themselves in a lazy, half-hearted way, like playful lions after a successful hunt. Their mental emanation, sluggishly booming through the water, grew steadily more blurred, more vague, more toneless.

And then it was overlaid and entirely masked by the pulsation of some new and awesome kind of mind ahead: one of enormous power, whose output beat upon the water with what was almost a physical force, like some massive metal chain being lashed against the surface of the ocean. Apparently the source of this gigantic output still lay at a considerable distance, for, strong as it was, it grew stronger still as the lobsters advanced toward it, until at last it was an overwhelming clangor, terrifying, bewildering. McCulloch could no longer remain quiescent under the impact of that monstrous sound. Breaking through to the sanctuary of his host, he cried:

—*What is it?*

—*We are approaching a god,* the lobster replied.

—*A god, did you say?*

—*A divine presence, yes. Did you think we were the rulers of this world?*

In fact McCulloch had, assuming automatically that this time-jaunt had deposited him within the consciousness of some member of this world's highest species, just as he would have expected to have landed, had he reached the twenty-second century as intended, in the consciousness of a human rather than in a frog or a horse. But obviously the division between humanity and all sub-sentient species in his own world did not have an exact parallel here; many races, perhaps all of them, had some sort of intelligence, and it was becoming clear that the lobsters, though a high life-form, were not the highest. He found that dismaying and even humbling; for the lobsters seemed quite adequately intelligent to him, quite the equals—for all his early condescension to them—of mankind itself. And now he was to meet one of their gods? How great a mind was a god likely to have?

The booming of that mind grew unbearably intense, nor was there any way to hide from it. McCulloch visualized himself doubled over in pain, pressing his hands to his ears, an image that drew a quizzical shaft of thought from his host. Still the lobsters pressed forward, but even they were responding now to the waves of mental energy that rippled outward from that unimaginable source. They had at last broken ranks, and were fanning out horizontally on the broad dark plain of the ocean floor, as though deploying themselves before a place of worship. Where was the god? McCulloch, striving with difficulty to see in this nearly lightless place, thought he made out some vast shape ahead, some dark entity, swollen and fearsome, that rose like a colossal boulder in the midst of the suddenly diminutive-looking lobsters. He saw eyes like bright yellow platters, gleaming furiously; he saw a huge frightful beak; he saw what he thought at first to be a nest of writhing serpents, and then realized to be tentacles, dozens of them, coiling and uncoiling with a terrible restless energy. To the host he said:

—*Is that your god?*

But he could not hear the reply, for an agonizing new force suddenly buffeted him, one even more powerful than that which was emanating from the giant creature that sat before him. It ripped upward through his soul like a spike. It cast him forth, and he tumbled over and over, helpless in some incomprehensible limbo, where nevertheless he could still hear the faint distant voice of his lobster host:

—*Friend human McCulloch? Friend human McCulloch?*

He was drowning. He had waded incautiously into the surf, deceived by the beauty of the transparent tropical water and the shimmering white sand below, and a wave had caught him and knocked him to his knees, and the next wave had come before he could arise, pulling him under. And now he tossed like a discarded doll in the suddenly turbulent sea, struggling to get his head above water and failing, failing, failing.

Maggie was standing on the shore, calling in panic to him, and somehow he could hear her words even through the tumult of the crashing waves: "This way, Jim, swim toward me! Oh, please, Jim, this way, this way!"

Bleier was there too, Mortenson, Bob Rodrigues, the whole group, ten or fifteen people, running about worriedly, beckoning to him, calling his name. It was odd that he could see them, if he was underwater. And he could hear them so clearly, too, Bleier telling him to stand up and walk ashore, the water wasn't deep at all, and Rodrigues saying to come in on hands and knees if he couldn't manage to get up, and Ybarra yelling that it was getting late, that they couldn't wait all the goddamned afternoon, that he had been swimming long enough. McCulloch wondered why they didn't come after him, if they were so eager to get him to shore. Obviously he was unable to help himself.

"Look," he said, "I'm drowning, can't you see? Throw me a line, for Christ's sake!" Water rushed into his mouth as he spoke. It filled his lungs, it pressed against his brain.

"We can't hear you, Jim!"

"Throw me a line!" he cried again, and felt the torrents pouring through his body. "I'm—drowning—drowning—"

And then he realized that he did not at all want them to rescue him, that it was worse to be rescued than to drown. He did not understand why he felt that way, but he made no attempt to question the feeling. All that concerned him now was preventing those people on the shore, those humans, from seizing him and taking him from the water. They were rushing about, assembling some kind of machine to pull him in, an arm at the end of a great boom. McCulloch signalled to them to leave him alone.

"I'm okay," he called. "I'm not drowning after all! I'm fine right where I am!"

But now they had their machine in operation, and its long metal arm was reaching out over the water toward him. He turned and dived, and swam as hard as he could away from the shore, but it was no use: the boom seemed to extend over an infinite distance, and no matter how fast he swam the boom moved faster, so that it hovered just above him now, and from its tip some sort of hook was descending.—

"No—no—let me be! I don't want to go ashore!"

Then he felt a hand on his wrist: firm, reassuring, taking control. All right, he thought. They've caught me after all, they're going to pull me in. There's nothing I can do about it. They have me, and that's all there is to it. But he realized, after a moment, that he was heading not toward shore but out to sea, beyond the waves, into the calm warm depths. And the hand that was on his wrist was not a hand; it was a tentacle, thick as heavy cable, a strong surdy tentacle lined on one side by rounded suction cups that held him in an unbreakable grip.

That was all right. Anything to be away from that wild crashing surf. It was much more peaceful out here. He could rest, catch his breath, get his equilibrium. And all the while that powerful tentacle towed him steadily seaward. He could still hear the voices of his friends on shore, but they were as faint as the cries of distant sea-birds now, and when he looked back he saw only tiny dots, like excited ants, moving along the beach. McCulloch waved at them. "See you some other time," he called. "I didn't want to come out of the water yet anyway."

Better here. Much much better. Peaceful. Warm. Like the womb.
And that tentacle around his wrist: So reassuring, so steady.
—*Friend human McCulloch? Friend human McCulloch?*
—*This is where I belong. Isn't it?*
—*Yes. This is where you belong. You are one of us, friend human McCulloch. You are one of us.*

Gradually the turbulence subsided, and he found himself re-gaining his balance. He was still within the lobster; the whole horde of lobsters was gathered around him, thousands upon thousands of them, a gentle solicitous community; and right in front of him was the largest octopus imaginable, a creature that must have been fifteen or twenty feet in diameter, with tentacles that extended an implausible distance on all sides. Somehow he did not find the sight frightening.

"He is recovered now," his host announced.
—*What happened to me?* McCulloch asked.
—*Your people called you again. But you did not want to make your homefaring, and you resisted them. And when we under-stood that you wanted to remain, the god aided you, and you broke free of their pull.*
—*The god?*
His host indicated the great octopus.
—*There.*

It did not seem at all improbable to McCulloch now. The infinite fullness of time brings about everything, he thought: even intelligent lobsters, even a divine octopus. He still could feel the mighty telepathic output of the vast creature, but though it had lost none of its power it no longer caused him discomfort; it was like the roaring thunder of some great waterfall, to which one becomes accustomed, and which, in time, one begins to love. The octopus sat motionless, its immense yellow eyes trained on McCulloch, its scarlet mantle rippling gently, its tentacles weaving in intricate patterns. McCulloch thought of an octopus he had once seen when he was diving in the West Indies: a small shy scuttling thing, hurrying to slither behind a snarled coral head. He felt chastened and awed by this evidence of the magnifi-cations wrought by the eons. A hundred million years? Half a billion? The numbers were without meaning. But that span of years had produced this creature. He sensed a serene intelligence of incomprehensible depth, benign, tranquil, all-penetrating: a god indeed. Yes. Truly a god. Why not?

The great cephalopod was partly sheltered by an overhanging wall of rock. Clustered about it were dozens of the scorpion-things, motionless, poised: plainly a guard force. Overhead swam a whole army of the big squids, doubtless guardians also, and for once the presence of those creatures did not trigger any emotion in the lobsters, as if they regarded squids in the service of the god as acceptable ones. The scene left McCulloch dazed with awe. He had never felt farther from home.

—*The god would speak with you,* said his host.

—*What shall I say?*

—*Listen, first.*

McCulloch's lobster moved forward until it stood virtually beneath the octopus's huge beak. From the octopus, then, came an outpouring of words that McCulloch did not immediately comprehend, but which, after a moment, he understood to be some kind of benediction that enfolded his soul like a warm blanket. And gradually he perceived that he was being spoken to.

"Can you tell us why you have come all this way, human McCulloch?"

"It was an error. They didn't mean to send me so far—only a hundred years or less, that was all we were trying to cross. But it was our first attempt. We didn't really know what we were doing. And I suppose I wound up halfway across time—a hundred million years, two hundred, maybe a billion—who knows?"

"It is a great distance. Do you feel no fear?"

"At the beginning I did. But not any longer. This world is alien to me, but not frightening."

"Do you prefer it to your own?"

"I don't understand," McCulloch said.

"Your people summoned you. You refused to go. You appealed to us for aid, and we aided you in resisting your homecalling, because it was what you seemed to require from us."

"I'm—not ready to go home yet," he said. "There's so much I haven't seen yet, and that I want to see. I want to see everything. I'll never have an opportunity like this again. Perhaps no one ever will. Besides, I have services to perform here. I'm the herald; I bring the Omen; I'm part of this pilgrimage. I think I ought to stay until the rites have been performed. I *want* to stay until then."

"Those rites will not be performed," said the octopus quietly.

"Not performed?"

"You are not the herald. You carry no Omen. The Time is not at hand."

McCulloch did not know what to reply. Confusion swirled within him. No Omen? Not the Time?

—*It is so,* said the host. *We were in error. The god has shown us that we came to our conclusion too quickly. The Time of the Molting may be near, but it is not yet upon us. You have many of the outer signs of a herald, but there is no Omen upon you. You are merely a visitor. An accident.*

McCulloch was assailed by a startlingly keen pang of disappointment. It was absurd; but for a time he had been the central figure in some apocalyptic ritual of immense significance, or at least had been thought to be, and all that suddenly was gone from him, and he felt strangely diminished, irrelevant, bereft of his bewildering grandeur. A visitor. An accident.

—*In that case I feel great shame and sorrow,* he said. *To have caused so much trouble for you. To have sent you off on this pointless pilgrimage.*

—*No blame attaches to you,* said the host. *We acted of our free choice, after considering the evidence.*

"Nor was the pilgrimage pointless," the octopus declared. "There are no pointless pilgrimages. And this one will continue."

"But if there's no Omen—if this is not the Time—"

"There are other needs to consider," replied the octopus, "and other observances to carry out. We must visit the dry place ourselves, from time to time, so that we may prepare ourselves for the world that is to succeed ours, for it will be very different from ours. It is time now for such a visit, and well past time. And also we must bring you to the dry place, for only there can we properly make you one of us."

"I don't understand," said McCulloch.

"You have asked to stay among us; and if you stay, you must become one of us, for your sake, and for ours. And that can best be done at the dry place. It is not necessary that you understand that now, human McCulloch."

—*Make no further reply,* said McCulloch's host. *The god has spoken. We must proceed.*

Shortly the lobsters resumed their march, chanting as before, though in a more subdued way, and, so it seemed to McCulloch, singing a different melody. From the context of his conversation with it, McCulloch had supposed that the octopus now would accompany them, which puzzled him, for the huge unwieldy creature did not seem capable of any extensive journey. That proved to be the case: the octopus did not go along, though the vast booming resonances of its mental output followed the procession for what must have been hundreds of miles.

Once more the line was a single one, with McCulloch's host at the end of the file. A short while after departure it said:

—*I am glad, friend human McCulloch, that you chose to continue with us. I would be sorry to lose you now.*

—*Do you mean that? Isn't it an inconvenience for you, to carry me around inside your mind?*

—*I have grown quite accustomed to it. You are part of me, friend human McCulloch. We are part of one another. At the place of the dry land we will celebrate our sharing of this body.*

—*I was lucky,* said McCulloch, *to have landed like this in a mind that would make me welcome.*

—*Any of us would have made you welcome,* responded the host.

McCulloch pondered that. Was it merely a courteous turn of phrase, or did the lobster mean him to take the answer literally? Most likely the latter: the host's words seemed always to have only a single level of meaning, a straightforwardly literal one. So any of the lobsters would have taken him in uncomplainingly? Perhaps so. They appeared to be virtually interchangeable beings, without distinctive individual personalities, without names, even. The host had remained silent when McCulloch had asked him its name, and had not seemed to understand what kind of label McCulloch's own name was. So powerful was their sense of community, then, that they must have little sense of private identity. He had never cared much for that sort of hive-mentality, where he had observed it in human society. But here it seemed not only appropriate but admirable.

—*How much longer will it be,* McCulloch asked, *before we reach the place of dry land?*

—*Long.*

—*Can you tell me where it is?*

—*It is in the place where the world grows narrower,* said the host.

McCulloch had realized, the moment he asked the question, that it was meaningless: what useful answer could the lobster possibly give? The old continents were gone and their names long forgotten. But the answer he had received was meaningless too: where, on a round planet, is the place where the world grows narrower? He wondered what sort of geography the lobsters understood. If I live among them a hundred years, he thought, I will probably just begin to comprehend what their perceptions are like.

Where the world grows narrower. All right. Possibly the place of the dry land was some surviving outcropping of the former world, the summit of Mount Everest, perhaps, Kilimanjaro, whatever. Or perhaps not: perhaps even those peaks had been ground down by time, and new ones had arisen—one of them, at least, tall enough to rise above the universal expanse of sea. It was folly to suppose that any shred at all of his world remained accessible: it was all down there beneath tons of water and millions of years of sediments, the old continents buried, hidden, rearranged by time like pieces scattered about a board.

The pulsations of the octopus's mind could no longer be felt. As the lobsters went tirelessly onward, moving always in that lithe skipping stride of theirs and never halting to rest or to feed, the terrain rose for a time and then began to dip again, slightly at first and then more than slightly. They entered into the waters that were deeper and significantly darker, and somewhat cooler as well. In this somber zone, where vision seemed all but useless, the pilgrims grew silent for long spells for the first time, neither chanting nor speaking to one another, and McCulloch's host, who had become increasingly quiet, disappeared once more into its impenetrable inner domain and rarely emerged.

In the gloom and darkness there began to appear a strange red glow off to the left, as though someone had left a lantern hanging midway between the ocean floor and the surface of the sea. The lobsters, when that mysterious light came into view, at once changed the direction of their line of march to go veering off to the right; but at the same time they resumed their chanting, and kept one eye trained on the glowing place as they walked.

The water felt warmer here. A zone of unusual heat was spreading outward from the glow. And the taste of the water, and what McCulloch persisted in thinking of as its smell, were peculiar, with a harsh choking salty flavor. Brimstone? Ashes?

McCulloch realized that what he was seeing was an undersea volcano, belching forth a stream of red-hot lava that was turning the sea into a boiling bubbling cauldron. The sight stirred him oddly. He felt that he was looking into the pulsing ancient core of the world, the primordial flame, the geological link that bound the otherwise vanished former worlds to this one. There awakened in him a powerful tide of awe, and a baffling unfocused yearning that he might have termed homesickness, except that it was not, for he was no longer sure where his true home lay.

—*Yes*, said the host. *It is a mountain on fire. We think it is a part of the older of the two former worlds that has endured both of the Moltings. It is a very sacred place.*

—An object of pilgrimage? McCulloch asked.

—Only to those who wish to end their lives. The fire devours all who approach it.

—In my world we had many such fiery mountains, McCulloch said. *They often did great destruction.*

—How strange your world must have been!

—It was very beautiful, said McCulloch.

—Surely. But strange. The dry land, the fire in the air—the sun, I mean—the air-breathing creatures—yes, strange, very strange. I can scarcely believe it really existed.

—There are times, now, when I begin to feel the same way, McCulloch said.

The volcano receded in the distance; its warmth could no longer be felt; the water was dark again, and cold, and growing colder, and McCulloch could no longer detect any trace of that sulphurous aroma. It seemed to him that they were moving now down an endless incline, where scarcely any creatures dwelled.

And then he realized that the marchers ahead had halted, and were drawn up in a long row as they had been when they came to the place where the octopus held its court. Another god? No. There was only blackness ahead.

—Where are we? he asked.

—It is the shore of the great abyss.

Indeed what lay before them looked like the Pit itself: lightless, without landmark, an empty landscape. McCulloch understood now that they had been marching all this while across some sunken continent's coastal plain, and at last they had come to—what?—the graveyard where one of Earth's lost oceans lay buried in ocean?

—Is it possible to continue? he asked.

—Of course, said the host. *But now we must swim.*

Already the lobsters before them were kicking off from shore with vigorous strokes of their tails and vanishing into the open sea beyond. A moment later McCulloch's host joined them. Almost at once there was no sense of a bottom beneath them—only a dark and infinitely deep void. Swimming across this, McCulloch thought, is like falling through time—an endless descent and no safety net.

The lobsters, he knew, were not true swimming creatures: like the lobsters of his own era they were bottom-dwellers, who walked to get where they needed to go. But they could never cross this abyss that way, and so they were swimming now, moving steadily by flexing their huge abdominal muscles and their tails. Was it terrifying to them to be setting forth into a place without landmarks like this? His host remained utterly calm, as though this were no more than an afternoon stroll.

McCulloch lost what little perception of the passage of time that he had had. Heave, stroke, onward, heave, stroke, onward, that was all, endless repetition. Out of the depths there occasionally came an upwelling of cold water, like a dull, heavy river miraculously flowing upward through air, and in that strange surging from below rose a fountain of nourishment, tiny transparent struggling creatures and even smaller flecks of some substance that must have been edible, for the lobsters, without missing a stroke, sucked in all they could hold. And swam on and on. McCulloch had a sense of being involved in a trek of epic magnitude, a once-in-many generations thing that would be legendary long after.

Enemies roved this open sea: the free-swimming creatures that had evolved out of God only knew which kinds of worms or slugs to become the contemporary equivalents of sharks and whales. Now and again one of these huge beasts dived through the horde of lobsters, harvesting it at will. But they could eat only so much; and the survivors kept going onward.

Until at last—months, years later?—the far shore came into view; the ocean floor, long invisible, reared up beneath them and afforded support; the swimmers at last put their legs down on the solid bottom, and with something that sounded much like gratitude in their voices began once again to chant in unison as they ascended the rising flank of a new continent.

The first rays of the sun, when they came into view an unknown span of time later, struck McCulloch with an astonishing, overwhelming impact. He perceived them first as a pale greenish glow resting in the upper levels of the sea just ahead, striking downward like illuminated wands; he did not then know what he was seeing, but the sight engendered wonder in him all the same; and later, when that radiance diminished and was gone and in a short while returned, he understood that the pilgrims were coming up out of the sea. So they had reached their goal: the still point of the turning world, the one remaining unsubmerged scrap of the former Earth.

—*Yes*, said the host. *This is it*.

In that same instant McCulloch felt another tug from the past: a summons dizzying in its imperative impact. He thought he could hear Maggie Caldwell's voice crying across the time-winds: "Jim, Jim, come back to us!" And Bleier, grouchy,

angered, muttering, "For Christ's sake, McCulloch, stop holding on up there! This is getting expensive!" Was it all his
imagination, that fantasy of hands on his wrists, familiar faces
hovering before his eyes?

"Leave me alone," he said. "I'm still not ready."

"Will you ever be?" That was Maggie. "Jim, you'll be
marooned. You'll be stranded there if you don't let us pull you
back now."

"I may be marooned already," he said, and brushed the
voices out of his mind with surprising ease.

He returned his attention to his companions and saw that they
had halted their trek a little way short of that zone of light which
now was but a quick scramble ahead of them. Their linear
formation was broken once again. Some of the lobsters, marching blindly forward, were piling up in confused-looking heaps in
the shallows, forming mounds fifteen or twenty lobsters deep.
Many of the others had begun a bizarre convulsive dance: a wild
twitchy cavorting, rearing up on their back legs, waving their
claws about, flicking their antennae in frantic circles.

—*What's happening?* McCulloch asked his host. *Is this the
beginning of a rite?*

But the host did not reply. The host did not appear to be
within their shared body at all. McCulloch felt a silence far
deeper than the host's earlier withdrawals; this seemed not a
withdrawal but an evacuation, leaving McCulloch in sole
possession. That new solitude came rolling in upon him with a
crushing force. He sent forth a tentative probe, found nothing,
found less than nothing. Perhaps it's meant to be this way, he
thought. Perhaps it was necessary for him to face this climactic
initiation unaided, unaccompanied.

Then he noticed that what he had taken to be a weird jerky
dance was actually the onset of a mass molting prodrome. Hundreds of the lobsters had been stricken simultaneously, he realized,
with that strange painful sense of inner expansion, of volcanic
upheaval and stress: that heaving and rearing about was the first
stage of the splitting of the shell.

And all of the molters were females.

Until that instant McCulloch had not been aware of any division into sexes among the lobsters. He had barely been able to
tell one from the next; they had no individual character, no shred
of uniqueness. Now, suddenly, strangely, he knew without being
told that half of his companions were females, and that they were
molting now because they were fertile only when they had shed
their old armor, and that the pilgrimage to the place of the dry

land was the appropriate time to engender the young. He had asked no questions of anyone to learn that; the knowledge was simply within him; and, reflecting on that, he saw that the host was absent from him because the host was wholly fused with him; he was the host, the host was Jim McCulloch.

He approached a female, knowing precisely which one was the appropriate one, and sang to her, and she acknowledged his song with a song of her own, and raised her third pair of legs to him, and let him plant his gametes beside her oviducts. There was no apparent pleasure in it, as he remembered pleasure from his days as a human. Yet it brought him a subtle but unmistakable sense of fulfillment, of the completion of biological destiny, that had a kind of orgasmic finality about it, and left him calm and anchored at the absolute dead center of his soul: yes, truly the still point of the turning world, he thought.

His mate moved away to begin her new Growing and the awaiting of her motherhood. And McCulloch, unbidden, began to ascend the slope that led to the land.

The bottom was fine sand here, soft, elegant. He barely touched it with his legs as he raced shoreward. Before him lay a world of light, radiant, heavenly, a bright irresistible beacon. He went on until the water, pearly-pink and transparent, was only a foot or two deep, and the domed upper curve of his back was reaching into the air. He felt no fear. There was no danger in this. Serenely he went forward—the leader, now, of the trek—and climbing out into the hot sunlight.

It was an island, low and sandy, so small that he imagined he could cross it in a day. The sky was intensely blue and the sun, hanging close to a noon position, looked swollen and fiery. A little grove of palm trees clustered a few hundred yards inland, but he saw nothing else, no birds, no insects, no animal life of any sort. Walking was difficult here—his breath was short, his shell seemed to be too tight, his stalked eyes were stinging in the air—but he pulled himself forward, almost to the trees. Other male lobsters, hundreds of them, thousands of them, were following. He felt himself linked to each of them: his people, his nation, his community, his brothers.

Now, at that moment of completion and communion, came one more call from the past.

There was no turbulence in it this time. No one was yanking at his wrists, no surf boiled and heaved in his mind and threatened to dash him on the reefs of the soul. The call was simple and clear: *This is the moment of coming back, Jim.*

Was it? Had he no choice? He belonged here. These were his people. This was where his loyalties lay.

And yet, and yet: he knew that he had been sent on a mission unique in human history, that he had been granted a vision beyond all dreams, that it was his duty to return and report on it. There was no ambiguity about that. He owed it to Bleier and Maggie and Ybarra and the rest to return, to tell them everything.

How clear it all was! He belonged *here*, and he belonged *there*, and an unbreakable net of loyalties and responsibilities held him to both places. It was a perfect equilibrium; and therefore he was tranquil and at ease. The pull was on him; he resisted nothing, for he was at last beyond all resistance to anything. The immense sun was a drumbeat in the heavens; the fiery warmth was a benediction; he had never known such peace.

"I must make my homefaring now," he said, and released himself, and let himself drift upward, light as a bubble, toward the sun.

Strange figures surrounded him, tall and narrow-bodied, with odd fleshy faces and huge moist mouths and bulbing staring eyes, and their kind of speech was a crude hubbub of sound-waves that bashed and battered against his sensibilities with painful intensity. "We were afraid the signal wasn't reaching you, Jim," they said. "We tried again and again, but there was no contact, nothing. And then just as we were giving up, suddenly your eyes were opening, you were stirring, you stretched your arms—"

He felt air pouring into his body, and dryness all about him. It was a struggle to understand the speech of these creatures who were bending over him, and he hated the reek that came from their flesh and the booming vibrations that they made with their mouths. But gradually he found himself returning to himself, like one who has been lost in a dream so profound that it eclipses reality for the first few moments of wakefulness.

"How long was I gone?" he asked.

"Four minutes and eighteen seconds," Ybarra said.

McCulloch shook his head. "Four minutes? Eighteen seconds? It was more like forty months, to me. Longer. I don't know how long."

"Where did you go, Jim? What was it like?"

"Wait," someone else said. "He's not ready for debriefing yet. Can't you see, he's about to collapse?"

McCulloch shrugged. "You sent me too far."

"How far?" Five hundred years?" Maggie asked.

"Millions," he said.

Someone gasped.

"He's dazed," a voice said at his left ear.

"Millions of years," McCulloch said in a slow, steady, determinedly articulate voice. "*Millions*. The whole earth was covered by the sea, except for one little island. The people are lobsters. They have a society, a culture. They worship a giant octopus."

Maggie was crying. "Jim, oh, Jim—"

"No. It's true. I went on migration with them. Intelligent lobsters is what they are. And I wanted to stay with them forever. I felt you pulling at me, but I—didn't—want—to—go—"

"Give him a sedative, Doc," Bleier said.

"You think I'm crazy? You think I'm deranged? They were lobsters, fellows. *Lobsters*.

After he had slept and showered and changed his clothes they came to see him again, and by that time he realized that he must have been behaving like a lunatic in the first moments of his return, blurting out his words, weeping, carrying on, crying out what surely had sounded like gibberish to them. Now he was rested, he was calm, he was at home in his own body once again.

He told them all that had befallen him, and from their faces he saw at first that they still thought he had gone around the bend: but as he kept speaking, quietly, straightforwardly, in rich detail, they began to acknowledge his report in subtle little ways, asking questions about the geography, about the ecological balance in a manner that showed him they were not simply humoring him. And after that, as it sank in upon them that he really had dwelled for a period of many months at the far end of time, beyond the span of the present world, they came to look upon him—it was unmistakable—as someone who was now wholly unlike them. In particular he saw the cold glassy stare in Maggie Caldwell's eyes.

Then they left him, for he was tiring again; and later Maggie came to see him alone, and took his hand and held it between hers, which were cold.

She said, "What do you want to do now, Jim?"

"To go back there."

"I thought you did."

"It's impossible, isn't it?" he said.

"We could try. But it couldn't ever work. We don't know what we're doing, yet, with that machine. We don't know where we'd send you. We might miss by a million years. By a billion."

"That's what I figured too."

"But you want to go back?"

He nodded. "I can't explain it. It was like being a member of some Buddhist monastery, do you see? Feeling *absolutely sure* that this is where you belong, that everything fits together perfectly, that you're an integral part of it. I've never felt anything like that before. I never will again."

"I'll talk to Bleier, Jim, about sending you back."

"No. Don't. I can't possibly get there. And I don't want to land anywhere else. Let Ybarra take the next trip. I'll stay here."

"Will you be happy?"

He smiled. "I'll do my best," he said.

When the others understood what the problem was, they saw to it that he went into re-entry therapy—Bleier had already foreseen something like that, and made preparations for it—and after a while the pain went from him, that sense of having undergone a violent separation, of having been ripped untimely from the womb. He resumed his work in the group and gradually recovered his mental balance and took an active part in the second transmission, which sent a young anthropologist named Ludwig off for two minutes and eight seconds. Ludwig did not see lobsters, to McCulloch's intense disappointment. He went sixty years into the future and came back glowing with wondrous tales of atomic fusion plants.

That was too bad, McCulloch thought. But soon he decided that it was just as well, that he preferred being the only one who had encountered the world beyond this world, probably the only human being who ever would.

He thought of that world with love, wondering about his mate and her millions of larvae, about the journey of his friends back across the great abyss, about the legends that were being spun about his visit in that unimaginably distant epoch. Sometimes the pain of separation returned, and Maggie found him crying in the night, and held him until he was whole again. And eventually the pain did not return. But still he did not forget, and in some part of his soul he longed to make his homefaring back to his true kind, and he rarely passed a day when he did not think he could hear the inaudible sound of delicate claws, scurrying over the sands of silent seas.